THE GRAPHIC NOVEL
William Shakespeare

PLAIN TEXT VERSION

Script Adaptation: John McDonald
American English Adaptation: Joe Sutliff Sanders
Character Designs & Original Artwork: Jon Haward
Inking: Gary Erskine
Coloring & Lettering: Nigel Dobbyn
Design & Layout: Jo Wheeler & Carl Andrews

Editor in Chief: Clive Bryant

The Tempest: The Graphic Novel
Plain Text Version

William Shakespeare

First US Edition

Published by: Classical Comics Ltd
Copyright ©2009 Classical Comics Ltd.

Acknowledgments: Every effort has been made to trace copyright holders of
material reproduced in this book. Any rights not acknowledged here will be
acknowledged in subsequent editions if notice is given to Classical Comics Ltd.

Images on page 135 reproduced with the kind permission of The Shakespeare Birthplace Trust.

All enquiries should be addressed to:
Classical Comics Ltd.
PO Box 7280
Litchborough
Towcester
NN12 9AR
United Kingdom
Tel: +44 (0)845 812 3000

info@classicalcomics.com
www.classicalcomics.com

ISBN: 978-1-906332-70-9

Printed in the USA

This book is printed by CG Book Printers using environmentally safe inks, on environmentally
friendly paper which is FSC (Forest Stewardship Council) certified (SW-COC-003110). This material
can be disposed of by recycling, incineration for energy recovery, composting and biodegradation.

The publisher wishes to acknowledge and thank Greg Powell
for his help in the completion of this book.

The rights of John McDonald, Joe Sutliff Sanders, Jon Haward, Gary Erskine and Nigel Dobbyn
to be identified as the artists of this work have been asserted in accordance with
the Copyright, Designs and Patents Act 1988 sections 77 and 78.

Contents

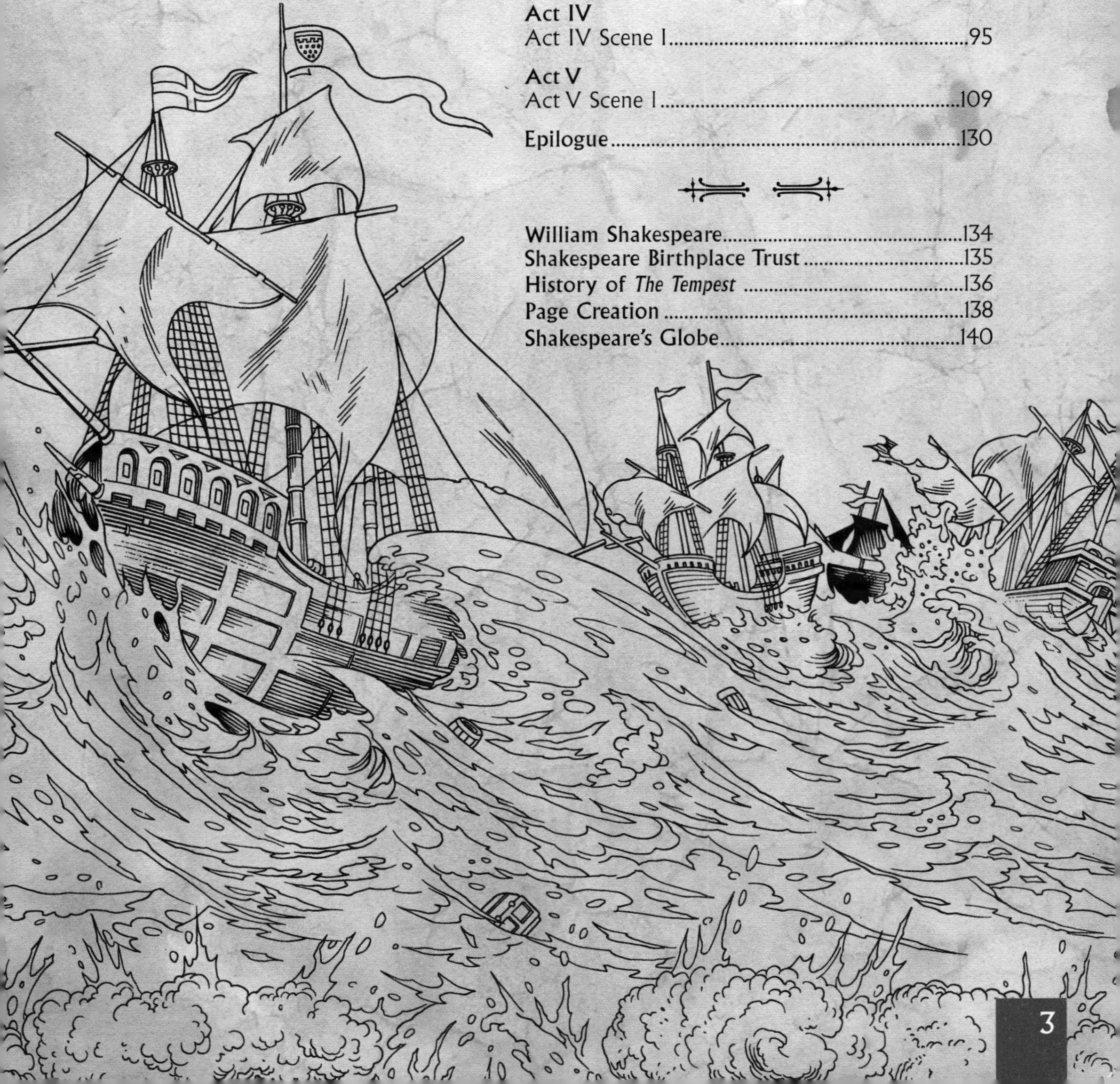

Dramatis Personæ

Prospero
The right Duke of Milan

Miranda
Prospero's daughter

Caliban
A savage and deformed slave

Ariel
An airy Spirit

Alonso
King of Naples

Ferdinand
The King's son

Sebastian
The King's brother

Antonio
Prospero's brother, the usurping Duke of Milan

Gonzalo
An honest old counselor

Adrian
A lord

Francisco
A lord

Stephano
A drunken butler

Trinculo
A jester

Master of the ship

Boatswain of the ship
(pronounced "Bosun")

Mariners of the ship

Ceres, Juno and Iris
Spirits, commanded by Prospero

Spirits and Reapers
Commanded by Prospero

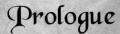

A royal ship, carrying the King of Naples and his entourage, is part of a small fleet sailing home from Tunis in North Africa. They are returning from the wedding of the King's daughter, Claribel, to the King of Tunis. The King of Naples is accompanied by his son Ferdinand, his brother Sebastian, and his trusty advisor Gonzalo. Also with the party is the King's friend Antonio, Duke of Milan. Antonio took the title of Duke from his older brother Prospero, who disappeared suddenly one night, never to be seen again…

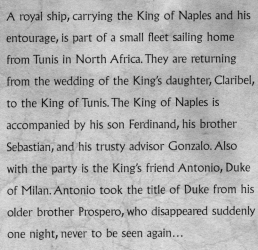

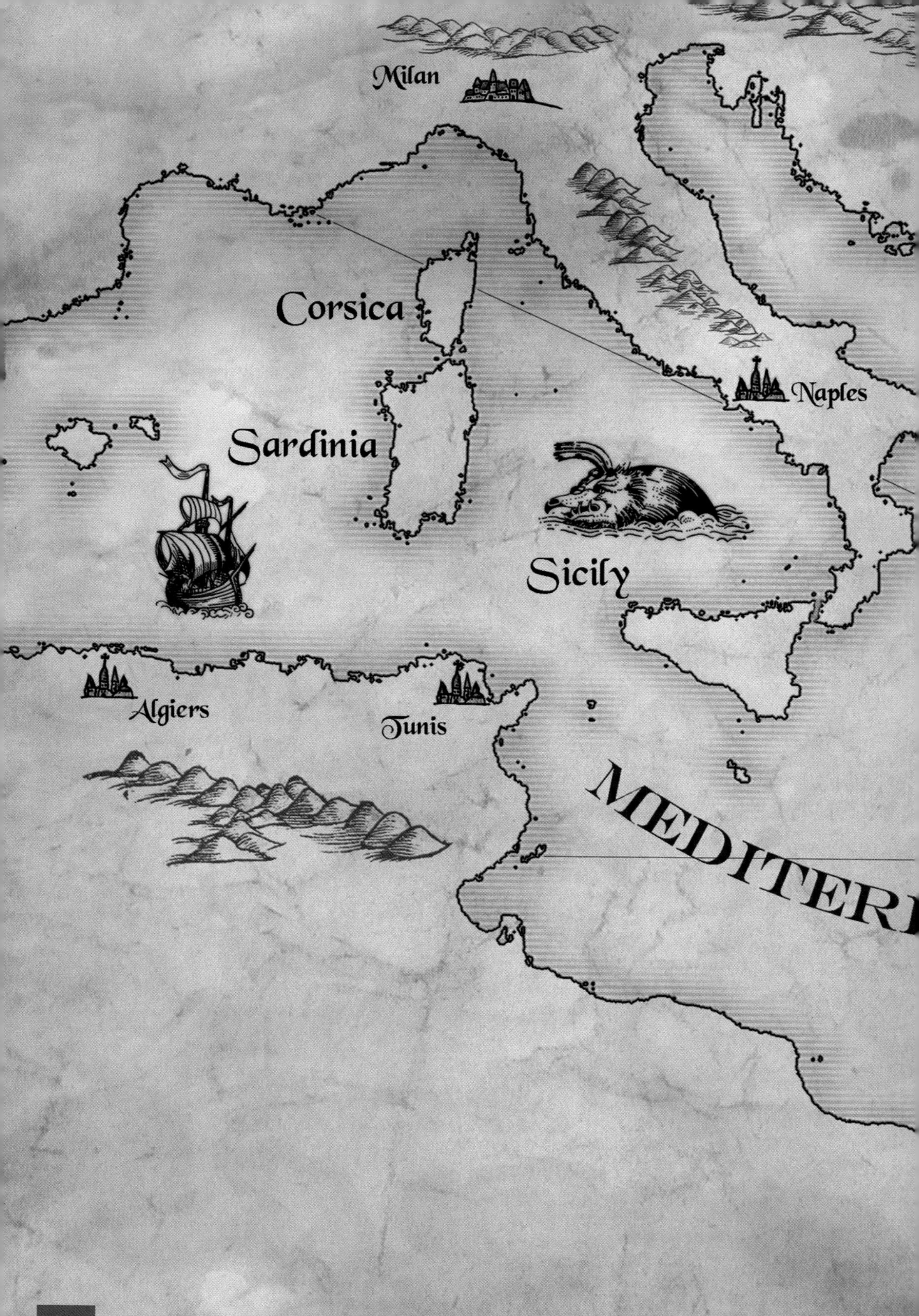
Milan
Corsica
Naples
Sardinia
Sicily
Algiers
Tunis
MEDITER

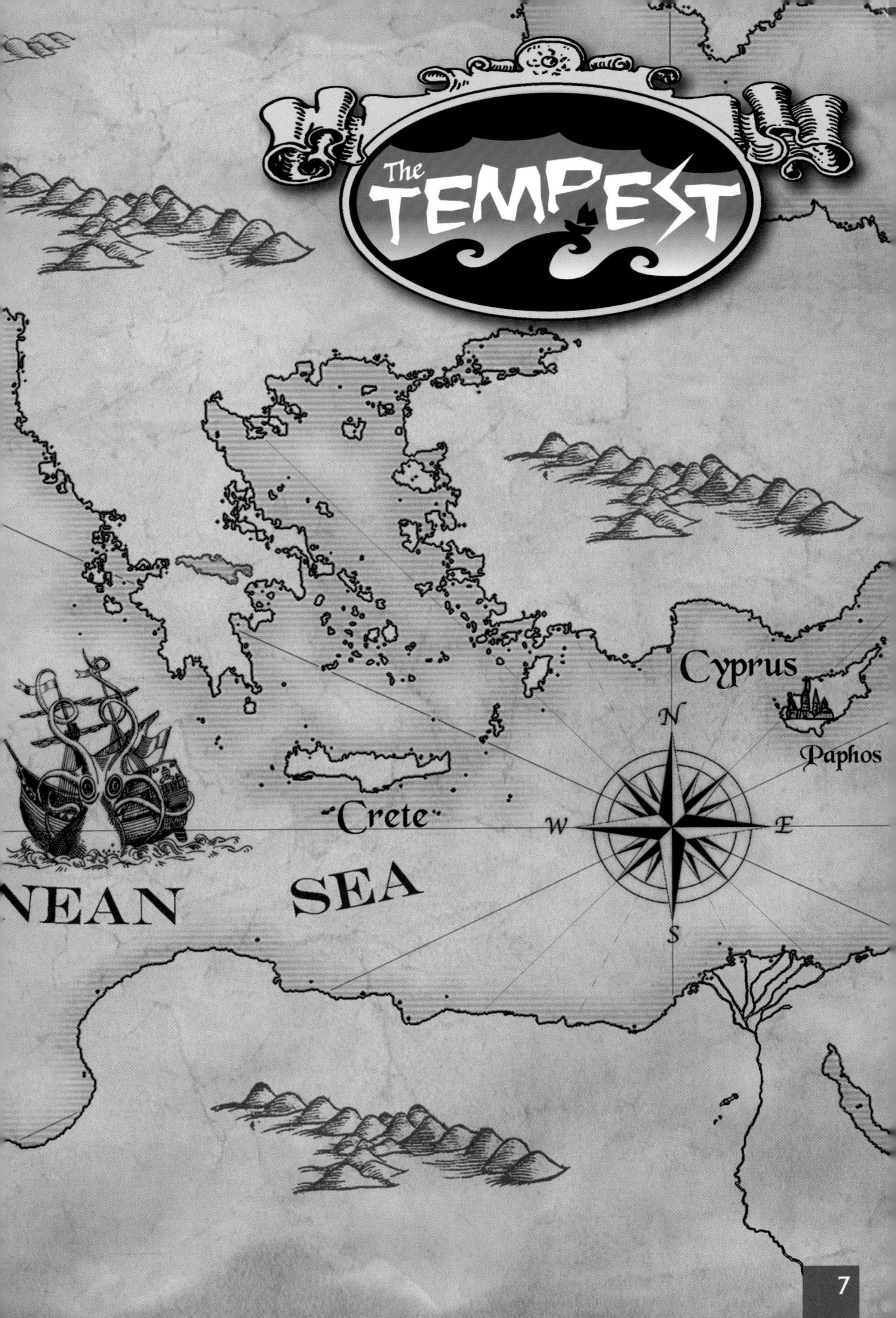
The TEMPEST
Cyprus
N
Paphos
Crete
W
E
S
NEAN
SEA

Act I

Scene I

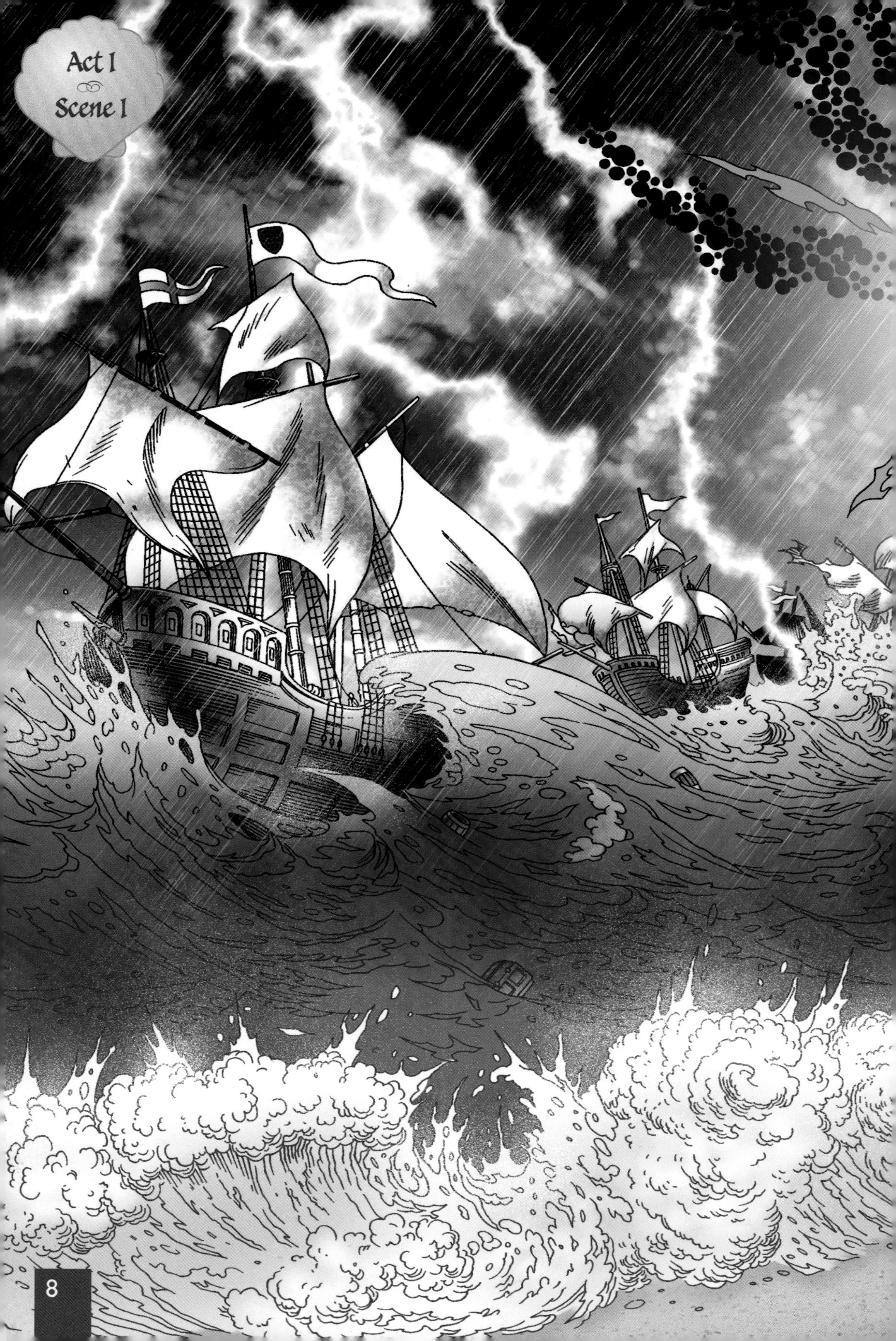

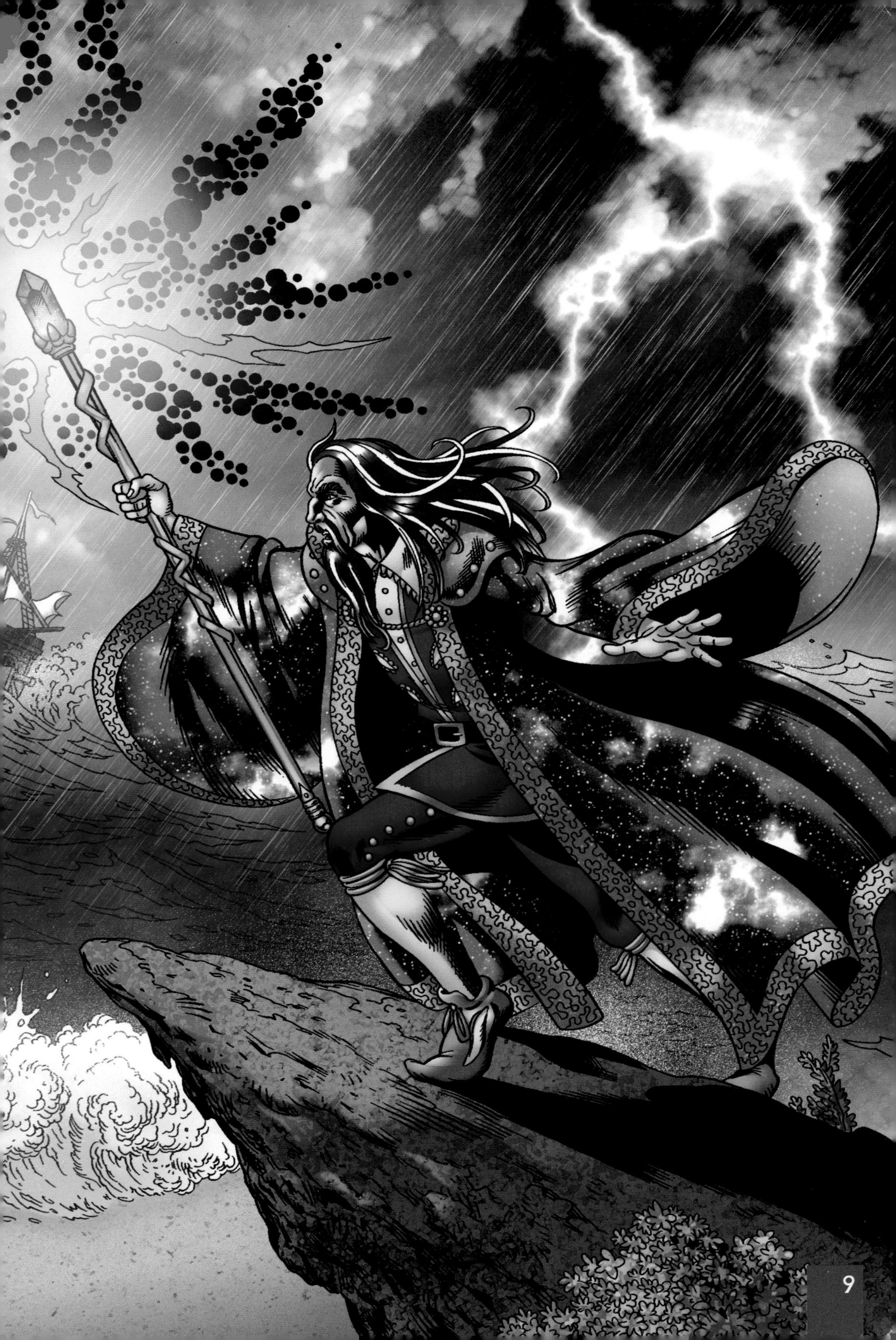

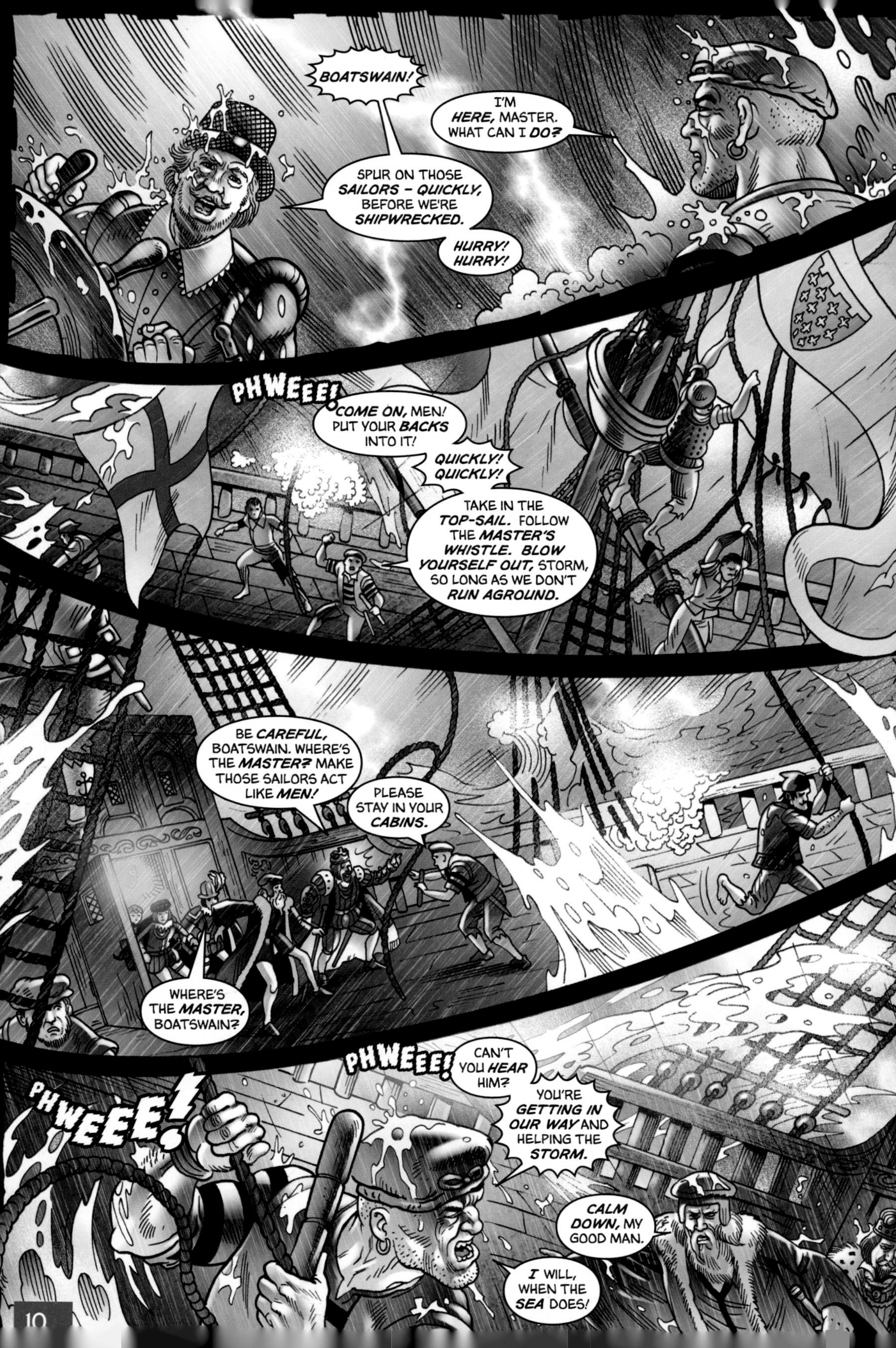
BOATSWAIN!
I'M HERE, MASTER. WHAT CAN I DO?
SPUR ON THOSE SAILORS – QUICKLY, BEFORE WE'RE SHIPWRECKED.
HURRY! HURRY!
PHWEEE!
COME ON, MEN! PUT YOUR BACKS INTO IT!
QUICKLY! QUICKLY!
TAKE IN THE TOP-SAIL. FOLLOW THE MASTER'S WHISTLE. BLOW YOURSELF OUT, STORM, SO LONG AS WE DON'T RUN AGROUND.
BE CAREFUL, BOATSWAIN. WHERE'S THE MASTER? MAKE THOSE SAILORS ACT LIKE MEN!
PLEASE STAY IN YOUR CABINS.
WHERE'S THE MASTER, BOATSWAIN?
PHWEEE!
PHWEEE!
CAN'T YOU HEAR HIM?
YOU'RE GETTING IN OUR WAY AND HELPING THE STORM.
CALM DOWN, MY GOOD MAN.
I WILL, WHEN THE SEA DOES!

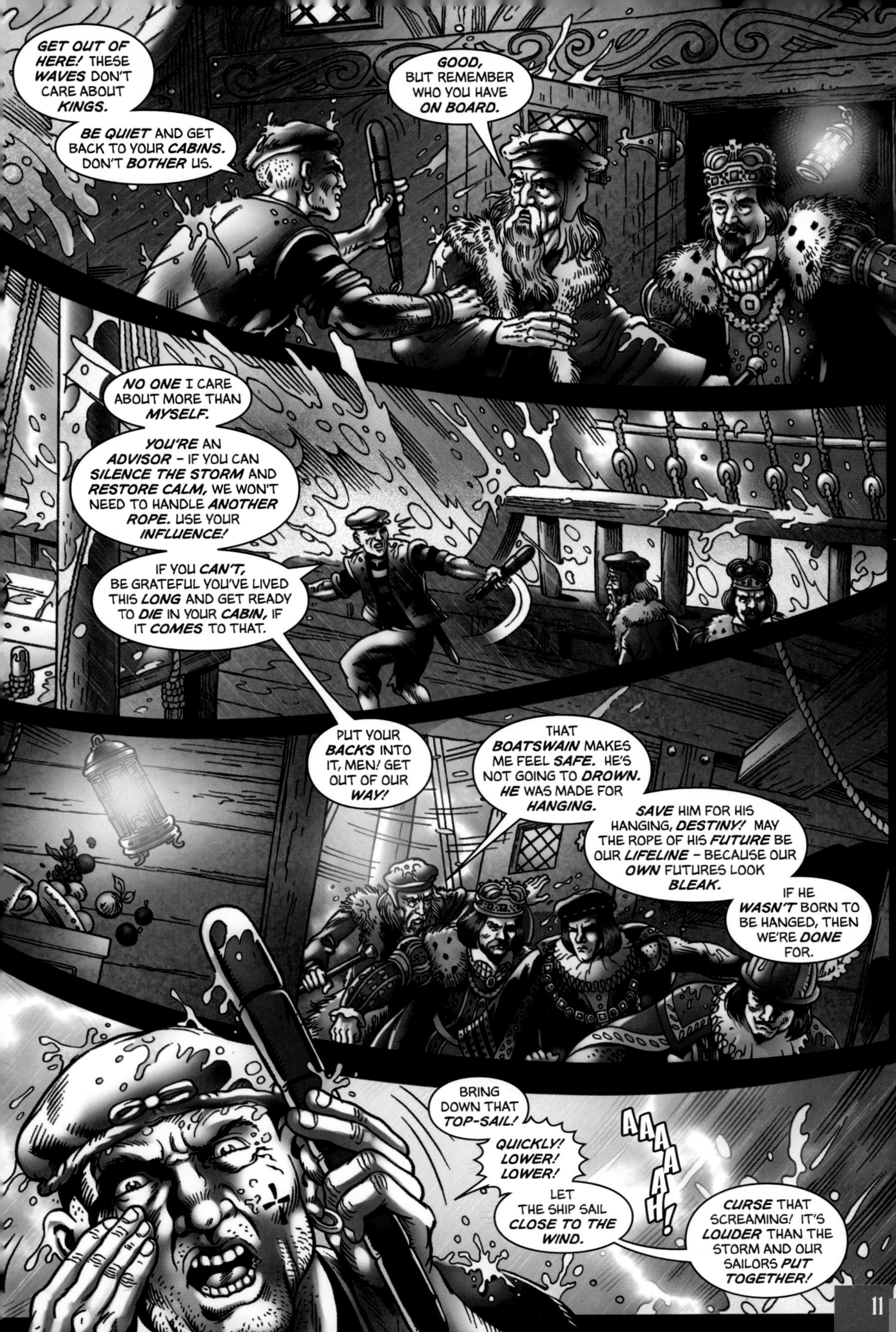
GET OUT OF HERE! THESE WAVES DON'T CARE ABOUT KINGS.
BE QUIET AND GET BACK TO YOUR CABINS. DON'T BOTHER US.
GOOD, BUT REMEMBER WHO YOU HAVE ON BOARD.
NO ONE I CARE ABOUT MORE THAN MYSELF.
YOU'RE AN ADVISOR – IF YOU CAN SILENCE THE STORM AND RESTORE CALM, WE WON'T NEED TO HANDLE ANOTHER ROPE. USE YOUR INFLUENCE!
IF YOU CAN'T, BE GRATEFUL YOU'VE LIVED THIS LONG AND GET READY TO DIE IN YOUR CABIN, IF IT COMES TO THAT.
PUT YOUR BACKS INTO IT, MEN! GET OUT OF OUR WAY!
THAT BOATSWAIN MAKES ME FEEL SAFE. HE'S NOT GOING TO DROWN. HE WAS MADE FOR HANGING.
SAVE HIM FOR HIS HANGING, DESTINY! MAY THE ROPE OF HIS FUTURE BE OUR LIFELINE – BECAUSE OUR OWN FUTURES LOOK BLEAK.
IF HE WASN'T BORN TO BE HANGED, THEN WE'RE DONE FOR.
BRING DOWN THAT TOP-SAIL!
QUICKLY! LOWER! LOWER!
LET THE SHIP SAIL CLOSE TO THE WIND.
AAAAAH!
CURSE THAT SCREAMING! IT'S LOUDER THAN THE STORM AND OUR SAILORS PUT TOGETHER!

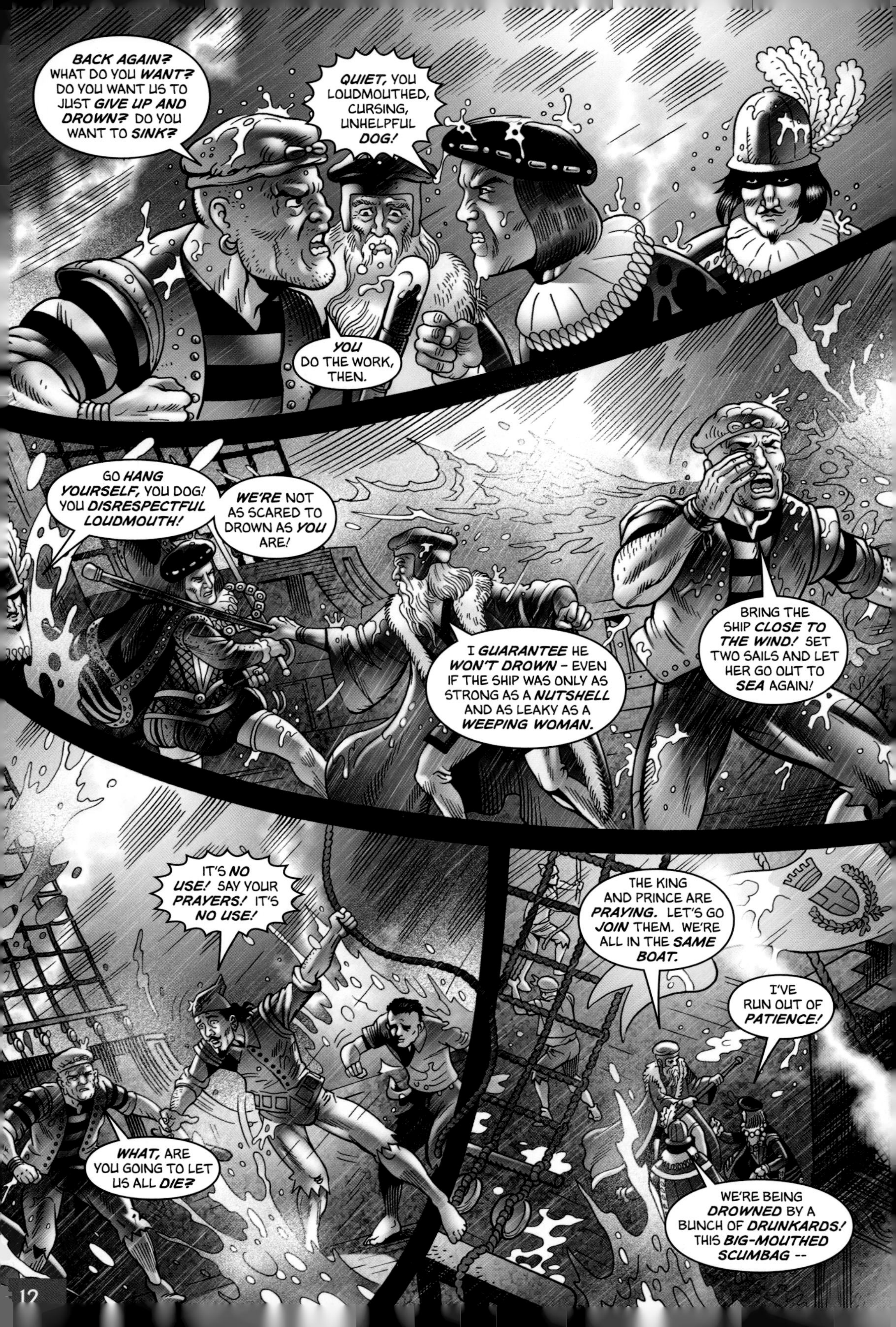
BACK AGAIN? WHAT DO YOU WANT? DO YOU WANT US TO JUST GIVE UP AND DROWN? DO YOU WANT TO SINK?
QUIET, YOU LOUDMOUTHED, CURSING, UNHELPFUL DOG!
YOU DO THE WORK, THEN.
GO HANG YOURSELF, YOU DOG! YOU DISRESPECTFUL LOUDMOUTH!
WE'RE NOT AS SCARED TO DROWN AS YOU ARE!
I GUARANTEE HE WON'T DROWN – EVEN IF THE SHIP WAS ONLY AS STRONG AS A NUTSHELL AND AS LEAKY AS A WEEPING WOMAN.
BRING THE SHIP CLOSE TO THE WIND! SET TWO SAILS AND LET HER GO OUT TO SEA AGAIN!
IT'S NO USE! SAY YOUR PRAYERS! IT'S NO USE!
WHAT, ARE YOU GOING TO LET US ALL DIE?
THE KING AND PRINCE ARE PRAYING. LET'S GO JOIN THEM. WE'RE ALL IN THE SAME BOAT.
I'VE RUN OUT OF PATIENCE!
WE'RE BEING DROWNED BY A BUNCH OF DRUNKARDS! THIS BIG-MOUTHED SCUMBAG --

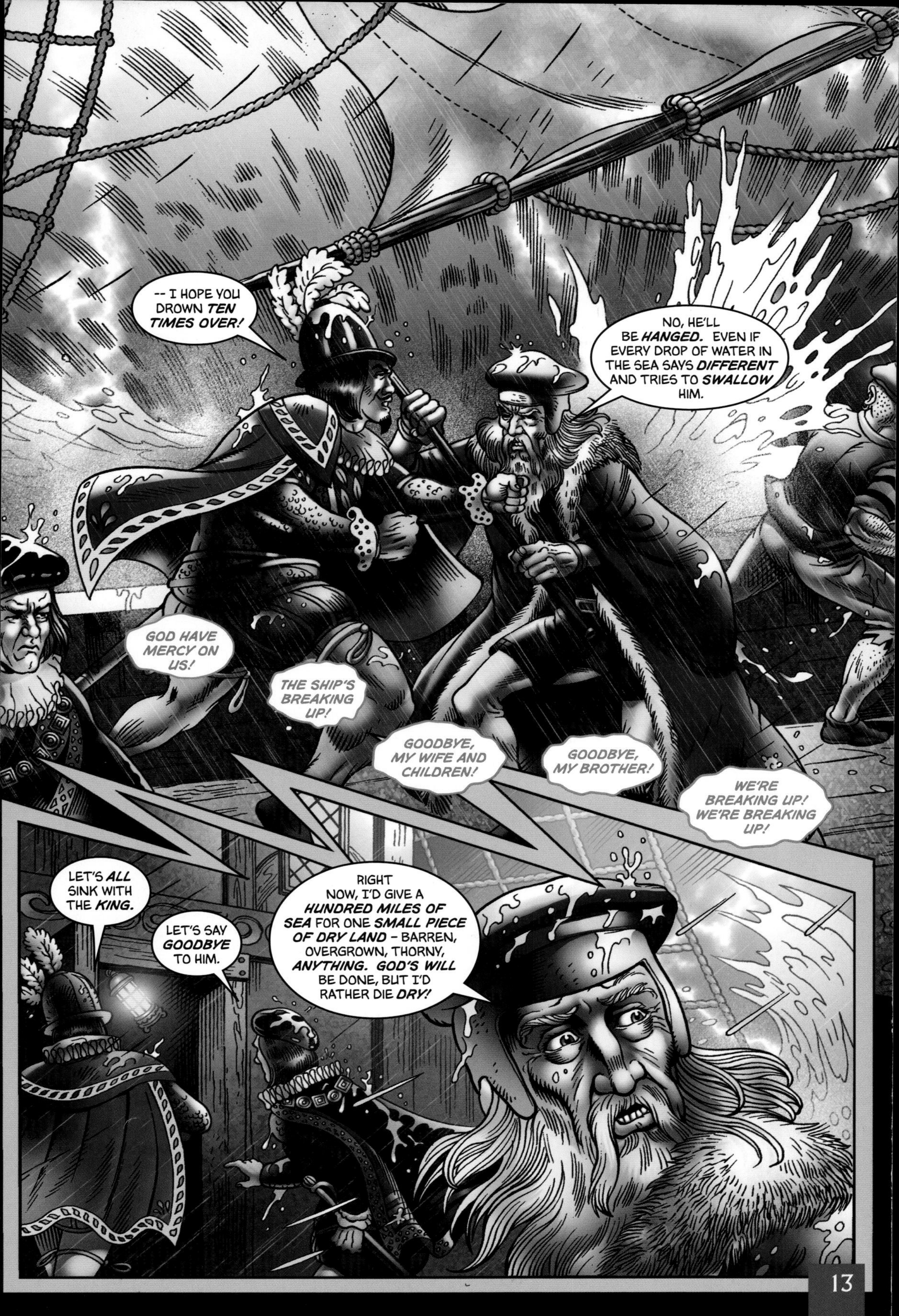
-- I HOPE YOU DROWN TEN TIMES OVER!
NO, HE'LL BE HANGED. EVEN IF EVERY DROP OF WATER IN THE SEA SAYS DIFFERENT AND TRIES TO SWALLOW HIM.
GOD HAVE MERCY ON US!
THE SHIP'S BREAKING UP!
GOODBYE, MY WIFE AND CHILDREN!
GOODBYE, MY BROTHER!
WE'RE BREAKING UP! WE'RE BREAKING UP!
LET'S ALL SINK WITH THE KING.
LET'S SAY GOODBYE TO HIM.
RIGHT NOW, I'D GIVE A HUNDRED MILES OF SEA FOR ONE SMALL PIECE OF DRY LAND – BARREN, OVERGROWN, THORNY, ANYTHING. GOD'S WILL BE DONE, BUT I'D RATHER DIE DRY!

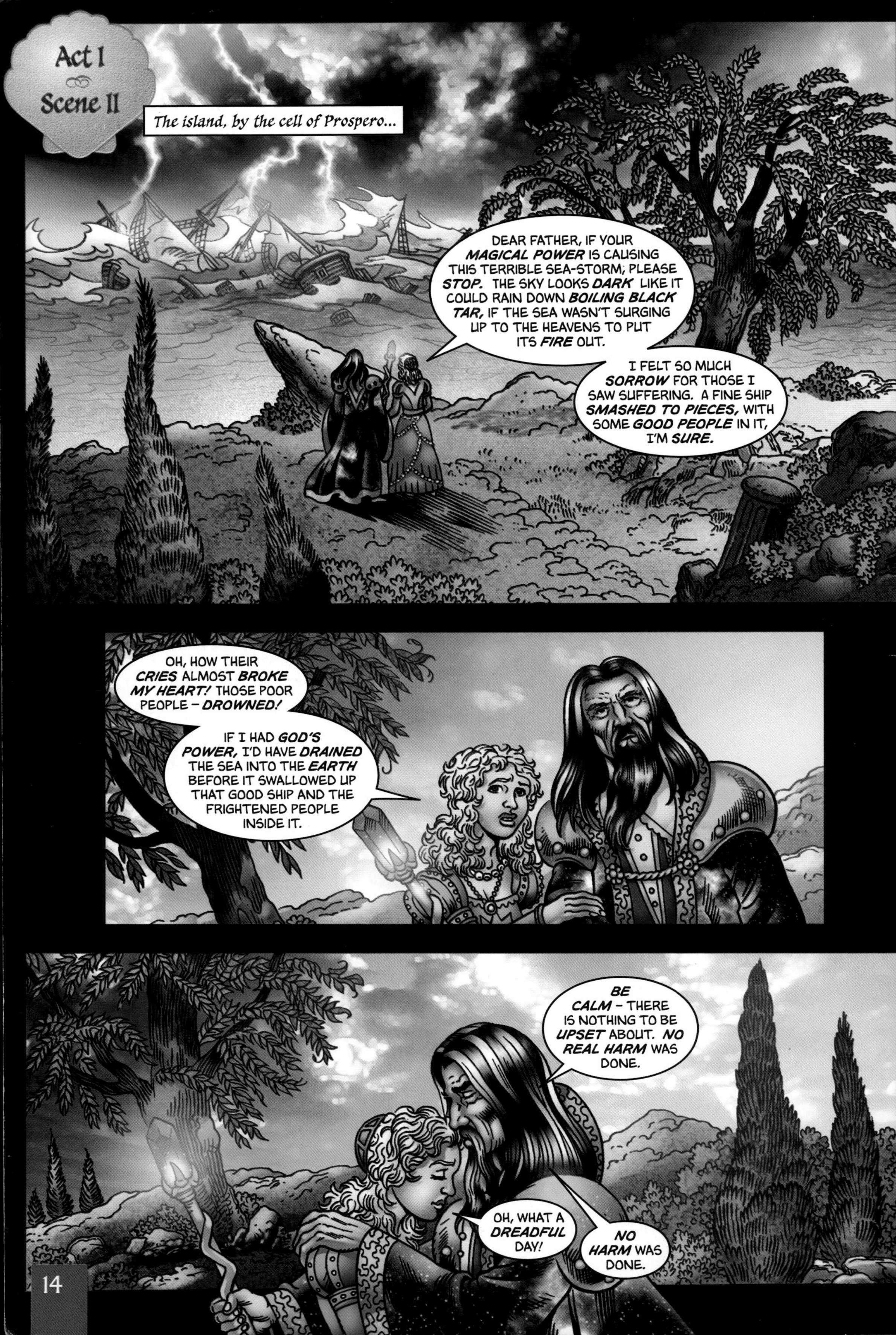
Act I
Scene II
The island, by the cell of Prospero...
DEAR FATHER, IF YOUR MAGICAL POWER IS CAUSING THIS TERRIBLE SEA-STORM; PLEASE STOP. THE SKY LOOKS DARK LIKE IT COULD RAIN DOWN BOILING BLACK TAR, IF THE SEA WASN'T SURGING UP TO THE HEAVENS TO PUT ITS FIRE OUT.
I FELT SO MUCH SORROW FOR THOSE I SAW SUFFERING. A FINE SHIP SMASHED TO PIECES, WITH SOME GOOD PEOPLE IN IT, I'M SURE.
OH, HOW THEIR CRIES ALMOST BROKE MY HEART! THOSE POOR PEOPLE – DROWNED!
IF I HAD GOD'S POWER, I'D HAVE DRAINED THE SEA INTO THE EARTH BEFORE IT SWALLOWED UP THAT GOOD SHIP AND THE FRIGHTENED PEOPLE INSIDE IT.
BE CALM – THERE IS NOTHING TO BE UPSET ABOUT. NO REAL HARM WAS DONE.
OH, WHAT A DREADFUL DAY!
NO HARM WAS DONE.

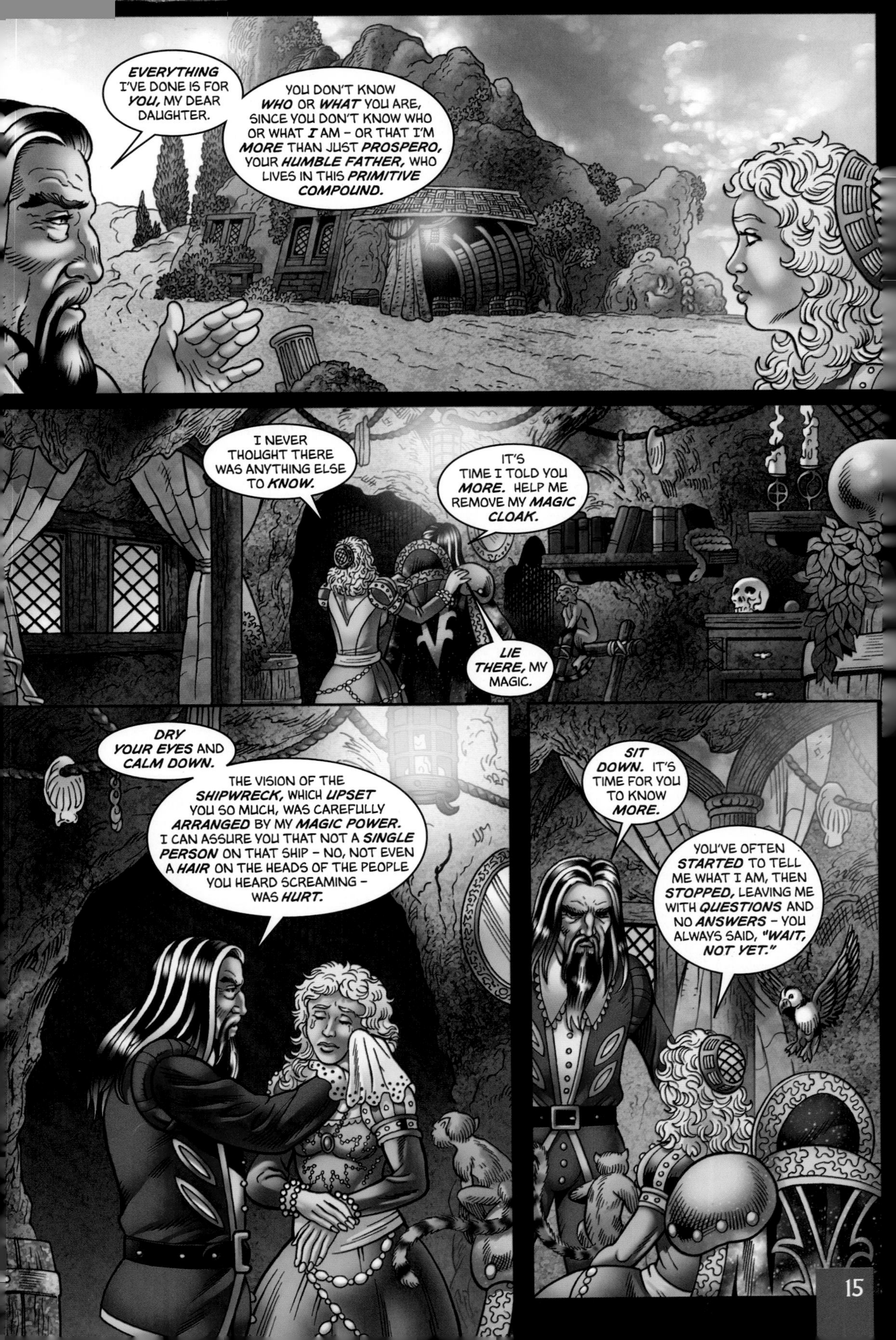
EVERYTHING I'VE DONE IS FOR YOU, MY DEAR DAUGHTER.
YOU DON'T KNOW WHO OR WHAT YOU ARE, SINCE YOU DON'T KNOW WHO OR WHAT I AM – OR THAT I'M MORE THAN JUST PROSPERO, YOUR HUMBLE FATHER, WHO LIVES IN THIS PRIMITIVE COMPOUND.
I NEVER THOUGHT THERE WAS ANYTHING ELSE TO KNOW.
IT'S TIME I TOLD YOU MORE. HELP ME REMOVE MY MAGIC CLOAK.
LIE THERE, MY MAGIC.
DRY YOUR EYES AND CALM DOWN.
THE VISION OF THE SHIPWRECK, WHICH UPSET YOU SO MUCH, WAS CAREFULLY ARRANGED BY MY MAGIC POWER. I CAN ASSURE YOU THAT NOT A SINGLE PERSON ON THAT SHIP – NO, NOT EVEN A HAIR ON THE HEADS OF THE PEOPLE YOU HEARD SCREAMING – WAS HURT.
SIT DOWN. IT'S TIME FOR YOU TO KNOW MORE.
YOU'VE OFTEN STARTED TO TELL ME WHAT I AM, THEN STOPPED, LEAVING ME WITH QUESTIONS AND NO ANSWERS – YOU ALWAYS SAID, "WAIT, NOT YET."

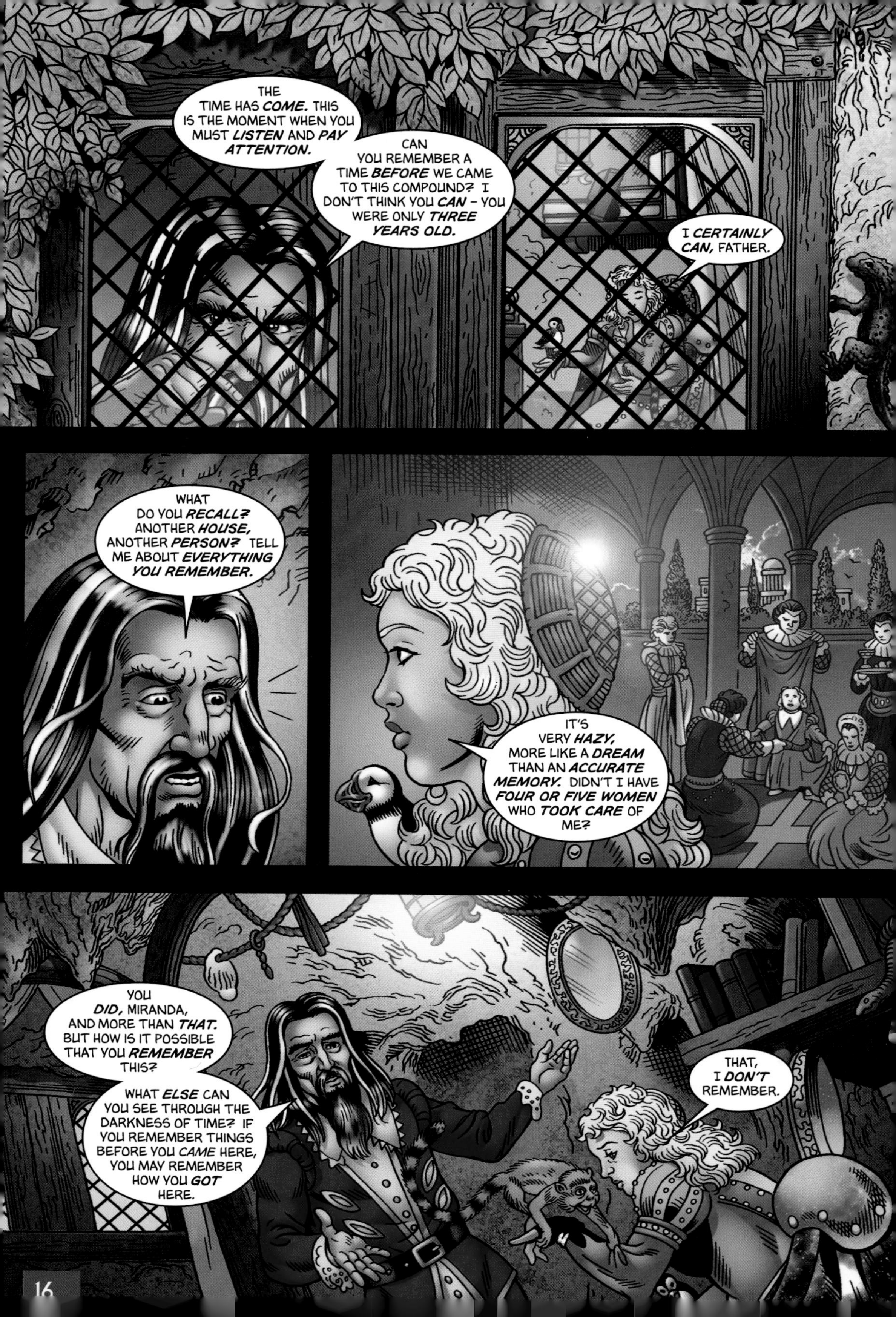
THE TIME HAS COME. THIS IS THE MOMENT WHEN YOU MUST LISTEN AND PAY ATTENTION.
CAN YOU REMEMBER A TIME BEFORE WE CAME TO THIS COMPOUND? I DON'T THINK YOU CAN – YOU WERE ONLY THREE YEARS OLD.
I CERTAINLY CAN, FATHER.
WHAT DO YOU RECALL? ANOTHER HOUSE, ANOTHER PERSON? TELL ME ABOUT EVERYTHING YOU REMEMBER.
IT'S VERY HAZY, MORE LIKE A DREAM THAN AN ACCURATE MEMORY. DIDN'T I HAVE FOUR OR FIVE WOMEN WHO TOOK CARE OF ME?
YOU DID, MIRANDA, AND MORE THAN THAT. BUT HOW IS IT POSSIBLE THAT YOU REMEMBER THIS?
WHAT ELSE CAN YOU SEE THROUGH THE DARKNESS OF TIME? IF YOU REMEMBER THINGS BEFORE YOU CAME HERE, YOU MAY REMEMBER HOW YOU GOT HERE.
THAT, I DON'T REMEMBER.

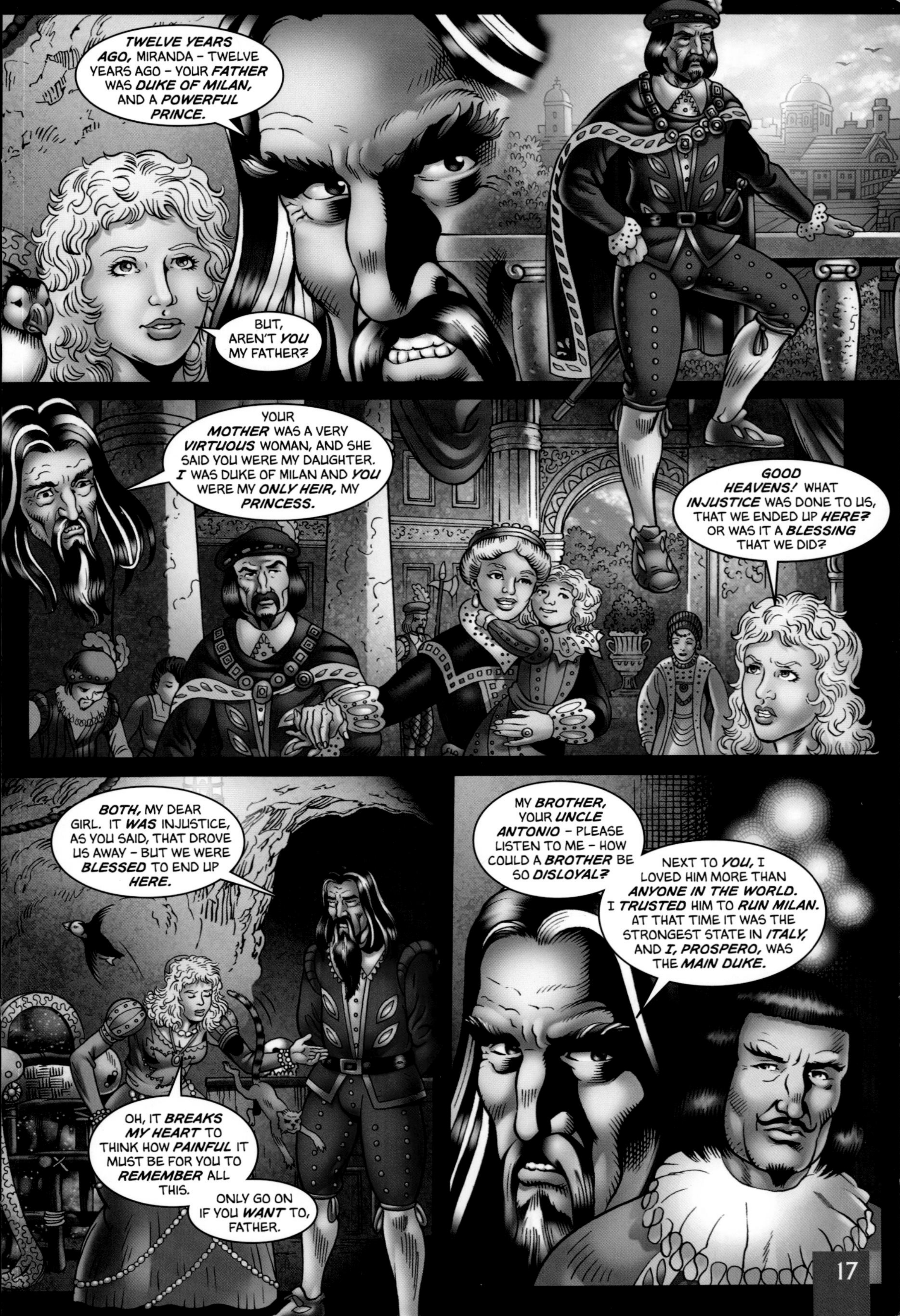

TWELVE YEARS AGO, MIRANDA – TWELVE YEARS AGO – YOUR FATHER WAS DUKE OF MILAN, AND A POWERFUL PRINCE.
BUT, AREN'T YOU MY FATHER?
YOUR MOTHER WAS A VERY VIRTUOUS WOMAN, AND SHE SAID YOU WERE MY DAUGHTER. I WAS DUKE OF MILAN AND YOU WERE MY ONLY HEIR, MY PRINCESS.
GOOD HEAVENS! WHAT INJUSTICE WAS DONE TO US, THAT WE ENDED UP HERE? OR WAS IT A BLESSING THAT WE DID?
BOTH, MY DEAR GIRL. IT WAS INJUSTICE, AS YOU SAID, THAT DROVE US AWAY – BUT WE WERE BLESSED TO END UP HERE.
OH, IT BREAKS MY HEART TO THINK HOW PAINFUL IT MUST BE FOR YOU TO REMEMBER ALL THIS.
ONLY GO ON IF YOU WANT TO, FATHER.
MY BROTHER, YOUR UNCLE ANTONIO – PLEASE LISTEN TO ME – HOW COULD A BROTHER BE SO DISLOYAL?
NEXT TO YOU, I LOVED HIM MORE THAN ANYONE IN THE WORLD. I TRUSTED HIM TO RUN MILAN. AT THAT TIME IT WAS THE STRONGEST STATE IN ITALY, AND I, PROSPERO, WAS THE MAIN DUKE.

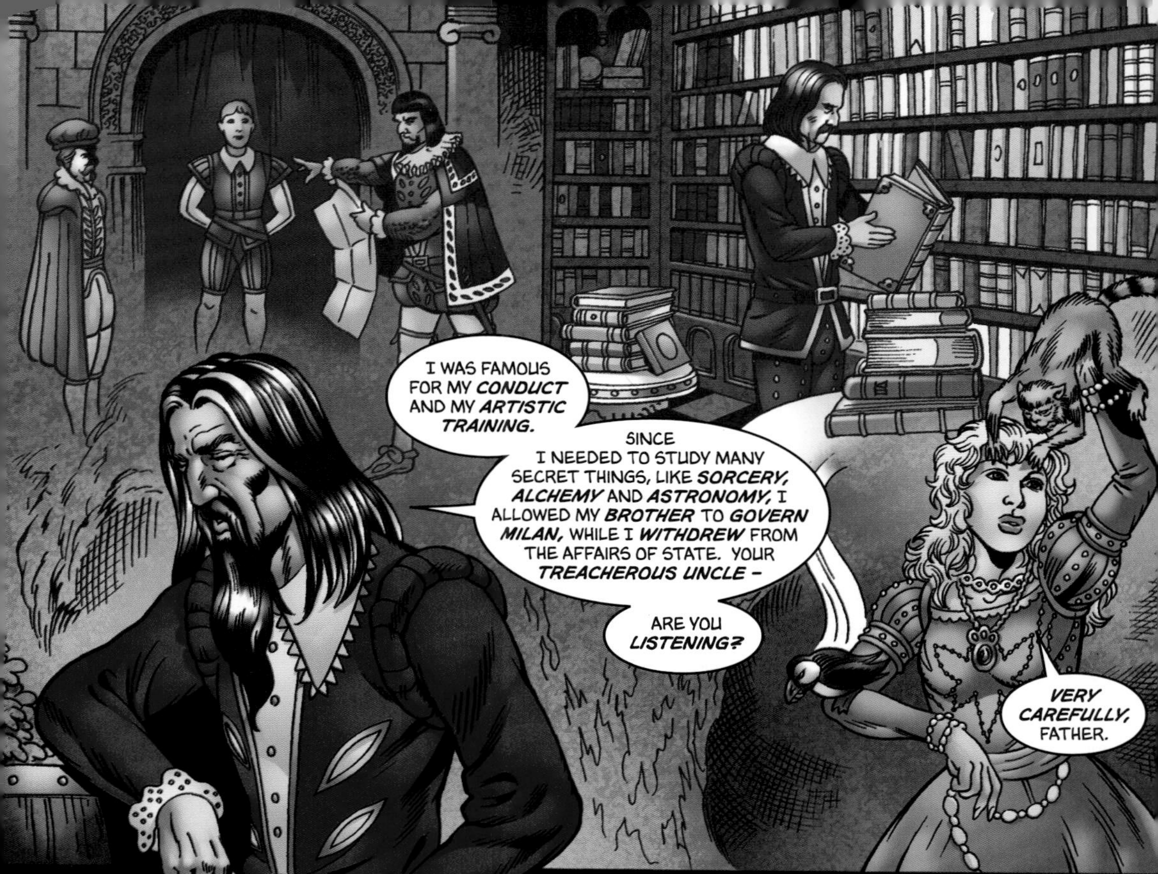
I WAS FAMOUS FOR MY CONDUCT AND MY ARTISTIC TRAINING.
SINCE I NEEDED TO STUDY MANY SECRET THINGS, LIKE SORCERY, ALCHEMY AND ASTRONOMY, I ALLOWED MY BROTHER TO GOVERN MILAN, WHILE I WITHDREW FROM THE AFFAIRS OF STATE. YOUR TREACHEROUS UNCLE –
ARE YOU LISTENING?
VERY CAREFULLY, FATHER.

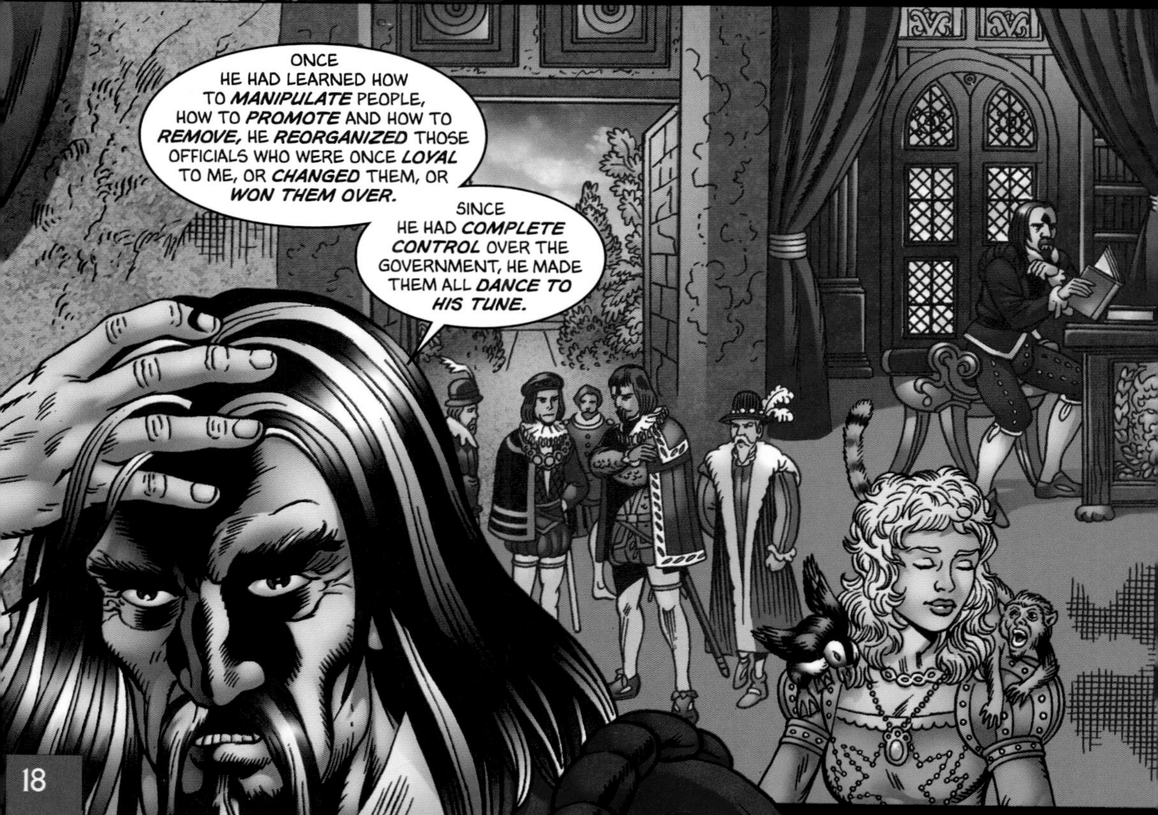
ONCE HE HAD LEARNED HOW TO MANIPULATE PEOPLE, HOW TO PROMOTE AND HOW TO REMOVE, HE REORGANIZED THOSE OFFICIALS WHO WERE ONCE LOYAL TO ME, OR CHANGED THEM, OR WON THEM OVER.
SINCE HE HAD COMPLETE CONTROL OVER THE GOVERNMENT, HE MADE THEM ALL DANCE TO HIS TUNE.

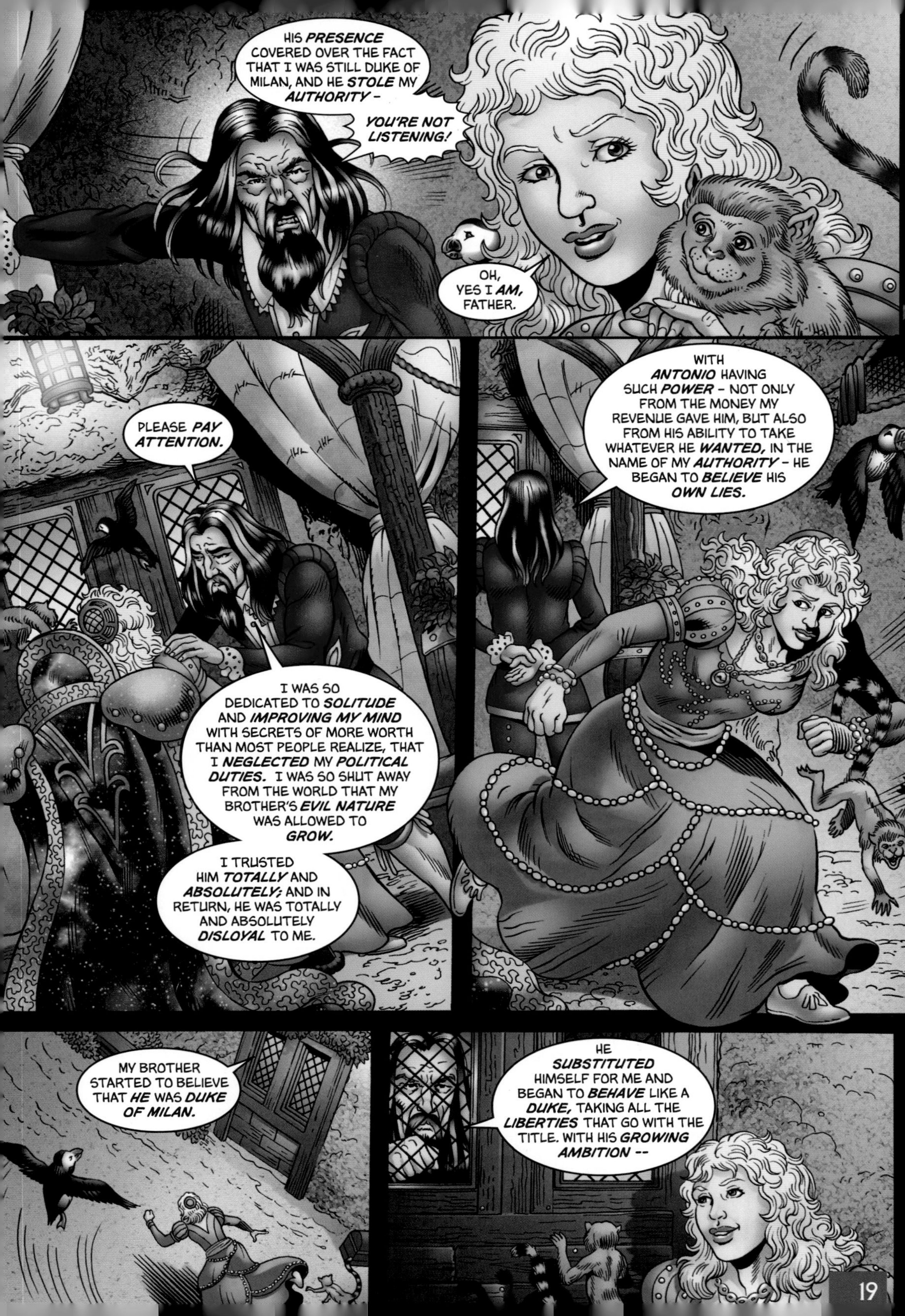
HIS PRESENCE COVERED OVER THE FACT THAT I WAS STILL DUKE OF MILAN, AND HE STOLE MY AUTHORITY –
YOU'RE NOT LISTENING!
OH, YES I AM, FATHER.
PLEASE PAY ATTENTION.
I WAS SO DEDICATED TO SOLITUDE AND IMPROVING MY MIND WITH SECRETS OF MORE WORTH THAN MOST PEOPLE REALIZE, THAT I NEGLECTED MY POLITICAL DUTIES. I WAS SO SHUT AWAY FROM THE WORLD THAT MY BROTHER'S EVIL NATURE WAS ALLOWED TO GROW.
I TRUSTED HIM TOTALLY AND ABSOLUTELY; AND IN RETURN, HE WAS TOTALLY AND ABSOLUTELY DISLOYAL TO ME.
WITH ANTONIO HAVING SUCH POWER – NOT ONLY FROM THE MONEY MY REVENUE GAVE HIM, BUT ALSO FROM HIS ABILITY TO TAKE WHATEVER HE WANTED, IN THE NAME OF MY AUTHORITY – HE BEGAN TO BELIEVE HIS OWN LIES.
MY BROTHER STARTED TO BELIEVE THAT HE WAS DUKE OF MILAN.
HE SUBSTITUTED HIMSELF FOR ME AND BEGAN TO BEHAVE LIKE A DUKE, TAKING ALL THE LIBERTIES THAT GO WITH THE TITLE. WITH HIS GROWING AMBITION --

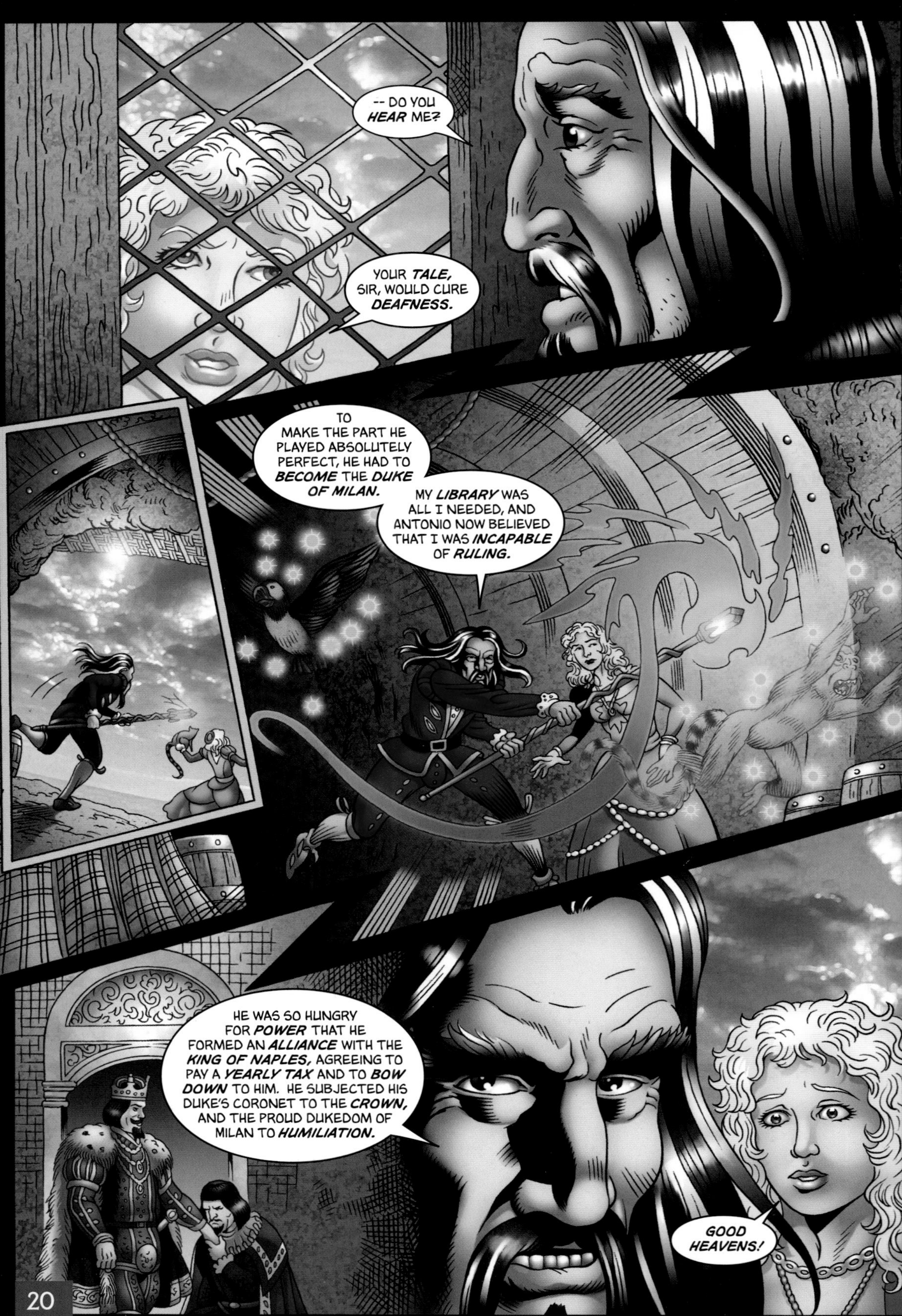
-- DO YOU HEAR ME?
YOUR TALE, SIR, WOULD CURE DEAFNESS.
TO MAKE THE PART HE PLAYED ABSOLUTELY PERFECT, HE HAD TO BECOME THE DUKE OF MILAN.
MY LIBRARY WAS ALL I NEEDED, AND ANTONIO NOW BELIEVED THAT I WAS INCAPABLE OF RULING.
HE WAS SO HUNGRY FOR POWER THAT HE FORMED AN ALLIANCE WITH THE KING OF NAPLES, AGREEING TO PAY A YEARLY TAX AND TO BOW DOWN TO HIM. HE SUBJECTED HIS DUKE'S CORONET TO THE CROWN, AND THE PROUD DUKEDOM OF MILAN TO HUMILIATION.
GOOD HEAVENS!

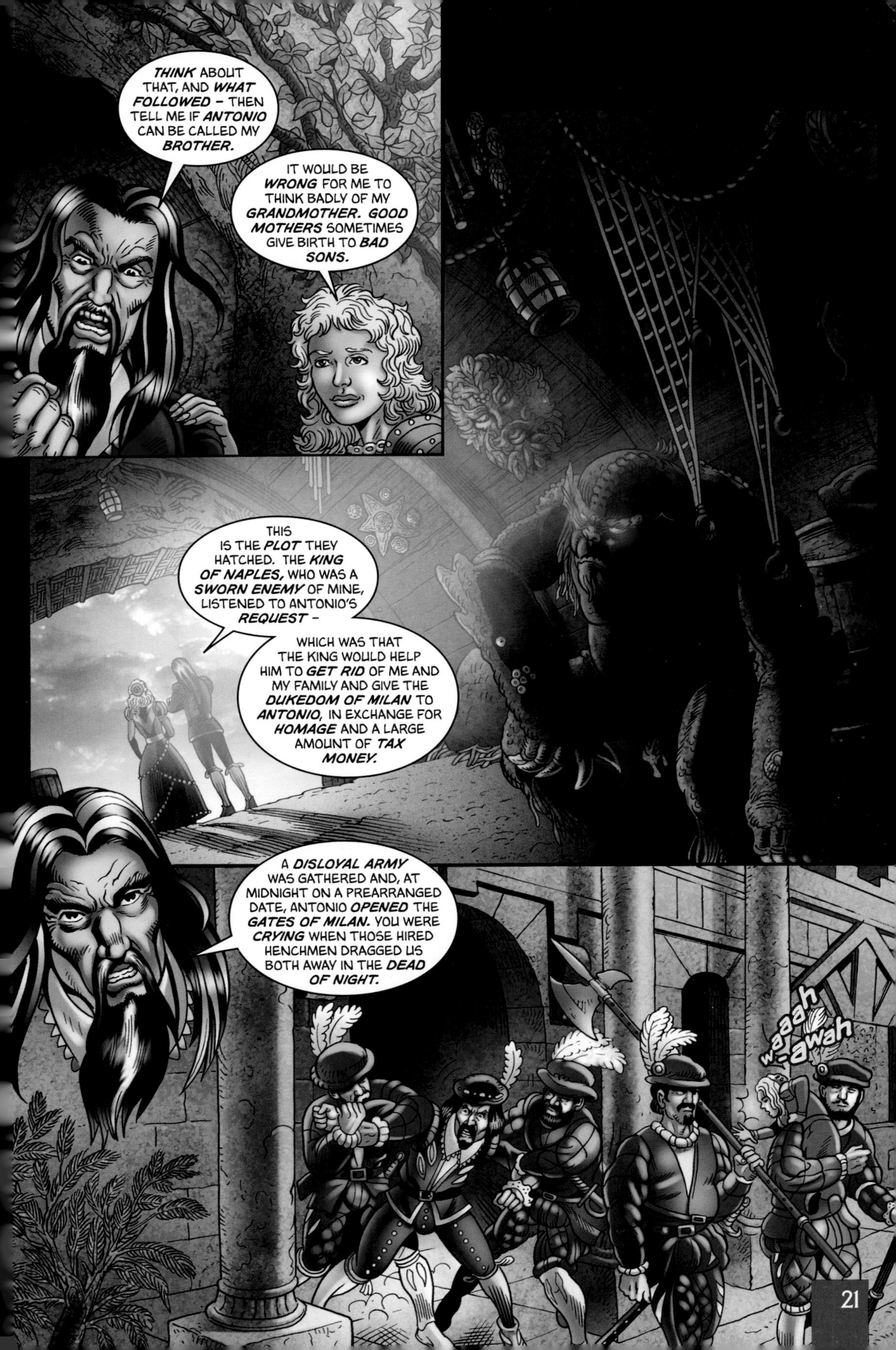
THINK ABOUT THAT, AND WHAT FOLLOWED – THEN TELL ME IF ANTONIO CAN BE CALLED MY BROTHER.
IT WOULD BE WRONG FOR ME TO THINK BADLY OF MY GRANDMOTHER. GOOD MOTHERS SOMETIMES GIVE BIRTH TO BAD SONS.
THIS IS THE PLOT THEY HATCHED. THE KING OF NAPLES, WHO WAS A SWORN ENEMY OF MINE, LISTENED TO ANTONIO'S REQUEST –
WHICH WAS THAT THE KING WOULD HELP HIM TO GET RID OF ME AND MY FAMILY AND GIVE THE DUKEDOM OF MILAN TO ANTONIO, IN EXCHANGE FOR HOMAGE AND A LARGE AMOUNT OF TAX MONEY.
A DISLOYAL ARMY WAS GATHERED AND, AT MIDNIGHT ON A PREARRANGED DATE, ANTONIO OPENED THE GATES OF MILAN. YOU WERE CRYING WHEN THOSE HIRED HENCHMEN DRAGGED US BOTH AWAY IN THE DEAD OF NIGHT.
waaah
-awah

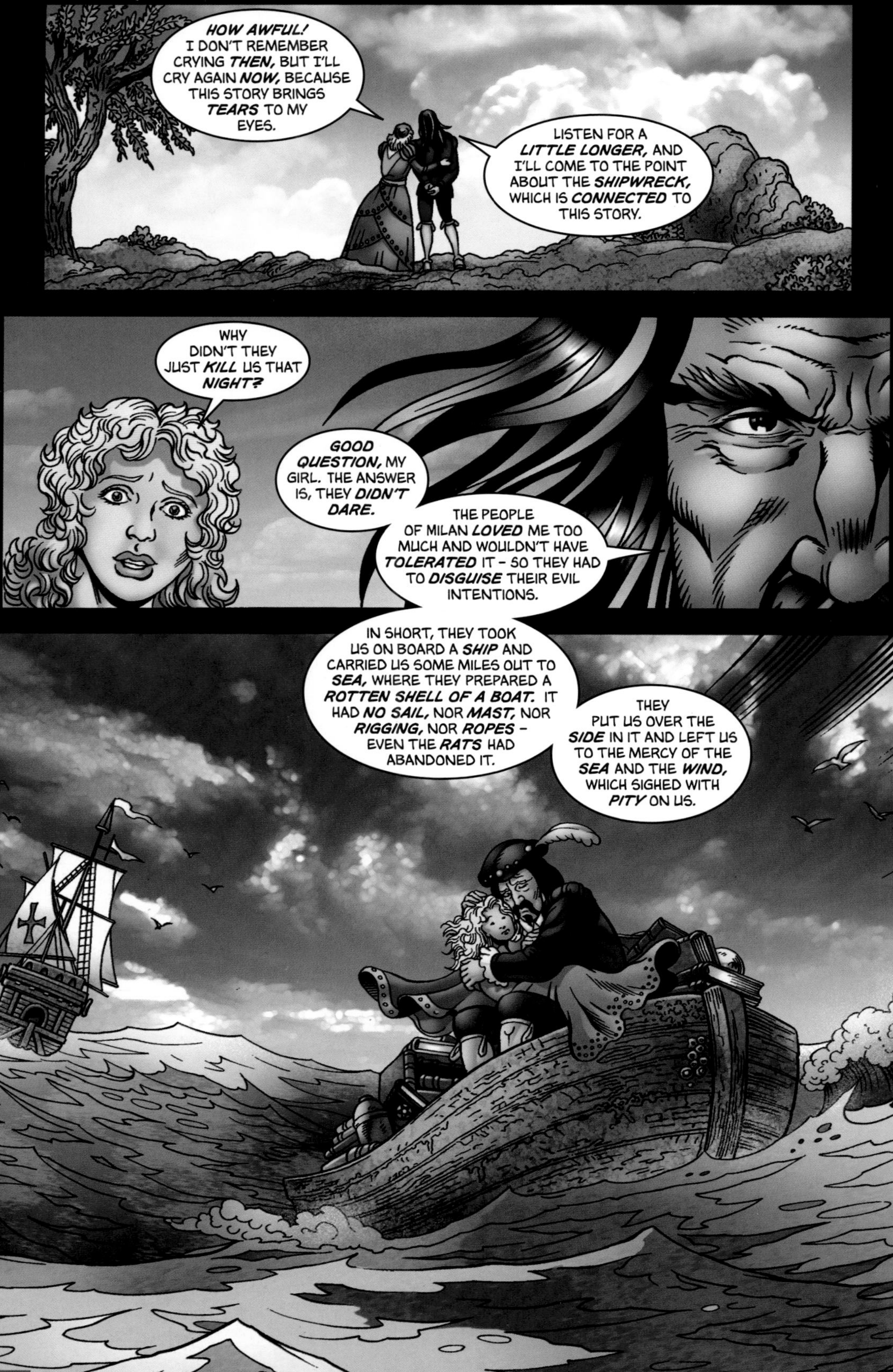
HOW AWFUL! I DON'T REMEMBER CRYING THEN, BUT I'LL CRY AGAIN NOW, BECAUSE THIS STORY BRINGS TEARS TO MY EYES.
LISTEN FOR A LITTLE LONGER, AND I'LL COME TO THE POINT ABOUT THE SHIPWRECK, WHICH IS CONNECTED TO THIS STORY.
WHY DIDN'T THEY JUST KILL US THAT NIGHT?
GOOD QUESTION, MY GIRL. THE ANSWER IS, THEY DIDN'T DARE.
THE PEOPLE OF MILAN LOVED ME TOO MUCH AND WOULDN'T HAVE TOLERATED IT – SO THEY HAD TO DISGUISE THEIR EVIL INTENTIONS.
IN SHORT, THEY TOOK US ON BOARD A SHIP AND CARRIED US SOME MILES OUT TO SEA, WHERE THEY PREPARED A ROTTEN SHELL OF A BOAT. IT HAD NO SAIL, NOR MAST, NOR RIGGING, NOR ROPES – EVEN THE RATS HAD ABANDONED IT.
THEY PUT US OVER THE SIDE IN IT AND LEFT US TO THE MERCY OF THE SEA AND THE WIND, WHICH SIGHED WITH PITY ON US.

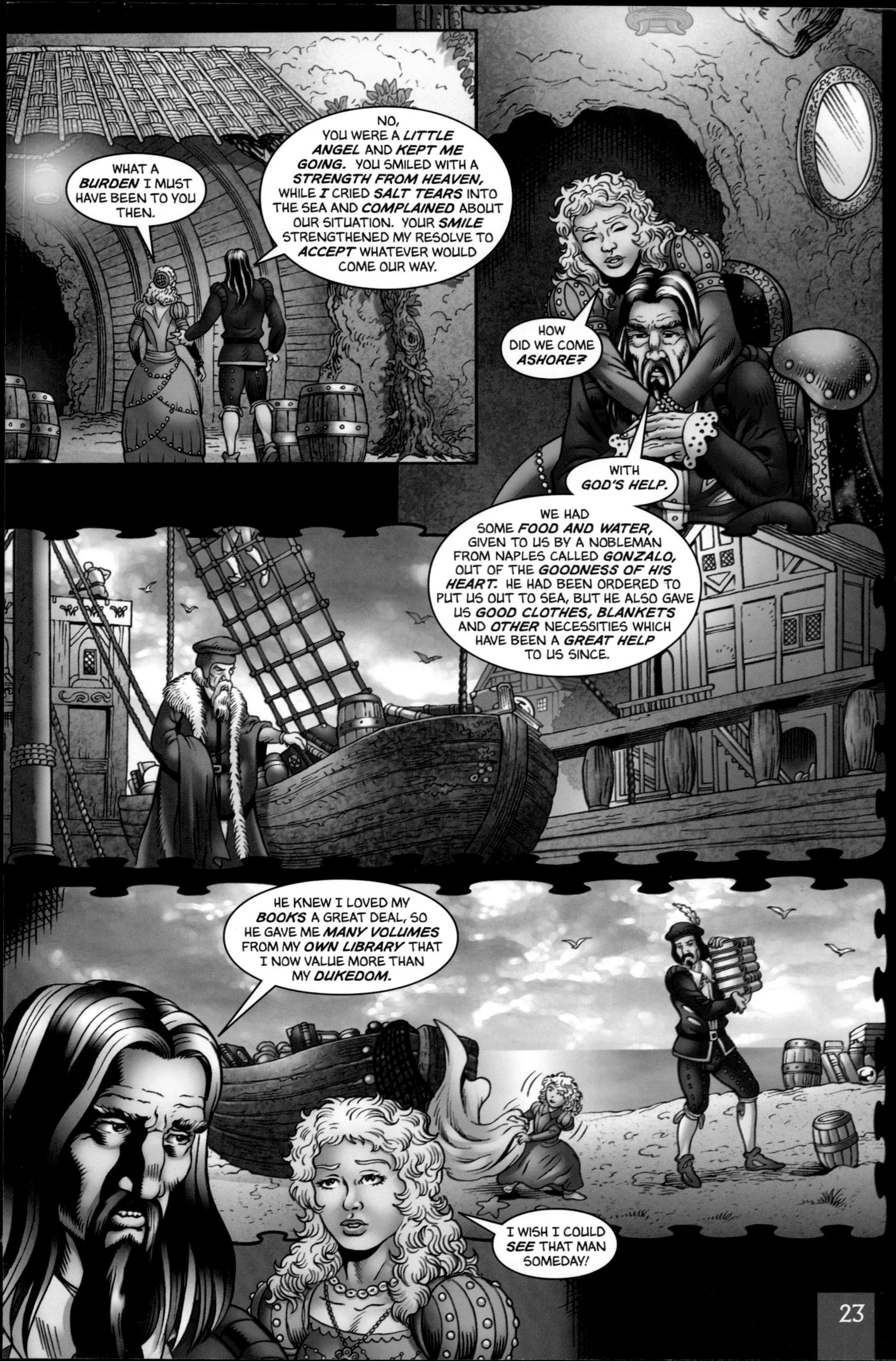
WHAT A BURDEN I MUST HAVE BEEN TO YOU THEN.
NO, YOU WERE A LITTLE ANGEL AND KEPT ME GOING. YOU SMILED WITH A STRENGTH FROM HEAVEN, WHILE I CRIED SALT TEARS INTO THE SEA AND COMPLAINED ABOUT OUR SITUATION. YOUR SMILE STRENGTHENED MY RESOLVE TO ACCEPT WHATEVER WOULD COME OUR WAY.
HOW DID WE COME ASHORE?
WITH GOD'S HELP.
WE HAD SOME FOOD AND WATER, GIVEN TO US BY A NOBLEMAN FROM NAPLES CALLED GONZALO, OUT OF THE GOODNESS OF HIS HEART. HE HAD BEEN ORDERED TO PUT US OUT TO SEA, BUT HE ALSO GAVE US GOOD CLOTHES, BLANKETS AND OTHER NECESSITIES WHICH HAVE BEEN A GREAT HELP TO US SINCE.
HE KNEW I LOVED MY BOOKS A GREAT DEAL, SO HE GAVE ME MANY VOLUMES FROM MY OWN LIBRARY THAT I NOW VALUE MORE THAN MY DUKEDOM.
I WISH I COULD SEE THAT MAN SOMEDAY!

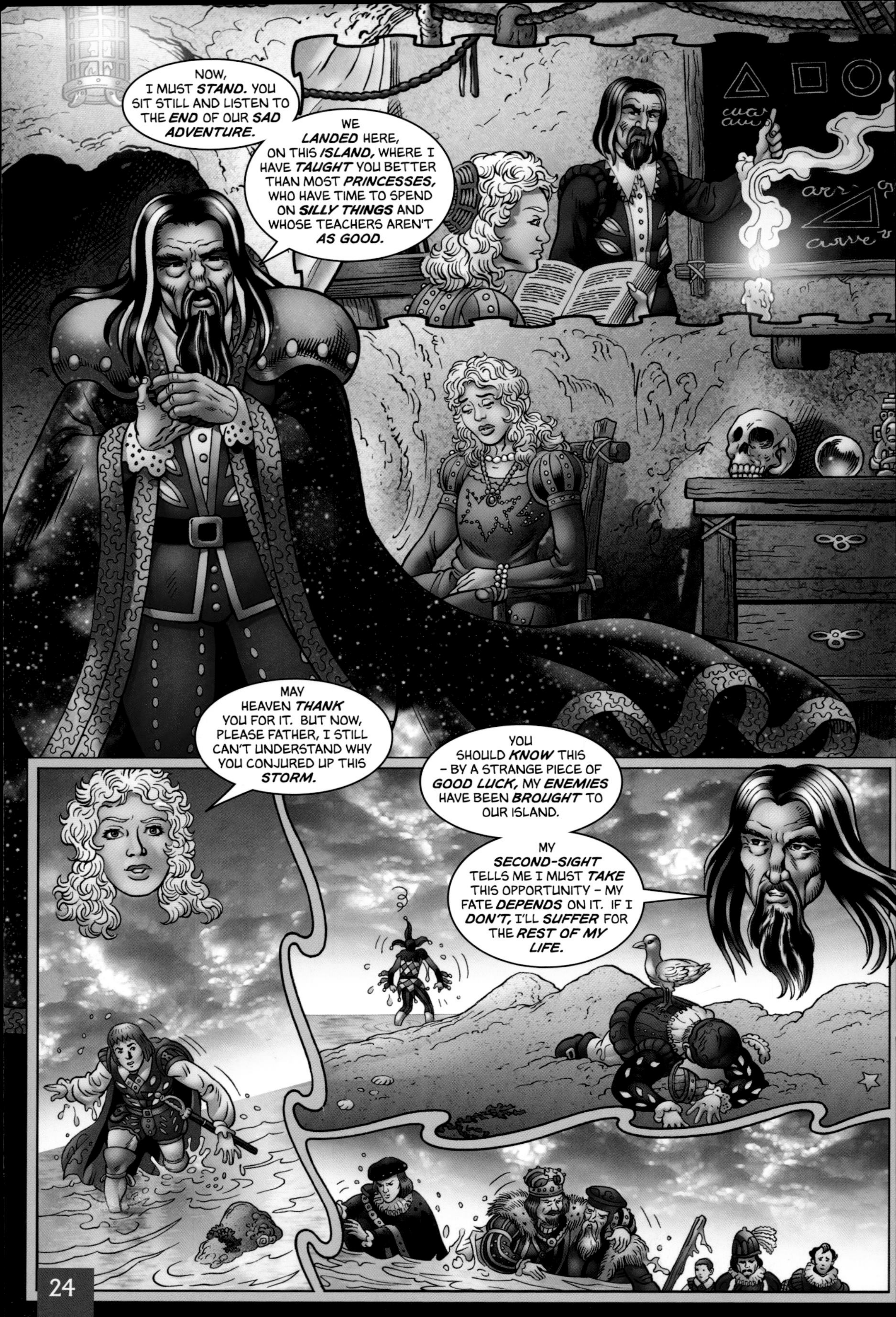
NOW, I MUST STAND. YOU SIT STILL AND LISTEN TO THE END OF OUR SAD ADVENTURE.
WE LANDED HERE, ON THIS ISLAND, WHERE I HAVE TAUGHT YOU BETTER THAN MOST PRINCESSES, WHO HAVE TIME TO SPEND ON SILLY THINGS AND WHOSE TEACHERS AREN'T AS GOOD.
MAY HEAVEN THANK YOU FOR IT. BUT NOW, PLEASE FATHER, I STILL CAN'T UNDERSTAND WHY YOU CONJURED UP THIS STORM.
YOU SHOULD KNOW THIS – BY A STRANGE PIECE OF GOOD LUCK, MY ENEMIES HAVE BEEN BROUGHT TO OUR ISLAND.
MY SECOND-SIGHT TELLS ME I MUST TAKE THIS OPPORTUNITY – MY FATE DEPENDS ON IT. IF I DON'T, I'LL SUFFER FOR THE REST OF MY LIFE.

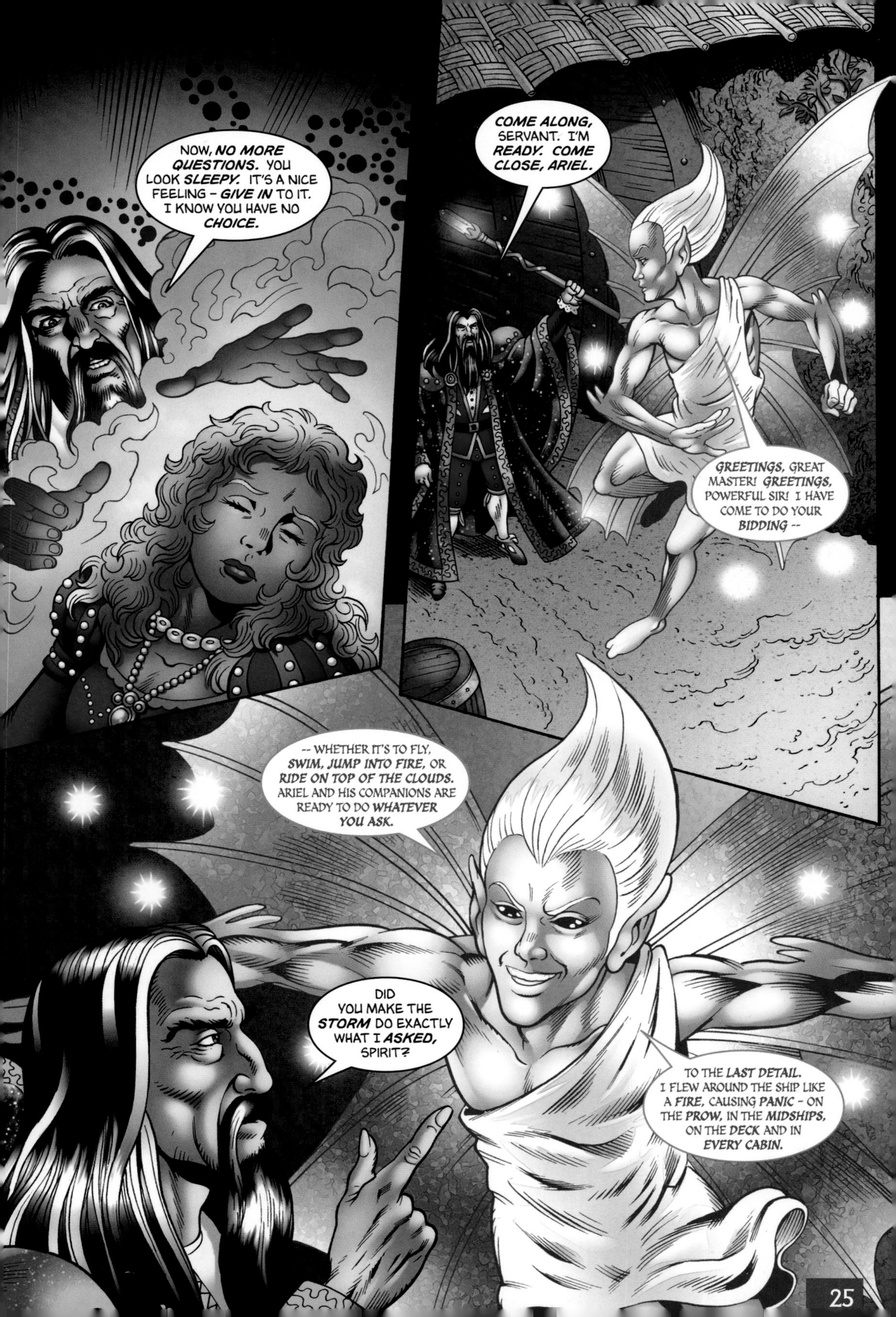
NOW, NO MORE QUESTIONS. YOU LOOK SLEEPY. IT'S A NICE FEELING – GIVE IN TO IT. I KNOW YOU HAVE NO CHOICE.
COME ALONG, SERVANT. I'M READY. COME CLOSE, ARIEL.
GREETINGS, GREAT MASTER! GREETINGS, POWERFUL SIR! I HAVE COME TO DO YOUR BIDDING --
-- WHETHER IT'S TO FLY, SWIM, JUMP INTO FIRE, OR RIDE ON TOP OF THE CLOUDS. ARIEL AND HIS COMPANIONS ARE READY TO DO WHATEVER YOU ASK.
DID YOU MAKE THE STORM DO EXACTLY WHAT I ASKED, SPIRIT?
TO THE LAST DETAIL. I FLEW AROUND THE SHIP LIKE A FIRE, CAUSING PANIC – ON THE PROW, IN THE MIDSHIPS, ON THE DECK AND IN EVERY CABIN.

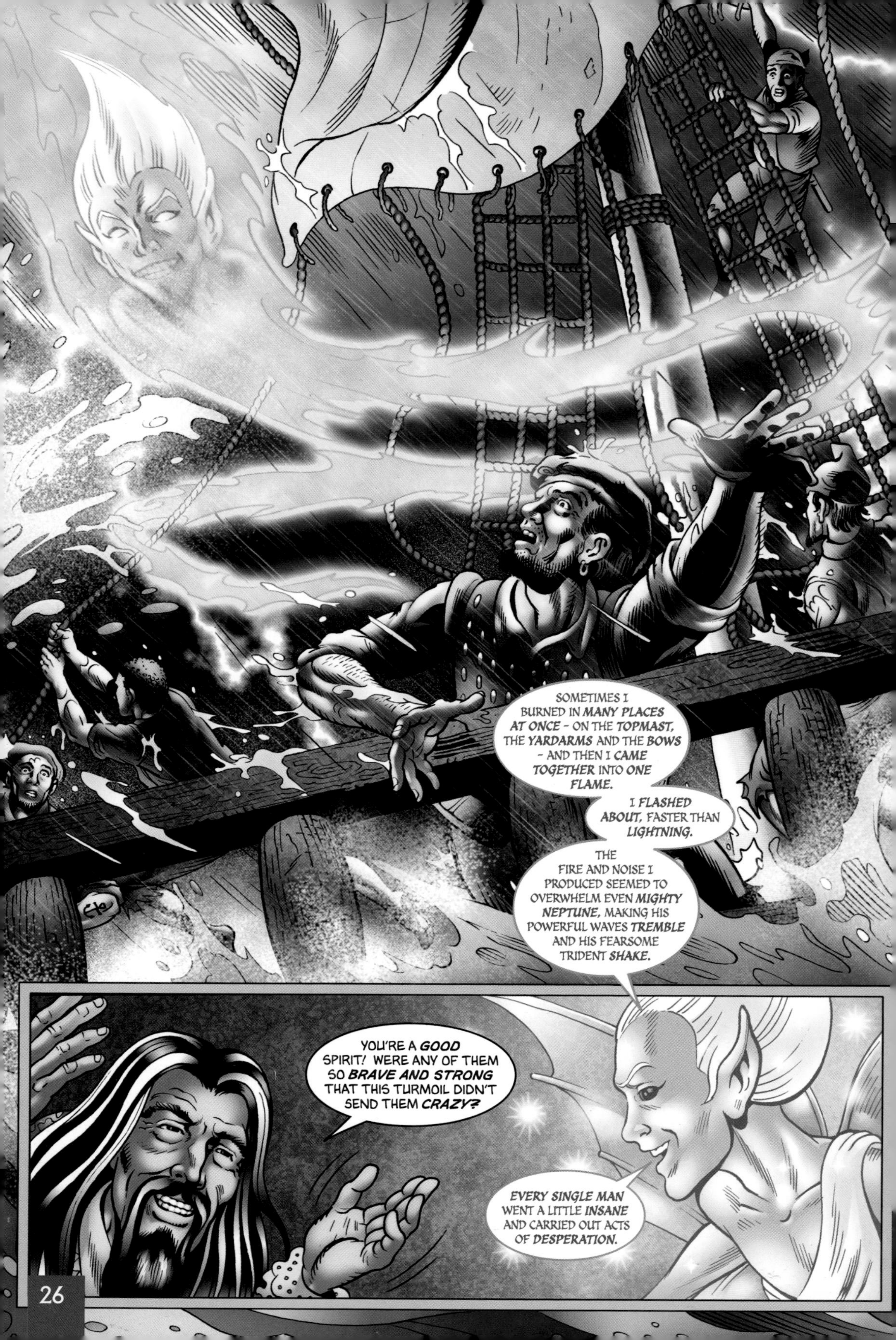
SOMETIMES I BURNED IN MANY PLACES AT ONCE - ON THE TOPMAST, THE YARDARMS AND THE BOWS - AND THEN I CAME TOGETHER INTO ONE FLAME.
I FLASHED ABOUT, FASTER THAN LIGHTNING.
THE FIRE AND NOISE I PRODUCED SEEMED TO OVERWHELM EVEN MIGHTY NEPTUNE, MAKING HIS POWERFUL WAVES TREMBLE AND HIS FEARSOME TRIDENT SHAKE.
YOU'RE A GOOD SPIRIT! WERE ANY OF THEM SO BRAVE AND STRONG THAT THIS TURMOIL DIDN'T SEND THEM CRAZY?
EVERY SINGLE MAN WENT A LITTLE INSANE AND CARRIED OUT ACTS OF DESPERATION.

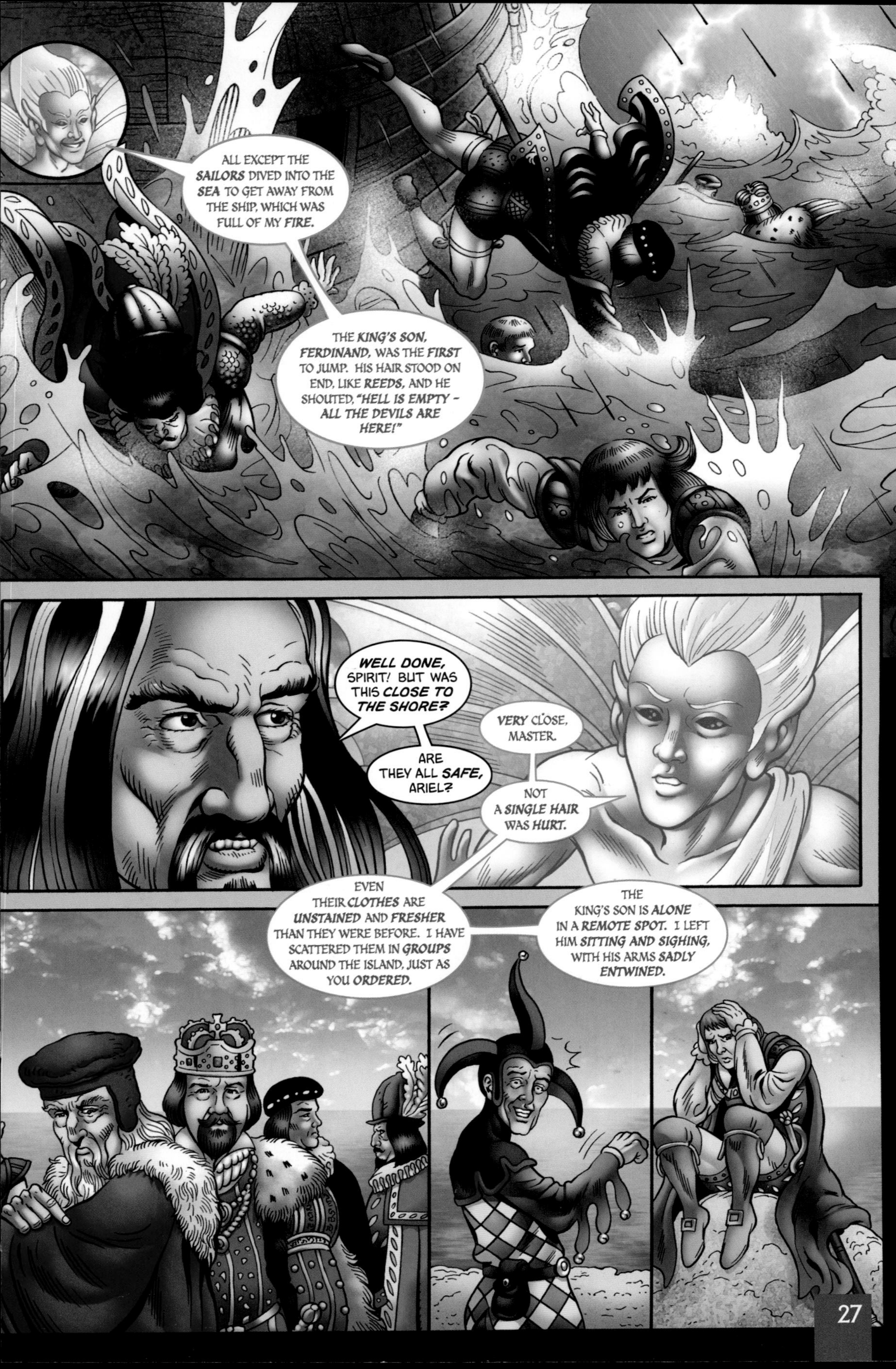
ALL EXCEPT THE SAILORS DIVED INTO THE SEA TO GET AWAY FROM THE SHIP, WHICH WAS FULL OF MY FIRE.
THE KING'S SON, FERDINAND, WAS THE FIRST TO JUMP. HIS HAIR STOOD ON END, LIKE REEDS, AND HE SHOUTED, "HELL IS EMPTY - ALL THE DEVILS ARE HERE!"
WELL DONE, SPIRIT! BUT WAS THIS CLOSE TO THE SHORE?
ARE THEY ALL SAFE, ARIEL?
VERY CLOSE, MASTER.
NOT A SINGLE HAIR WAS HURT.
EVEN THEIR CLOTHES ARE UNSTAINED AND FRESHER THAN THEY WERE BEFORE. I HAVE SCATTERED THEM IN GROUPS AROUND THE ISLAND, JUST AS YOU ORDERED.
THE KING'S SON IS ALONE IN A REMOTE SPOT. I LEFT HIM SITTING AND SIGHING, WITH HIS ARMS SADLY ENTWINED.

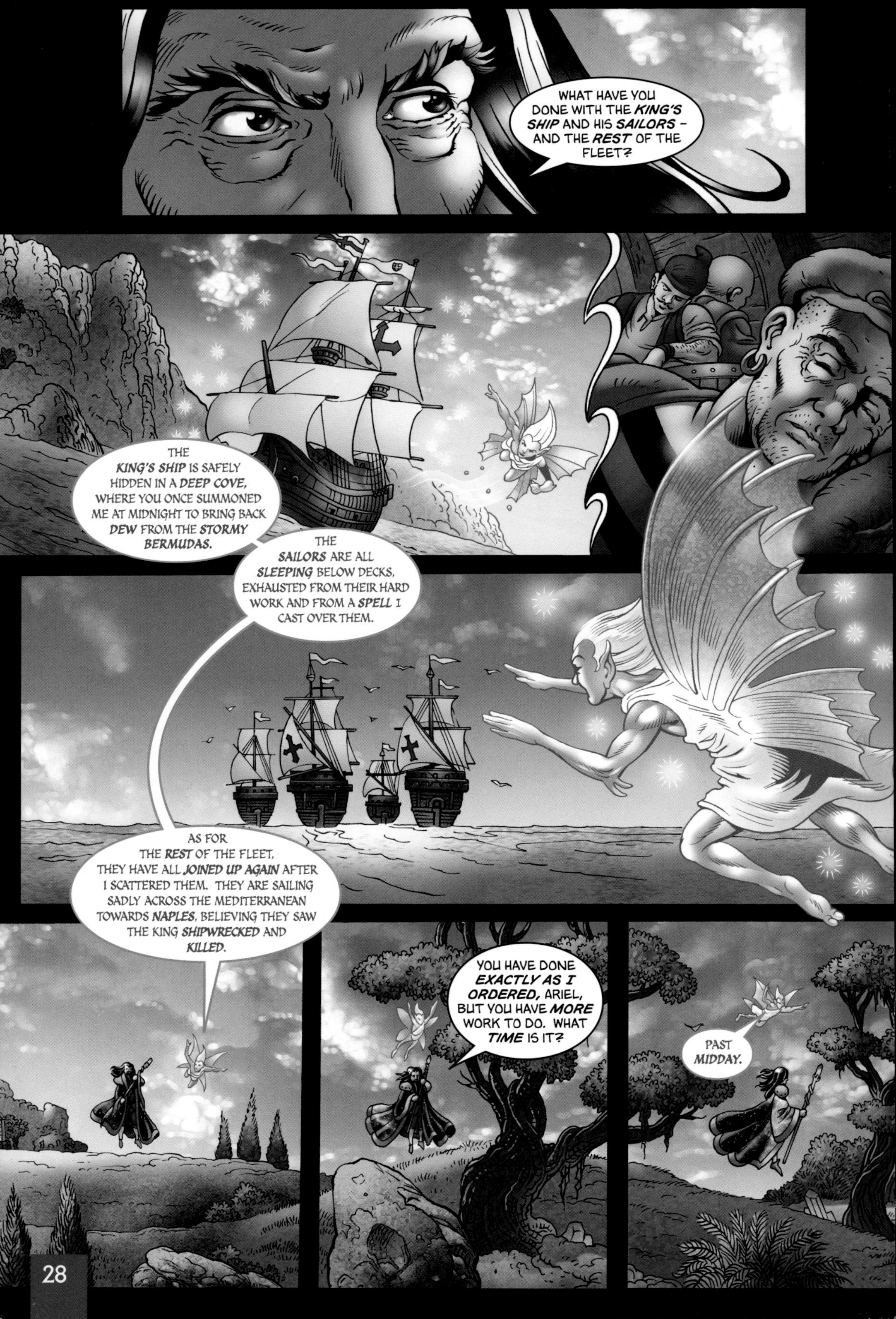

WHAT HAVE YOU DONE WITH THE KING'S SHIP AND HIS SAILORS – AND THE REST OF THE FLEET?
THE KING'S SHIP IS SAFELY HIDDEN IN A DEEP COVE, WHERE YOU ONCE SUMMONED ME AT MIDNIGHT TO BRING BACK DEW FROM THE STORMY BERMUDAS.
THE SAILORS ARE ALL SLEEPING BELOW DECKS, EXHAUSTED FROM THEIR HARD WORK AND FROM A SPELL I CAST OVER THEM.
AS FOR THE REST OF THE FLEET, THEY HAVE ALL JOINED UP AGAIN AFTER I SCATTERED THEM. THEY ARE SAILING SADLY ACROSS THE MEDITERRANEAN TOWARDS NAPLES, BELIEVING THEY SAW THE KING SHIPWRECKED AND KILLED.
YOU HAVE DONE EXACTLY AS I ORDERED, ARIEL, BUT YOU HAVE MORE WORK TO DO. WHAT TIME IS IT?
PAST MIDDAY.

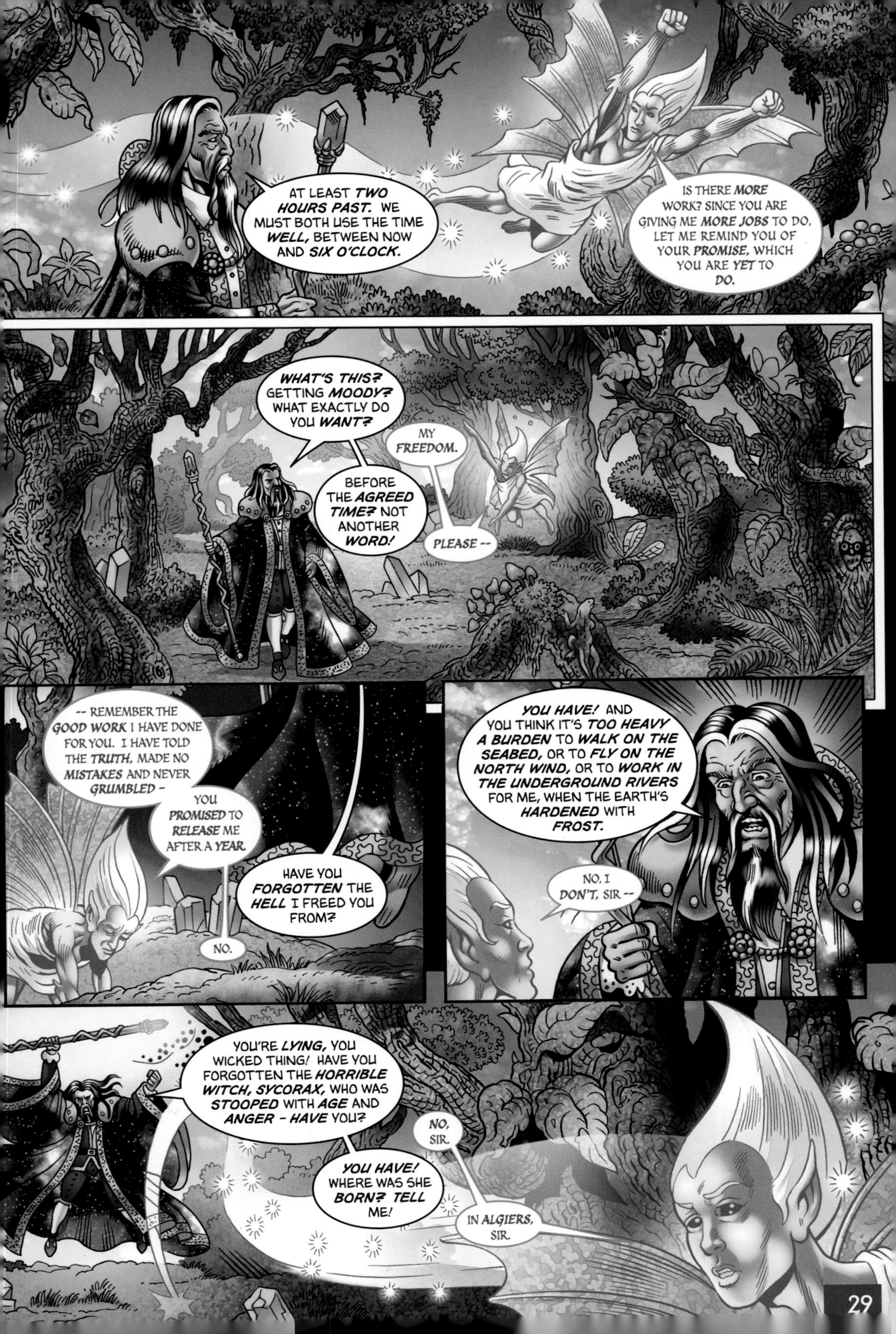
AT LEAST TWO HOURS PAST. WE MUST BOTH USE THE TIME WELL, BETWEEN NOW AND SIX O'CLOCK.
IS THERE MORE WORK? SINCE YOU ARE GIVING ME MORE JOBS TO DO, LET ME REMIND YOU OF YOUR PROMISE, WHICH YOU ARE YET TO DO.
WHAT'S THIS? GETTING MOODY? WHAT EXACTLY DO YOU WANT?
MY FREEDOM.
BEFORE THE AGREED TIME? NOT ANOTHER WORD!
PLEASE --
-- REMEMBER THE GOOD WORK I HAVE DONE FOR YOU. I HAVE TOLD THE TRUTH, MADE NO MISTAKES AND NEVER GRUMBLED -
YOU PROMISED TO RELEASE ME AFTER A YEAR.
HAVE YOU FORGOTTEN THE HELL I FREED YOU FROM?
NO.
YOU HAVE! AND YOU THINK IT'S TOO HEAVY A BURDEN TO WALK ON THE SEABED, OR TO FLY ON THE NORTH WIND, OR TO WORK IN THE UNDERGROUND RIVERS FOR ME, WHEN THE EARTH'S HARDENED WITH FROST.
NO, I DON'T, SIR --
YOU'RE LYING, YOU WICKED THING! HAVE YOU FORGOTTEN THE HORRIBLE WITCH, SYCORAX, WHO WAS STOOPED WITH AGE AND ANGER - HAVE YOU?
NO, SIR.
YOU HAVE! WHERE WAS SHE BORN? TELL ME!
IN ALGIERS, SIR.

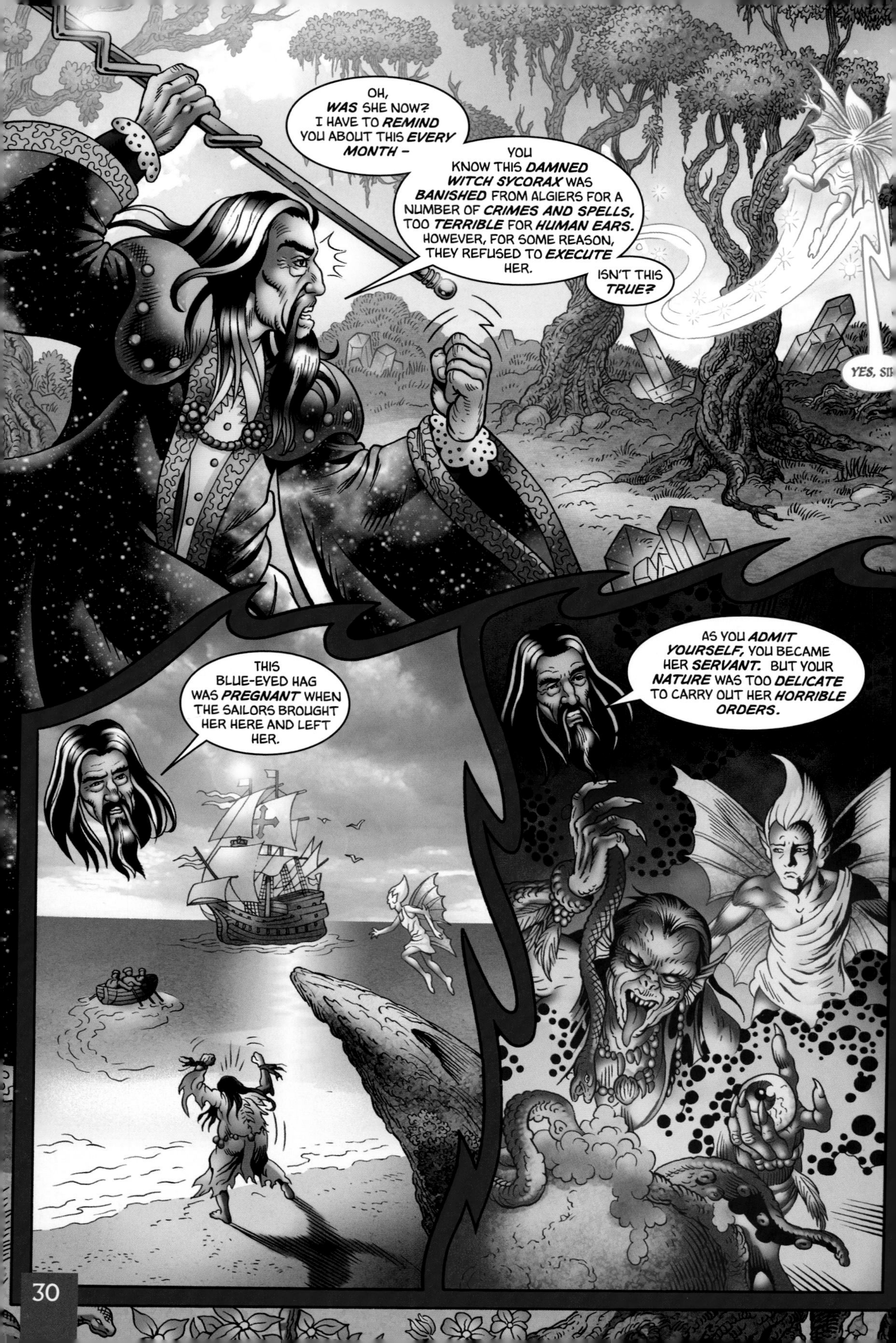
OH, WAS SHE NOW? I HAVE TO REMIND YOU ABOUT THIS EVERY MONTH –
YOU KNOW THIS DAMNED WITCH SYCORAX WAS BANISHED FROM ALGIERS FOR A NUMBER OF CRIMES AND SPELLS, TOO TERRIBLE FOR HUMAN EARS. HOWEVER, FOR SOME REASON, THEY REFUSED TO EXECUTE HER.
ISN'T THIS TRUE?
THIS BLUE-EYED HAG WAS PREGNANT WHEN THE SAILORS BROUGHT HER HERE AND LEFT HER.
AS YOU ADMIT YOURSELF, YOU BECAME HER SERVANT. BUT YOUR NATURE WAS TOO DELICATE TO CARRY OUT HER HORRIBLE ORDERS.

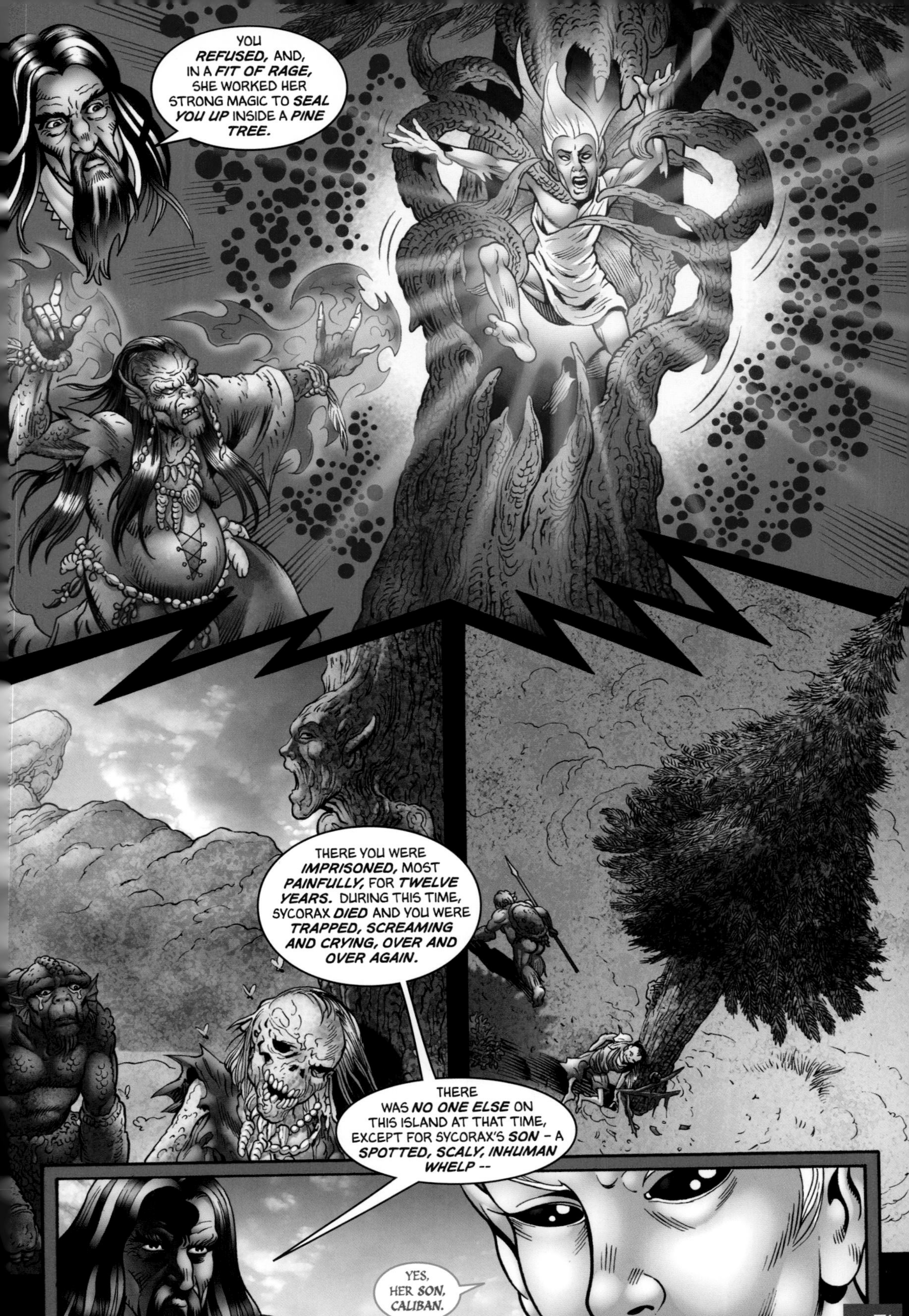
YOU REFUSED, AND, IN A FIT OF RAGE, SHE WORKED HER STRONG MAGIC TO SEAL YOU UP INSIDE A PINE TREE.
THERE YOU WERE IMPRISONED, MOST PAINFULLY, FOR TWELVE YEARS. DURING THIS TIME, SYCORAX DIED AND YOU WERE TRAPPED, SCREAMING AND CRYING, OVER AND OVER AGAIN.
THERE WAS NO ONE ELSE ON THIS ISLAND AT THAT TIME, EXCEPT FOR SYCORAX'S SON – A SPOTTED, SCALY, INHUMAN WHELP --
YES, HER SON, CALIBAN.

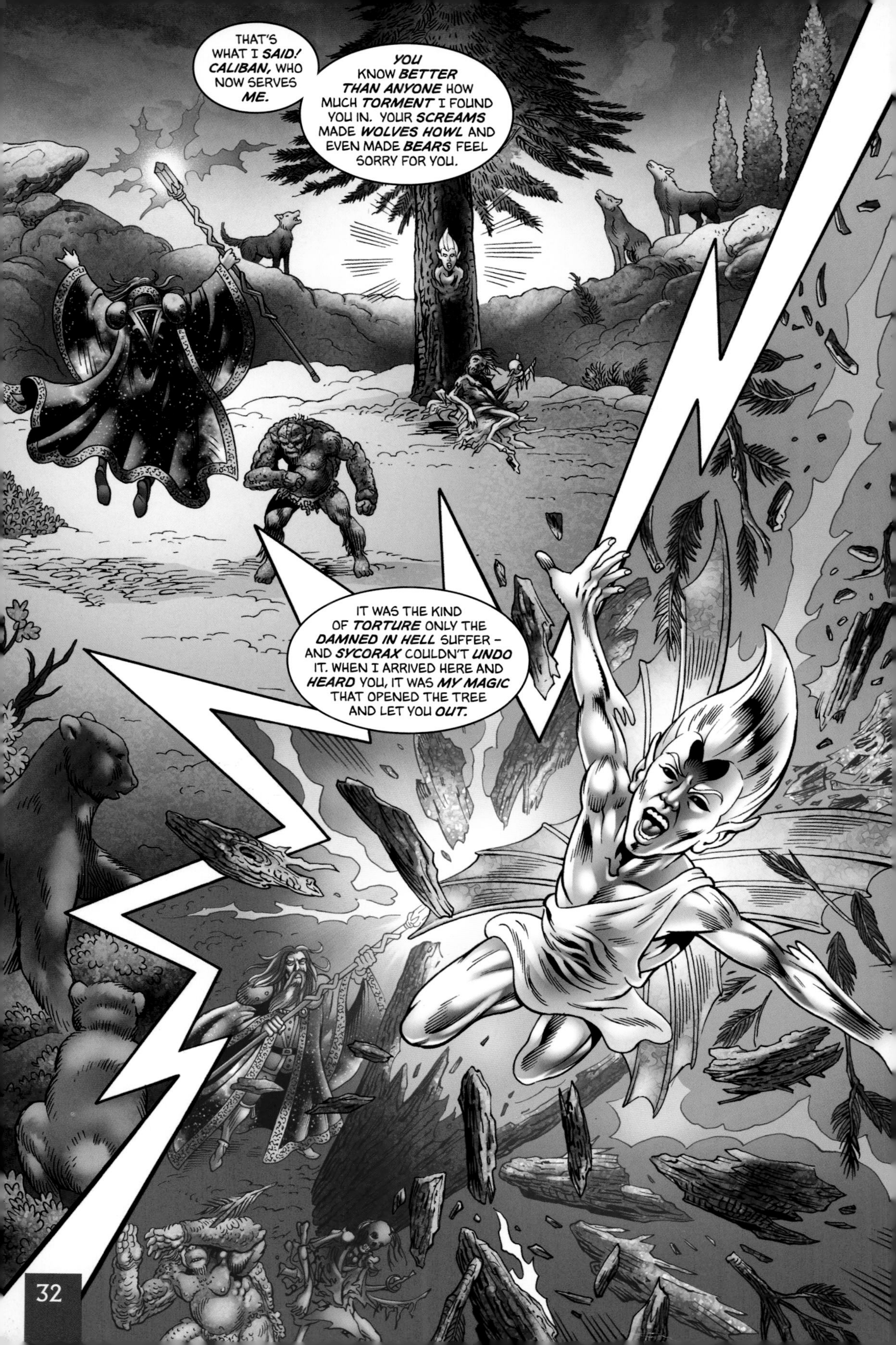
THAT'S WHAT I SAID! CALIBAN, WHO NOW SERVES ME.
YOU KNOW BETTER THAN ANYONE HOW MUCH TORMENT I FOUND YOU IN. YOUR SCREAMS MADE WOLVES HOWL AND EVEN MADE BEARS FEEL SORRY FOR YOU.
IT WAS THE KIND OF TORTURE ONLY THE DAMNED IN HELL SUFFER – AND SYCORAX COULDN'T UNDO IT. WHEN I ARRIVED HERE AND HEARD YOU, IT WAS MY MAGIC THAT OPENED THE TREE AND LET YOU OUT.

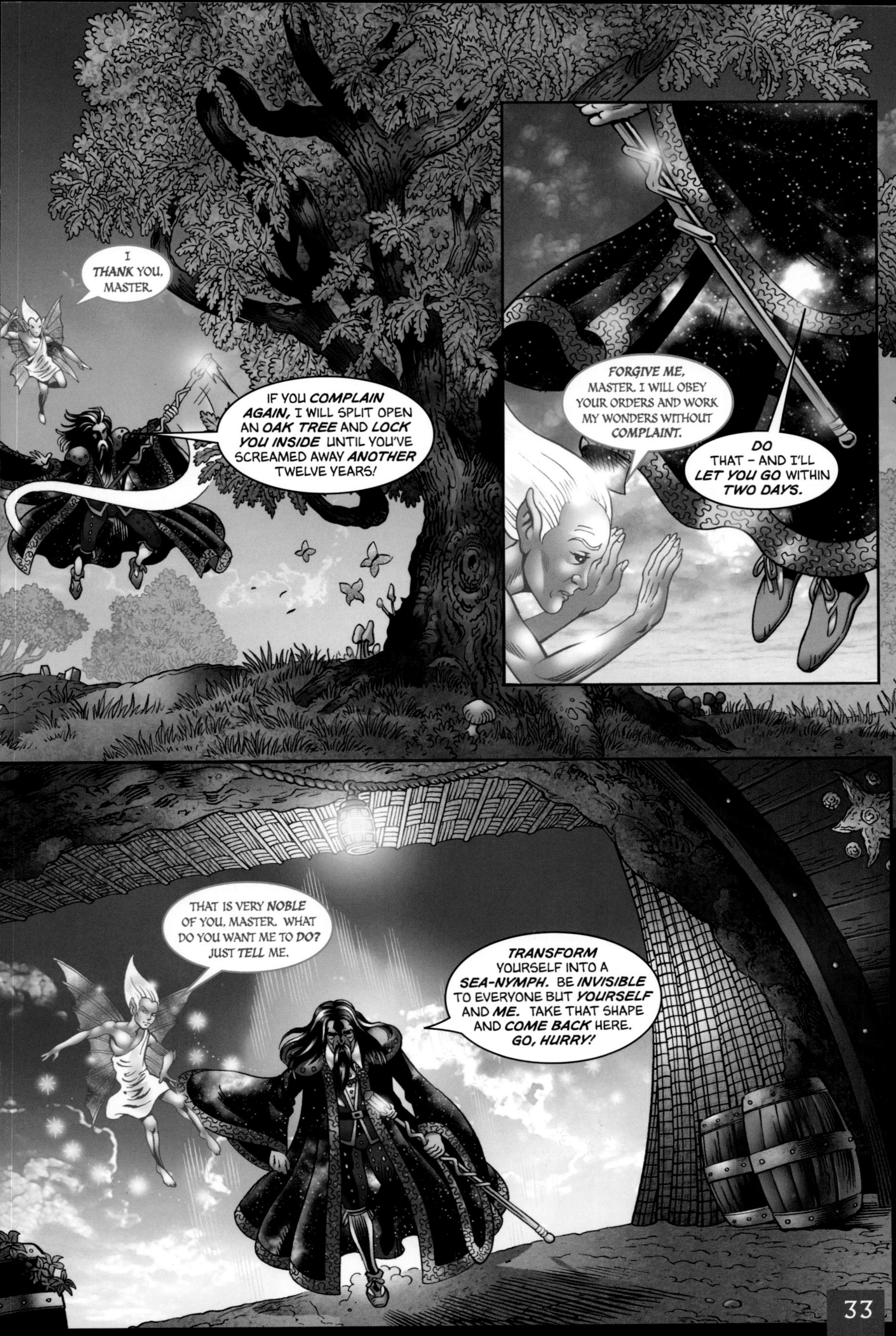
I THANK YOU, MASTER.
IF YOU COMPLAIN AGAIN, I WILL SPLIT OPEN AN OAK TREE AND LOCK YOU INSIDE UNTIL YOU'VE SCREAMED AWAY ANOTHER TWELVE YEARS!
FORGIVE ME, MASTER. I WILL OBEY YOUR ORDERS AND WORK MY WONDERS WITHOUT COMPLAINT.
DO THAT – AND I'LL LET YOU GO WITHIN TWO DAYS.
THAT IS VERY NOBLE OF YOU, MASTER. WHAT DO YOU WANT ME TO DO? JUST TELL ME.
TRANSFORM YOURSELF INTO A SEA-NYMPH. BE INVISIBLE TO EVERYONE BUT YOURSELF AND ME. TAKE THAT SHAPE AND COME BACK HERE. GO, HURRY!

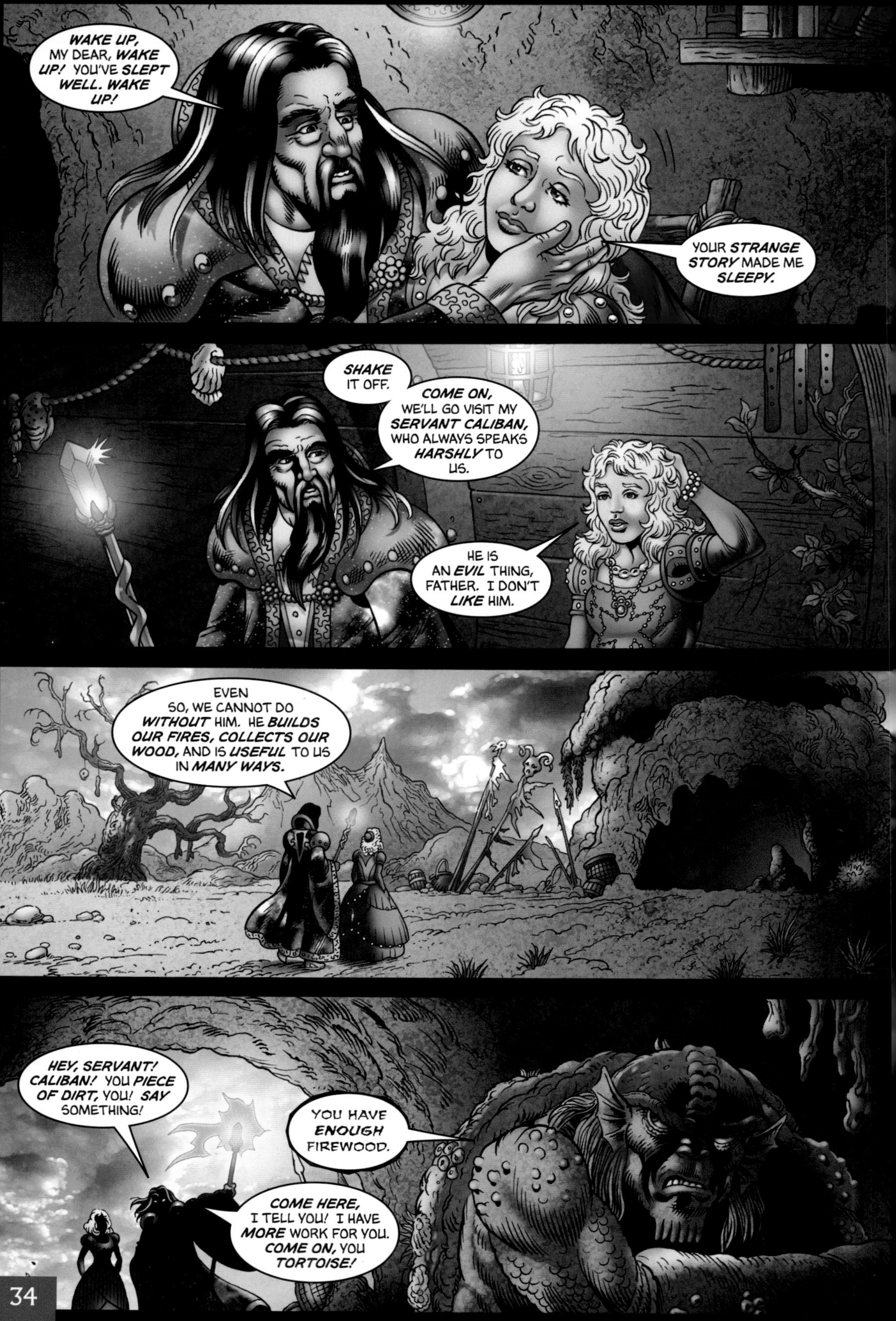

WAKE UP, MY DEAR, WAKE UP! YOU'VE SLEPT WELL. WAKE UP!
YOUR STRANGE STORY MADE ME SLEEPY.
SHAKE IT OFF.
COME ON, WE'LL GO VISIT MY SERVANT CALIBAN, WHO ALWAYS SPEAKS HARSHLY TO US.
HE IS AN EVIL THING, FATHER. I DON'T LIKE HIM.
EVEN SO, WE CANNOT DO WITHOUT HIM. HE BUILDS OUR FIRES, COLLECTS OUR WOOD, AND IS USEFUL TO US IN MANY WAYS.
HEY, SERVANT! CALIBAN! YOU PIECE OF DIRT, YOU! SAY SOMETHING!
YOU HAVE ENOUGH FIREWOOD.
COME HERE, I TELL YOU! I HAVE MORE WORK FOR YOU. COME ON, YOU TORTOISE!

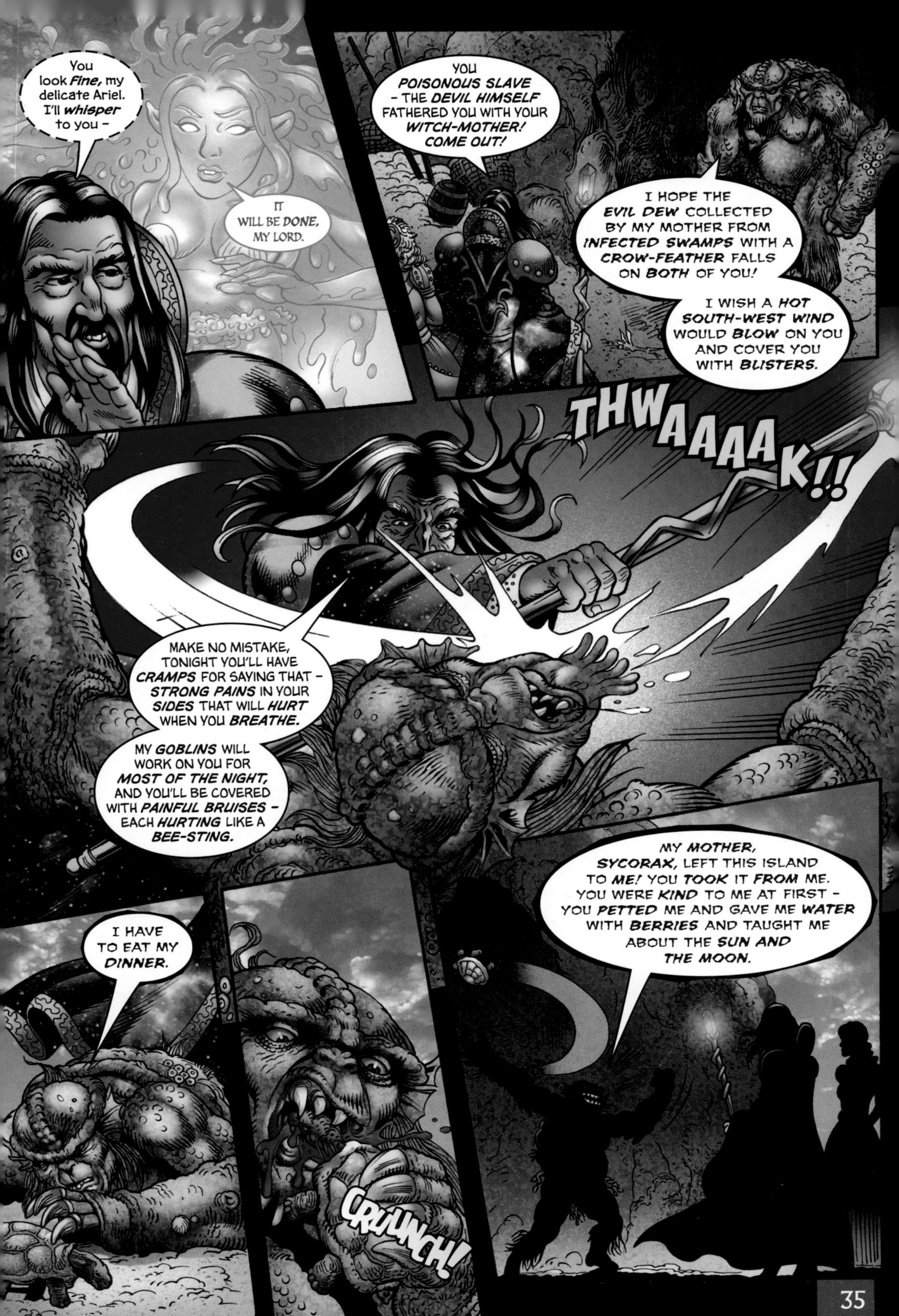
You look Fine, my delicate Ariel. I'll whisper to you -
IT WILL BE DONE, MY LORD.
YOU POISONOUS SLAVE - THE DEVIL HIMSELF FATHERED YOU WITH YOUR WITCH-MOTHER! COME OUT!
I HOPE THE EVIL DEW COLLECTED BY MY MOTHER FROM INFECTED SWAMPS WITH A CROW-FEATHER FALLS ON BOTH OF YOU!
I WISH A HOT SOUTH-WEST WIND WOULD BLOW ON YOU AND COVER YOU WITH BLISTERS.
THWAAAAK!!
MAKE NO MISTAKE, TONIGHT YOU'LL HAVE CRAMPS FOR SAYING THAT - STRONG PAINS IN YOUR SIDES THAT WILL HURT WHEN YOU BREATHE.
MY GOBLINS WILL WORK ON YOU FOR MOST OF THE NIGHT, AND YOU'LL BE COVERED WITH PAINFUL BRUISES - EACH HURTING LIKE A BEE-STING.
I HAVE TO EAT MY DINNER.
CRUUNCH!
MY MOTHER, SYCORAX, LEFT THIS ISLAND TO ME! YOU TOOK IT FROM ME. YOU WERE KIND TO ME AT FIRST - YOU PETTED ME AND GAVE ME WATER WITH BERRIES AND TAUGHT ME ABOUT THE SUN AND THE MOON.

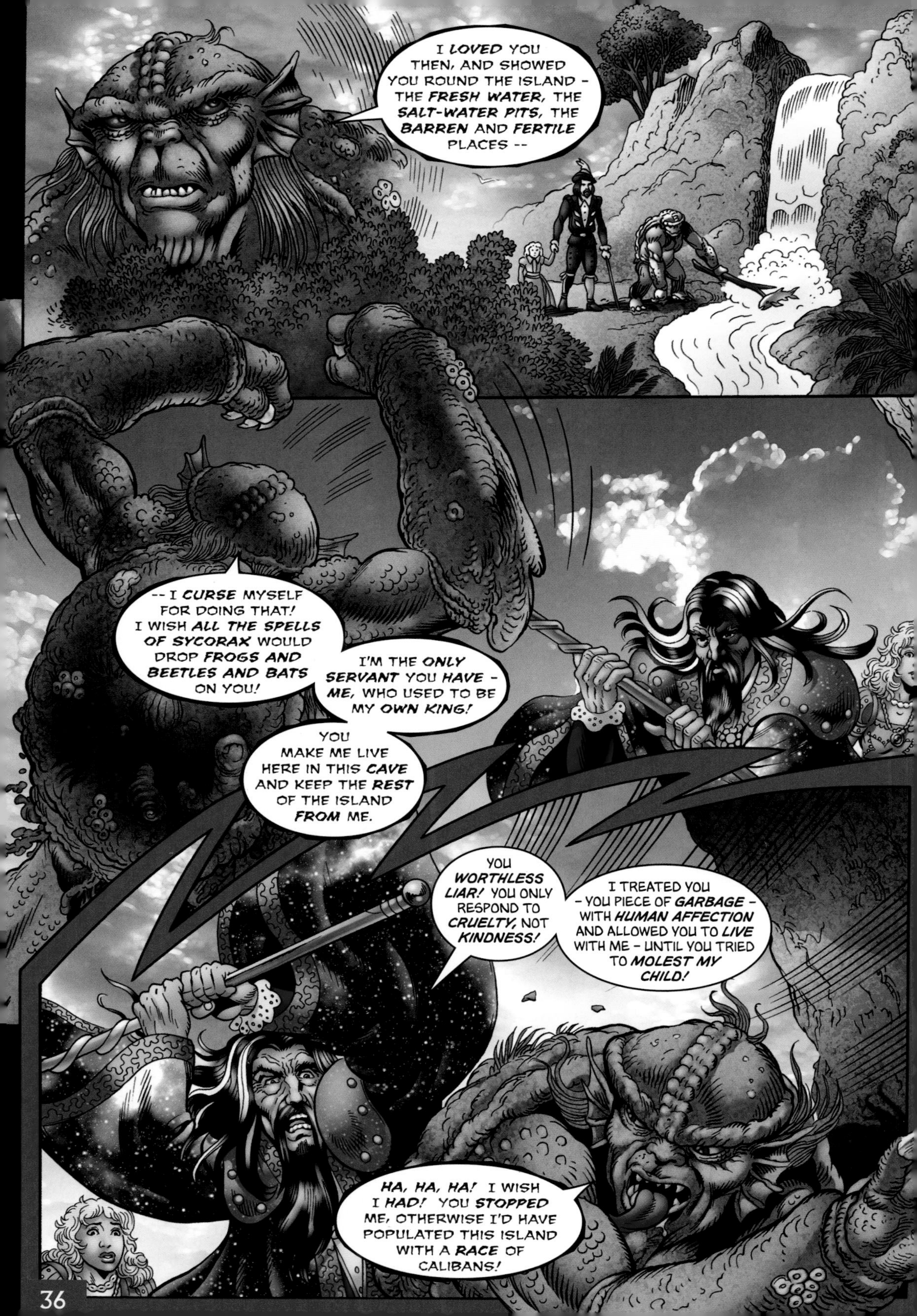
I LOVED YOU THEN, AND SHOWED YOU ROUND THE ISLAND - THE FRESH WATER, THE SALT-WATER PITS, THE BARREN AND FERTILE PLACES --
-- I CURSE MYSELF FOR DOING THAT! I WISH ALL THE SPELLS OF SYCORAX WOULD DROP FROGS AND BEETLES AND BATS ON YOU!
I'M THE ONLY SERVANT YOU HAVE - ME, WHO USED TO BE MY OWN KING!
YOU MAKE ME LIVE HERE IN THIS CAVE AND KEEP THE REST OF THE ISLAND FROM ME.
YOU WORTHLESS LIAR! YOU ONLY RESPOND TO CRUELTY, NOT KINDNESS!
I TREATED YOU - YOU PIECE OF GARBAGE - WITH HUMAN AFFECTION AND ALLOWED YOU TO LIVE WITH ME - UNTIL YOU TRIED TO MOLEST MY CHILD!
HA, HA, HA! I WISH I HAD! YOU STOPPED ME, OTHERWISE I'D HAVE POPULATED THIS ISLAND WITH A RACE OF CALIBANS!

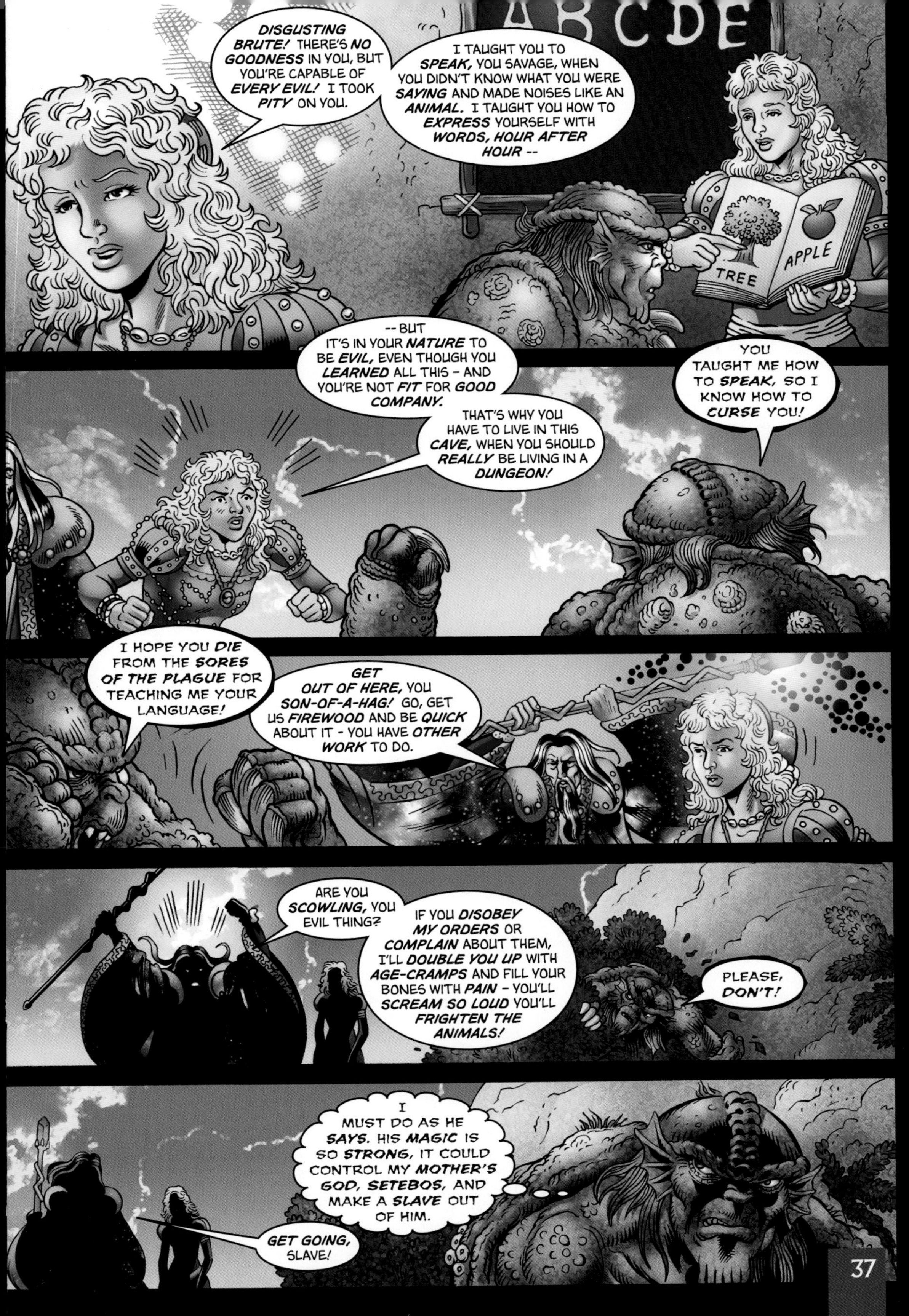
A B C D E
DISGUSTING BRUTE! THERE'S NO GOODNESS IN YOU, BUT YOU'RE CAPABLE OF EVERY EVIL! I TOOK PITY ON YOU.
I TAUGHT YOU TO SPEAK, YOU SAVAGE, WHEN YOU DIDN'T KNOW WHAT YOU WERE SAYING AND MADE NOISES LIKE AN ANIMAL. I TAUGHT YOU HOW TO EXPRESS YOURSELF WITH WORDS, HOUR AFTER HOUR --
TREE
APPLE
-- BUT IT'S IN YOUR NATURE TO BE EVIL, EVEN THOUGH YOU LEARNED ALL THIS - AND YOU'RE NOT FIT FOR GOOD COMPANY.
THAT'S WHY YOU HAVE TO LIVE IN THIS CAVE, WHEN YOU SHOULD REALLY BE LIVING IN A DUNGEON!
YOU TAUGHT ME HOW TO SPEAK, SO I KNOW HOW TO CURSE YOU!
I HOPE YOU DIE FROM THE SORES OF THE PLAGUE FOR TEACHING ME YOUR LANGUAGE!
GET OUT OF HERE, YOU SON-OF-A-HAG! GO, GET US FIREWOOD AND BE QUICK ABOUT IT - YOU HAVE OTHER WORK TO DO.
ARE YOU SCOWLING, YOU EVIL THING?
IF YOU DISOBEY MY ORDERS OR COMPLAIN ABOUT THEM, I'LL DOUBLE YOU UP WITH AGE-CRAMPS AND FILL YOUR BONES WITH PAIN - YOU'LL SCREAM SO LOUD YOU'LL FRIGHTEN THE ANIMALS!
PLEASE, DON'T!
I MUST DO AS HE SAYS. HIS MAGIC IS SO STRONG, IT COULD CONTROL MY MOTHER'S GOD, SETEBOS, AND MAKE A SLAVE OUT OF HIM.
GET GOING, SLAVE!

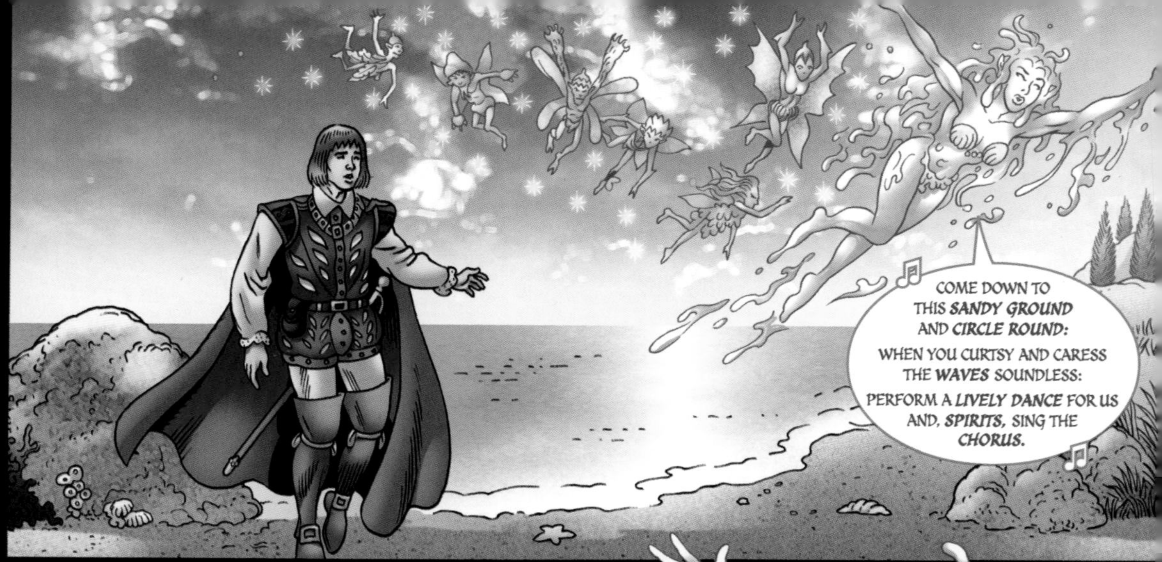
COME DOWN TO THIS SANDY GROUND AND CIRCLE ROUND: WHEN YOU CURTSY AND CARESS THE WAVES SOUNDLESS: PERFORM A LIVELY DANCE FOR US AND, SPIRITS, SING THE CHORUS.

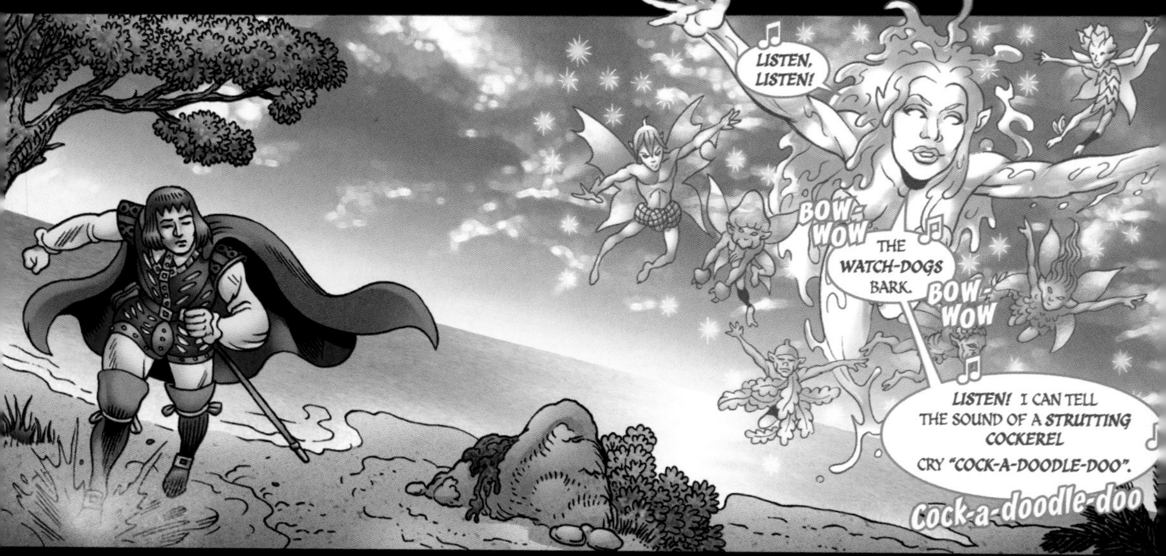
LISTEN, LISTEN!
BOW-WOW
THE WATCH-DOGS BARK.
BOW-WOW
LISTEN! I CAN TELL THE SOUND OF A STRUTTING COCKEREL CRY "COCK-A-DOODLE-DOO".
Cock-a-doodle-doo

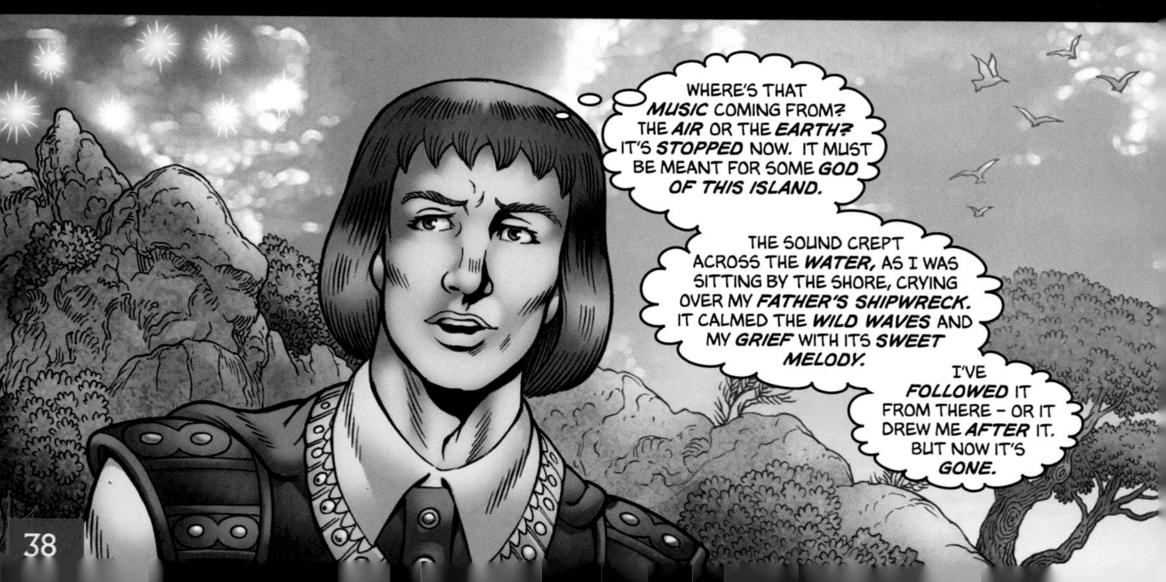
WHERE'S THAT MUSIC COMING FROM? THE AIR OR THE EARTH? IT'S STOPPED NOW. IT MUST BE MEANT FOR SOME GOD OF THIS ISLAND.
THE SOUND CREPT ACROSS THE WATER, AS I WAS SITTING BY THE SHORE, CRYING OVER MY FATHER'S SHIPWRECK. IT CALMED THE WILD WAVES AND MY GRIEF WITH ITS SWEET MELODY.
I'VE FOLLOWED IT FROM THERE – OR IT DREW ME AFTER IT. BUT NOW IT'S GONE.

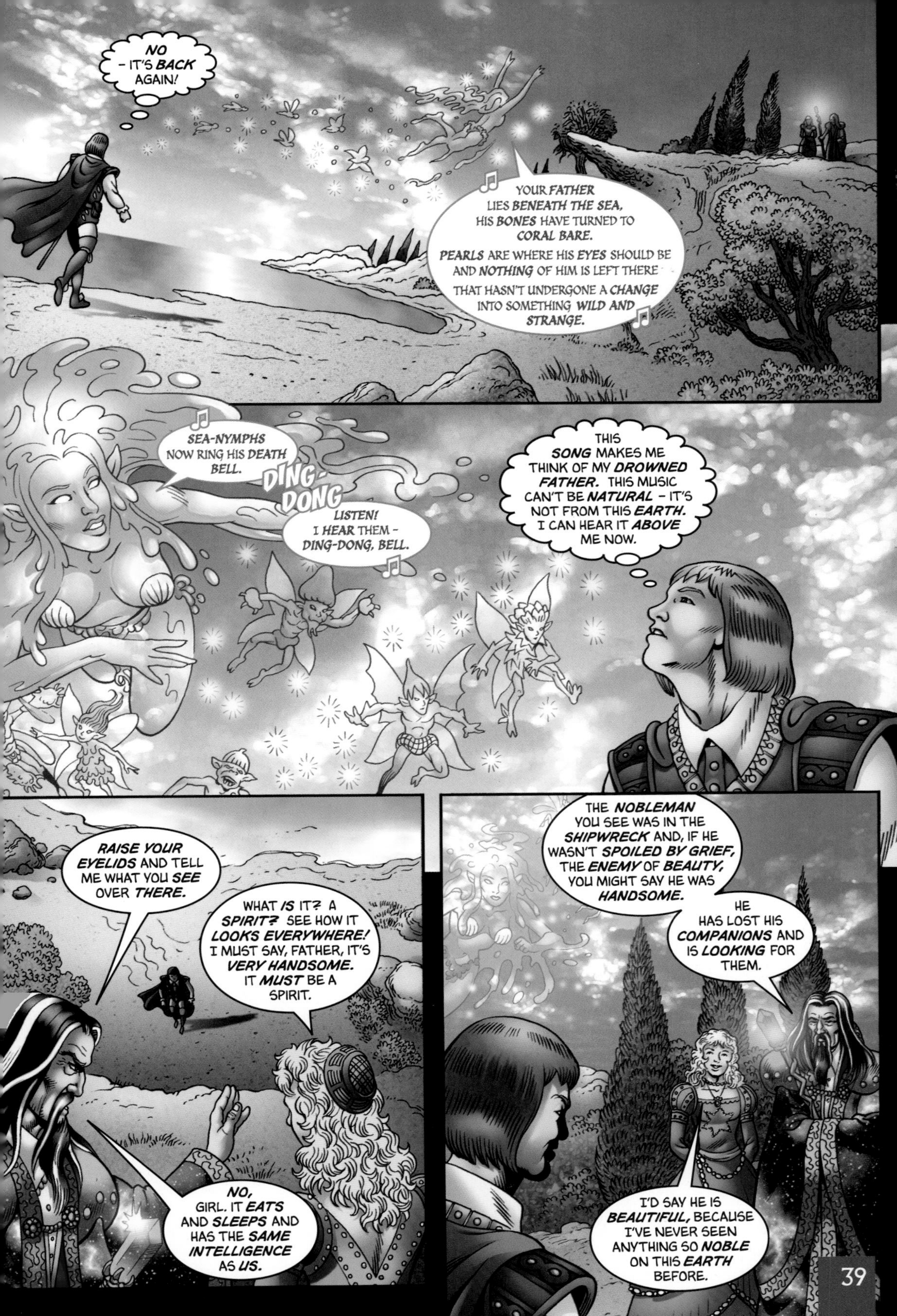
NO – IT'S BACK AGAIN!
YOUR FATHER LIES BENEATH THE SEA, HIS BONES HAVE TURNED TO CORAL BARE.
PEARLS ARE WHERE HIS EYES SHOULD BE AND NOTHING OF HIM IS LEFT THERE
THAT HASN'T UNDERGONE A CHANGE INTO SOMETHING WILD AND STRANGE.
SEA-NYMPHS NOW RING HIS DEATH BELL.
DING-DONG
LISTEN! I HEAR THEM – DING-DONG, BELL.
THIS SONG MAKES ME THINK OF MY DROWNED FATHER. THIS MUSIC CAN'T BE NATURAL – IT'S NOT FROM THIS EARTH. I CAN HEAR IT ABOVE ME NOW.
RAISE YOUR EYELIDS AND TELL ME WHAT YOU SEE OVER THERE.
WHAT IS IT? A SPIRIT? SEE HOW IT LOOKS EVERYWHERE! I MUST SAY, FATHER, IT'S VERY HANDSOME. IT MUST BE A SPIRIT.
NO, GIRL. IT EATS AND SLEEPS AND HAS THE SAME INTELLIGENCE AS US.
THE NOBLEMAN YOU SEE WAS IN THE SHIPWRECK AND, IF HE WASN'T SPOILED BY GRIEF, THE ENEMY OF BEAUTY, YOU MIGHT SAY HE WAS HANDSOME.
HE HAS LOST HIS COMPANIONS AND IS LOOKING FOR THEM.
I'D SAY HE IS BEAUTIFUL, BECAUSE I'VE NEVER SEEN ANYTHING SO NOBLE ON THIS EARTH BEFORE.

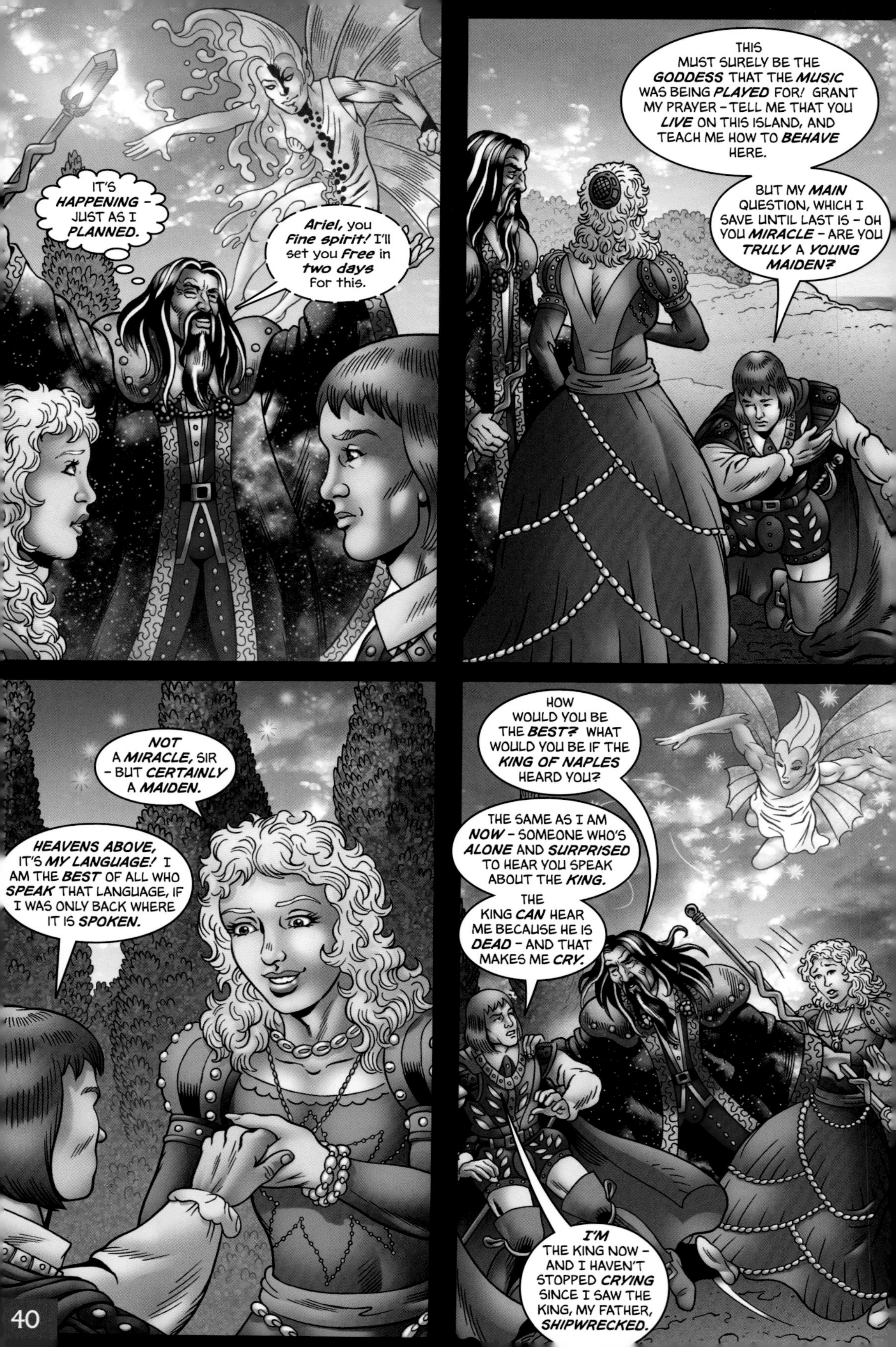
IT'S HAPPENING – JUST AS I PLANNED.
Ariel, you Fine spirit! I'll set you Free in two days For this.
THIS MUST SURELY BE THE GODDESS THAT THE MUSIC WAS BEING PLAYED FOR! GRANT MY PRAYER – TELL ME THAT YOU LIVE ON THIS ISLAND, AND TEACH ME HOW TO BEHAVE HERE.
BUT MY MAIN QUESTION, WHICH I SAVE UNTIL LAST IS – OH YOU MIRACLE – ARE YOU TRULY A YOUNG MAIDEN?
NOT A MIRACLE, SIR – BUT CERTAINLY A MAIDEN.
HEAVENS ABOVE, IT'S MY LANGUAGE! I AM THE BEST OF ALL WHO SPEAK THAT LANGUAGE, IF I WAS ONLY BACK WHERE IT IS SPOKEN.
HOW WOULD YOU BE THE BEST? WHAT WOULD YOU BE IF THE KING OF NAPLES HEARD YOU?
THE SAME AS I AM NOW – SOMEONE WHO'S ALONE AND SURPRISED TO HEAR YOU SPEAK ABOUT THE KING.
THE KING CAN HEAR ME BECAUSE HE IS DEAD – AND THAT MAKES ME CRY.
I'M THE KING NOW – AND I HAVEN'T STOPPED CRYING SINCE I SAW THE KING, MY FATHER, SHIPWRECKED.

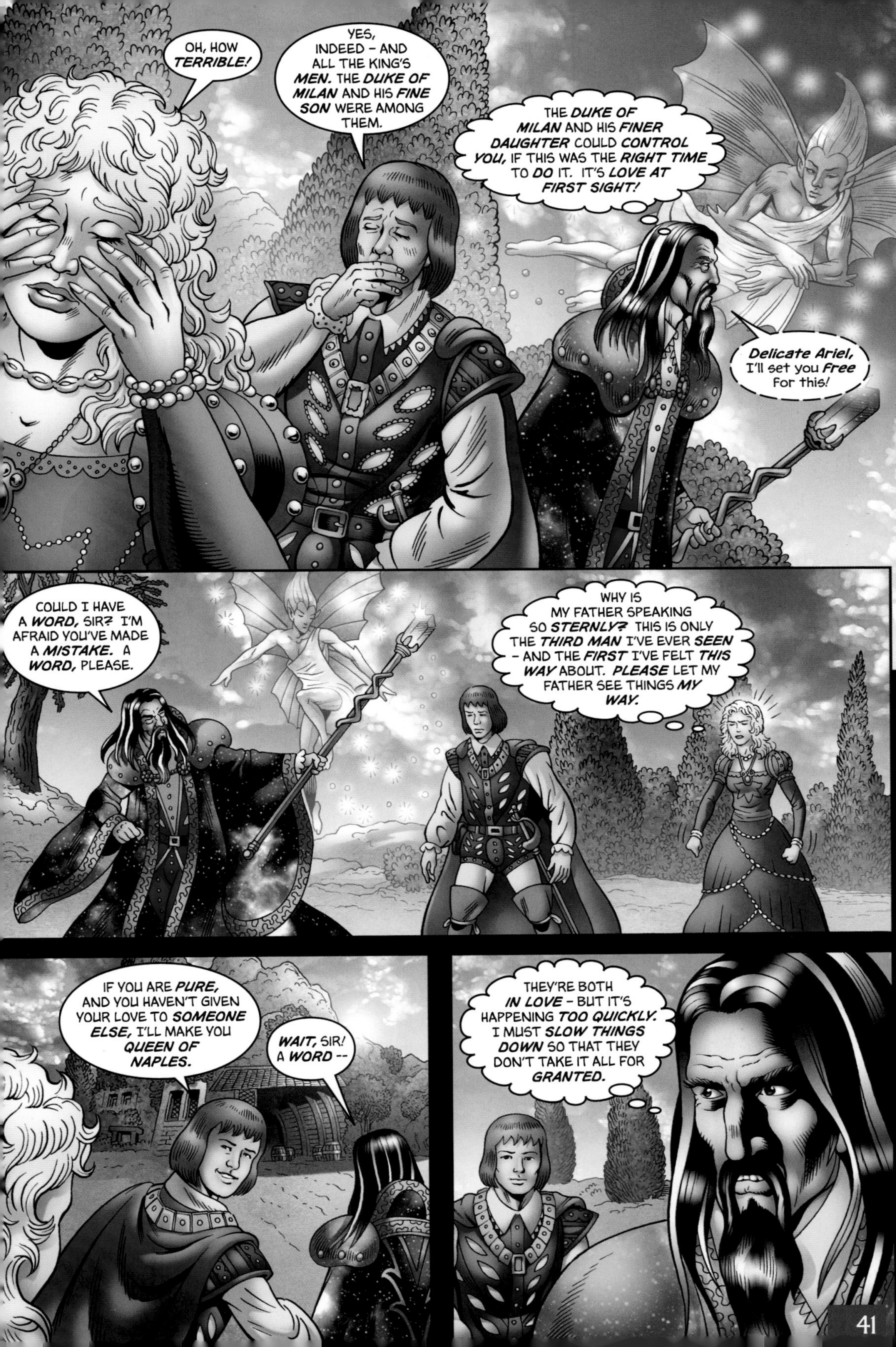
OH, HOW TERRIBLE!
YES, INDEED – AND ALL THE KING'S MEN. THE DUKE OF MILAN AND HIS FINE SON WERE AMONG THEM.
THE DUKE OF MILAN AND HIS FINER DAUGHTER COULD CONTROL YOU, IF THIS WAS THE RIGHT TIME TO DO IT. IT'S LOVE AT FIRST SIGHT!
Delicate Ariel, I'll set you Free for this!
COULD I HAVE A WORD, SIR? I'M AFRAID YOU'VE MADE A MISTAKE. A WORD, PLEASE.
WHY IS MY FATHER SPEAKING SO STERNLY? THIS IS ONLY THE THIRD MAN I'VE EVER SEEN – AND THE FIRST I'VE FELT THIS WAY ABOUT. PLEASE LET MY FATHER SEE THINGS MY WAY.
IF YOU ARE PURE, AND YOU HAVEN'T GIVEN YOUR LOVE TO SOMEONE ELSE, I'LL MAKE YOU QUEEN OF NAPLES.
WAIT, SIR! A WORD --
THEY'RE BOTH IN LOVE – BUT IT'S HAPPENING TOO QUICKLY. I MUST SLOW THINGS DOWN SO THAT THEY DON'T TAKE IT ALL FOR GRANTED.

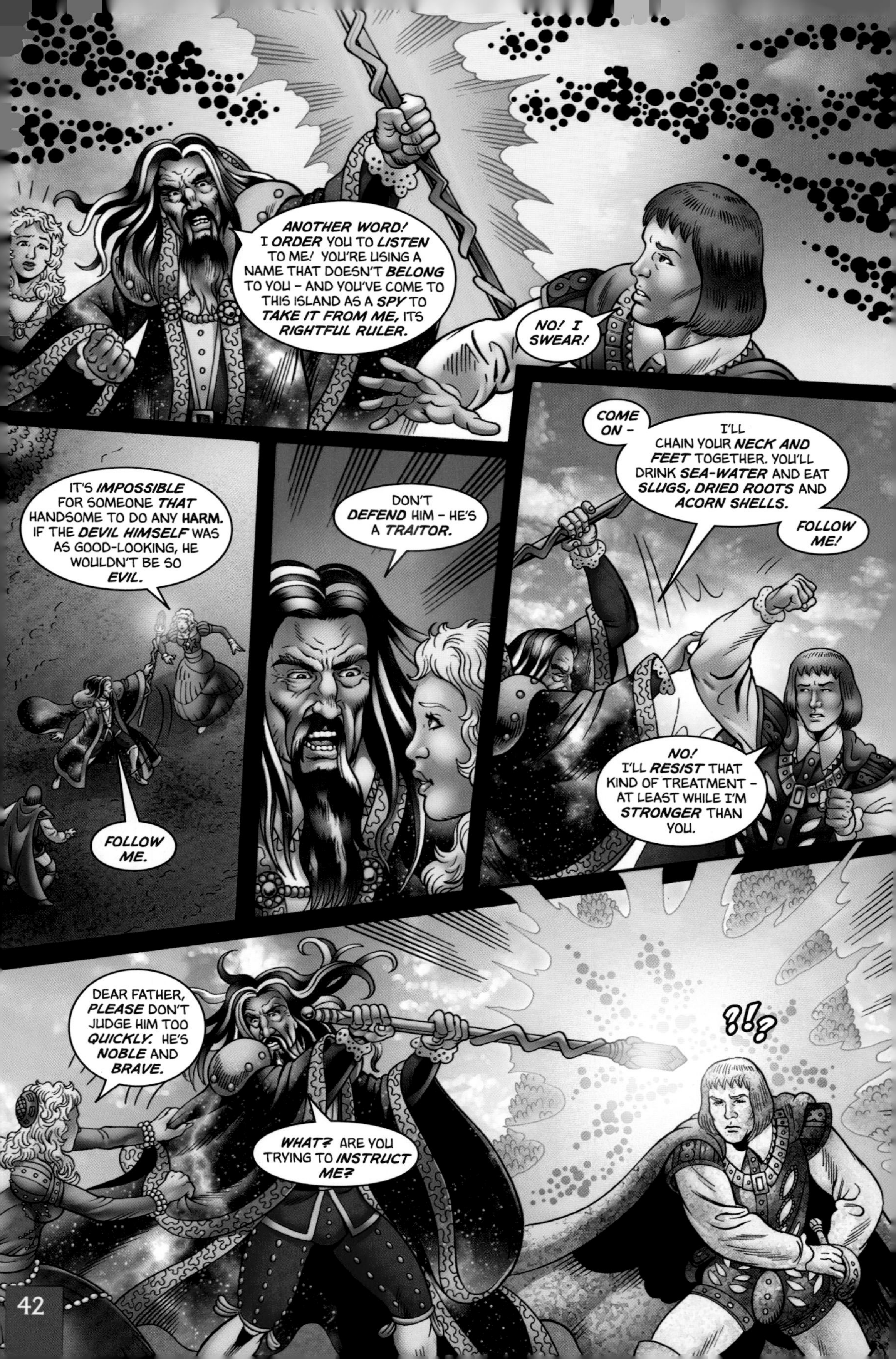
ANOTHER WORD! I ORDER YOU TO LISTEN TO ME! YOU'RE USING A NAME THAT DOESN'T BELONG TO YOU – AND YOU'VE COME TO THIS ISLAND AS A SPY TO TAKE IT FROM ME, ITS RIGHTFUL RULER.
NO! I SWEAR!
IT'S IMPOSSIBLE FOR SOMEONE THAT HANDSOME TO DO ANY HARM. IF THE DEVIL HIMSELF WAS AS GOOD-LOOKING, HE WOULDN'T BE SO EVIL.
FOLLOW ME.
DON'T DEFEND HIM – HE'S A TRAITOR.
COME ON –
I'LL CHAIN YOUR NECK AND FEET TOGETHER. YOU'LL DRINK SEA-WATER AND EAT SLUGS, DRIED ROOTS AND ACORN SHELLS.
FOLLOW ME!
NO! I'LL RESIST THAT KIND OF TREATMENT – AT LEAST WHILE I'M STRONGER THAN YOU.
DEAR FATHER, PLEASE DON'T JUDGE HIM TOO QUICKLY. HE'S NOBLE AND BRAVE.
WHAT? ARE YOU TRYING TO INSTRUCT ME?
?!?

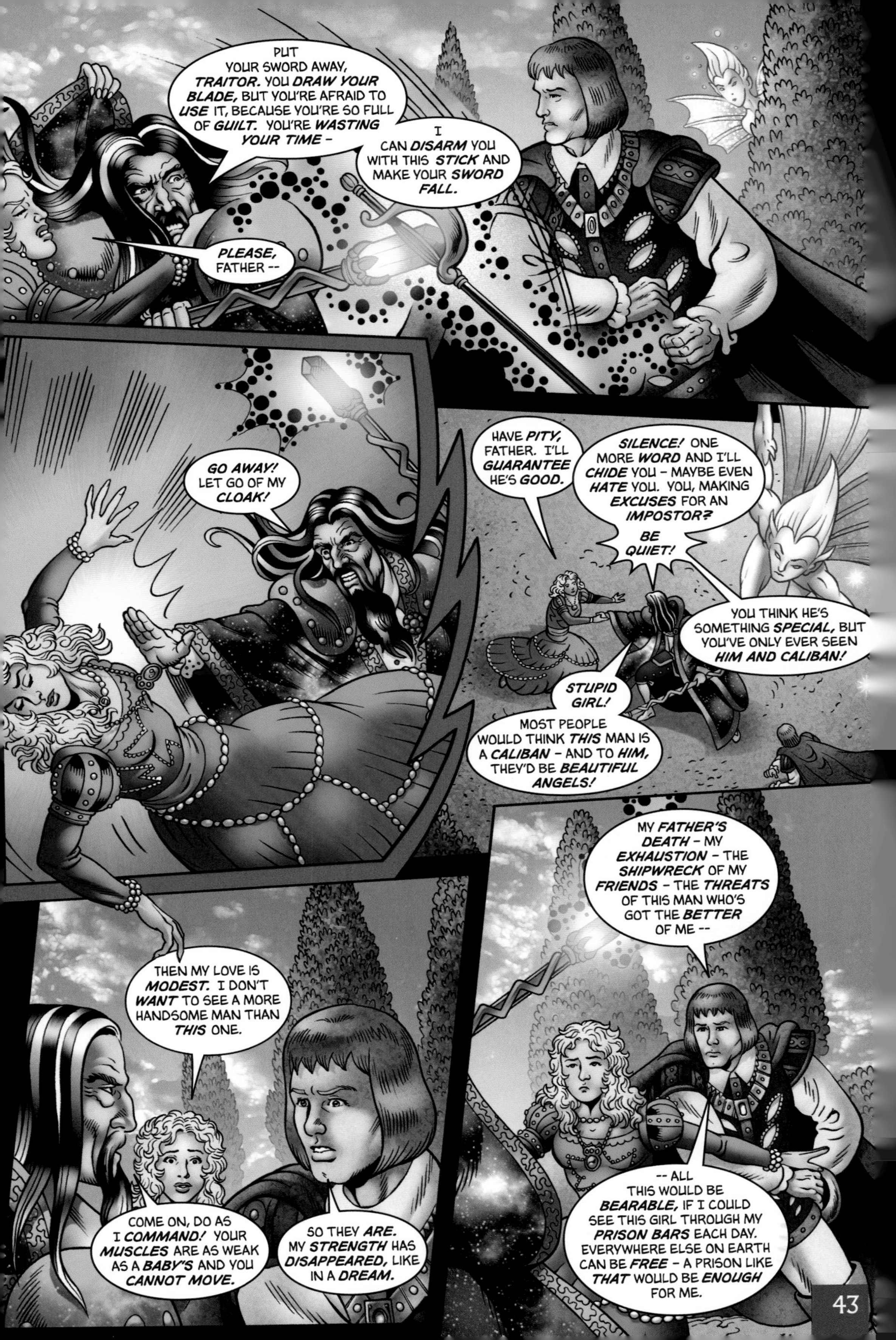
PUT YOUR SWORD AWAY, TRAITOR. YOU DRAW YOUR BLADE, BUT YOU'RE AFRAID TO USE IT, BECAUSE YOU'RE SO FULL OF GUILT. YOU'RE WASTING YOUR TIME -
I CAN DISARM YOU WITH THIS STICK AND MAKE YOUR SWORD FALL.
PLEASE, FATHER --
GO AWAY! LET GO OF MY CLOAK!
HAVE PITY, FATHER. I'LL GUARANTEE HE'S GOOD.
SILENCE! ONE MORE WORD AND I'LL CHIDE YOU - MAYBE EVEN HATE YOU. YOU, MAKING EXCUSES FOR AN IMPOSTOR?
BE QUIET!
YOU THINK HE'S SOMETHING SPECIAL, BUT YOU'VE ONLY EVER SEEN HIM AND CALIBAN!
STUPID GIRL!
MOST PEOPLE WOULD THINK THIS MAN IS A CALIBAN - AND TO HIM, THEY'D BE BEAUTIFUL ANGELS!
THEN MY LOVE IS MODEST. I DON'T WANT TO SEE A MORE HANDSOME MAN THAN THIS ONE.
COME ON, DO AS I COMMAND! YOUR MUSCLES ARE AS WEAK AS A BABY'S AND YOU CANNOT MOVE.
SO THEY ARE. MY STRENGTH HAS DISAPPEARED, LIKE IN A DREAM.
MY FATHER'S DEATH - MY EXHAUSTION - THE SHIPWRECK OF MY FRIENDS - THE THREATS OF THIS MAN WHO'S GOT THE BETTER OF ME --
-- ALL THIS WOULD BE BEARABLE, IF I COULD SEE THIS GIRL THROUGH MY PRISON BARS EACH DAY. EVERYWHERE ELSE ON EARTH CAN BE FREE - A PRISON LIKE THAT WOULD BE ENOUGH FOR ME.

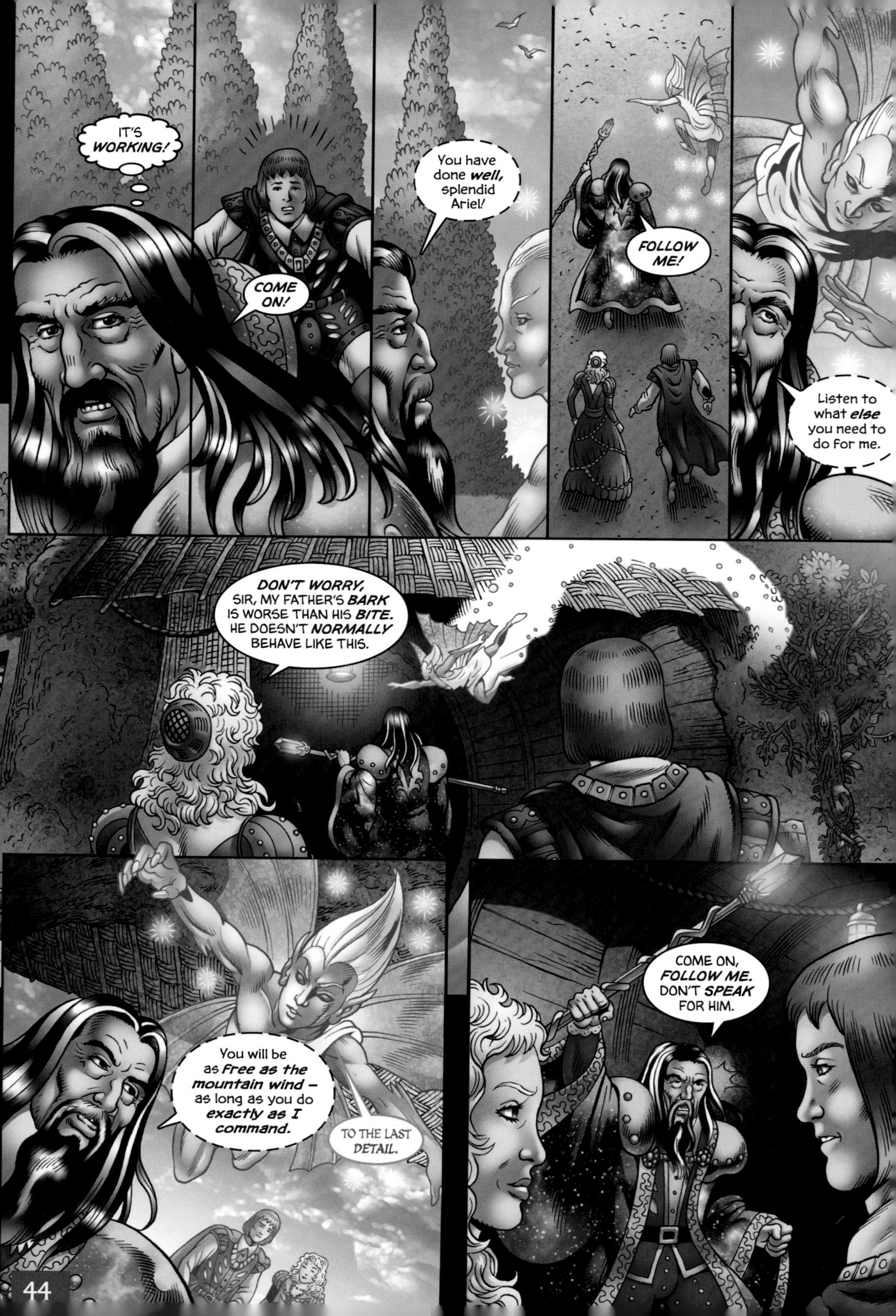
IT'S *WORKING!*
COME ON!
You have done *well,* splendid Ariel!
FOLLOW ME!
Listen to what *else* you need to do for me.
DON'T WORRY, SIR, MY FATHER'S *BARK* IS WORSE THAN HIS *BITE.* HE DOESN'T *NORMALLY* BEHAVE LIKE THIS.
You will be as *free as the mountain wind* – as long as you do *exactly as I command.*
TO THE LAST *DETAIL.*
COME ON, *FOLLOW ME.* DON'T *SPEAK* FOR HIM.

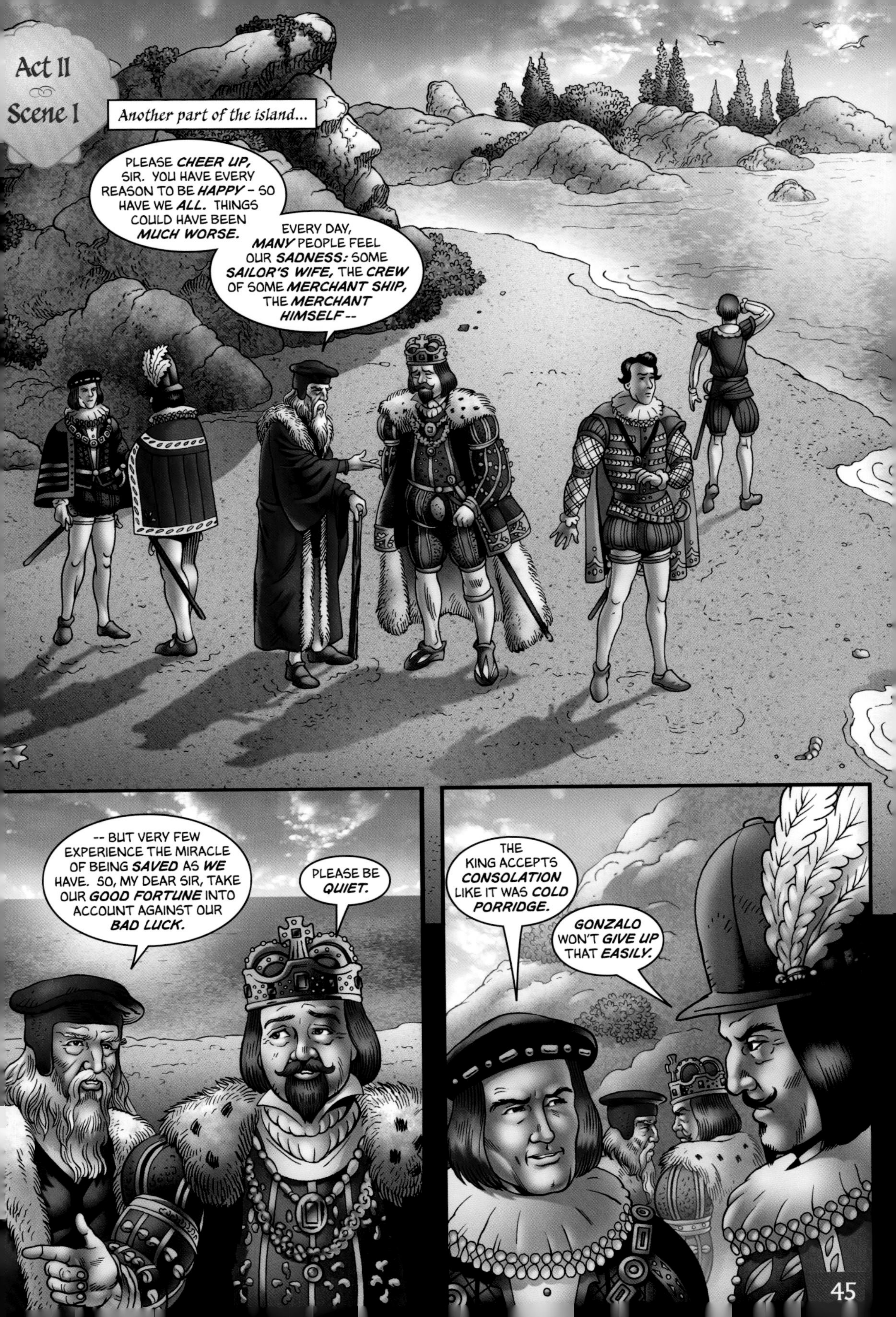
Act II
Scene I
Another part of the island...
PLEASE CHEER UP, SIR. YOU HAVE EVERY REASON TO BE HAPPY – SO HAVE WE ALL. THINGS COULD HAVE BEEN MUCH WORSE.
EVERY DAY, MANY PEOPLE FEEL OUR SADNESS: SOME SAILOR'S WIFE, THE CREW OF SOME MERCHANT SHIP, THE MERCHANT HIMSELF--
-- BUT VERY FEW EXPERIENCE THE MIRACLE OF BEING SAVED AS WE HAVE. SO, MY DEAR SIR, TAKE OUR GOOD FORTUNE INTO ACCOUNT AGAINST OUR BAD LUCK.
PLEASE BE QUIET.
THE KING ACCEPTS CONSOLATION LIKE IT WAS COLD PORRIDGE.
GONZALO WON'T GIVE UP THAT EASILY.

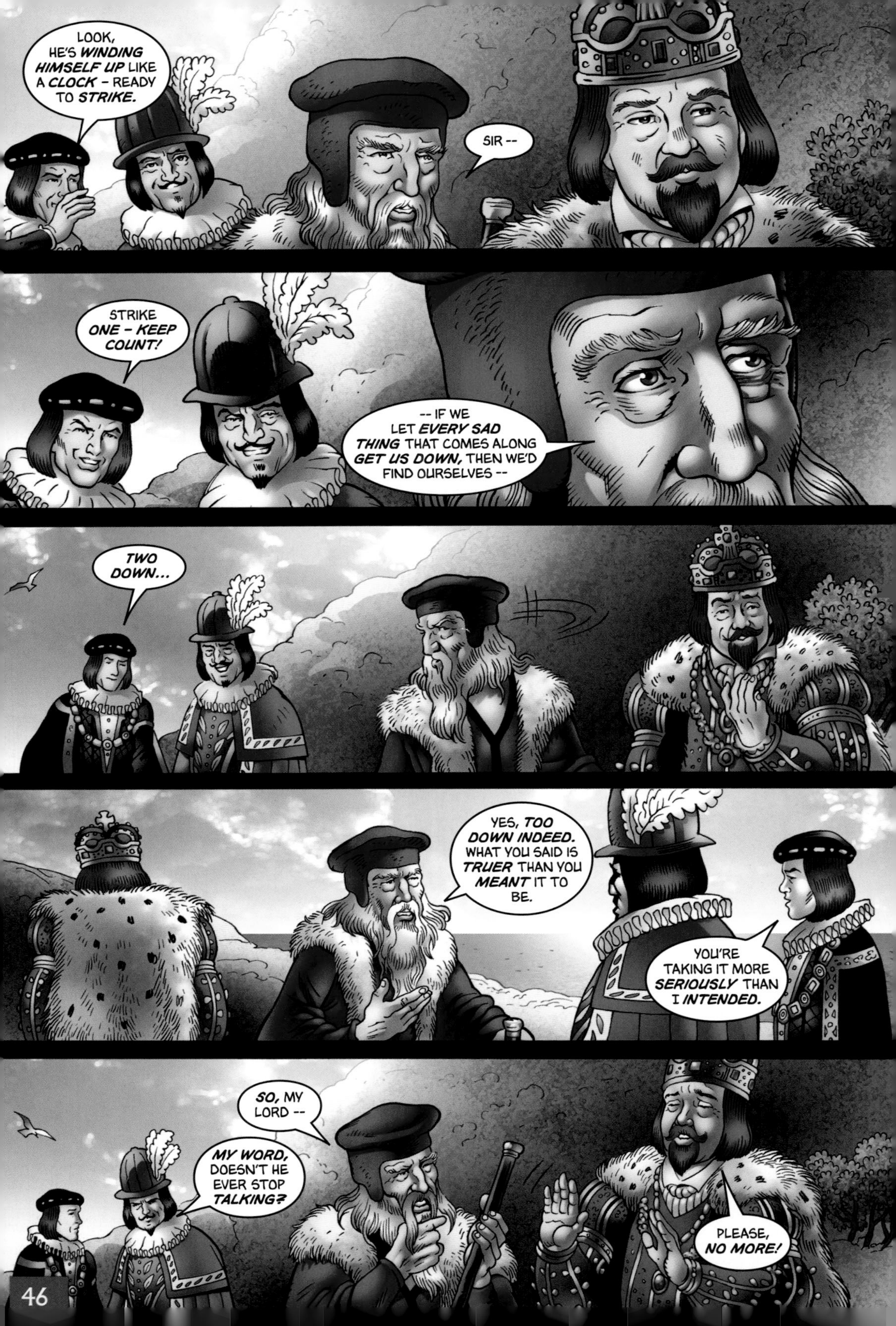
LOOK, HE'S WINDING HIMSELF UP LIKE A CLOCK – READY TO STRIKE.
SIR --
STRIKE ONE – KEEP COUNT!
-- IF WE LET EVERY SAD THING THAT COMES ALONG GET US DOWN, THEN WE'D FIND OURSELVES --
TWO DOWN...
YES, TOO DOWN INDEED. WHAT YOU SAID IS TRUER THAN YOU MEANT IT TO BE.
YOU'RE TAKING IT MORE SERIOUSLY THAN I INTENDED.
SO, MY LORD --
MY WORD, DOESN'T HE EVER STOP TALKING?
PLEASE, NO MORE!

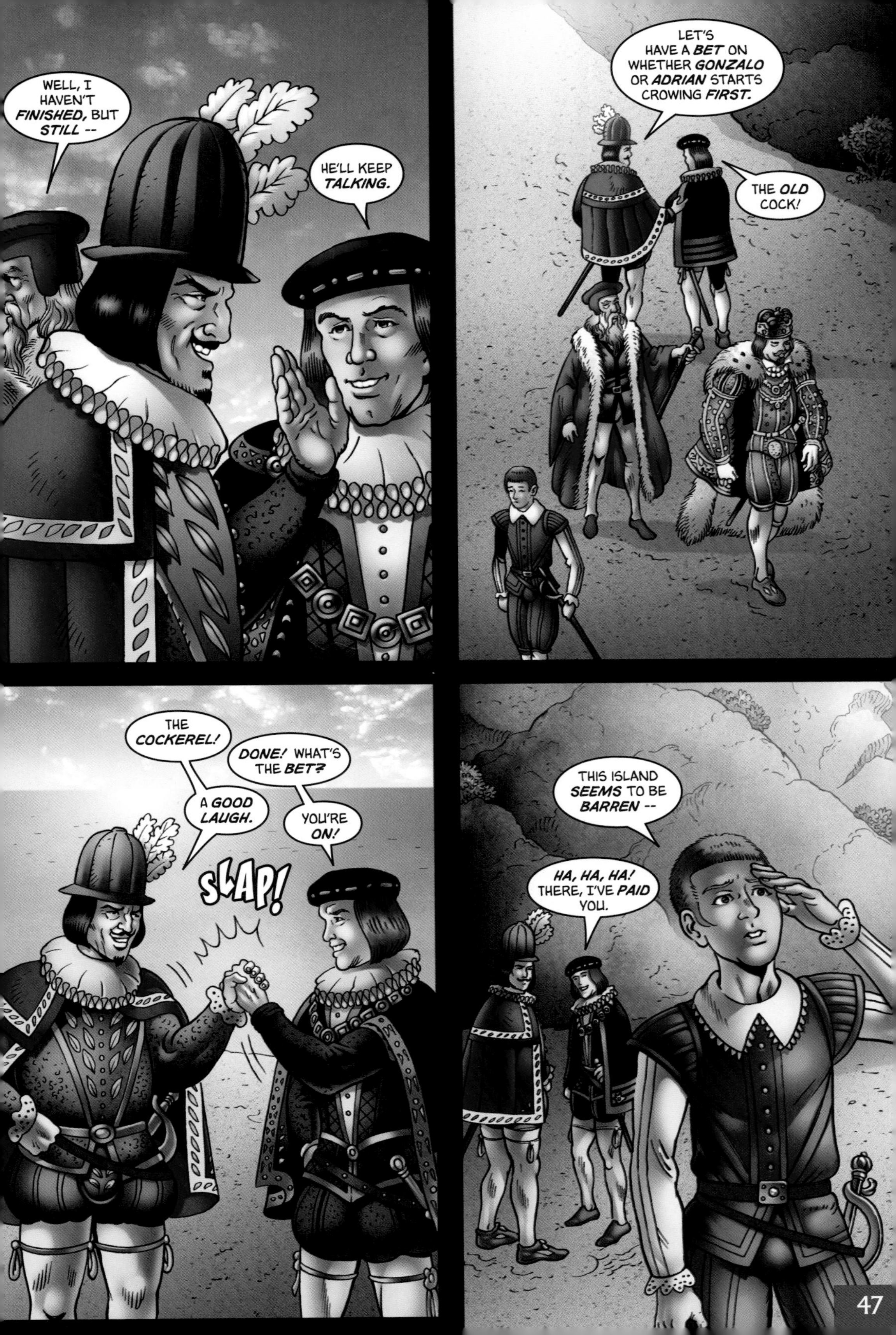
WELL, I HAVEN'T FINISHED, BUT STILL --
HE'LL KEEP TALKING.
LET'S HAVE A BET ON WHETHER GONZALO OR ADRIAN STARTS CROWING FIRST.
THE OLD COCK!
THE COCKEREL!
DONE! WHAT'S THE BET?
A GOOD LAUGH.
YOU'RE ON!
SLAP!
THIS ISLAND SEEMS TO BE BARREN --
HA, HA, HA! THERE, I'VE PAID YOU.

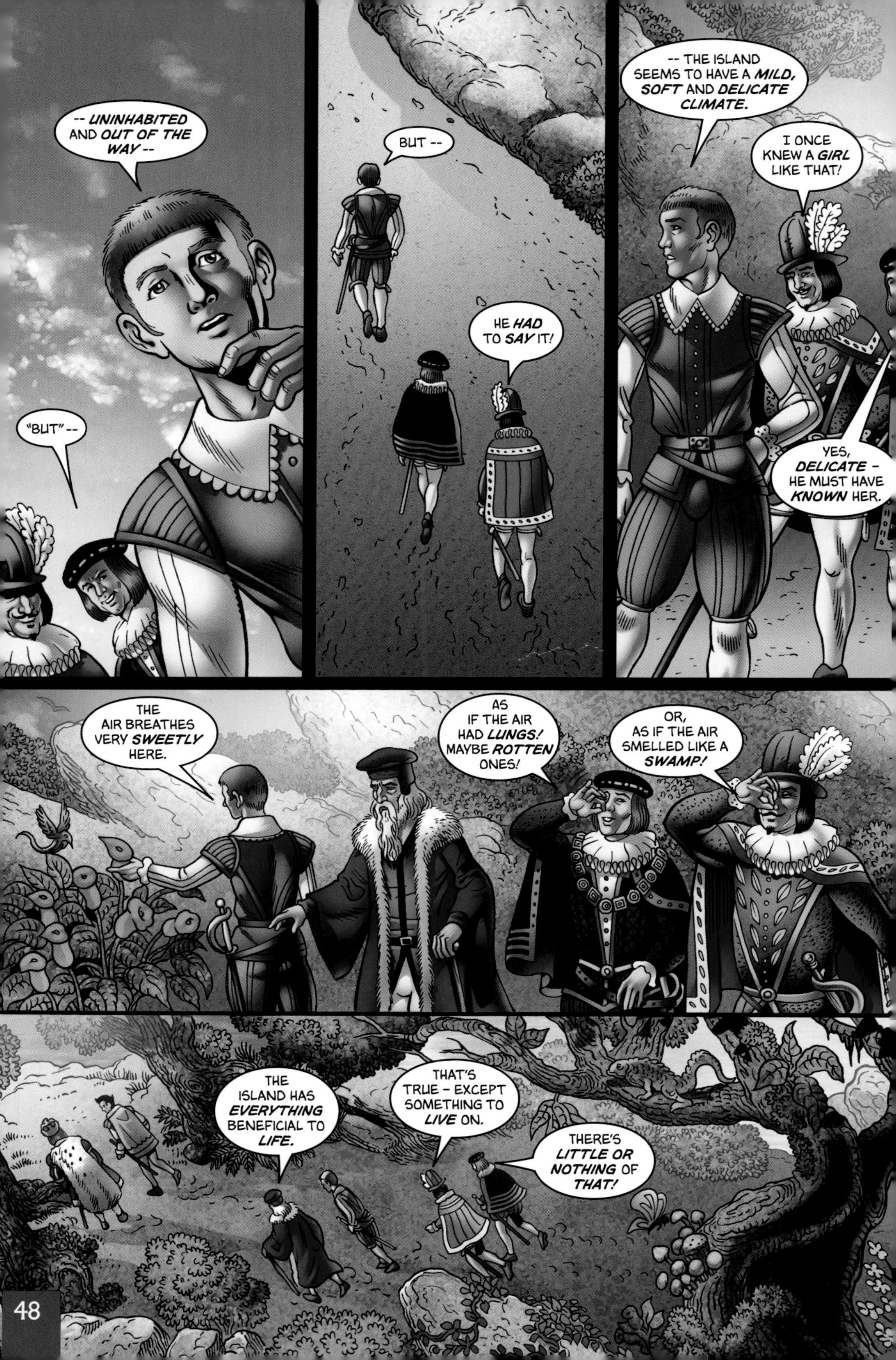
-- UNINHABITED AND OUT OF THE WAY --
"BUT" --
BUT --
HE HAD TO SAY IT!
-- THE ISLAND SEEMS TO HAVE A MILD, SOFT AND DELICATE CLIMATE.
I ONCE KNEW A GIRL LIKE THAT!
YES, DELICATE - HE MUST HAVE KNOWN HER.
THE AIR BREATHES VERY SWEETLY HERE.
AS IF THE AIR HAD LUNGS! MAYBE ROTTEN ONES!
OR, AS IF THE AIR SMELLED LIKE A SWAMP!
THE ISLAND HAS EVERYTHING BENEFICIAL TO LIFE.
THAT'S TRUE - EXCEPT SOMETHING TO LIVE ON.
THERE'S LITTLE OR NOTHING OF THAT!

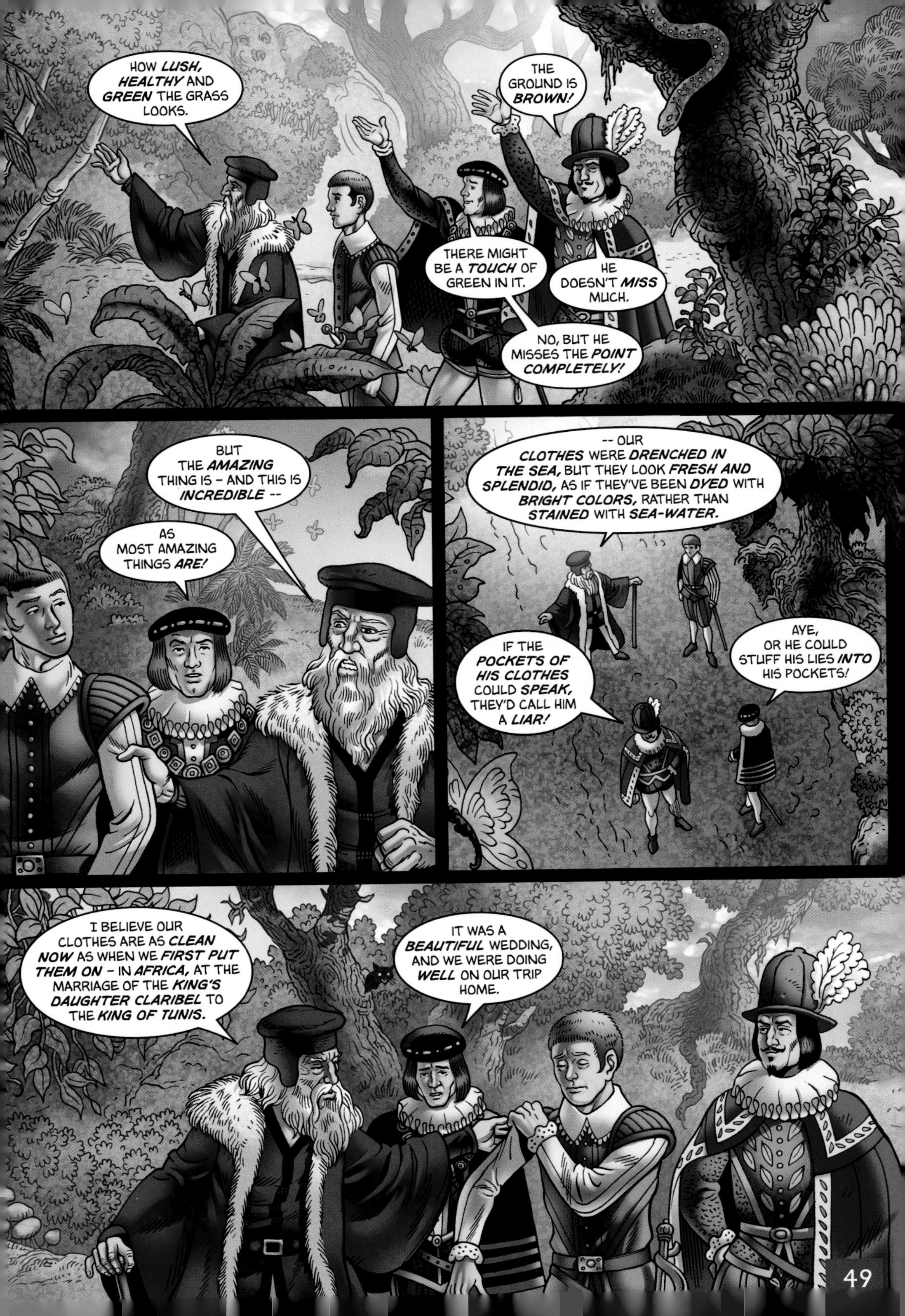
HOW LUSH, HEALTHY AND GREEN THE GRASS LOOKS.
THE GROUND IS BROWN!
THERE MIGHT BE A TOUCH OF GREEN IN IT.
HE DOESN'T MISS MUCH.
NO, BUT HE MISSES THE POINT COMPLETELY!
BUT THE AMAZING THING IS - AND THIS IS INCREDIBLE --
AS MOST AMAZING THINGS ARE!
-- OUR CLOTHES WERE DRENCHED IN THE SEA, BUT THEY LOOK FRESH AND SPLENDID, AS IF THEY'VE BEEN DYED WITH BRIGHT COLORS, RATHER THAN STAINED WITH SEA-WATER.
IF THE POCKETS OF HIS CLOTHES COULD SPEAK, THEY'D CALL HIM A LIAR!
AYE, OR HE COULD STUFF HIS LIES INTO HIS POCKETS!
I BELIEVE OUR CLOTHES ARE AS CLEAN NOW AS WHEN WE FIRST PUT THEM ON - IN AFRICA, AT THE MARRIAGE OF THE KING'S DAUGHTER CLARIBEL TO THE KING OF TUNIS.
IT WAS A BEAUTIFUL WEDDING, AND WE WERE DOING WELL ON OUR TRIP HOME.

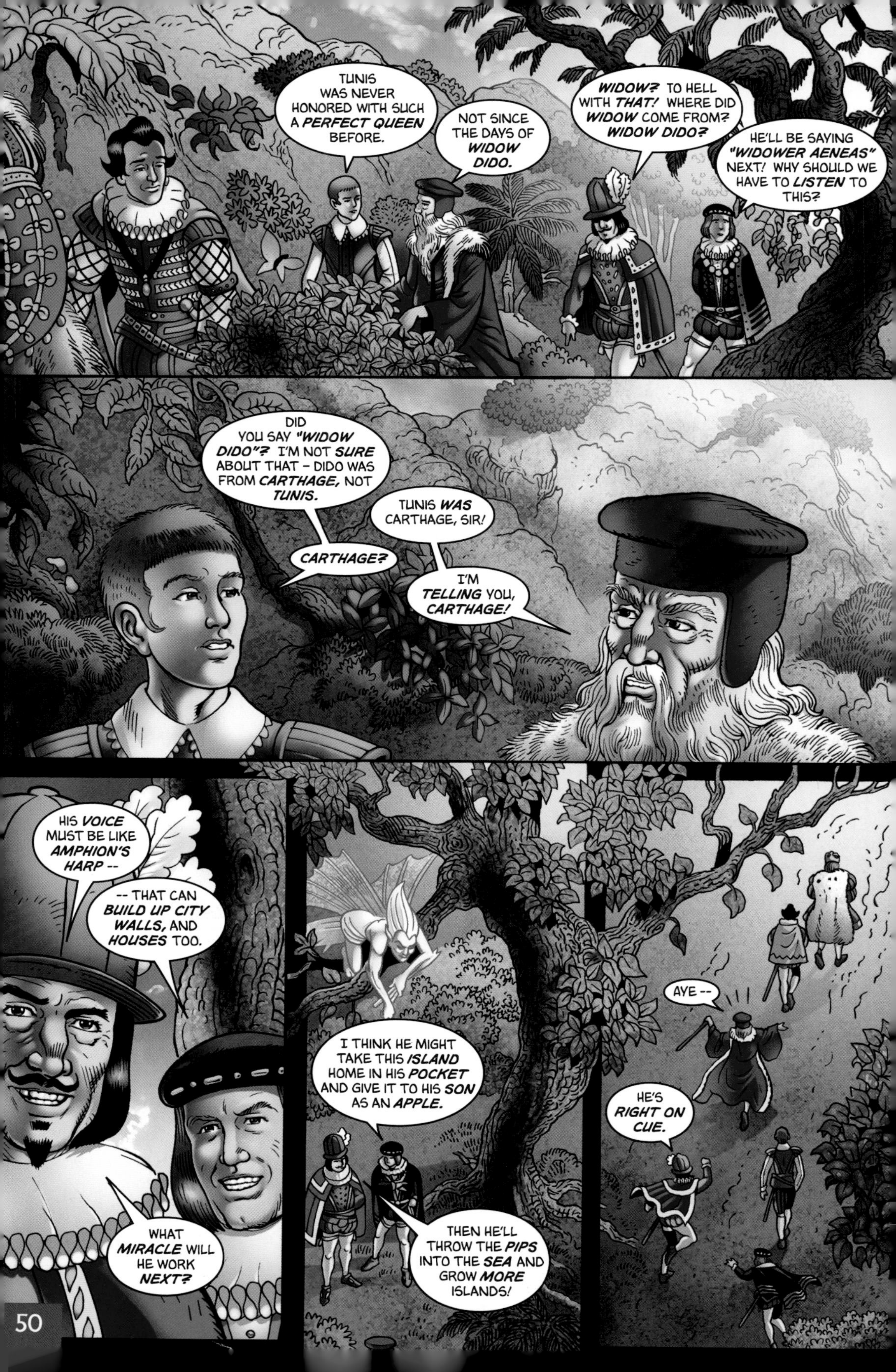
TUNIS WAS NEVER HONORED WITH SUCH A PERFECT QUEEN BEFORE.
NOT SINCE THE DAYS OF WIDOW DIDO.
WIDOW? TO HELL WITH THAT! WHERE DID WIDOW COME FROM? WIDOW DIDO?
HE'LL BE SAYING "WIDOWER AENEAS" NEXT! WHY SHOULD WE HAVE TO LISTEN TO THIS?
DID YOU SAY "WIDOW DIDO"? I'M NOT SURE ABOUT THAT - DIDO WAS FROM CARTHAGE, NOT TUNIS.
TUNIS WAS CARTHAGE, SIR!
CARTHAGE?
I'M TELLING YOU, CARTHAGE!
HIS VOICE MUST BE LIKE AMPHION'S HARP --
-- THAT CAN BUILD UP CITY WALLS, AND HOUSES TOO.
WHAT MIRACLE WILL HE WORK NEXT?
I THINK HE MIGHT TAKE THIS ISLAND HOME IN HIS POCKET AND GIVE IT TO HIS SON AS AN APPLE.
THEN HE'LL THROW THE PIPS INTO THE SEA AND GROW MORE ISLANDS!
AYE --
HE'S RIGHT ON CUE.

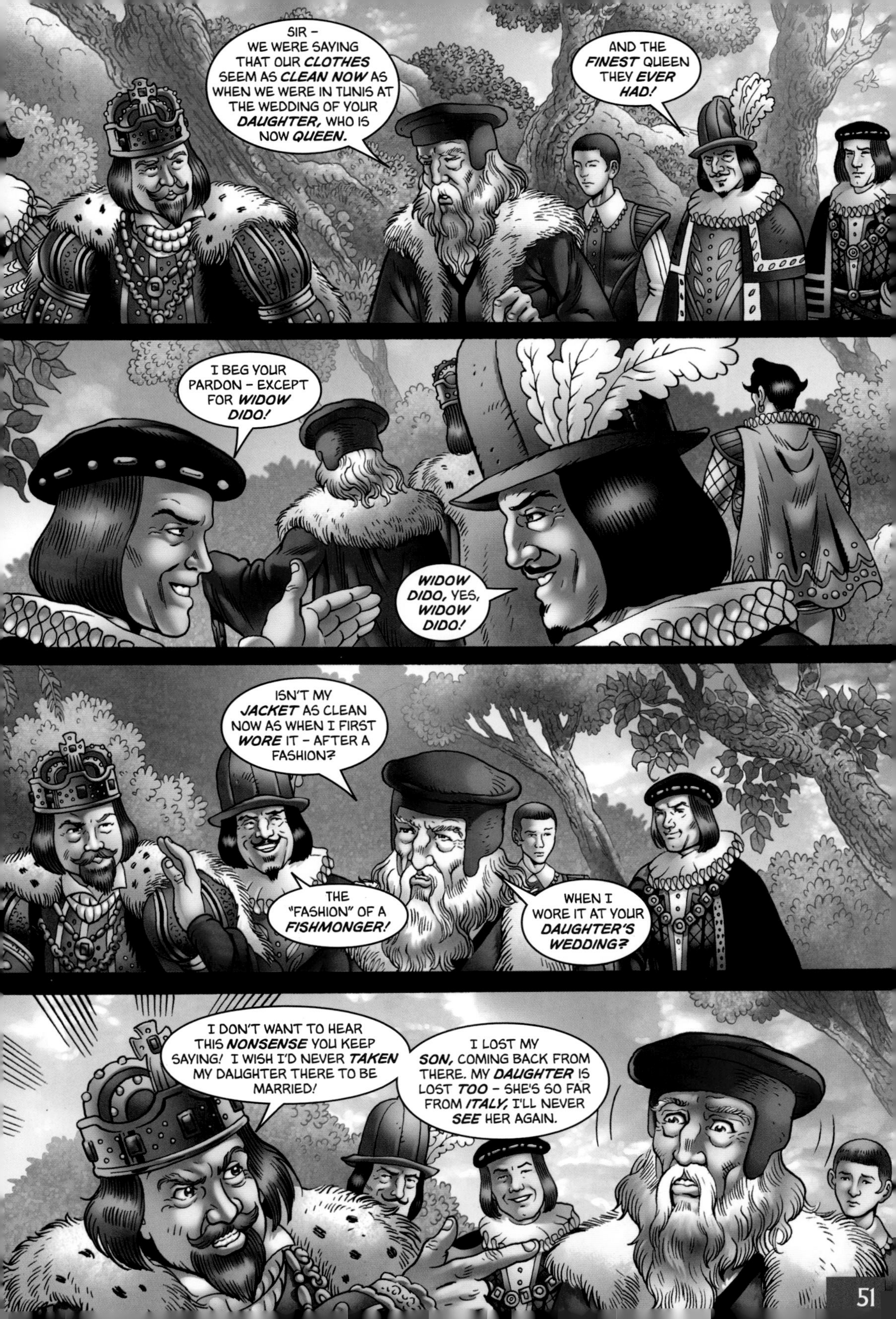
SIR – WE WERE SAYING THAT OUR CLOTHES SEEM AS CLEAN NOW AS WHEN WE WERE IN TUNIS AT THE WEDDING OF YOUR DAUGHTER, WHO IS NOW QUEEN.
AND THE FINEST QUEEN THEY EVER HAD!
I BEG YOUR PARDON – EXCEPT FOR WIDOW DIDO!
WIDOW DIDO, YES, WIDOW DIDO!
ISN'T MY JACKET AS CLEAN NOW AS WHEN I FIRST WORE IT – AFTER A FASHION?
THE "FASHION" OF A FISHMONGER!
WHEN I WORE IT AT YOUR DAUGHTER'S WEDDING?
I DON'T WANT TO HEAR THIS NONSENSE YOU KEEP SAYING! I WISH I'D NEVER TAKEN MY DAUGHTER THERE TO BE MARRIED!
I LOST MY SON, COMING BACK FROM THERE. MY DAUGHTER IS LOST TOO – SHE'S SO FAR FROM ITALY, I'LL NEVER SEE HER AGAIN.

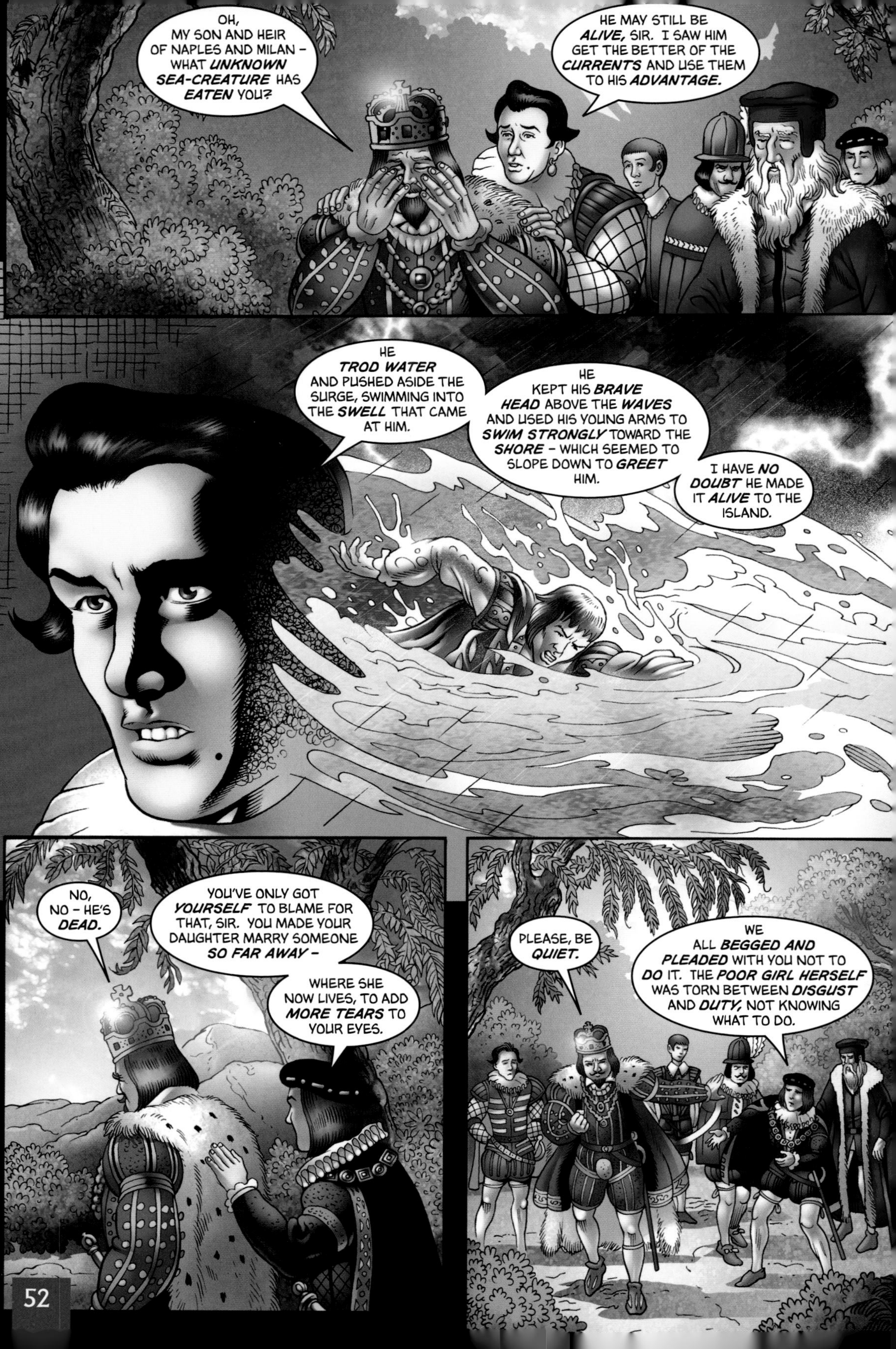
OH, MY SON AND HEIR OF NAPLES AND MILAN – WHAT UNKNOWN SEA-CREATURE HAS EATEN YOU?
HE MAY STILL BE ALIVE, SIR. I SAW HIM GET THE BETTER OF THE CURRENTS AND USE THEM TO HIS ADVANTAGE.
HE TROD WATER AND PUSHED ASIDE THE SURGE, SWIMMING INTO THE SWELL THAT CAME AT HIM.
HE KEPT HIS BRAVE HEAD ABOVE THE WAVES AND USED HIS YOUNG ARMS TO SWIM STRONGLY TOWARD THE SHORE – WHICH SEEMED TO SLOPE DOWN TO GREET HIM.
I HAVE NO DOUBT HE MADE IT ALIVE TO THE ISLAND.
NO, NO – HE'S DEAD.
YOU'VE ONLY GOT YOURSELF TO BLAME FOR THAT, SIR. YOU MADE YOUR DAUGHTER MARRY SOMEONE SO FAR AWAY –
WHERE SHE NOW LIVES, TO ADD MORE TEARS TO YOUR EYES.
PLEASE, BE QUIET.
WE ALL BEGGED AND PLEADED WITH YOU NOT TO DO IT. THE POOR GIRL HERSELF WAS TORN BETWEEN DISGUST AND DUTY, NOT KNOWING WHAT TO DO.

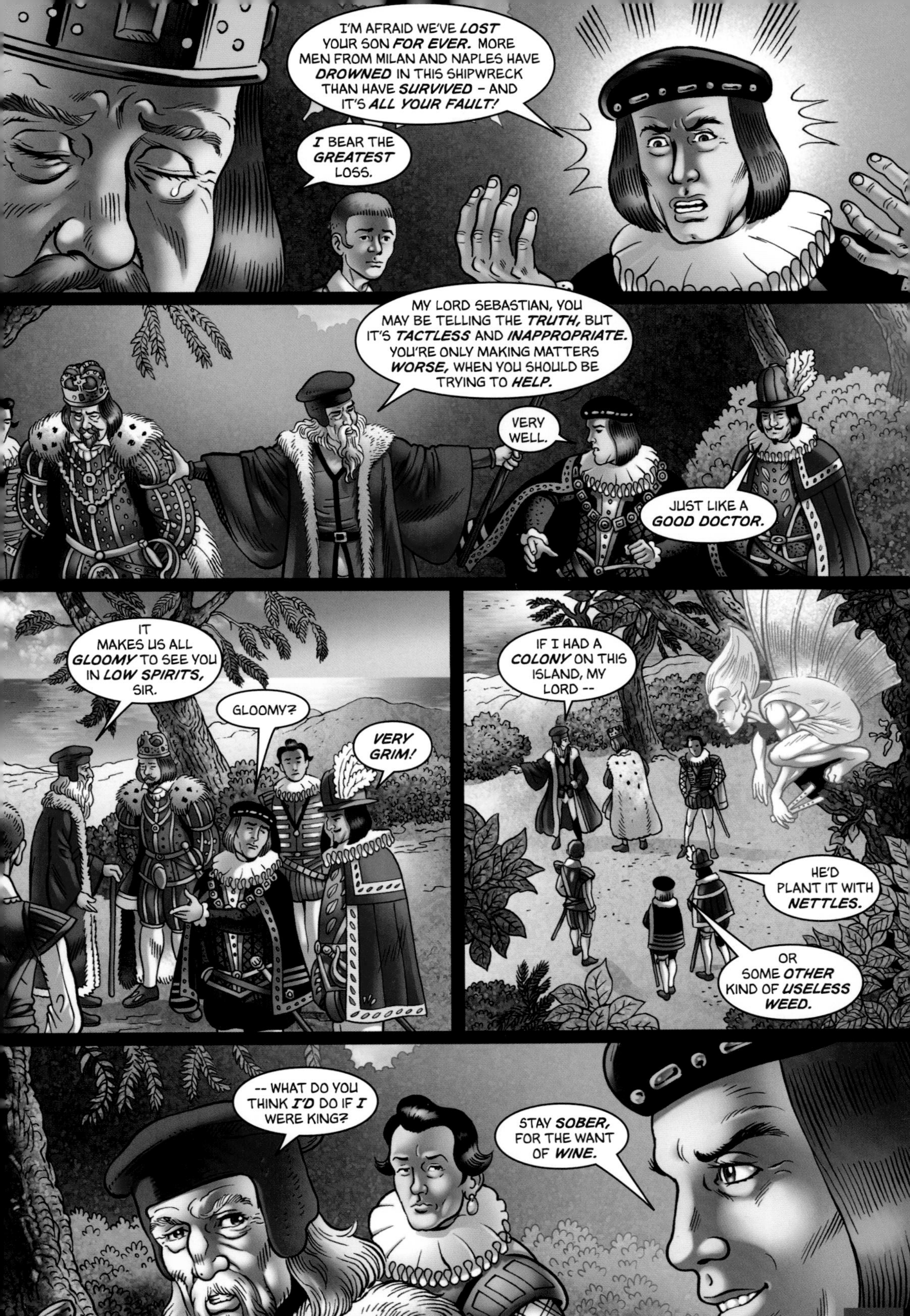
I'M AFRAID WE'VE LOST YOUR SON FOR EVER. MORE MEN FROM MILAN AND NAPLES HAVE DROWNED IN THIS SHIPWRECK THAN HAVE SURVIVED – AND IT'S ALL YOUR FAULT!
I BEAR THE GREATEST LOSS.
MY LORD SEBASTIAN, YOU MAY BE TELLING THE TRUTH, BUT IT'S TACTLESS AND INAPPROPRIATE. YOU'RE ONLY MAKING MATTERS WORSE, WHEN YOU SHOULD BE TRYING TO HELP.
VERY WELL.
JUST LIKE A GOOD DOCTOR.
IT MAKES US ALL GLOOMY TO SEE YOU IN LOW SPIRITS, SIR.
GLOOMY?
VERY GRIM!
IF I HAD A COLONY ON THIS ISLAND, MY LORD --
HE'D PLANT IT WITH NETTLES.
OR SOME OTHER KIND OF USELESS WEED.
-- WHAT DO YOU THINK I'D DO IF I WERE KING?
STAY SOBER, FOR THE WANT OF WINE.

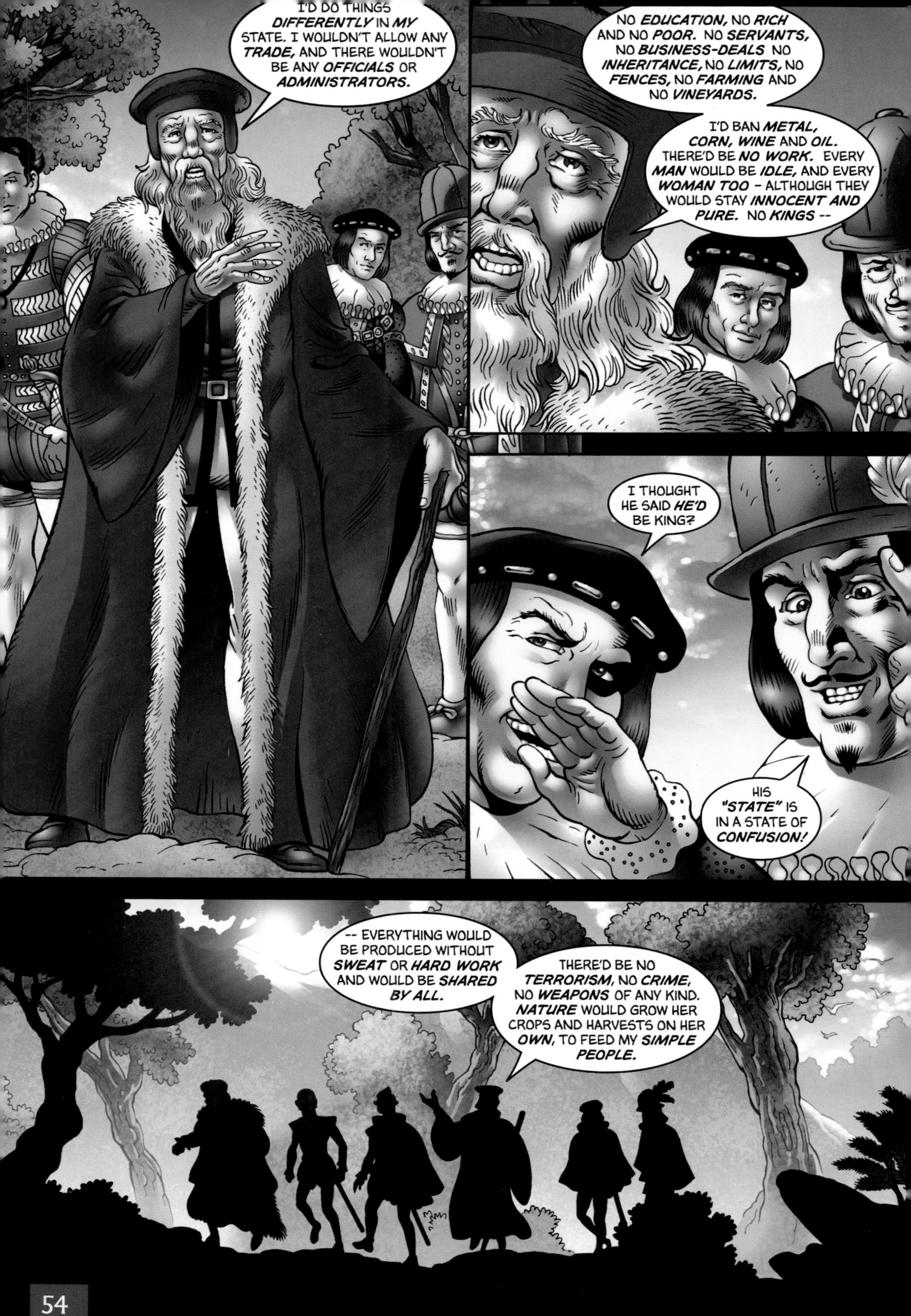
I'D DO THINGS DIFFERENTLY IN MY STATE. I WOULDN'T ALLOW ANY TRADE, AND THERE WOULDN'T BE ANY OFFICIALS OR ADMINISTRATORS.
NO EDUCATION, NO RICH AND NO POOR. NO SERVANTS, NO BUSINESS-DEALS NO INHERITANCE, NO LIMITS, NO FENCES, NO FARMING AND NO VINEYARDS.
I'D BAN METAL, CORN, WINE AND OIL. THERE'D BE NO WORK. EVERY MAN WOULD BE IDLE, AND EVERY WOMAN TOO – ALTHOUGH THEY WOULD STAY INNOCENT AND PURE. NO KINGS --
I THOUGHT HE SAID HE'D BE KING?
HIS "STATE" IS IN A STATE OF CONFUSION!
-- EVERYTHING WOULD BE PRODUCED WITHOUT SWEAT OR HARD WORK AND WOULD BE SHARED BY ALL.
THERE'D BE NO TERRORISM, NO CRIME, NO WEAPONS OF ANY KIND. NATURE WOULD GROW HER CROPS AND HARVESTS ON HER OWN, TO FEED MY SIMPLE PEOPLE.

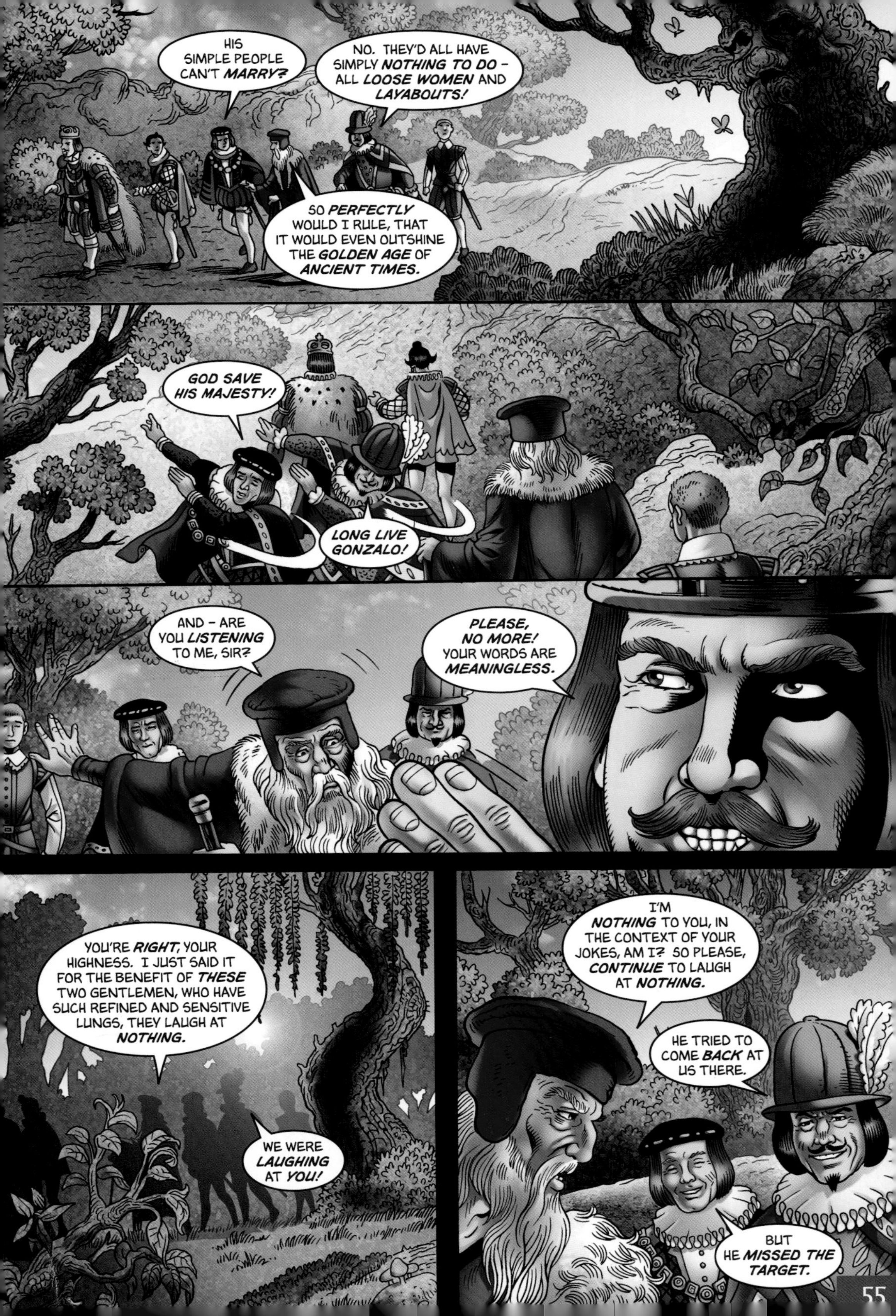
HIS SIMPLE PEOPLE CAN'T MARRY?
NO. THEY'D ALL HAVE SIMPLY NOTHING TO DO - ALL LOOSE WOMEN AND LAYABOUTS!
SO PERFECTLY WOULD I RULE, THAT IT WOULD EVEN OUTSHINE THE GOLDEN AGE OF ANCIENT TIMES.
GOD SAVE HIS MAJESTY!
LONG LIVE GONZALO!
AND - ARE YOU LISTENING TO ME, SIR?
PLEASE, NO MORE! YOUR WORDS ARE MEANINGLESS.
YOU'RE RIGHT, YOUR HIGHNESS. I JUST SAID IT FOR THE BENEFIT OF THESE TWO GENTLEMEN, WHO HAVE SUCH REFINED AND SENSITIVE LUNGS, THEY LAUGH AT NOTHING.
WE WERE LAUGHING AT YOU!
I'M NOTHING TO YOU, IN THE CONTEXT OF YOUR JOKES, AM I? SO PLEASE, CONTINUE TO LAUGH AT NOTHING.
HE TRIED TO COME BACK AT US THERE.
BUT HE MISSED THE TARGET.

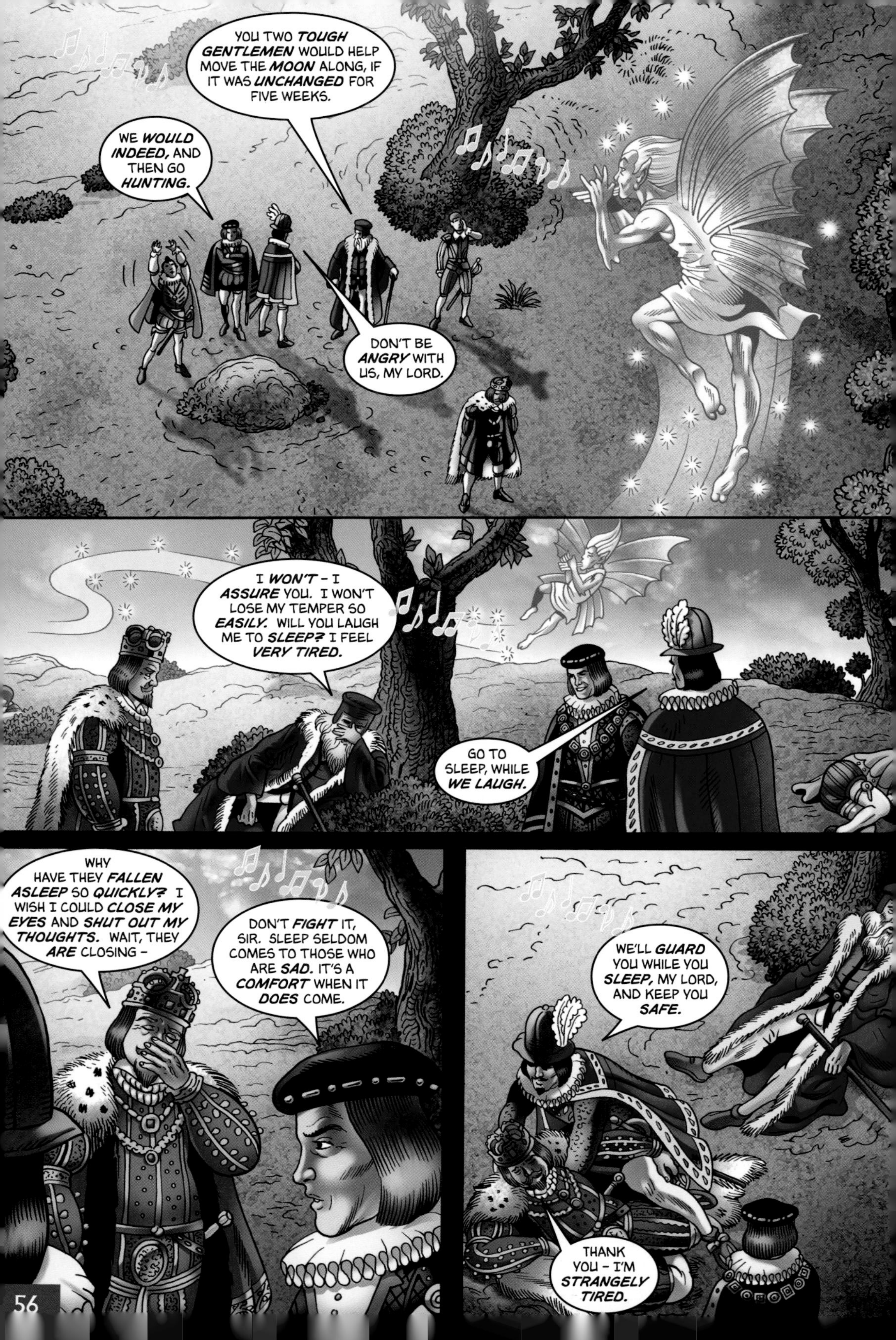

YOU TWO TOUGH GENTLEMEN WOULD HELP MOVE THE MOON ALONG, IF IT WAS UNCHANGED FOR FIVE WEEKS.
WE WOULD INDEED, AND THEN GO HUNTING.
DON'T BE ANGRY WITH US, MY LORD.
I WON'T – I ASSURE YOU. I WON'T LOSE MY TEMPER SO EASILY. WILL YOU LAUGH ME TO SLEEP? I FEEL VERY TIRED.
GO TO SLEEP, WHILE WE LAUGH.
WHY HAVE THEY FALLEN ASLEEP SO QUICKLY? I WISH I COULD CLOSE MY EYES AND SHUT OUT MY THOUGHTS. WAIT, THEY ARE CLOSING –
DON'T FIGHT IT, SIR. SLEEP SELDOM COMES TO THOSE WHO ARE SAD. IT'S A COMFORT WHEN IT DOES COME.
WE'LL GUARD YOU WHILE YOU SLEEP, MY LORD, AND KEEP YOU SAFE.
THANK YOU – I'M STRANGELY TIRED.

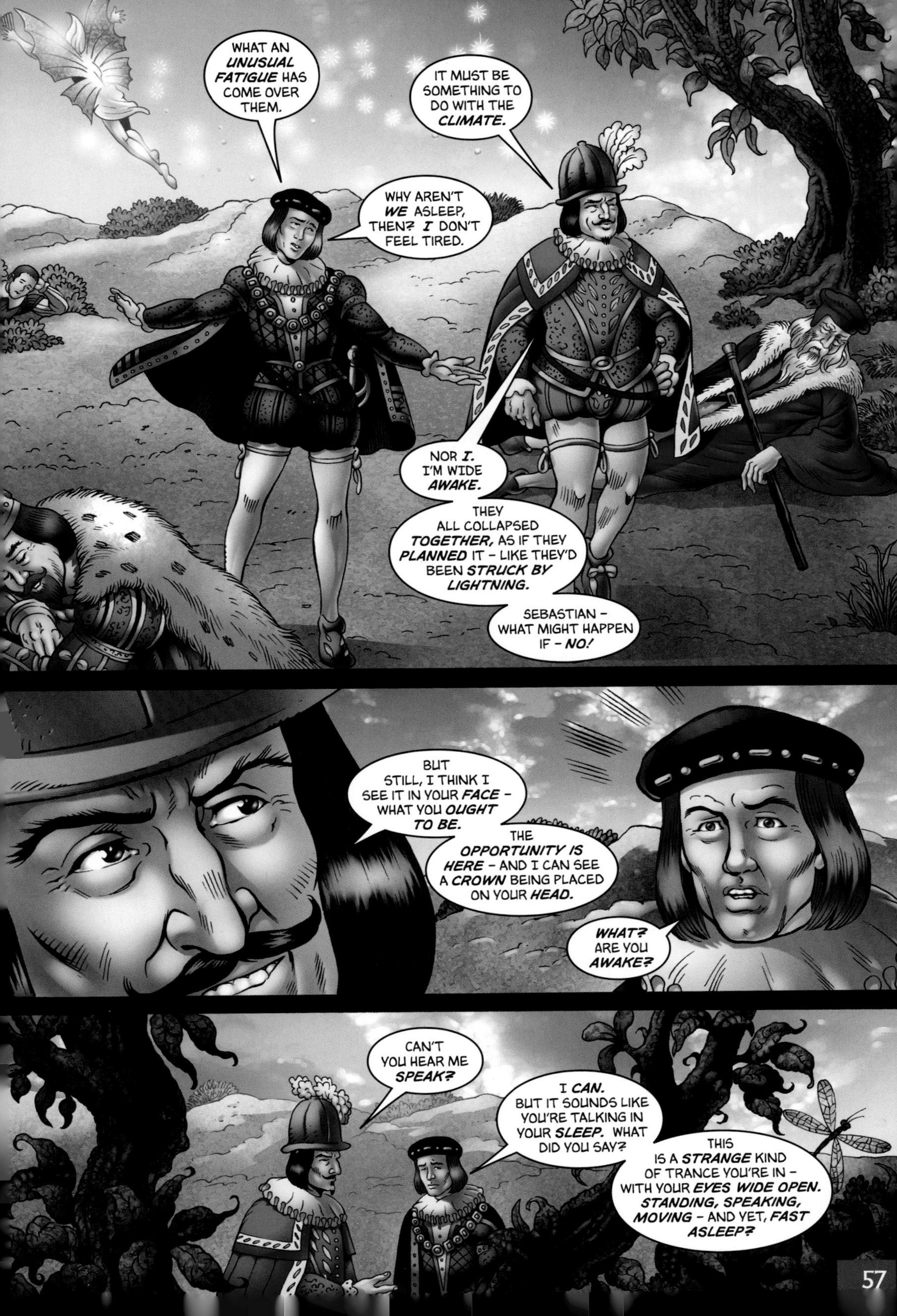
WHAT AN UNUSUAL FATIGUE HAS COME OVER THEM.
IT MUST BE SOMETHING TO DO WITH THE CLIMATE.
WHY AREN'T WE ASLEEP, THEN? I DON'T FEEL TIRED.
NOR I. I'M WIDE AWAKE.
THEY ALL COLLAPSED TOGETHER, AS IF THEY PLANNED IT – LIKE THEY'D BEEN STRUCK BY LIGHTNING.
SEBASTIAN – WHAT MIGHT HAPPEN IF – NO!
BUT STILL, I THINK I SEE IT IN YOUR FACE – WHAT YOU OUGHT TO BE.
THE OPPORTUNITY IS HERE – AND I CAN SEE A CROWN BEING PLACED ON YOUR HEAD.
WHAT? ARE YOU AWAKE?
CAN'T YOU HEAR ME SPEAK?
I CAN. BUT IT SOUNDS LIKE YOU'RE TALKING IN YOUR SLEEP. WHAT DID YOU SAY?
THIS IS A STRANGE KIND OF TRANCE YOU'RE IN – WITH YOUR EYES WIDE OPEN. STANDING, SPEAKING, MOVING – AND YET, FAST ASLEEP?

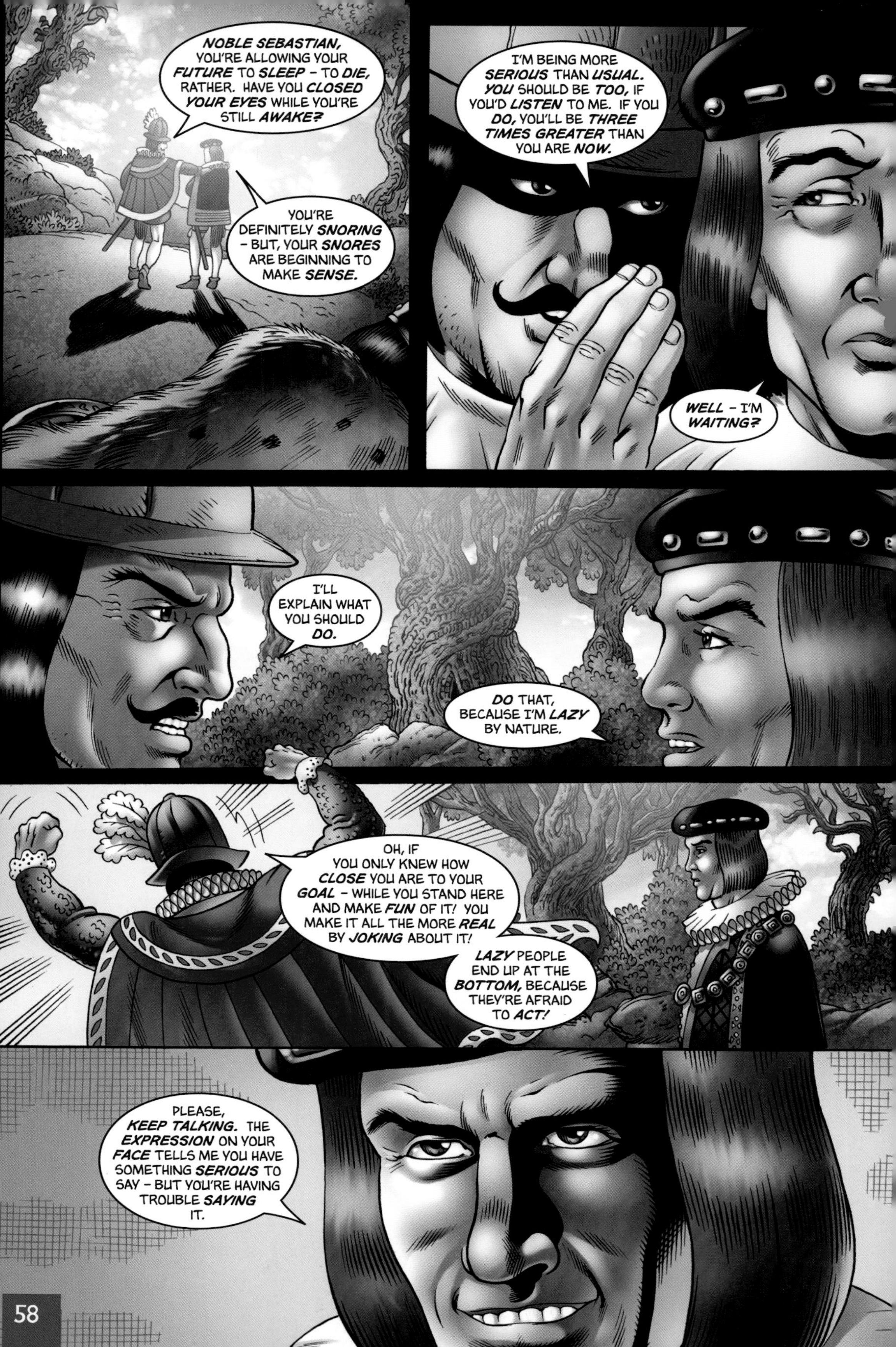
NOBLE SEBASTIAN, YOU'RE ALLOWING YOUR FUTURE TO SLEEP – TO DIE, RATHER. HAVE YOU CLOSED YOUR EYES WHILE YOU'RE STILL AWAKE?
YOU'RE DEFINITELY SNORING – BUT, YOUR SNORES ARE BEGINNING TO MAKE SENSE.
I'M BEING MORE SERIOUS THAN USUAL. YOU SHOULD BE TOO, IF YOU'D LISTEN TO ME. IF YOU DO, YOU'LL BE THREE TIMES GREATER THAN YOU ARE NOW.
WELL – I'M WAITING?
I'LL EXPLAIN WHAT YOU SHOULD DO.
DO THAT, BECAUSE I'M LAZY BY NATURE.
OH, IF YOU ONLY KNEW HOW CLOSE YOU ARE TO YOUR GOAL – WHILE YOU STAND HERE AND MAKE FUN OF IT! YOU MAKE IT ALL THE MORE REAL BY JOKING ABOUT IT!
LAZY PEOPLE END UP AT THE BOTTOM, BECAUSE THEY'RE AFRAID TO ACT!
PLEASE, KEEP TALKING. THE EXPRESSION ON YOUR FACE TELLS ME YOU HAVE SOMETHING SERIOUS TO SAY – BUT YOU'RE HAVING TROUBLE SAYING IT.

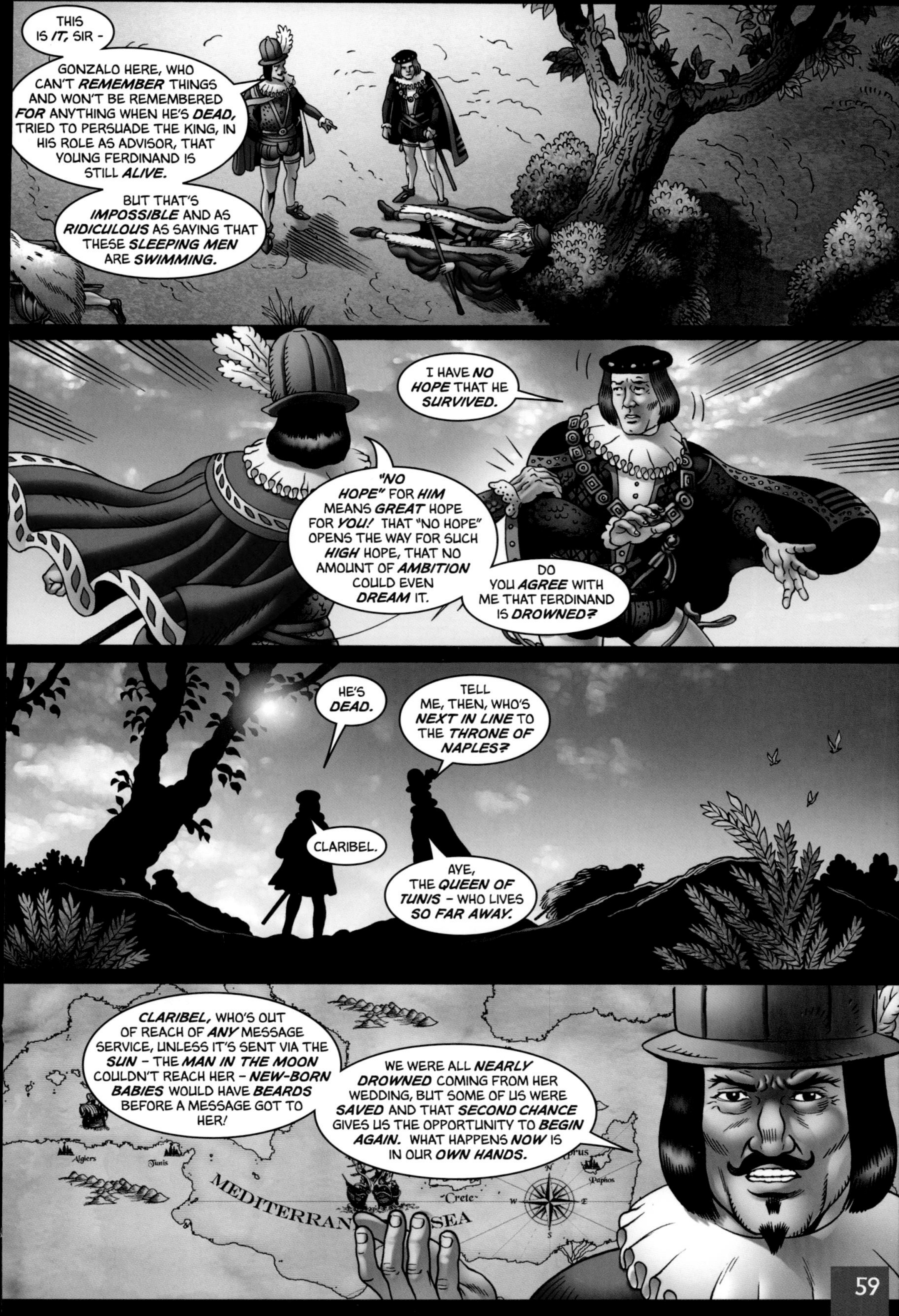

THIS IS *IT,* SIR -
GONZALO HERE, WHO CAN'T ***REMEMBER*** THINGS AND WON'T BE REMEMBERED ***FOR*** ANYTHING WHEN HE'S ***DEAD,*** TRIED TO PERSUADE THE KING, IN HIS ROLE AS ADVISOR, THAT YOUNG FERDINAND IS STILL ***ALIVE.***
BUT THAT'S ***IMPOSSIBLE*** AND AS ***RIDICULOUS*** AS SAYING THAT THESE ***SLEEPING MEN*** ARE ***SWIMMING.***
I HAVE ***NO HOPE*** THAT HE ***SURVIVED.***
"NO HOPE" FOR ***HIM*** MEANS ***GREAT*** HOPE FOR ***YOU!*** THAT "NO HOPE" OPENS THE WAY FOR SUCH ***HIGH*** HOPE, THAT NO AMOUNT OF ***AMBITION*** COULD EVEN ***DREAM*** IT.
DO YOU ***AGREE*** WITH ME THAT FERDINAND IS ***DROWNED?***
HE'S ***DEAD.***
TELL ME, THEN, WHO'S ***NEXT IN LINE*** TO THE ***THRONE OF NAPLES?***
CLARIBEL.
AYE, THE ***QUEEN OF TUNIS*** - WHO LIVES ***SO FAR AWAY.***
CLARIBEL, WHO'S OUT OF REACH OF ***ANY*** MESSAGE SERVICE, UNLESS IT'S SENT VIA THE ***SUN*** - THE ***MAN IN THE MOON*** COULDN'T REACH HER - ***NEW-BORN BABIES*** WOULD HAVE ***BEARDS*** BEFORE A MESSAGE GOT TO HER!
WE WERE ALL ***NEARLY DROWNED*** COMING FROM HER WEDDING, BUT SOME OF US WERE ***SAVED*** AND THAT ***SECOND CHANCE*** GIVES US THE OPPORTUNITY TO ***BEGIN AGAIN.*** WHAT HAPPENS ***NOW*** IS IN OUR ***OWN HANDS.***
Algiers
Tunis
MEDITERRAN
SEA
Crete
Paphos

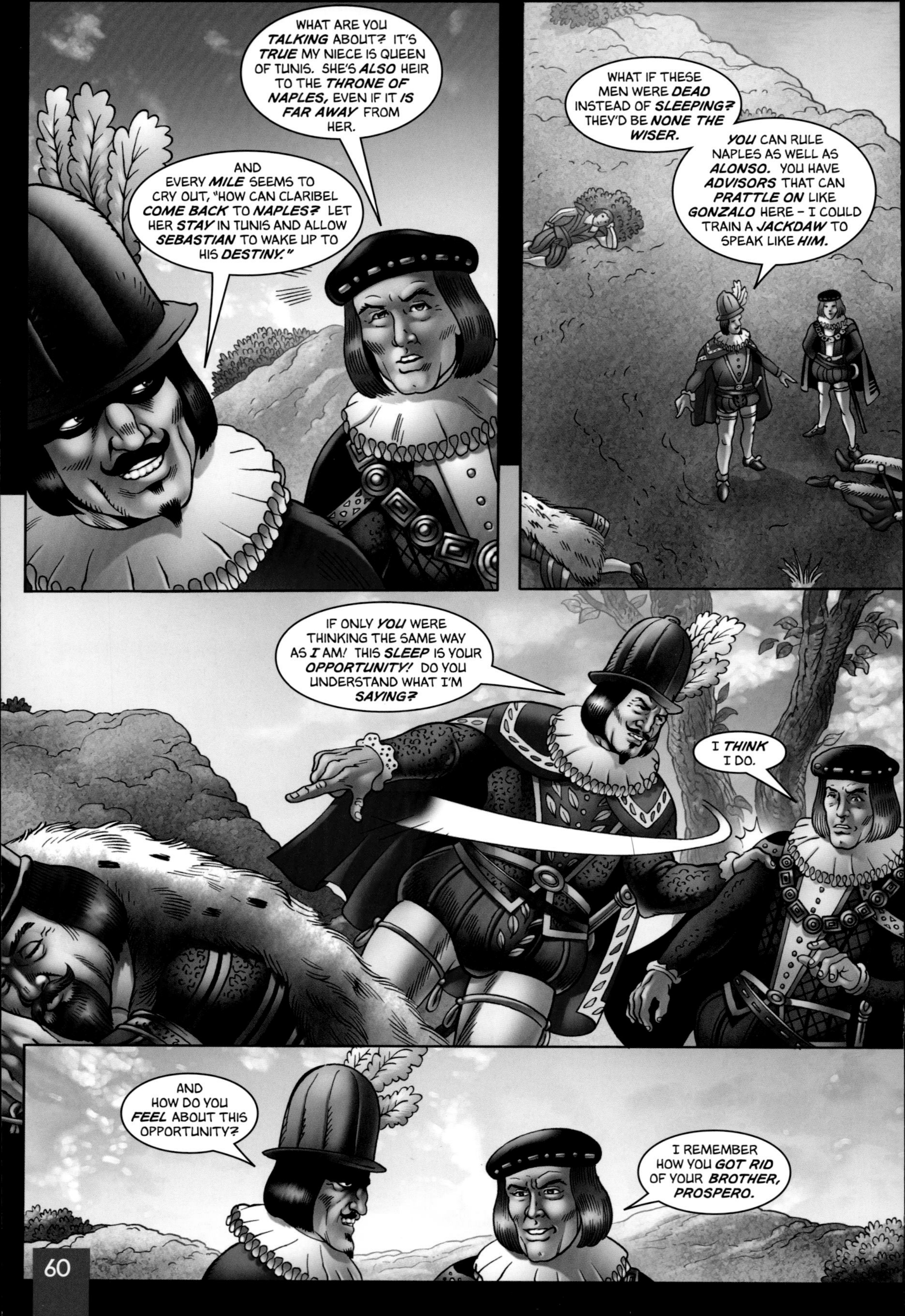
WHAT ARE YOU TALKING ABOUT? IT'S TRUE MY NIECE IS QUEEN OF TUNIS. SHE'S ALSO HEIR TO THE THRONE OF NAPLES, EVEN IF IT IS FAR AWAY FROM HER.
AND EVERY MILE SEEMS TO CRY OUT, "HOW CAN CLARIBEL COME BACK TO NAPLES? LET HER STAY IN TUNIS AND ALLOW SEBASTIAN TO WAKE UP TO HIS DESTINY."
WHAT IF THESE MEN WERE DEAD INSTEAD OF SLEEPING? THEY'D BE NONE THE WISER.
YOU CAN RULE NAPLES AS WELL AS ALONSO. YOU HAVE ADVISORS THAT CAN PRATTLE ON LIKE GONZALO HERE - I COULD TRAIN A JACKDAW TO SPEAK LIKE HIM.
IF ONLY YOU WERE THINKING THE SAME WAY AS I AM! THIS SLEEP IS YOUR OPPORTUNITY! DO YOU UNDERSTAND WHAT I'M SAYING?
I THINK I DO.
AND HOW DO YOU FEEL ABOUT THIS OPPORTUNITY?
I REMEMBER HOW YOU GOT RID OF YOUR BROTHER, PROSPERO.

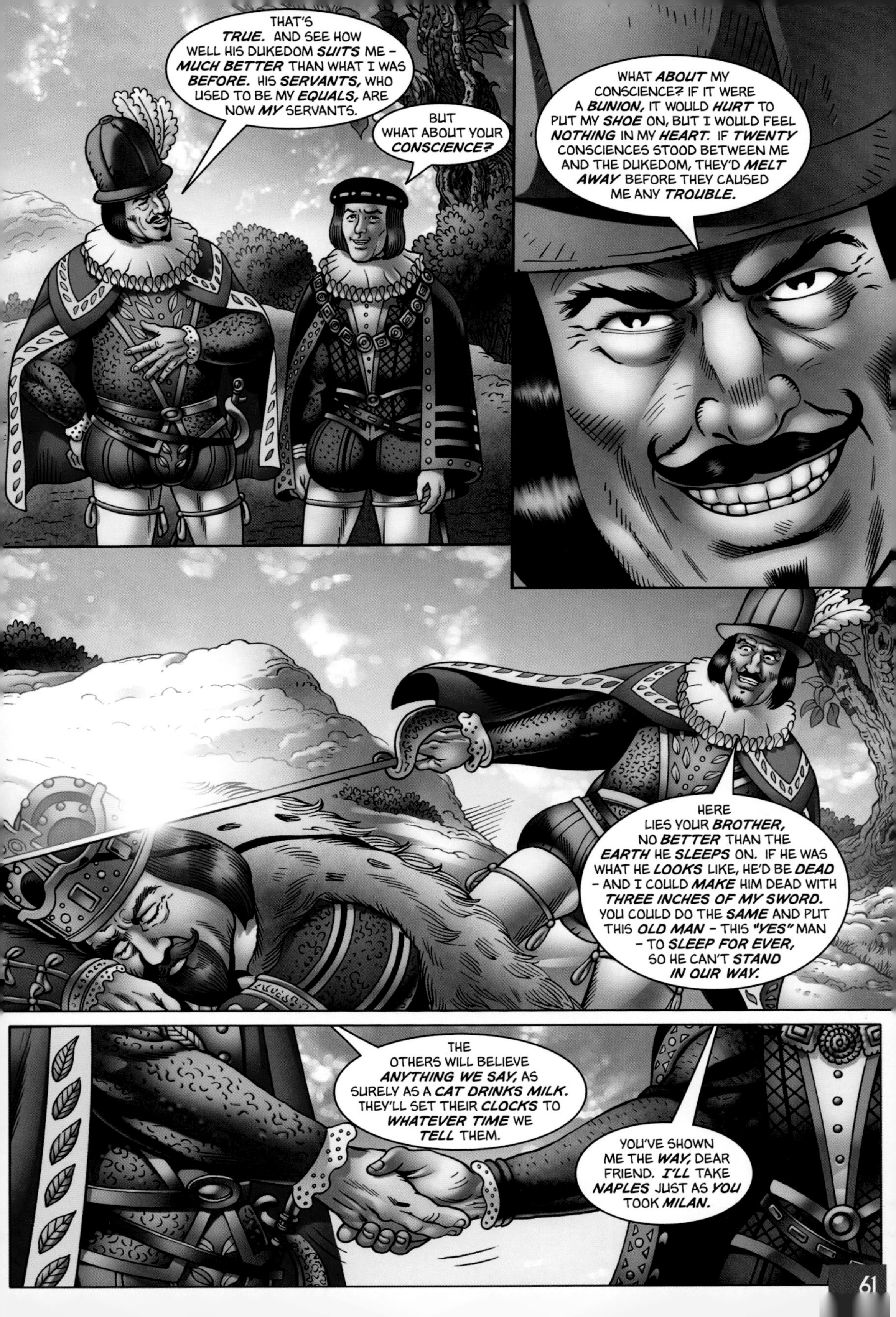

THAT'S TRUE. AND SEE HOW WELL HIS DUKEDOM SUITS ME - MUCH BETTER THAN WHAT I WAS BEFORE. HIS SERVANTS, WHO USED TO BE MY EQUALS, ARE NOW MY SERVANTS.
BUT WHAT ABOUT YOUR CONSCIENCE?
WHAT ABOUT MY CONSCIENCE? IF IT WERE A BUNION, IT WOULD HURT TO PUT MY SHOE ON, BUT I WOULD FEEL NOTHING IN MY HEART. IF TWENTY CONSCIENCES STOOD BETWEEN ME AND THE DUKEDOM, THEY'D MELT AWAY BEFORE THEY CAUSED ME ANY TROUBLE.
HERE LIES YOUR BROTHER, NO BETTER THAN THE EARTH HE SLEEPS ON. IF HE WAS WHAT HE LOOKS LIKE, HE'D BE DEAD - AND I COULD MAKE HIM DEAD WITH THREE INCHES OF MY SWORD. YOU COULD DO THE SAME AND PUT THIS OLD MAN - THIS "YES" MAN - TO SLEEP FOR EVER, SO HE CAN'T STAND IN OUR WAY.
THE OTHERS WILL BELIEVE ANYTHING WE SAY, AS SURELY AS A CAT DRINKS MILK. THEY'LL SET THEIR CLOCKS TO WHATEVER TIME WE TELL THEM.
YOU'VE SHOWN ME THE WAY, DEAR FRIEND. I'LL TAKE NAPLES JUST AS YOU TOOK MILAN.

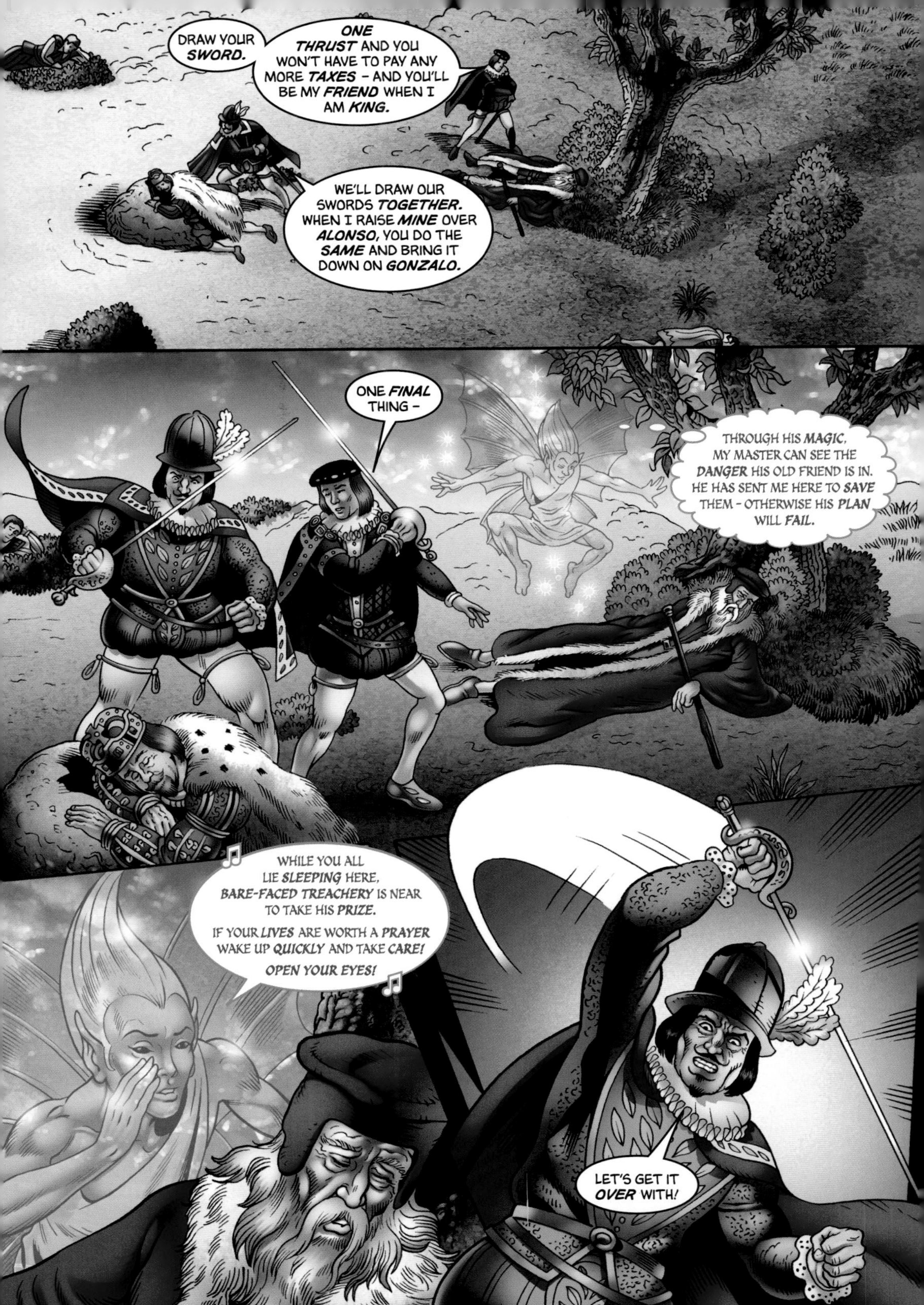
DRAW YOUR SWORD.
ONE THRUST AND YOU WON'T HAVE TO PAY ANY MORE TAXES – AND YOU'LL BE MY FRIEND WHEN I AM KING.
WE'LL DRAW OUR SWORDS TOGETHER. WHEN I RAISE MINE OVER ALONSO, YOU DO THE SAME AND BRING IT DOWN ON GONZALO.
ONE FINAL THING –
THROUGH HIS MAGIC, MY MASTER CAN SEE THE DANGER HIS OLD FRIEND IS IN. HE HAS SENT ME HERE TO SAVE THEM – OTHERWISE HIS PLAN WILL FAIL.
WHILE YOU ALL LIE SLEEPING HERE, BARE-FACED TREACHERY IS NEAR TO TAKE HIS PRIZE.
IF YOUR LIVES ARE WORTH A PRAYER WAKE UP QUICKLY AND TAKE CARE!
OPEN YOUR EYES!
LET'S GET IT OVER WITH!

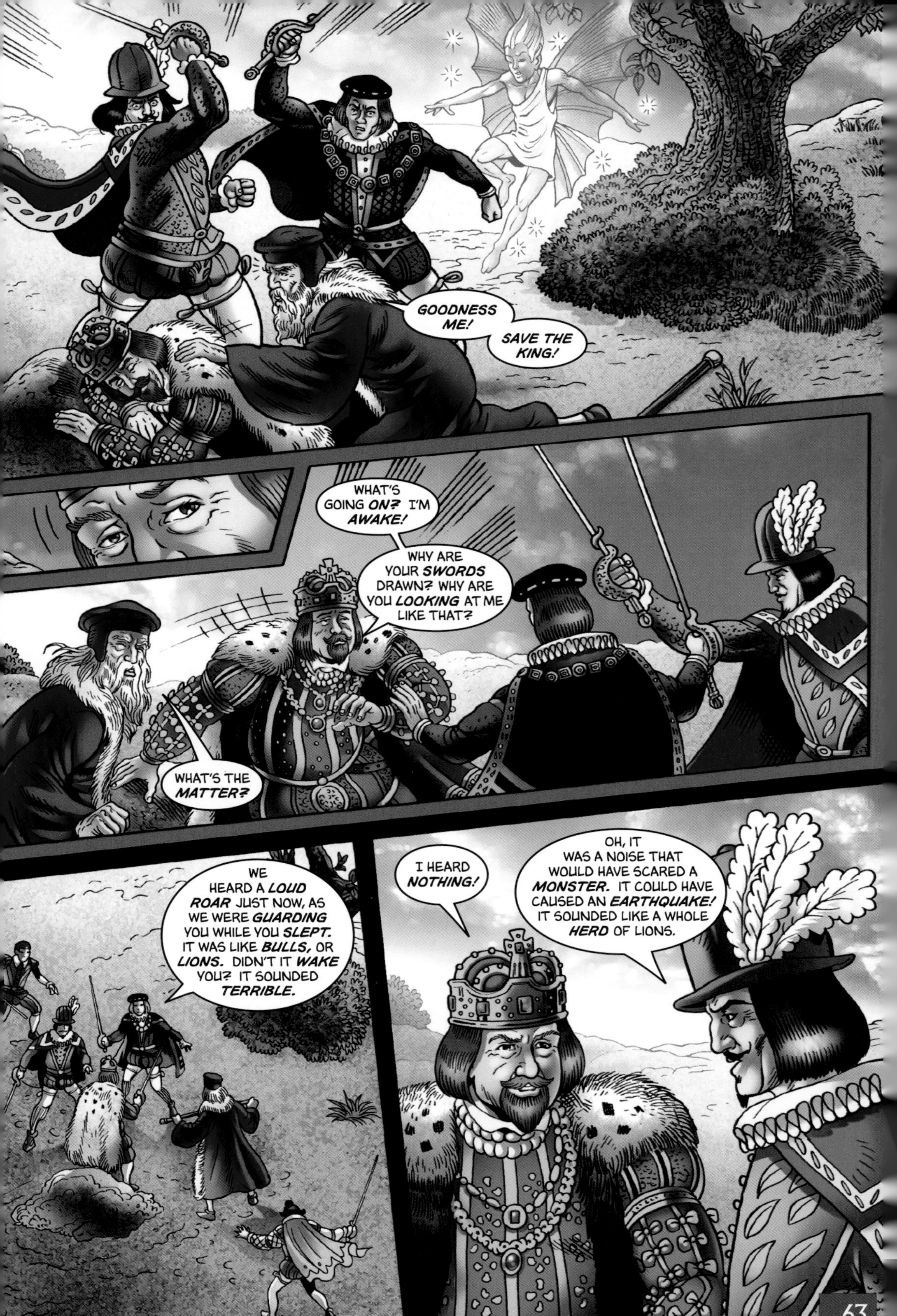
GOODNESS ME!
SAVE THE KING!
WHAT'S GOING ON? I'M AWAKE!
WHY ARE YOUR SWORDS DRAWN? WHY ARE YOU LOOKING AT ME LIKE THAT?
WHAT'S THE MATTER?
WE HEARD A LOUD ROAR JUST NOW, AS WE WERE GUARDING YOU WHILE YOU SLEPT. IT WAS LIKE BULLS, OR LIONS. DIDN'T IT WAKE YOU? IT SOUNDED TERRIBLE.
I HEARD NOTHING!
OH, IT WAS A NOISE THAT WOULD HAVE SCARED A MONSTER. IT COULD HAVE CAUSED AN EARTHQUAKE! IT SOUNDED LIKE A WHOLE HERD OF LIONS.

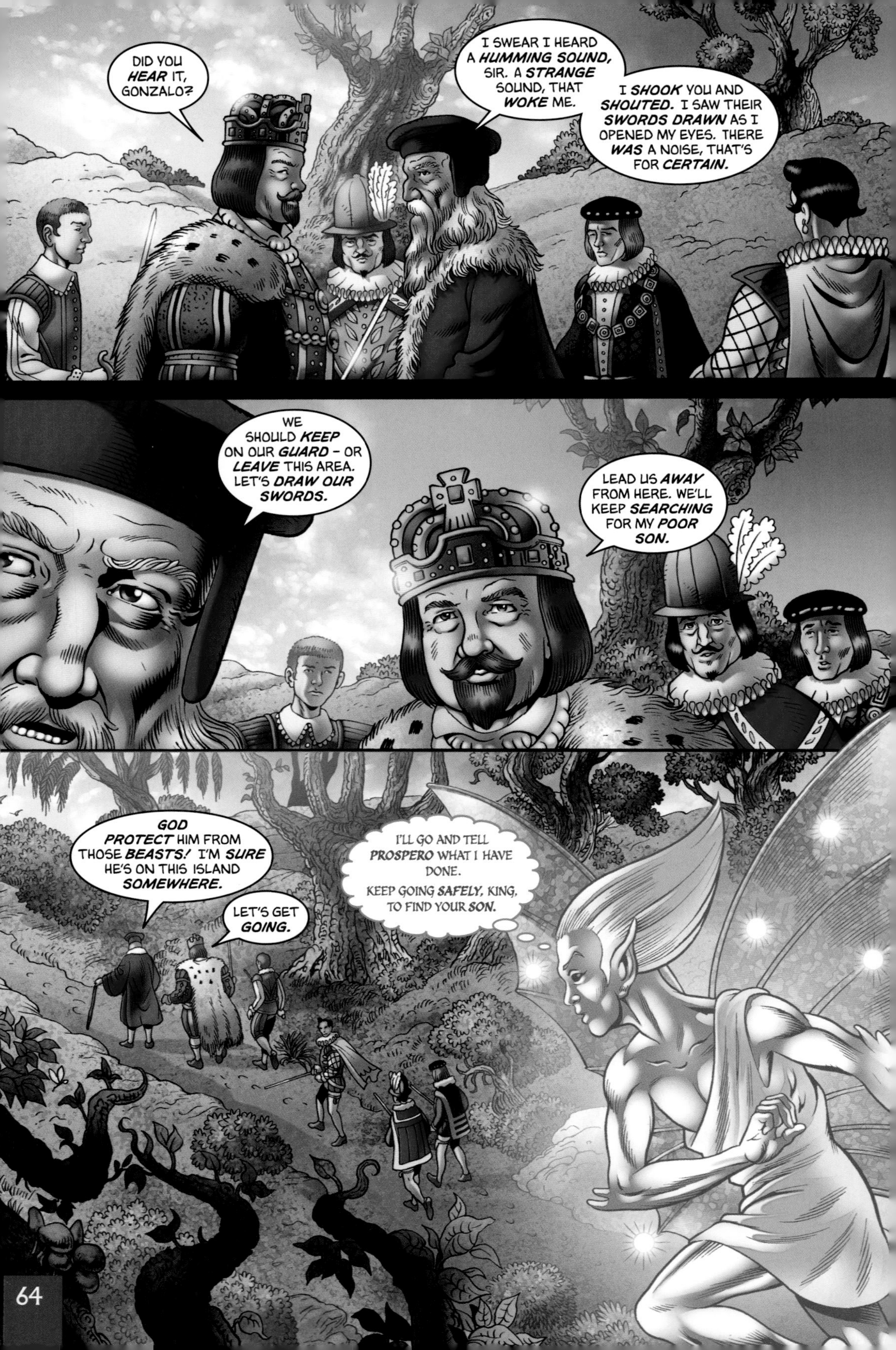
DID YOU HEAR IT, GONZALO?
I SWEAR I HEARD A HUMMING SOUND, SIR. A STRANGE SOUND, THAT WOKE ME.
I SHOOK YOU AND SHOUTED. I SAW THEIR SWORDS DRAWN AS I OPENED MY EYES. THERE WAS A NOISE, THAT'S FOR CERTAIN.
WE SHOULD KEEP ON OUR GUARD – OR LEAVE THIS AREA. LET'S DRAW OUR SWORDS.
LEAD US AWAY FROM HERE. WE'LL KEEP SEARCHING FOR MY POOR SON.
GOD PROTECT HIM FROM THOSE BEASTS! I'M SURE HE'S ON THIS ISLAND SOMEWHERE.
LET'S GET GOING.
I'LL GO AND TELL PROSPERO WHAT I HAVE DONE.
KEEP GOING SAFELY, KING, TO FIND YOUR SON.

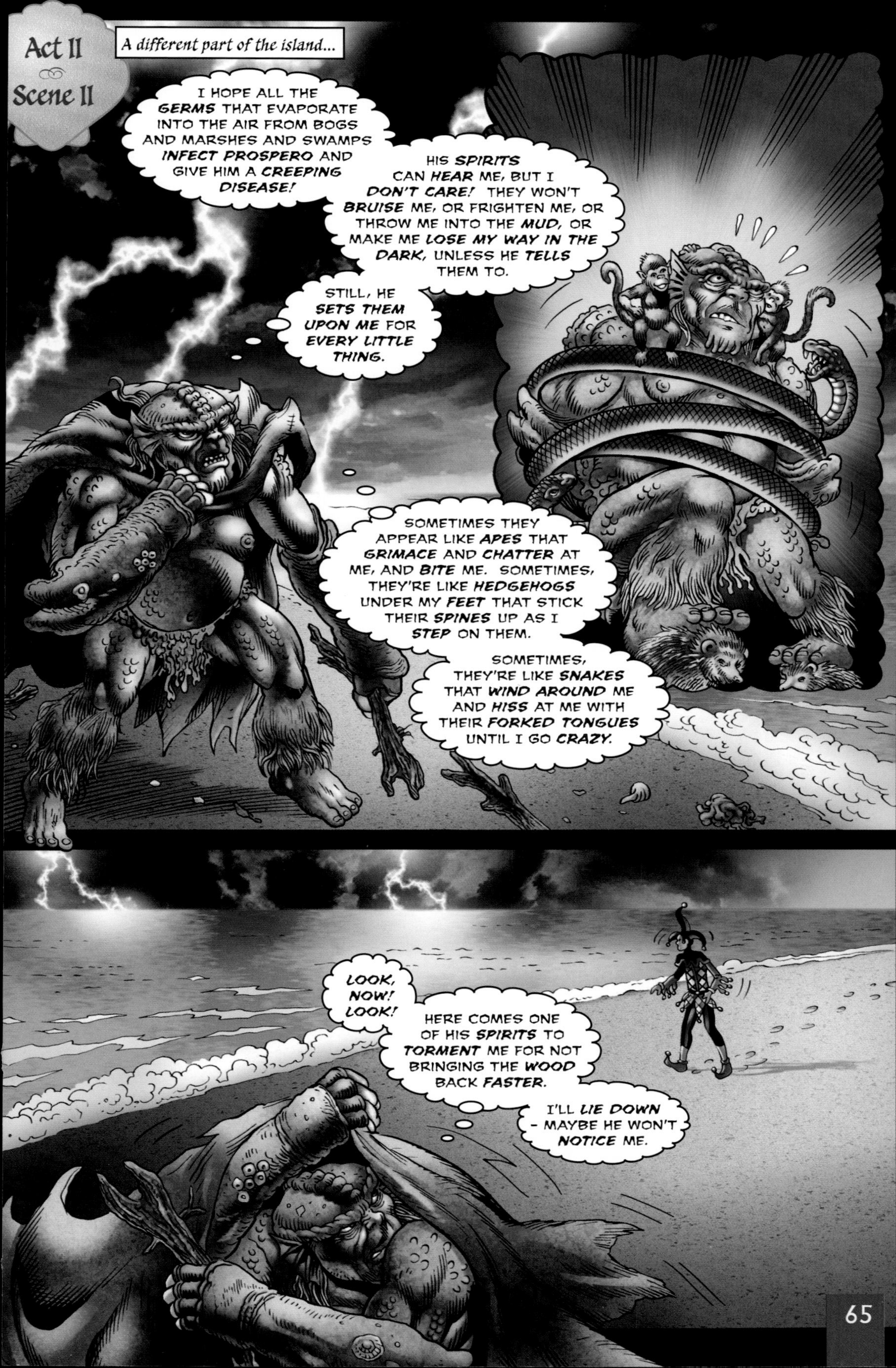

Act II Scene II
A different part of the island...
I HOPE ALL THE GERMS THAT EVAPORATE INTO THE AIR FROM BOGS AND MARSHES AND SWAMPS INFECT PROSPERO AND GIVE HIM A CREEPING DISEASE!
HIS SPIRITS CAN HEAR ME, BUT I DON'T CARE! THEY WON'T BRUISE ME, OR FRIGHTEN ME, OR THROW ME INTO THE MUD, OR MAKE ME LOSE MY WAY IN THE DARK, UNLESS HE TELLS THEM TO.
STILL, HE SETS THEM UPON ME FOR EVERY LITTLE THING.
SOMETIMES THEY APPEAR LIKE APES THAT GRIMACE AND CHATTER AT ME, AND BITE ME. SOMETIMES, THEY'RE LIKE HEDGEHOGS UNDER MY FEET THAT STICK THEIR SPINES UP AS I STEP ON THEM.
SOMETIMES, THEY'RE LIKE SNAKES THAT WIND AROUND ME AND HISS AT ME WITH THEIR FORKED TONGUES UNTIL I GO CRAZY.
LOOK, NOW! LOOK!
HERE COMES ONE OF HIS SPIRITS TO TORMENT ME FOR NOT BRINGING THE WOOD BACK FASTER.
I'LL LIE DOWN - MAYBE HE WON'T NOTICE ME.

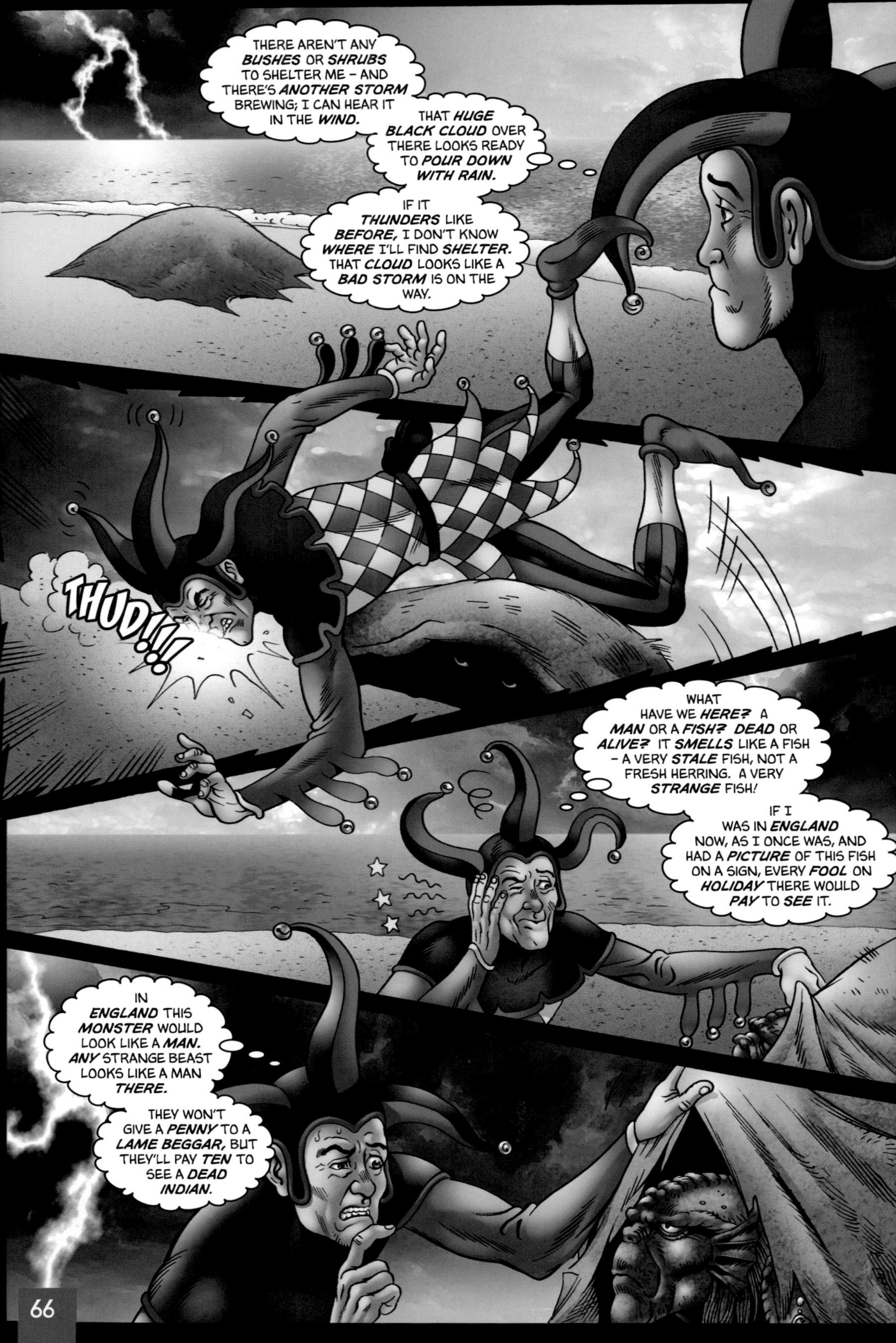
THERE AREN'T ANY BUSHES OR SHRUBS TO SHELTER ME – AND THERE'S ANOTHER STORM BREWING; I CAN HEAR IT IN THE WIND.
THAT HUGE BLACK CLOUD OVER THERE LOOKS READY TO POUR DOWN WITH RAIN.
IF IT THUNDERS LIKE BEFORE, I DON'T KNOW WHERE I'LL FIND SHELTER. THAT CLOUD LOOKS LIKE A BAD STORM IS ON THE WAY.
THUD!!!
WHAT HAVE WE HERE? A MAN OR A FISH? DEAD OR ALIVE? IT SMELLS LIKE A FISH – A VERY STALE FISH, NOT A FRESH HERRING. A VERY STRANGE FISH!
IF I WAS IN ENGLAND NOW, AS I ONCE WAS, AND HAD A PICTURE OF THIS FISH ON A SIGN, EVERY FOOL ON HOLIDAY THERE WOULD PAY TO SEE IT.
IN ENGLAND THIS MONSTER WOULD LOOK LIKE A MAN. ANY STRANGE BEAST LOOKS LIKE A MAN THERE.
THEY WON'T GIVE A PENNY TO A LAME BEGGAR, BUT THEY'LL PAY TEN TO SEE A DEAD INDIAN.

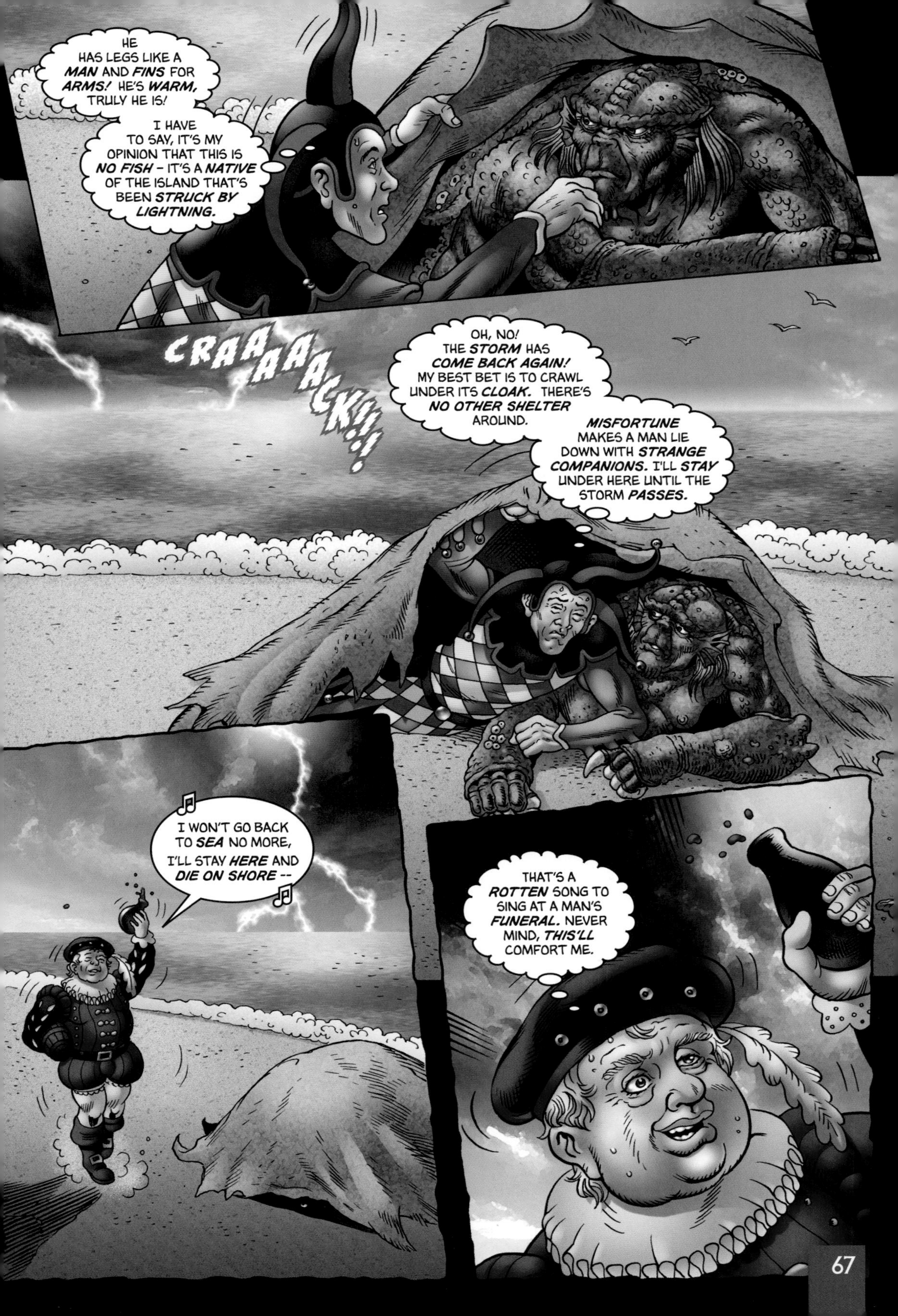

HE HAS LEGS LIKE A MAN AND FINS FOR ARMS! HE'S WARM, TRULY HE IS!
I HAVE TO SAY, IT'S MY OPINION THAT THIS IS NO FISH – IT'S A NATIVE OF THE ISLAND THAT'S BEEN STRUCK BY LIGHTNING.
CRAAAAACK!!!
OH, NO! THE STORM HAS COME BACK AGAIN! MY BEST BET IS TO CRAWL UNDER ITS CLOAK. THERE'S NO OTHER SHELTER AROUND.
MISFORTUNE MAKES A MAN LIE DOWN WITH STRANGE COMPANIONS. I'LL STAY UNDER HERE UNTIL THE STORM PASSES.
I WON'T GO BACK TO SEA NO MORE, I'LL STAY HERE AND DIE ON SHORE --
THAT'S A ROTTEN SONG TO SING AT A MAN'S FUNERAL. NEVER MIND, THIS'LL COMFORT ME.

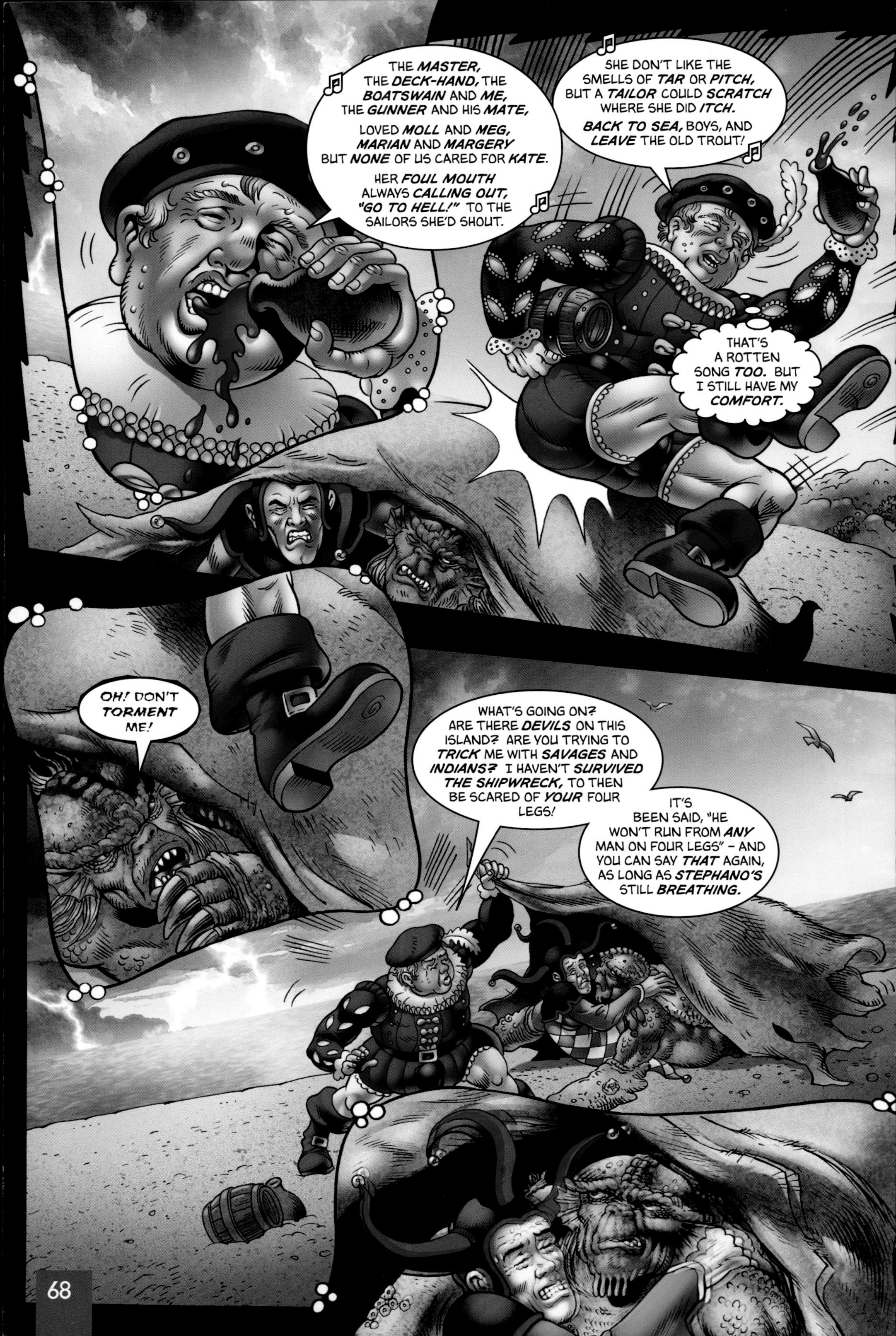
THE MASTER, THE DECK-HAND, THE BOATSWAIN AND ME, THE GUNNER AND HIS MATE, LOVED MOLL AND MEG, MARIAN AND MARGERY BUT NONE OF US CARED FOR KATE. HER FOUL MOUTH ALWAYS CALLING OUT, "GO TO HELL!" TO THE SAILORS SHE'D SHOUT.
SHE DON'T LIKE THE SMELLS OF TAR OR PITCH, BUT A TAILOR COULD SCRATCH WHERE SHE DID ITCH. BACK TO SEA, BOYS, AND LEAVE THE OLD TROUT!
THAT'S A ROTTEN SONG TOO. BUT I STILL HAVE MY COMFORT.
OH! DON'T TORMENT ME!
WHAT'S GOING ON? ARE THERE DEVILS ON THIS ISLAND? ARE YOU TRYING TO TRICK ME WITH SAVAGES AND INDIANS? I HAVEN'T SURVIVED THE SHIPWRECK, TO THEN BE SCARED OF YOUR FOUR LEGS!
IT'S BEEN SAID, "HE WON'T RUN FROM ANY MAN ON FOUR LEGS" – AND YOU CAN SAY THAT AGAIN, AS LONG AS STEPHANO'S STILL BREATHING.

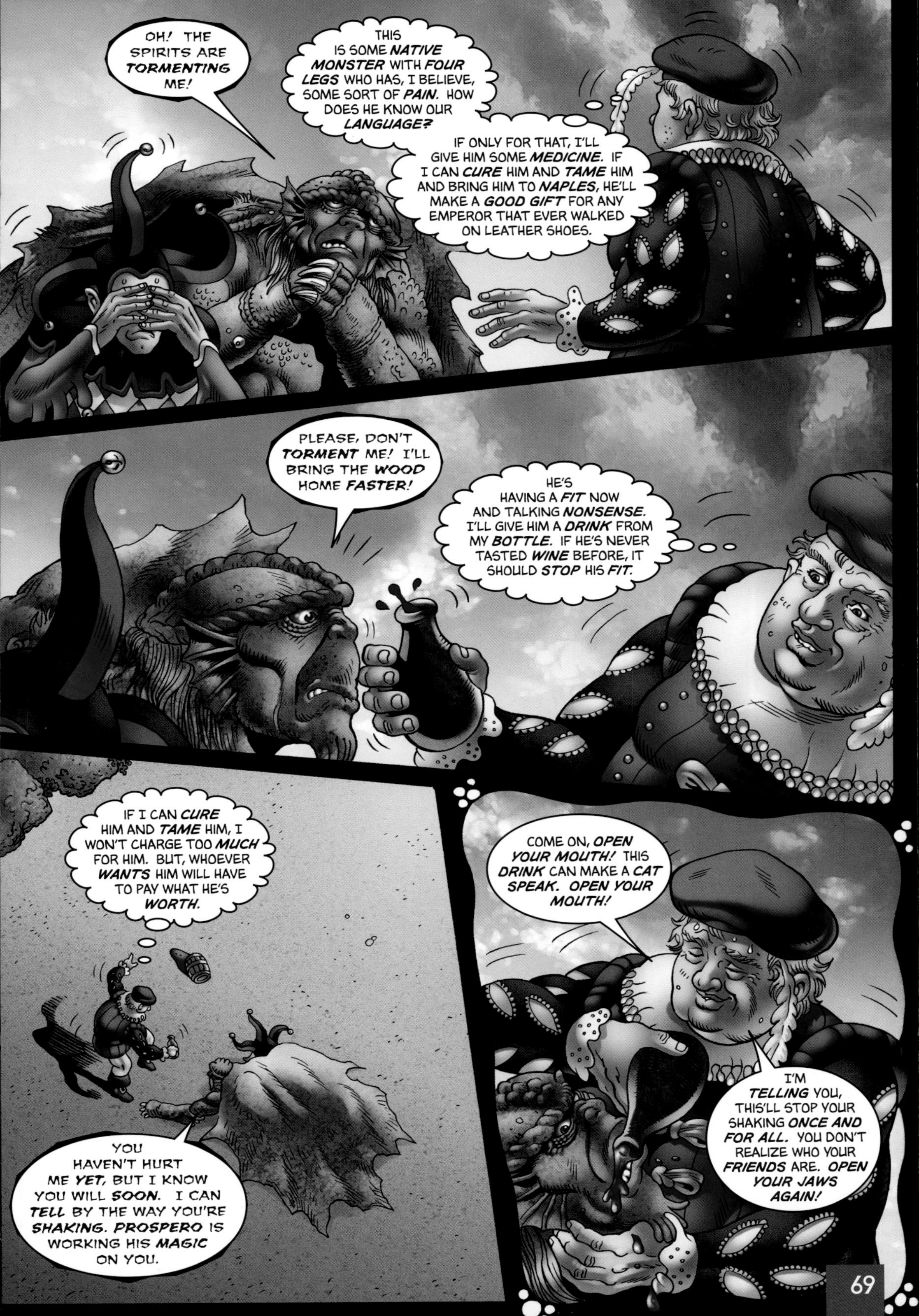

OH! THE SPIRITS ARE TORMENTING ME!
THIS IS SOME NATIVE MONSTER WITH FOUR LEGS WHO HAS, I BELIEVE, SOME SORT OF PAIN. HOW DOES HE KNOW OUR LANGUAGE?
IF ONLY FOR THAT, I'LL GIVE HIM SOME MEDICINE. IF I CAN CURE HIM AND TAME HIM AND BRING HIM TO NAPLES, HE'LL MAKE A GOOD GIFT FOR ANY EMPEROR THAT EVER WALKED ON LEATHER SHOES.
PLEASE, DON'T TORMENT ME! I'LL BRING THE WOOD HOME FASTER!
HE'S HAVING A FIT NOW AND TALKING NONSENSE. I'LL GIVE HIM A DRINK FROM MY BOTTLE. IF HE'S NEVER TASTED WINE BEFORE, IT SHOULD STOP HIS FIT.
IF I CAN CURE HIM AND TAME HIM, I WON'T CHARGE TOO MUCH FOR HIM. BUT, WHOEVER WANTS HIM WILL HAVE TO PAY WHAT HE'S WORTH.
YOU HAVEN'T HURT ME YET, BUT I KNOW YOU WILL SOON. I CAN TELL BY THE WAY YOU'RE SHAKING. PROSPERO IS WORKING HIS MAGIC ON YOU.
COME ON, OPEN YOUR MOUTH! THIS DRINK CAN MAKE A CAT SPEAK. OPEN YOUR MOUTH!
I'M TELLING YOU, THIS'LL STOP YOUR SHAKING ONCE AND FOR ALL. YOU DON'T REALIZE WHO YOUR FRIENDS ARE. OPEN YOUR JAWS AGAIN!

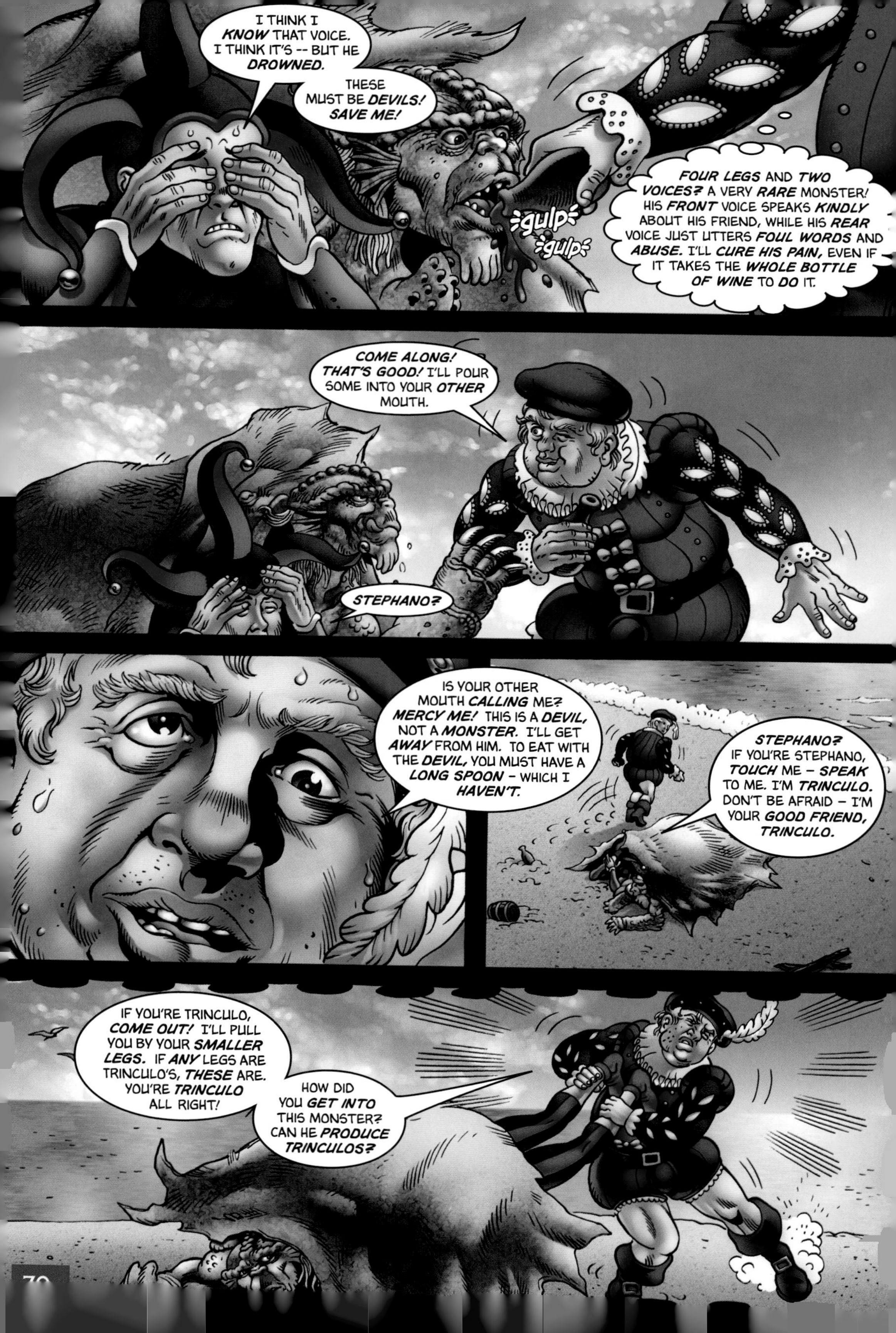
I THINK I KNOW THAT VOICE. I THINK IT'S -- BUT HE DROWNED.
THESE MUST BE DEVILS! SAVE ME!
gulp
gulp
FOUR LEGS AND TWO VOICES? A VERY RARE MONSTER! HIS FRONT VOICE SPEAKS KINDLY ABOUT HIS FRIEND, WHILE HIS REAR VOICE JUST UTTERS FOUL WORDS AND ABUSE. I'LL CURE HIS PAIN, EVEN IF IT TAKES THE WHOLE BOTTLE OF WINE TO DO IT.
COME ALONG! THAT'S GOOD! I'LL POUR SOME INTO YOUR OTHER MOUTH.
STEPHANO?
IS YOUR OTHER MOUTH CALLING ME? MERCY ME! THIS IS A DEVIL, NOT A MONSTER. I'LL GET AWAY FROM HIM. TO EAT WITH THE DEVIL, YOU MUST HAVE A LONG SPOON – WHICH I HAVEN'T.
STEPHANO? IF YOU'RE STEPHANO, TOUCH ME – SPEAK TO ME. I'M TRINCULO. DON'T BE AFRAID – I'M YOUR GOOD FRIEND, TRINCULO.
IF YOU'RE TRINCULO, COME OUT! I'LL PULL YOU BY YOUR SMALLER LEGS. IF ANY LEGS ARE TRINCULO'S, THESE ARE. YOU'RE TRINCULO ALL RIGHT!
HOW DID YOU GET INTO THIS MONSTER? CAN HE PRODUCE TRINCULOS?

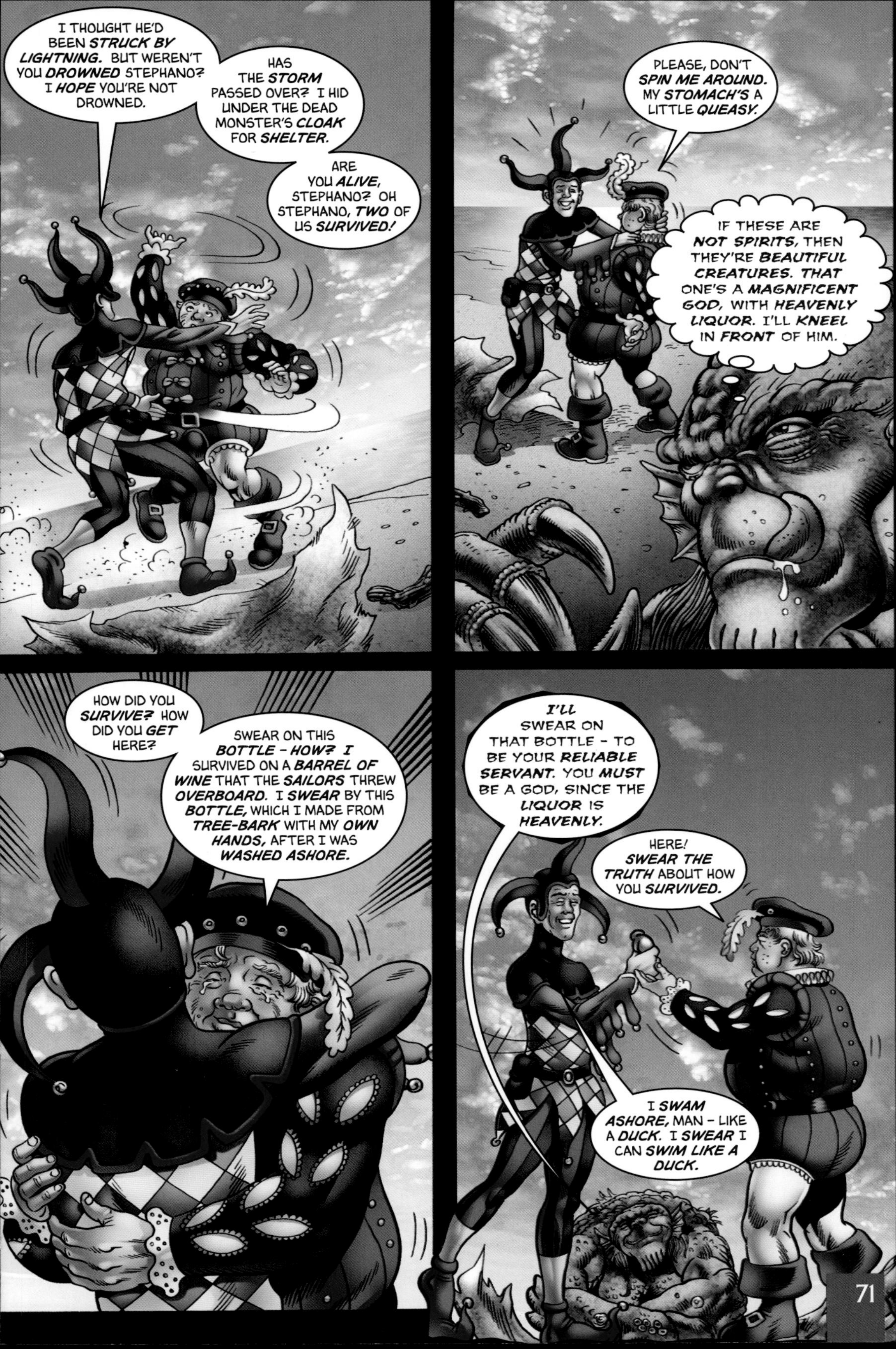
I THOUGHT HE'D BEEN STRUCK BY LIGHTNING. BUT WEREN'T YOU DROWNED STEPHANO? I HOPE YOU'RE NOT DROWNED.
HAS THE STORM PASSED OVER? I HID UNDER THE DEAD MONSTER'S CLOAK FOR SHELTER.
ARE YOU ALIVE, STEPHANO? OH STEPHANO, TWO OF US SURVIVED!
PLEASE, DON'T SPIN ME AROUND. MY STOMACH'S A LITTLE QUEASY.
IF THESE ARE NOT SPIRITS, THEN THEY'RE BEAUTIFUL CREATURES. THAT ONE'S A MAGNIFICENT GOD, WITH HEAVENLY LIQUOR. I'LL KNEEL IN FRONT OF HIM.
HOW DID YOU SURVIVE? HOW DID YOU GET HERE?
SWEAR ON THIS BOTTLE - HOW? I SURVIVED ON A BARREL OF WINE THAT THE SAILORS THREW OVERBOARD. I SWEAR BY THIS BOTTLE, WHICH I MADE FROM TREE-BARK WITH MY OWN HANDS, AFTER I WAS WASHED ASHORE.
I'LL SWEAR ON THAT BOTTLE - TO BE YOUR RELIABLE SERVANT. YOU MUST BE A GOD, SINCE THE LIQUOR IS HEAVENLY.
HERE! SWEAR THE TRUTH ABOUT HOW YOU SURVIVED.
I SWAM ASHORE, MAN - LIKE A DUCK. I SWEAR I CAN SWIM LIKE A DUCK.

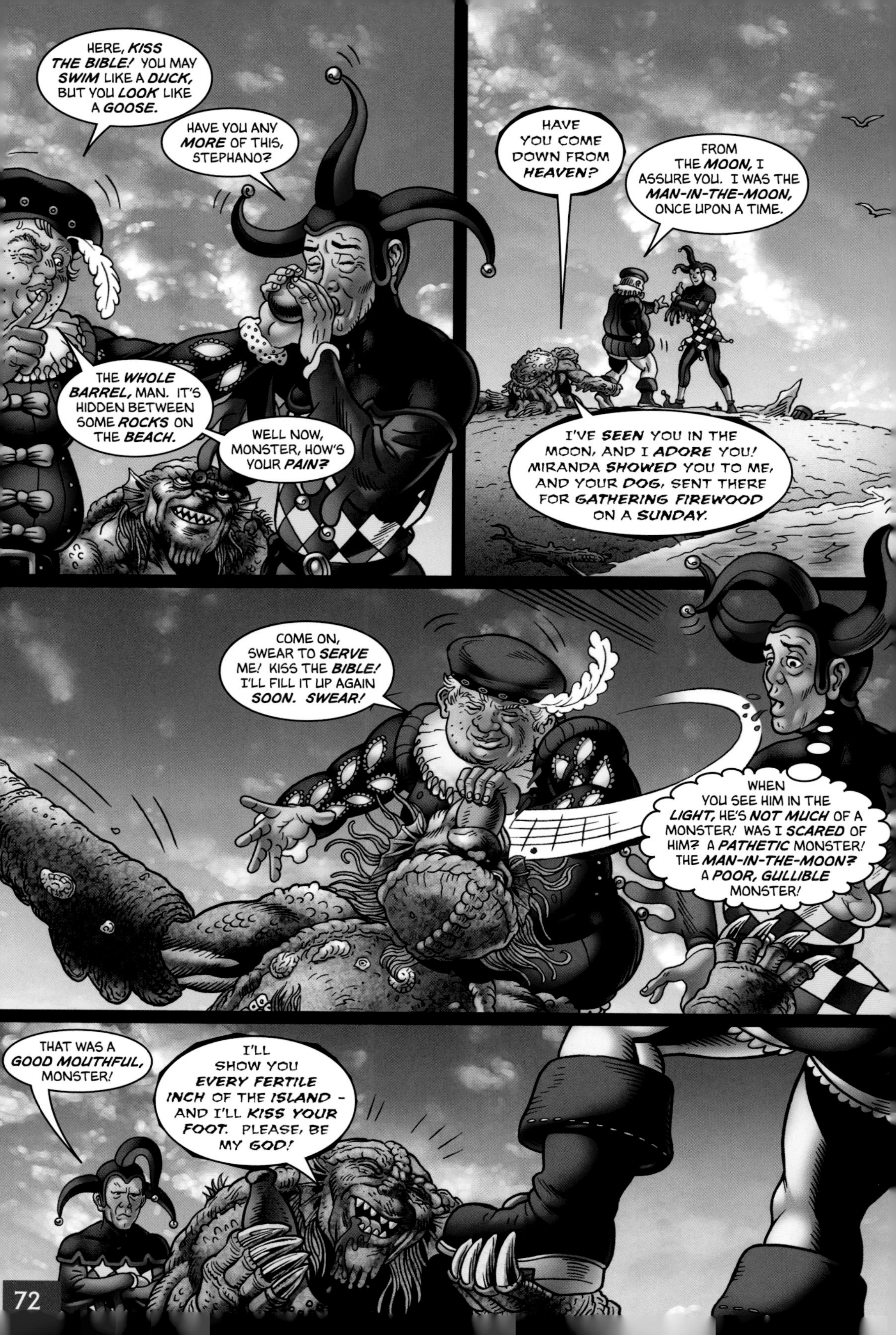
HERE, KISS THE BIBLE! YOU MAY SWIM LIKE A DUCK, BUT YOU LOOK LIKE A GOOSE.
HAVE YOU ANY MORE OF THIS, STEPHANO?
THE WHOLE BARREL, MAN. IT'S HIDDEN BETWEEN SOME ROCKS ON THE BEACH.
WELL NOW, MONSTER, HOW'S YOUR PAIN?
HAVE YOU COME DOWN FROM HEAVEN?
FROM THE MOON, I ASSURE YOU. I WAS THE MAN-IN-THE-MOON, ONCE UPON A TIME.
I'VE SEEN YOU IN THE MOON, AND I ADORE YOU! MIRANDA SHOWED YOU TO ME, AND YOUR DOG, SENT THERE FOR GATHERING FIREWOOD ON A SUNDAY.
COME ON, SWEAR TO SERVE ME! KISS THE BIBLE! I'LL FILL IT UP AGAIN SOON. SWEAR!
WHEN YOU SEE HIM IN THE LIGHT, HE'S NOT MUCH OF A MONSTER! WAS I SCARED OF HIM? A PATHETIC MONSTER! THE MAN-IN-THE-MOON? A POOR, GULLIBLE MONSTER!
THAT WAS A GOOD MOUTHFUL, MONSTER!
I'LL SHOW YOU EVERY FERTILE INCH OF THE ISLAND - AND I'LL KISS YOUR FOOT. PLEASE, BE MY GOD!

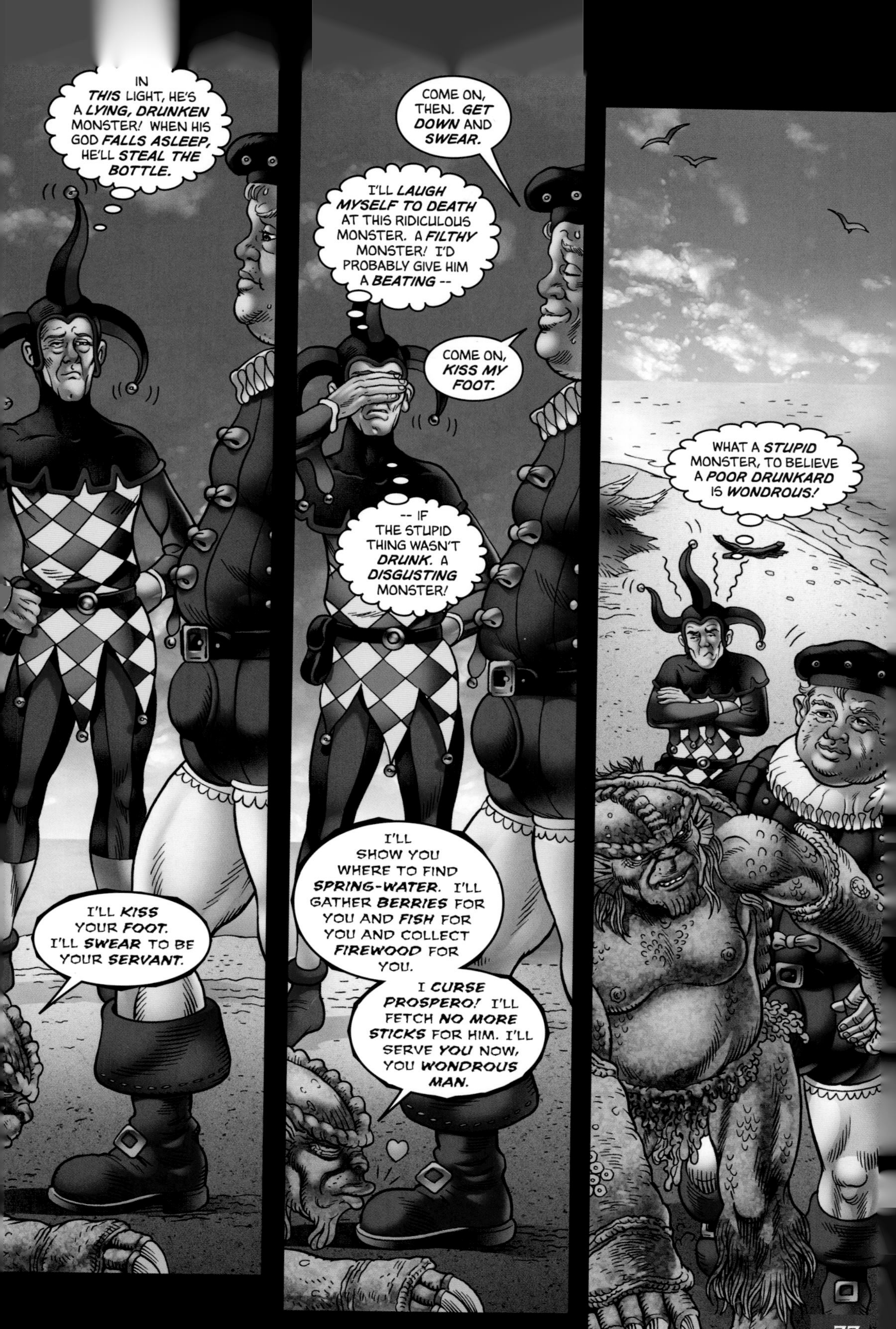
IN THIS LIGHT, HE'S A LYING, DRUNKEN MONSTER! WHEN HIS GOD FALLS ASLEEP, HE'LL STEAL THE BOTTLE.
I'LL KISS YOUR FOOT. I'LL SWEAR TO BE YOUR SERVANT.
COME ON, THEN. GET DOWN AND SWEAR.
I'LL LAUGH MYSELF TO DEATH AT THIS RIDICULOUS MONSTER. A FILTHY MONSTER! I'D PROBABLY GIVE HIM A BEATING --
COME ON, KISS MY FOOT.
-- IF THE STUPID THING WASN'T DRUNK. A DISGUSTING MONSTER!
I'LL SHOW YOU WHERE TO FIND SPRING-WATER. I'LL GATHER BERRIES FOR YOU AND FISH FOR YOU AND COLLECT FIREWOOD FOR YOU.
I CURSE PROSPERO! I'LL FETCH NO MORE STICKS FOR HIM. I'LL SERVE YOU NOW, YOU WONDROUS MAN.
WHAT A STUPID MONSTER, TO BELIEVE A POOR DRUNKARD IS WONDROUS!

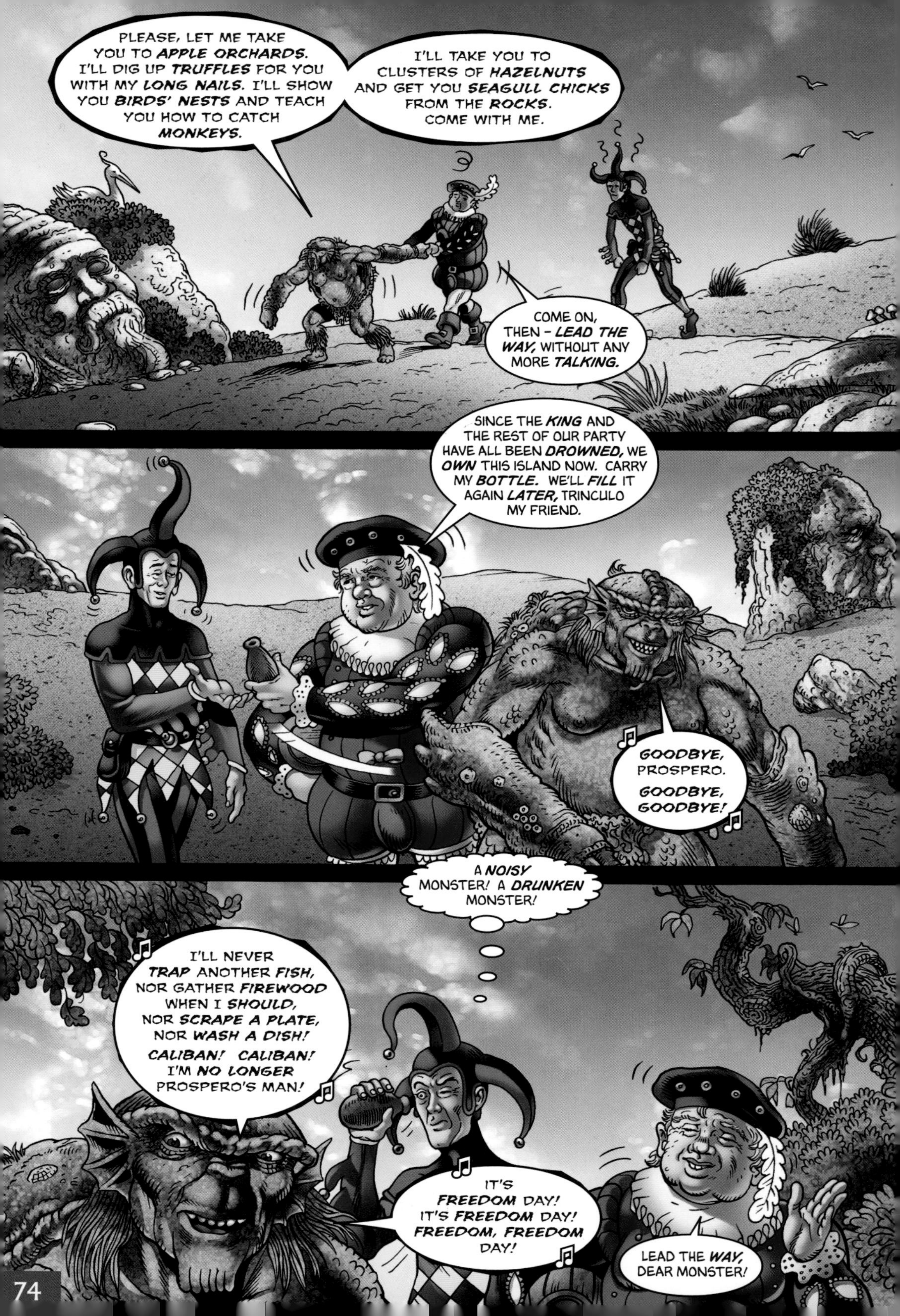
PLEASE, LET ME TAKE YOU TO APPLE ORCHARDS. I'LL DIG UP TRUFFLES FOR YOU WITH MY LONG NAILS. I'LL SHOW YOU BIRDS' NESTS AND TEACH YOU HOW TO CATCH MONKEYS.
I'LL TAKE YOU TO CLUSTERS OF HAZELNUTS AND GET YOU SEAGULL CHICKS FROM THE ROCKS. COME WITH ME.
COME ON, THEN – LEAD THE WAY, WITHOUT ANY MORE TALKING.
SINCE THE KING AND THE REST OF OUR PARTY HAVE ALL BEEN DROWNED, WE OWN THIS ISLAND NOW. CARRY MY BOTTLE. WE'LL FILL IT AGAIN LATER, TRINCULO MY FRIEND.
GOODBYE, PROSPERO. GOODBYE, GOODBYE!
A NOISY MONSTER! A DRUNKEN MONSTER!
I'LL NEVER TRAP ANOTHER FISH, NOR GATHER FIREWOOD WHEN I SHOULD, NOR SCRAPE A PLATE, NOR WASH A DISH! CALIBAN! CALIBAN! I'M NO LONGER PROSPERO'S MAN!
IT'S FREEDOM DAY! IT'S FREEDOM DAY! FREEDOM, FREEDOM DAY!
LEAD THE WAY, DEAR MONSTER!

Act III
Scene I

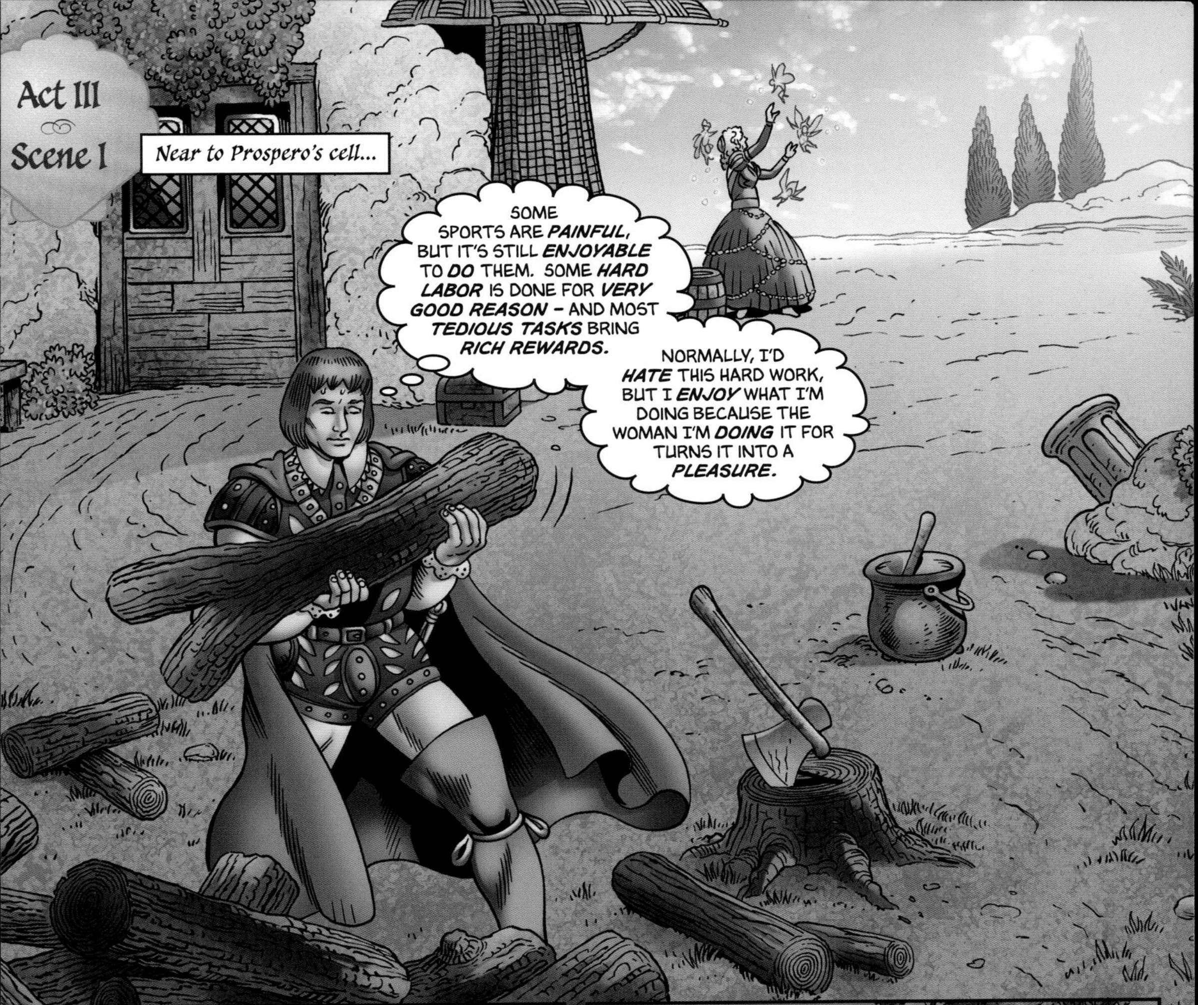
Near to Prospero's cell...
SOME SPORTS ARE PAINFUL, BUT IT'S STILL ENJOYABLE TO DO THEM. SOME HARD LABOR IS DONE FOR VERY GOOD REASON – AND MOST TEDIOUS TASKS BRING RICH REWARDS.
NORMALLY, I'D HATE THIS HARD WORK, BUT I ENJOY WHAT I'M DOING BECAUSE THE WOMAN I'M DOING IT FOR TURNS IT INTO A PLEASURE.

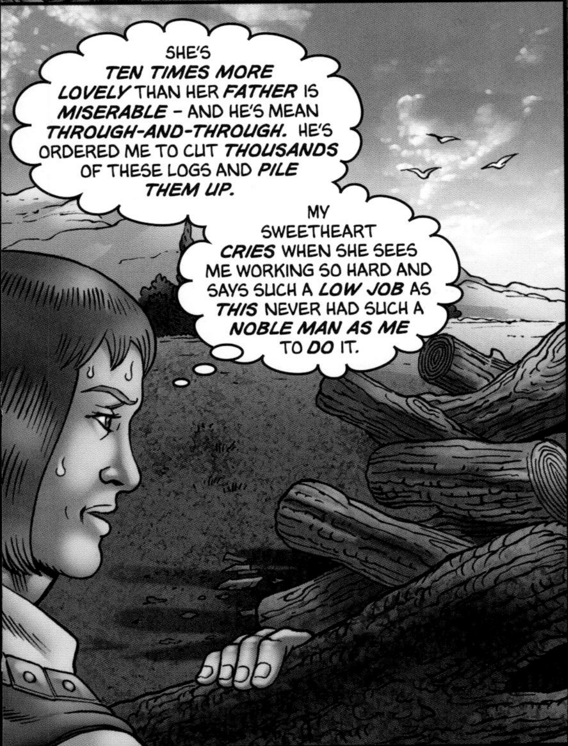
SHE'S TEN TIMES MORE LOVELY THAN HER FATHER IS MISERABLE – AND HE'S MEAN THROUGH-AND-THROUGH. HE'S ORDERED ME TO CUT THOUSANDS OF THESE LOGS AND PILE THEM UP.
MY SWEETHEART CRIES WHEN SHE SEES ME WORKING SO HARD AND SAYS SUCH A LOW JOB AS THIS NEVER HAD SUCH A NOBLE MAN AS ME TO DO IT.

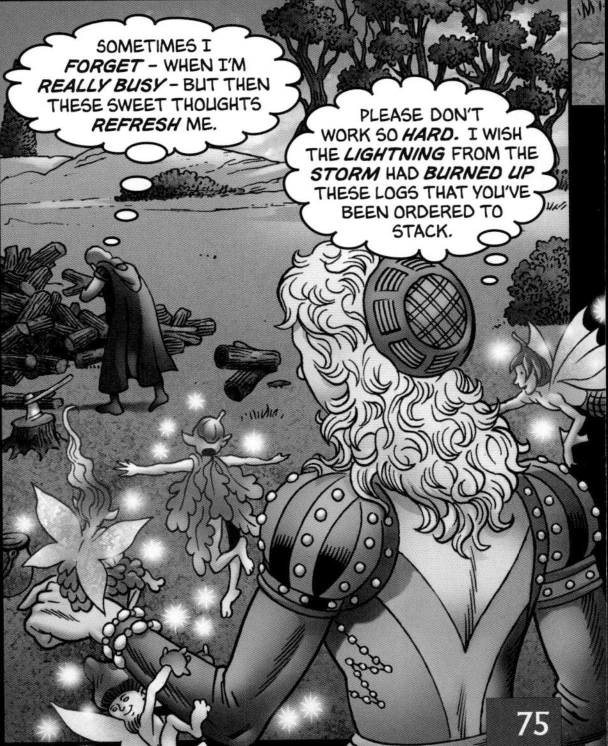
SOMETIMES I FORGET – WHEN I'M REALLY BUSY – BUT THEN THESE SWEET THOUGHTS REFRESH ME.
PLEASE DON'T WORK SO HARD. I WISH THE LIGHTNING FROM THE STORM HAD BURNED UP THESE LOGS THAT YOU'VE BEEN ORDERED TO STACK.

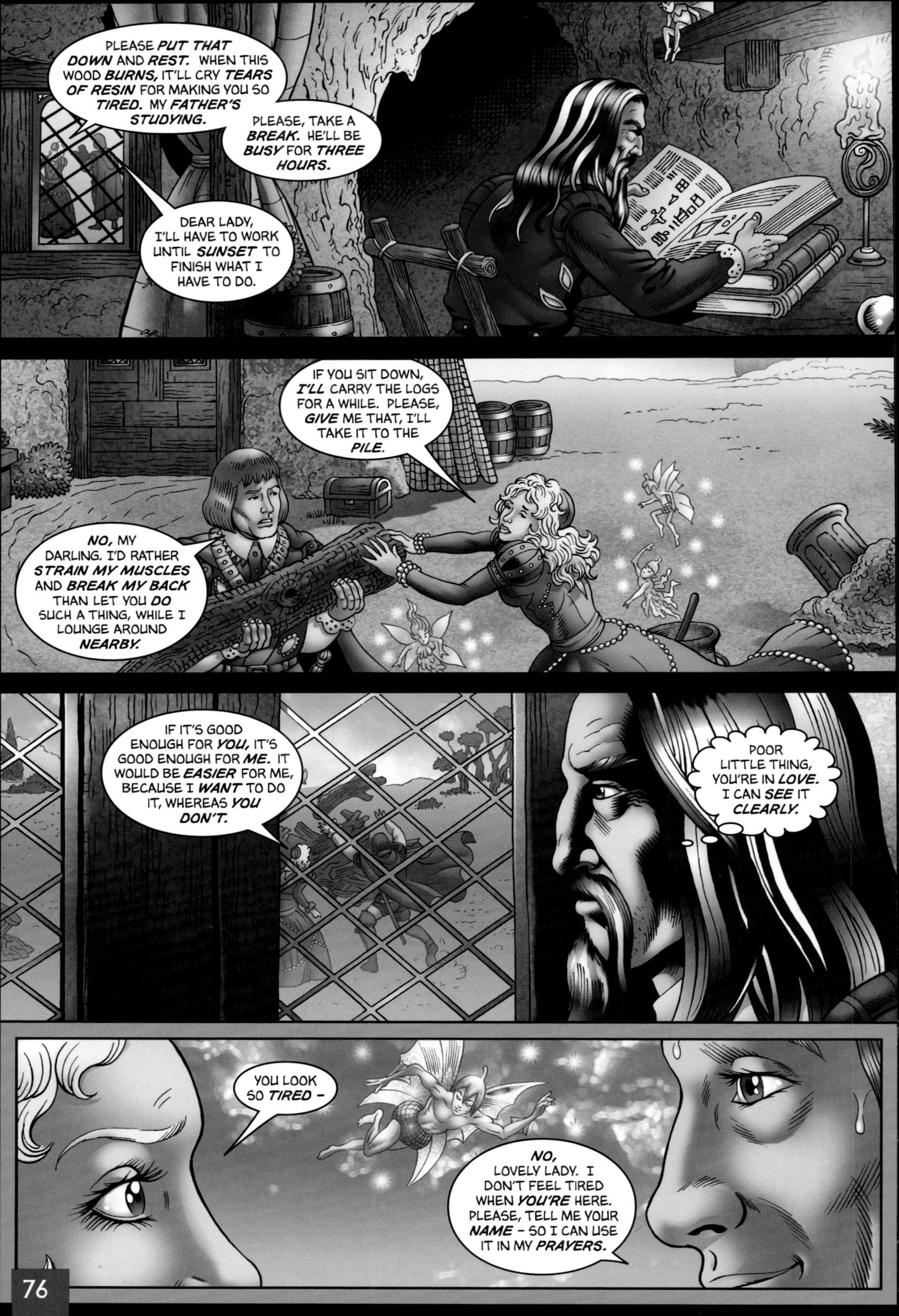
PLEASE PUT THAT DOWN AND REST. WHEN THIS WOOD BURNS, IT'LL CRY TEARS OF RESIN FOR MAKING YOU SO TIRED. MY FATHER'S STUDYING.
PLEASE, TAKE A BREAK. HE'LL BE BUSY FOR THREE HOURS.
DEAR LADY, I'LL HAVE TO WORK UNTIL SUNSET TO FINISH WHAT I HAVE TO DO.
IF YOU SIT DOWN, I'LL CARRY THE LOGS FOR A WHILE. PLEASE, GIVE ME THAT, I'LL TAKE IT TO THE PILE.
NO, MY DARLING. I'D RATHER STRAIN MY MUSCLES AND BREAK MY BACK THAN LET YOU DO SUCH A THING, WHILE I LOUNGE AROUND NEARBY.
IF IT'S GOOD ENOUGH FOR YOU, IT'S GOOD ENOUGH FOR ME. IT WOULD BE EASIER FOR ME, BECAUSE I WANT TO DO IT, WHEREAS YOU DON'T.
POOR LITTLE THING, YOU'RE IN LOVE. I CAN SEE IT CLEARLY.
YOU LOOK SO TIRED –
NO, LOVELY LADY. I DON'T FEEL TIRED WHEN YOU'RE HERE. PLEASE, TELL ME YOUR NAME – SO I CAN USE IT IN MY PRAYERS.

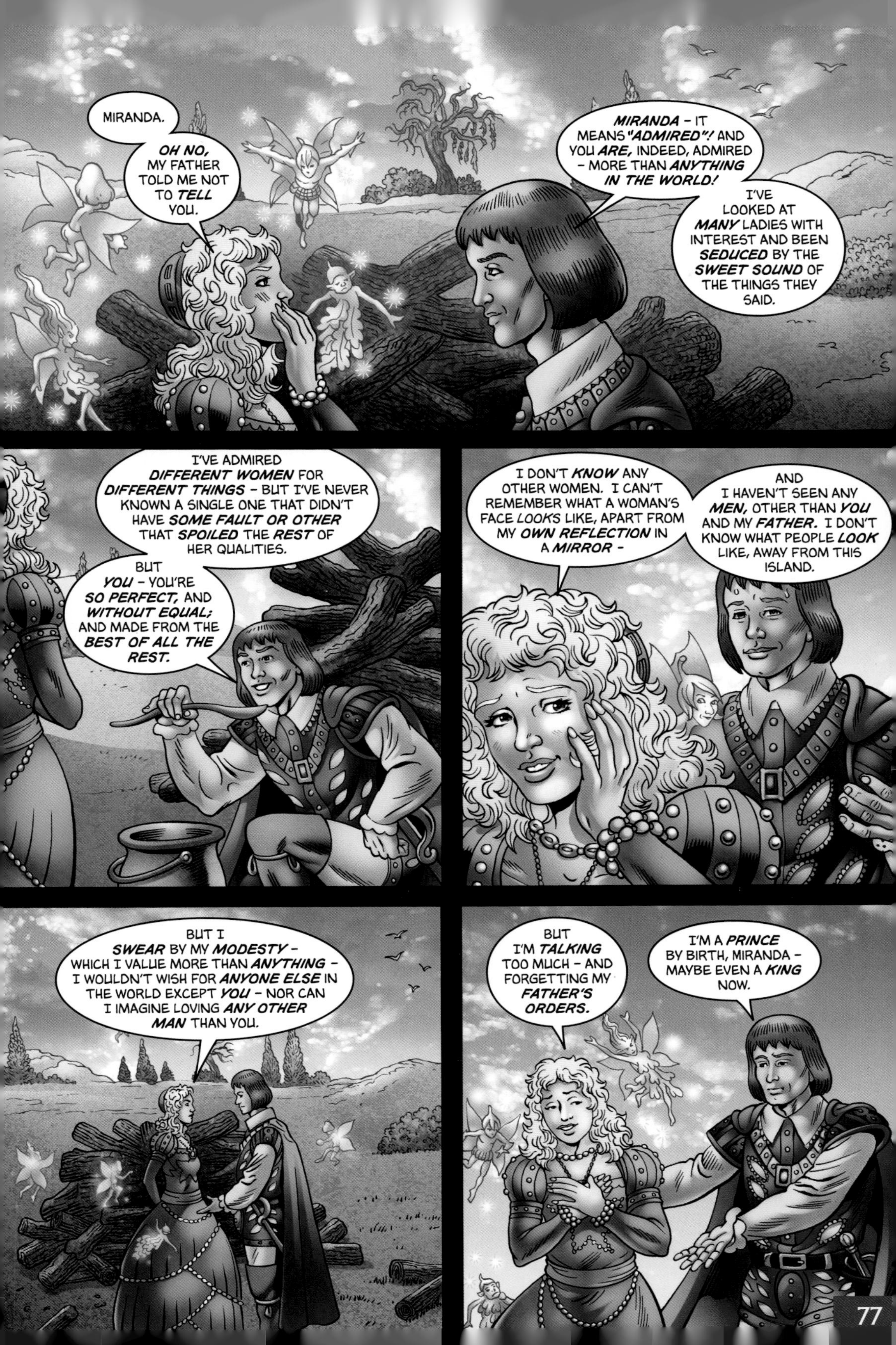
MIRANDA.
OH NO, MY FATHER TOLD ME NOT TO TELL YOU.
MIRANDA – IT MEANS "ADMIRED"! AND YOU ARE, INDEED, ADMIRED – MORE THAN ANYTHING IN THE WORLD!
I'VE LOOKED AT MANY LADIES WITH INTEREST AND BEEN SEDUCED BY THE SWEET SOUND OF THE THINGS THEY SAID.
I'VE ADMIRED DIFFERENT WOMEN FOR DIFFERENT THINGS – BUT I'VE NEVER KNOWN A SINGLE ONE THAT DIDN'T HAVE SOME FAULT OR OTHER THAT SPOILED THE REST OF HER QUALITIES.
BUT YOU – YOU'RE SO PERFECT, AND WITHOUT EQUAL; AND MADE FROM THE BEST OF ALL THE REST.
I DON'T KNOW ANY OTHER WOMEN. I CAN'T REMEMBER WHAT A WOMAN'S FACE LOOKS LIKE, APART FROM MY OWN REFLECTION IN A MIRROR –
AND I HAVEN'T SEEN ANY MEN, OTHER THAN YOU AND MY FATHER. I DON'T KNOW WHAT PEOPLE LOOK LIKE, AWAY FROM THIS ISLAND.
BUT I SWEAR BY MY MODESTY – WHICH I VALUE MORE THAN ANYTHING – I WOULDN'T WISH FOR ANYONE ELSE IN THE WORLD EXCEPT YOU – NOR CAN I IMAGINE LOVING ANY OTHER MAN THAN YOU.
BUT I'M TALKING TOO MUCH – AND FORGETTING MY FATHER'S ORDERS.
I'M A PRINCE BY BIRTH, MIRANDA – MAYBE EVEN A KING NOW.

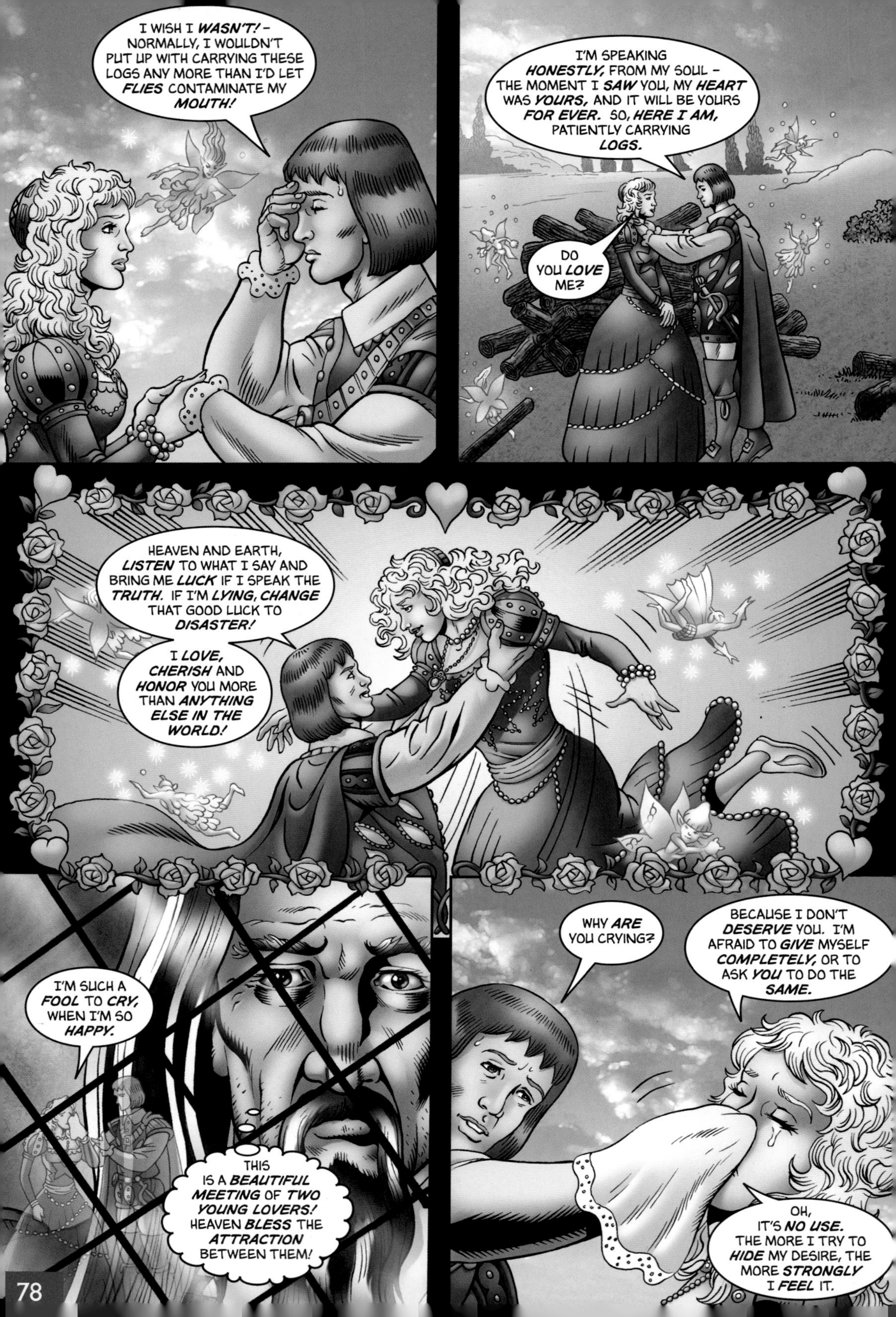
I WISH I WASN'T! – NORMALLY, I WOULDN'T PUT UP WITH CARRYING THESE LOGS ANY MORE THAN I'D LET FLIES CONTAMINATE MY MOUTH!
I'M SPEAKING HONESTLY, FROM MY SOUL – THE MOMENT I SAW YOU, MY HEART WAS YOURS, AND IT WILL BE YOURS FOR EVER. SO, HERE I AM, PATIENTLY CARRYING LOGS.
DO YOU LOVE ME?
HEAVEN AND EARTH, LISTEN TO WHAT I SAY AND BRING ME LUCK IF I SPEAK THE TRUTH. IF I'M LYING, CHANGE THAT GOOD LUCK TO DISASTER!
I LOVE, CHERISH AND HONOR YOU MORE THAN ANYTHING ELSE IN THE WORLD!
I'M SUCH A FOOL TO CRY, WHEN I'M SO HAPPY.
THIS IS A BEAUTIFUL MEETING OF TWO YOUNG LOVERS! HEAVEN BLESS THE ATTRACTION BETWEEN THEM!
WHY ARE YOU CRYING?
BECAUSE I DON'T DESERVE YOU. I'M AFRAID TO GIVE MYSELF COMPLETELY, OR TO ASK YOU TO DO THE SAME.
OH, IT'S NO USE. THE MORE I TRY TO HIDE MY DESIRE, THE MORE STRONGLY I FEEL IT.

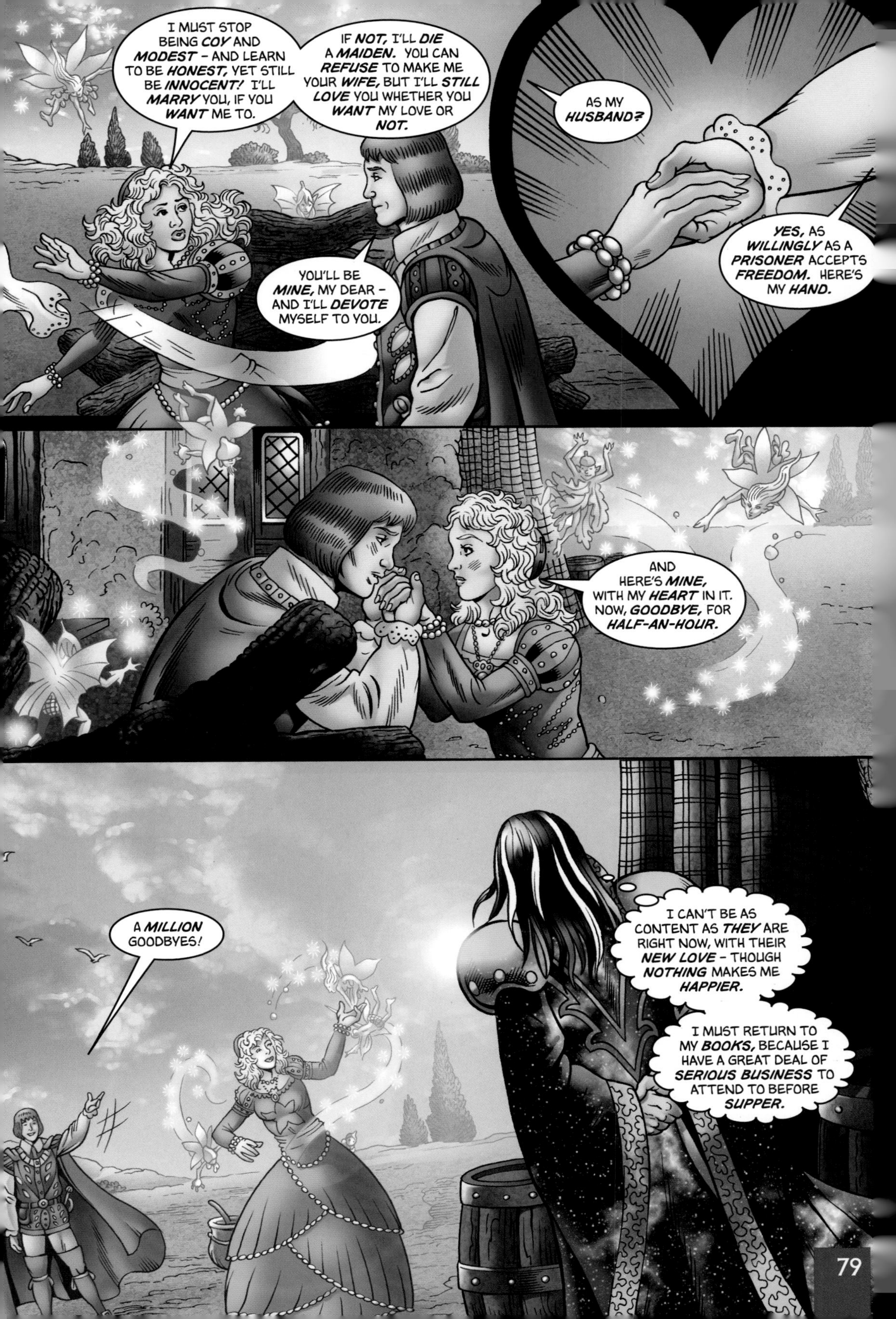

I MUST STOP BEING COY AND MODEST – AND LEARN TO BE HONEST, YET STILL BE INNOCENT! I'LL MARRY YOU, IF YOU WANT ME TO.
IF NOT, I'LL DIE A MAIDEN. YOU CAN REFUSE TO MAKE ME YOUR WIFE, BUT I'LL STILL LOVE YOU WHETHER YOU WANT MY LOVE OR NOT.
YOU'LL BE MINE, MY DEAR – AND I'LL DEVOTE MYSELF TO YOU.
AS MY HUSBAND?
YES, AS WILLINGLY AS A PRISONER ACCEPTS FREEDOM. HERE'S MY HAND.
AND HERE'S MINE, WITH MY HEART IN IT. NOW, GOODBYE, FOR HALF-AN-HOUR.
A MILLION GOODBYES!
I CAN'T BE AS CONTENT AS THEY ARE RIGHT NOW, WITH THEIR NEW LOVE – THOUGH NOTHING MAKES ME HAPPIER.
I MUST RETURN TO MY BOOKS, BECAUSE I HAVE A GREAT DEAL OF SERIOUS BUSINESS TO ATTEND TO BEFORE SUPPER.

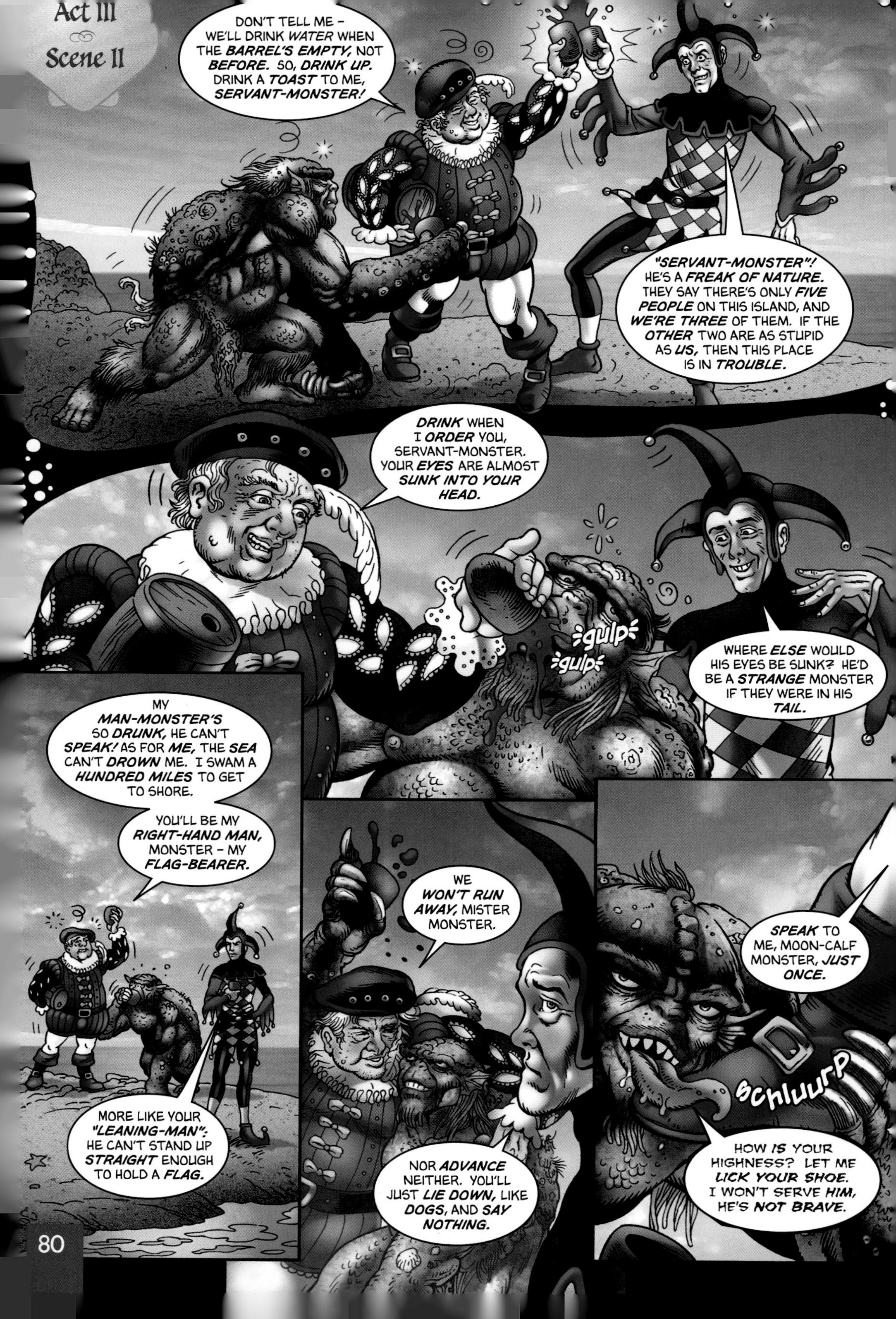
Act III
Scene II
DON'T TELL ME – WE'LL DRINK WATER WHEN THE BARREL'S EMPTY, NOT BEFORE. SO, DRINK UP. DRINK A TOAST TO ME, SERVANT-MONSTER!
"SERVANT-MONSTER"! HE'S A FREAK OF NATURE. THEY SAY THERE'S ONLY FIVE PEOPLE ON THIS ISLAND, AND WE'RE THREE OF THEM. IF THE OTHER TWO ARE AS STUPID AS US, THEN THIS PLACE IS IN TROUBLE.
DRINK WHEN I ORDER YOU, SERVANT-MONSTER. YOUR EYES ARE ALMOST SUNK INTO YOUR HEAD.
gulp
gulp
WHERE ELSE WOULD HIS EYES BE SUNK? HE'D BE A STRANGE MONSTER IF THEY WERE IN HIS TAIL.
MY MAN-MONSTER'S SO DRUNK, HE CAN'T SPEAK! AS FOR ME, THE SEA CAN'T DROWN ME. I SWAM A HUNDRED MILES TO GET TO SHORE.
YOU'LL BE MY RIGHT-HAND MAN, MONSTER – MY FLAG-BEARER.
MORE LIKE YOUR "LEANING-MAN": HE CAN'T STAND UP STRAIGHT ENOUGH TO HOLD A FLAG.
WE WON'T RUN AWAY, MISTER MONSTER.
NOR ADVANCE NEITHER. YOU'LL JUST LIE DOWN, LIKE DOGS, AND SAY NOTHING.
SPEAK TO ME, MOON-CALF MONSTER, JUST ONCE.
schluurp
HOW IS YOUR HIGHNESS? LET ME LICK YOUR SHOE. I WON'T SERVE HIM, HE'S NOT BRAVE.

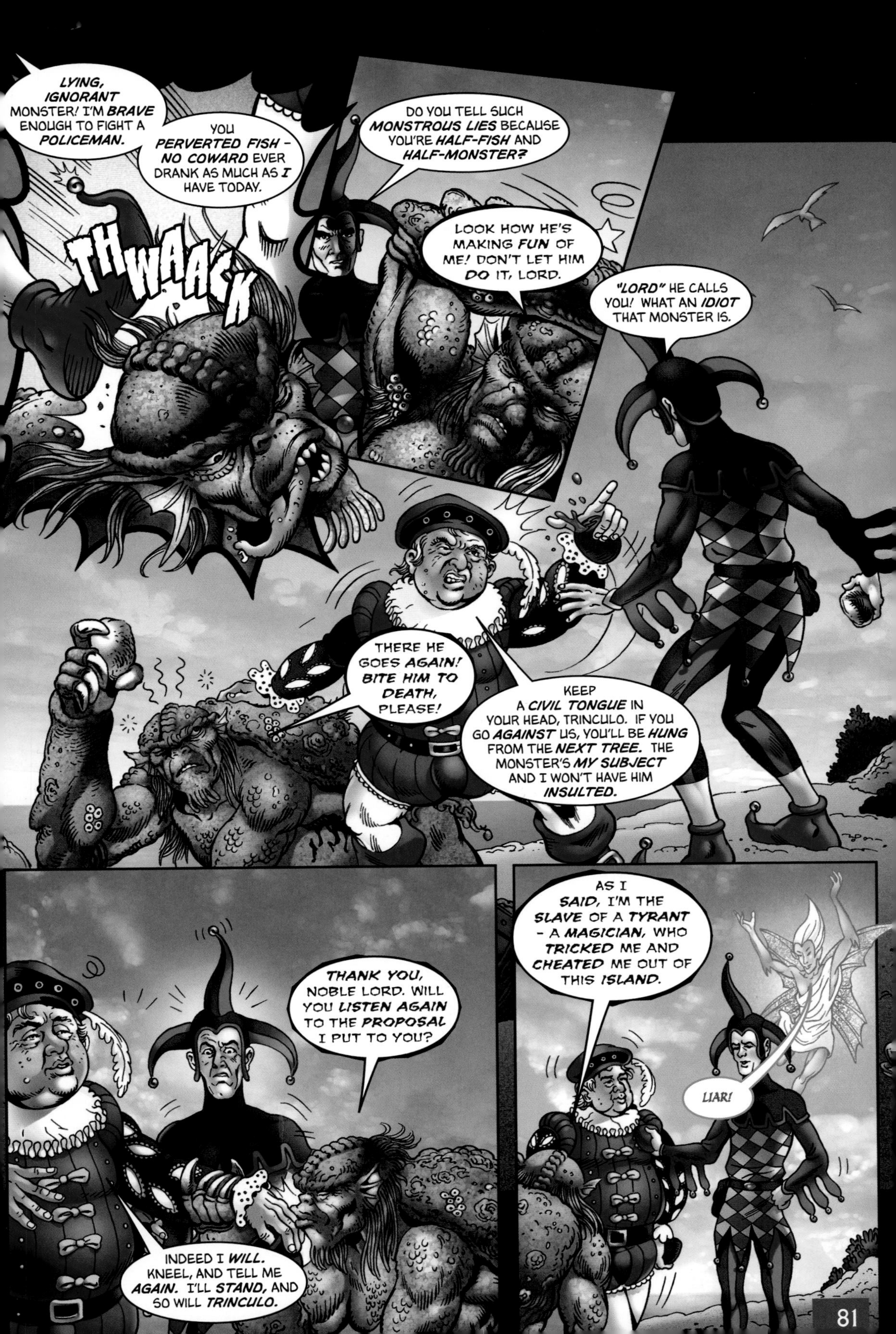
LYING, IGNORANT MONSTER! I'M BRAVE ENOUGH TO FIGHT A POLICEMAN.
YOU PERVERTED FISH - NO COWARD EVER DRANK AS MUCH AS I HAVE TODAY.
DO YOU TELL SUCH MONSTROUS LIES BECAUSE YOU'RE HALF-FISH AND HALF-MONSTER?
THWAACK
LOOK HOW HE'S MAKING FUN OF ME! DON'T LET HIM DO IT, LORD.
"LORD" HE CALLS YOU! WHAT AN IDIOT THAT MONSTER IS.
THERE HE GOES AGAIN! BITE HIM TO DEATH, PLEASE!
KEEP A CIVIL TONGUE IN YOUR HEAD, TRINCULO. IF YOU GO AGAINST US, YOU'LL BE HUNG FROM THE NEXT TREE. THE MONSTER'S MY SUBJECT AND I WON'T HAVE HIM INSULTED.
THANK YOU, NOBLE LORD. WILL YOU LISTEN AGAIN TO THE PROPOSAL I PUT TO YOU?
INDEED I WILL. KNEEL, AND TELL ME AGAIN. I'LL STAND, AND SO WILL TRINCULO.
AS I SAID, I'M THE SLAVE OF A TYRANT - A MAGICIAN, WHO TRICKED ME AND CHEATED ME OUT OF THIS ISLAND.
LIAR!

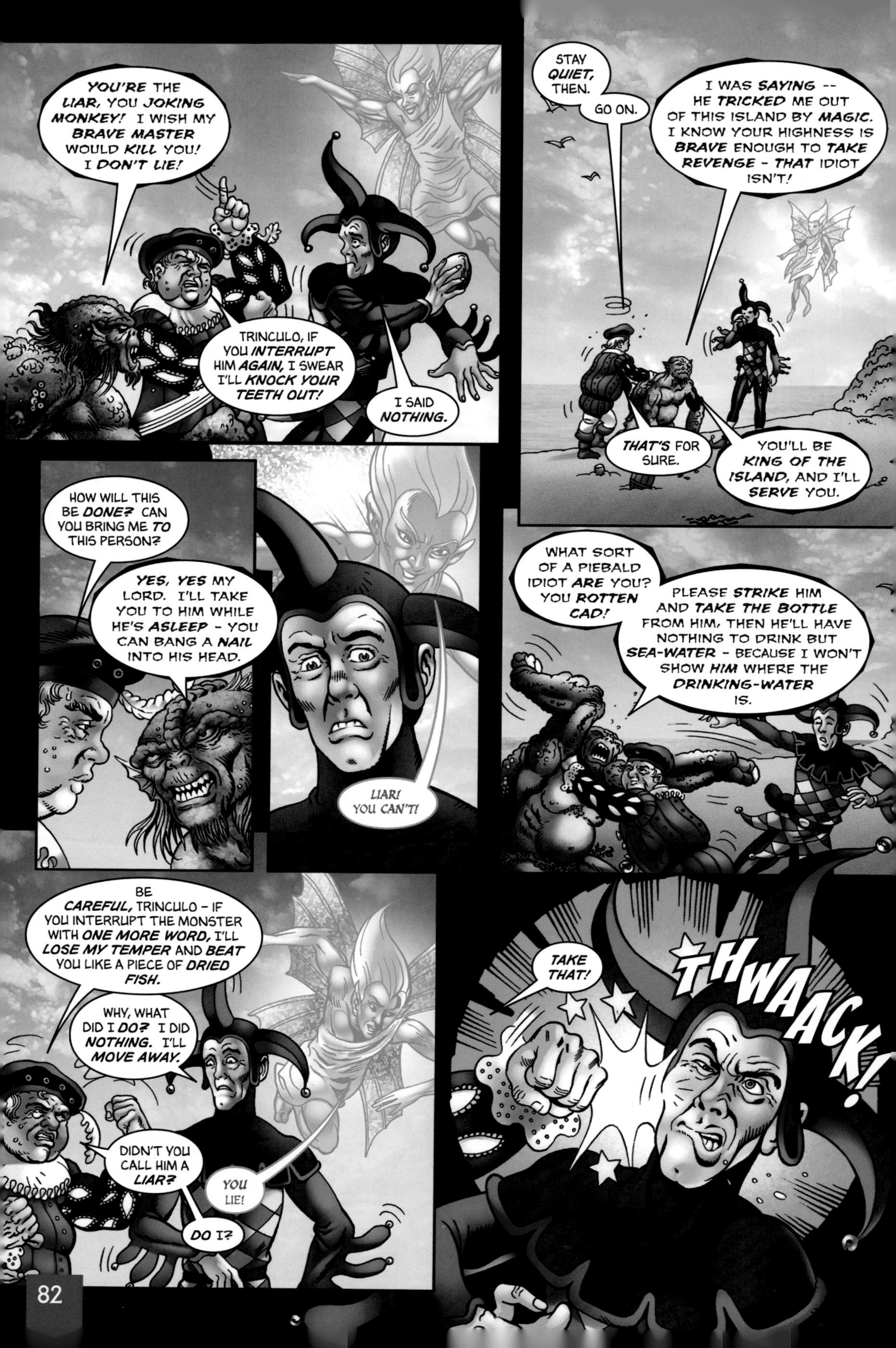

YOU'RE THE LIAR, YOU JOKING MONKEY! I WISH MY BRAVE MASTER WOULD KILL YOU! I DON'T LIE!
TRINCULO, IF YOU INTERRUPT HIM AGAIN, I SWEAR I'LL KNOCK YOUR TEETH OUT!
I SAID NOTHING.
STAY QUIET, THEN.
GO ON.
I WAS SAYING -- HE TRICKED ME OUT OF THIS ISLAND BY MAGIC. I KNOW YOUR HIGHNESS IS BRAVE ENOUGH TO TAKE REVENGE - THAT IDIOT ISN'T!
THAT'S FOR SURE.
YOU'LL BE KING OF THE ISLAND, AND I'LL SERVE YOU.
HOW WILL THIS BE DONE? CAN YOU BRING ME TO THIS PERSON?
YES, YES MY LORD. I'LL TAKE YOU TO HIM WHILE HE'S ASLEEP - YOU CAN BANG A NAIL INTO HIS HEAD.
LIAR! YOU CAN'T!
WHAT SORT OF A PIEBALD IDIOT ARE YOU? YOU ROTTEN CAD!
PLEASE STRIKE HIM AND TAKE THE BOTTLE FROM HIM, THEN HE'LL HAVE NOTHING TO DRINK BUT SEA-WATER - BECAUSE I WON'T SHOW HIM WHERE THE DRINKING-WATER IS.
BE CAREFUL, TRINCULO - IF YOU INTERRUPT THE MONSTER WITH ONE MORE WORD, I'LL LOSE MY TEMPER AND BEAT YOU LIKE A PIECE OF DRIED FISH.
WHY, WHAT DID I DO? I DID NOTHING. I'LL MOVE AWAY.
DIDN'T YOU CALL HIM A LIAR?
YOU LIE!
DO I?
TAKE THAT!
THWAACK!

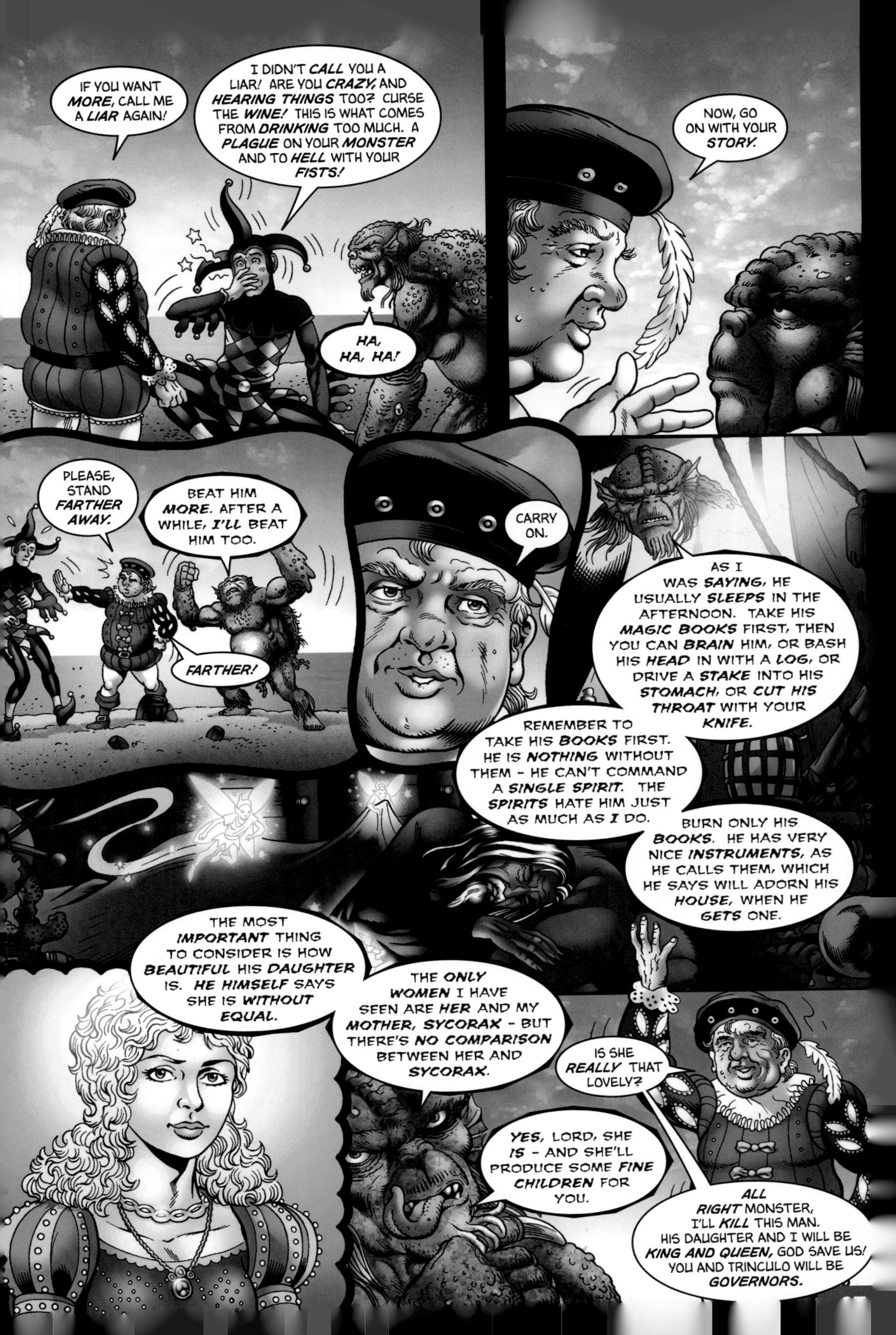
IF YOU WANT MORE, CALL ME A LIAR AGAIN!
I DIDN'T CALL YOU A LIAR! ARE YOU CRAZY, AND HEARING THINGS TOO? CURSE THE WINE! THIS IS WHAT COMES FROM DRINKING TOO MUCH. A PLAGUE ON YOUR MONSTER AND TO HELL WITH YOUR FISTS!
HA, HA, HA!
NOW, GO ON WITH YOUR STORY.
PLEASE, STAND FARTHER AWAY.
BEAT HIM MORE. AFTER A WHILE, I'LL BEAT HIM TOO.
FARTHER!
CARRY ON.
AS I WAS SAYING, HE USUALLY SLEEPS IN THE AFTERNOON. TAKE HIS MAGIC BOOKS FIRST, THEN YOU CAN BRAIN HIM, OR BASH HIS HEAD IN WITH A LOG, OR DRIVE A STAKE INTO HIS STOMACH, OR CUT HIS THROAT WITH YOUR KNIFE.
REMEMBER TO TAKE HIS BOOKS FIRST. HE IS NOTHING WITHOUT THEM - HE CAN'T COMMAND A SINGLE SPIRIT. THE SPIRITS HATE HIM JUST AS MUCH AS I DO.
BURN ONLY HIS BOOKS. HE HAS VERY NICE INSTRUMENTS, AS HE CALLS THEM, WHICH HE SAYS WILL ADORN HIS HOUSE, WHEN HE GETS ONE.
THE MOST IMPORTANT THING TO CONSIDER IS HOW BEAUTIFUL HIS DAUGHTER IS. HE HIMSELF SAYS SHE IS WITHOUT EQUAL.
THE ONLY WOMEN I HAVE SEEN ARE HER AND MY MOTHER, SYCORAX - BUT THERE'S NO COMPARISON BETWEEN HER AND SYCORAX.
IS SHE REALLY THAT LOVELY?
YES, LORD, SHE IS - AND SHE'LL PRODUCE SOME FINE CHILDREN FOR YOU.
ALL RIGHT MONSTER, I'LL KILL THIS MAN. HIS DAUGHTER AND I WILL BE KING AND QUEEN, GOD SAVE US! YOU AND TRINCULO WILL BE GOVERNORS.

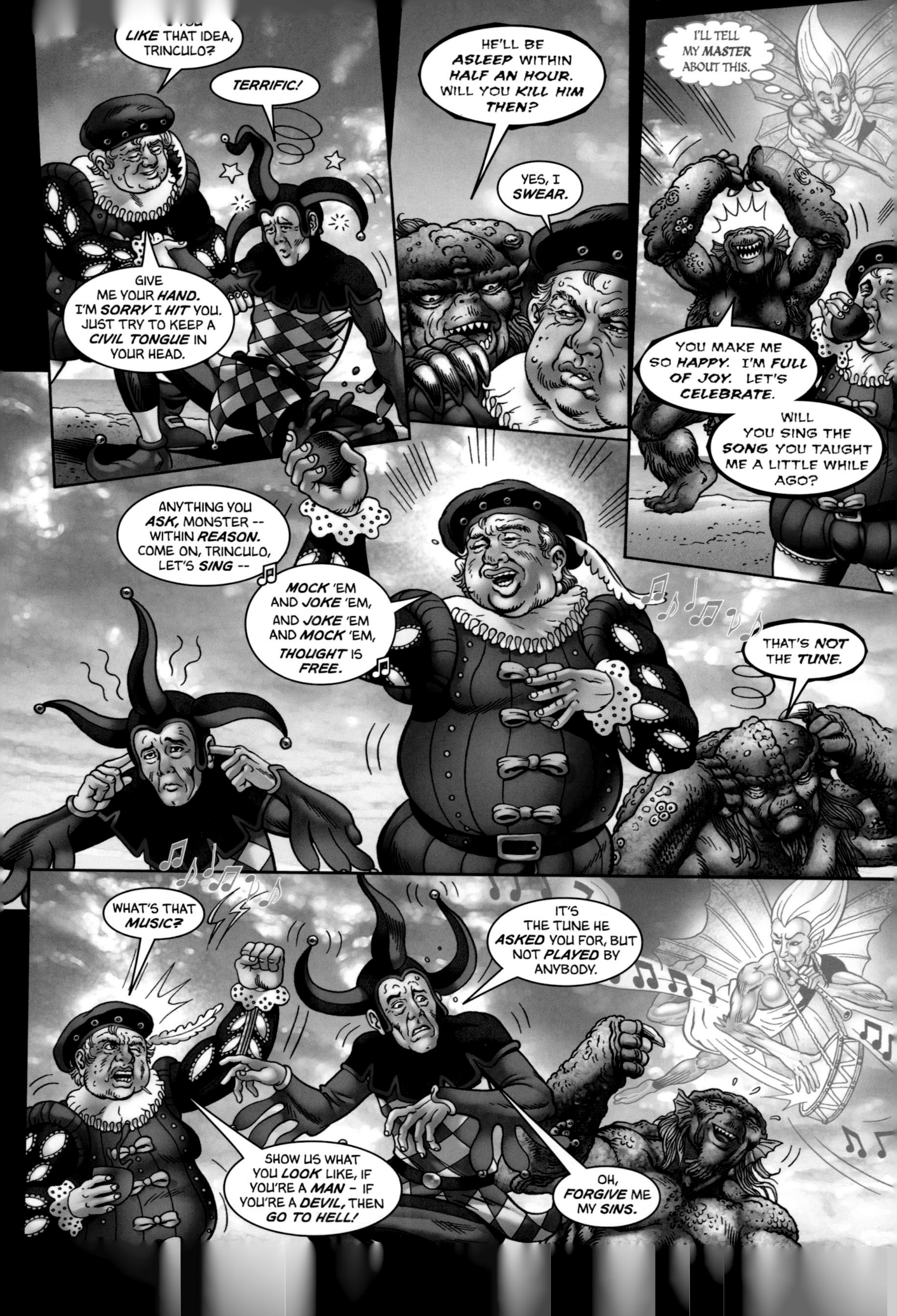
LIKE THAT IDEA, TRINCULO?
TERRIFIC!
GIVE ME YOUR HAND. I'M SORRY I HIT YOU. JUST TRY TO KEEP A CIVIL TONGUE IN YOUR HEAD.
HE'LL BE ASLEEP WITHIN HALF AN HOUR. WILL YOU KILL HIM THEN?
YES, I SWEAR.
I'LL TELL MY MASTER ABOUT THIS.
YOU MAKE ME SO HAPPY. I'M FULL OF JOY. LET'S CELEBRATE.
WILL YOU SING THE SONG YOU TAUGHT ME A LITTLE WHILE AGO?
ANYTHING YOU ASK, MONSTER -- WITHIN REASON. COME ON, TRINCULO, LET'S SING --
MOCK 'EM AND JOKE 'EM, AND JOKE 'EM AND MOCK 'EM, THOUGHT IS FREE.
THAT'S NOT THE TUNE.
WHAT'S THAT MUSIC?
IT'S THE TUNE HE ASKED YOU FOR, BUT NOT PLAYED BY ANYBODY.
SHOW US WHAT YOU LOOK LIKE, IF YOU'RE A MAN – IF YOU'RE A DEVIL, THEN GO TO HELL!
OH, FORGIVE ME MY SINS.

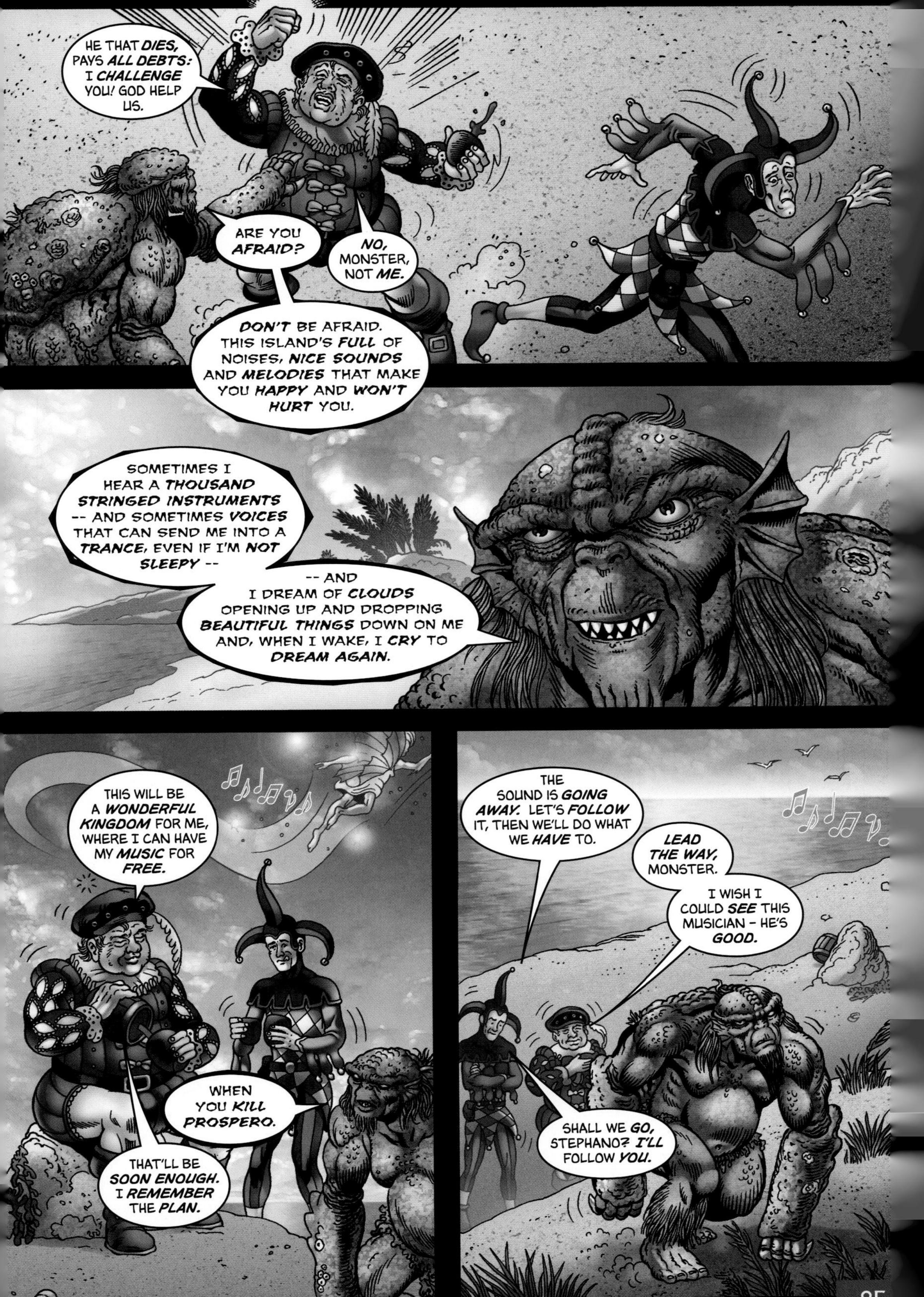
HE THAT DIES, PAYS ALL DEBTS: I CHALLENGE YOU! GOD HELP US.
ARE YOU AFRAID?
NO, MONSTER, NOT ME.
DON'T BE AFRAID. THIS ISLAND'S FULL OF NOISES, NICE SOUNDS AND MELODIES THAT MAKE YOU HAPPY AND WON'T HURT YOU.
SOMETIMES I HEAR A THOUSAND STRINGED INSTRUMENTS -- AND SOMETIMES VOICES THAT CAN SEND ME INTO A TRANCE, EVEN IF I'M NOT SLEEPY --
-- AND I DREAM OF CLOUDS OPENING UP AND DROPPING BEAUTIFUL THINGS DOWN ON ME AND, WHEN I WAKE, I CRY TO DREAM AGAIN.
THIS WILL BE A WONDERFUL KINGDOM FOR ME, WHERE I CAN HAVE MY MUSIC FOR FREE.
WHEN YOU KILL PROSPERO.
THAT'LL BE SOON ENOUGH. I REMEMBER THE PLAN.
THE SOUND IS GOING AWAY. LET'S FOLLOW IT, THEN WE'LL DO WHAT WE HAVE TO.
LEAD THE WAY, MONSTER.
I WISH I COULD SEE THIS MUSICIAN – HE'S GOOD.
SHALL WE GO, STEPHANO? I'LL FOLLOW YOU.

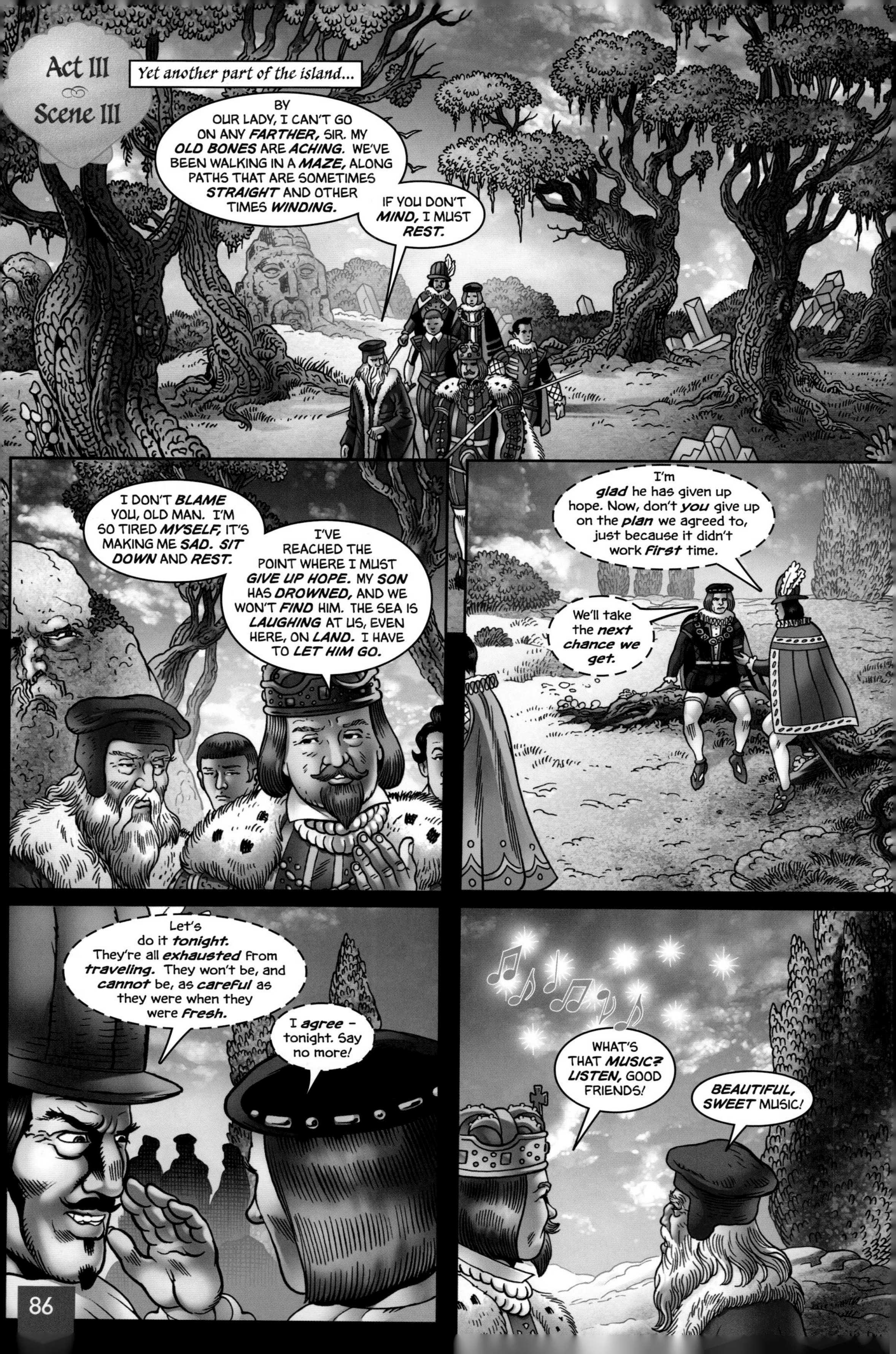
Act III
Scene III
Yet another part of the island...
BY OUR LADY, I CAN'T GO ON ANY FARTHER, SIR. MY OLD BONES ARE ACHING. WE'VE BEEN WALKING IN A MAZE, ALONG PATHS THAT ARE SOMETIMES STRAIGHT AND OTHER TIMES WINDING.
IF YOU DON'T MIND, I MUST REST.
I DON'T BLAME YOU, OLD MAN. I'M SO TIRED MYSELF, IT'S MAKING ME SAD. SIT DOWN AND REST.
I'VE REACHED THE POINT WHERE I MUST GIVE UP HOPE. MY SON HAS DROWNED, AND WE WON'T FIND HIM. THE SEA IS LAUGHING AT US, EVEN HERE, ON LAND. I HAVE TO LET HIM GO.
I'm glad he has given up hope. Now, don't you give up on the plan we agreed to, just because it didn't work first time.
We'll take the next chance we get.
Let's do it tonight. They're all exhausted from traveling. They won't be, and cannot be, as careful as they were when they were fresh.
I agree - tonight. Say no more!
WHAT'S THAT MUSIC? LISTEN, GOOD FRIENDS!
BEAUTIFUL, SWEET MUSIC!

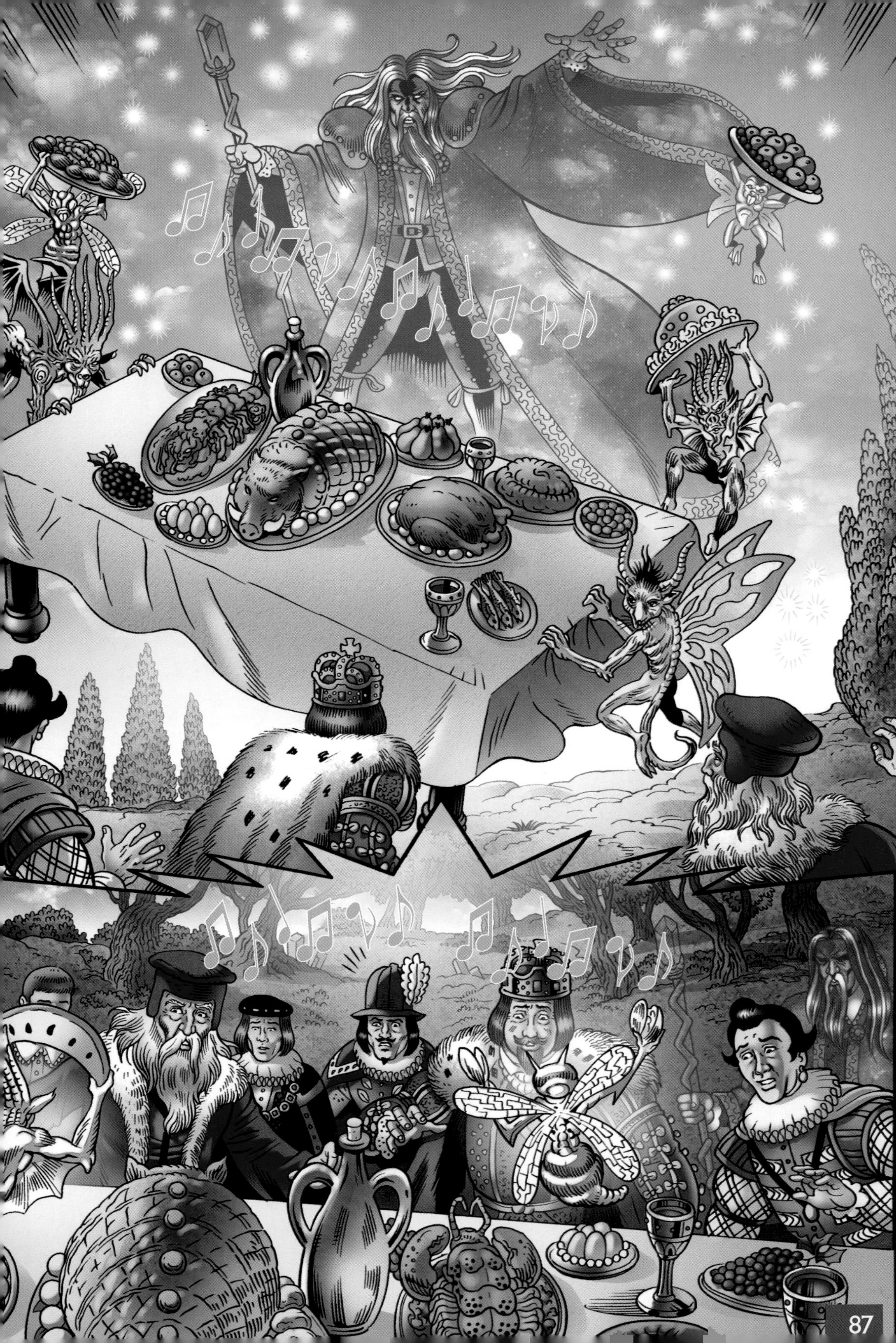

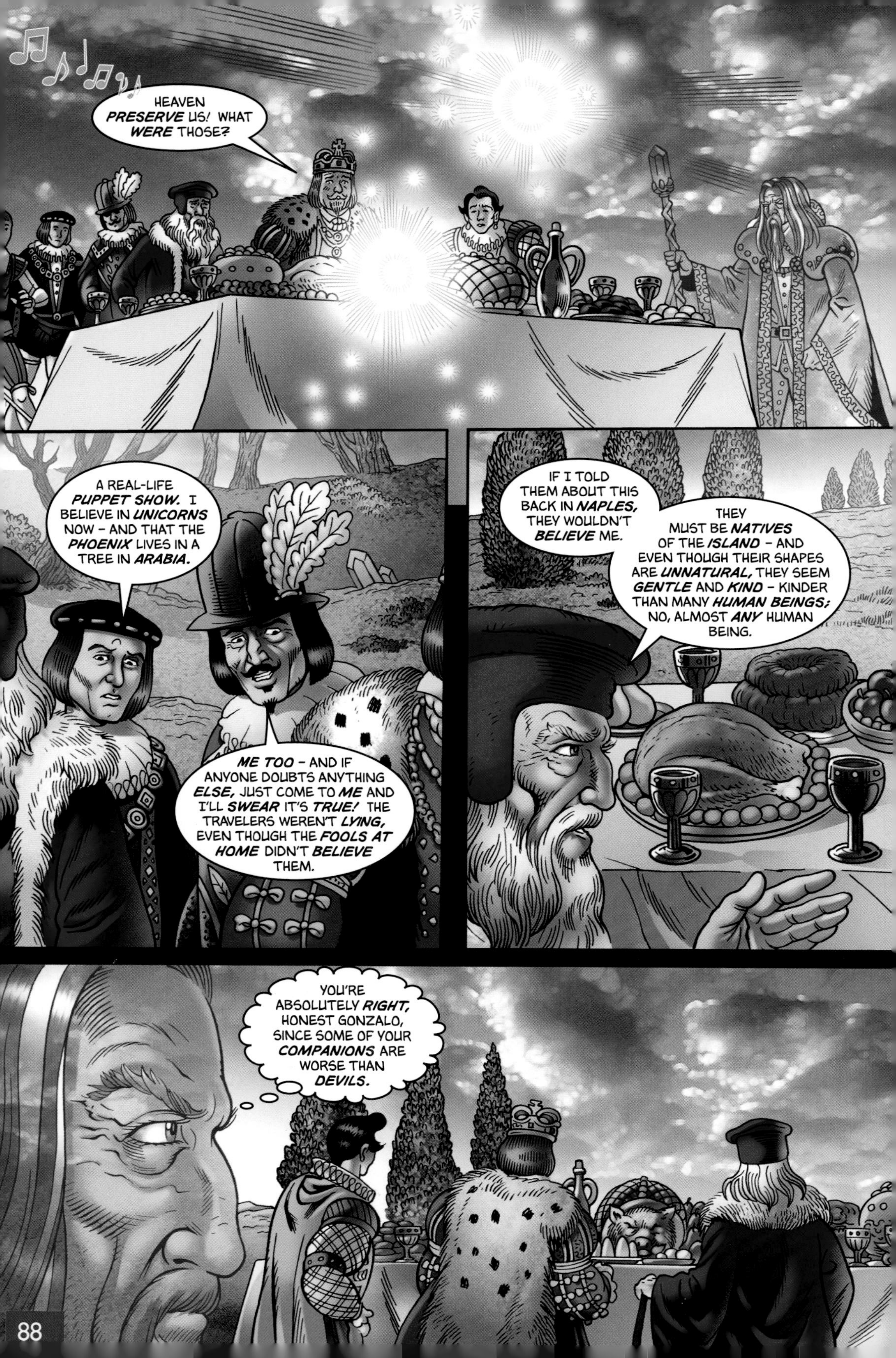
HEAVEN PRESERVE US! WHAT WERE THOSE?
A REAL-LIFE PUPPET SHOW. I BELIEVE IN UNICORNS NOW – AND THAT THE PHOENIX LIVES IN A TREE IN ARABIA.
ME TOO – AND IF ANYONE DOUBTS ANYTHING ELSE, JUST COME TO ME AND I'LL SWEAR IT'S TRUE! THE TRAVELERS WEREN'T LYING, EVEN THOUGH THE FOOLS AT HOME DIDN'T BELIEVE THEM.
IF I TOLD THEM ABOUT THIS BACK IN NAPLES, THEY WOULDN'T BELIEVE ME.
THEY MUST BE NATIVES OF THE ISLAND – AND EVEN THOUGH THEIR SHAPES ARE UNNATURAL, THEY SEEM GENTLE AND KIND – KINDER THAN MANY HUMAN BEINGS; NO, ALMOST ANY HUMAN BEING.
YOU'RE ABSOLUTELY RIGHT, HONEST GONZALO, SINCE SOME OF YOUR COMPANIONS ARE WORSE THAN DEVILS.

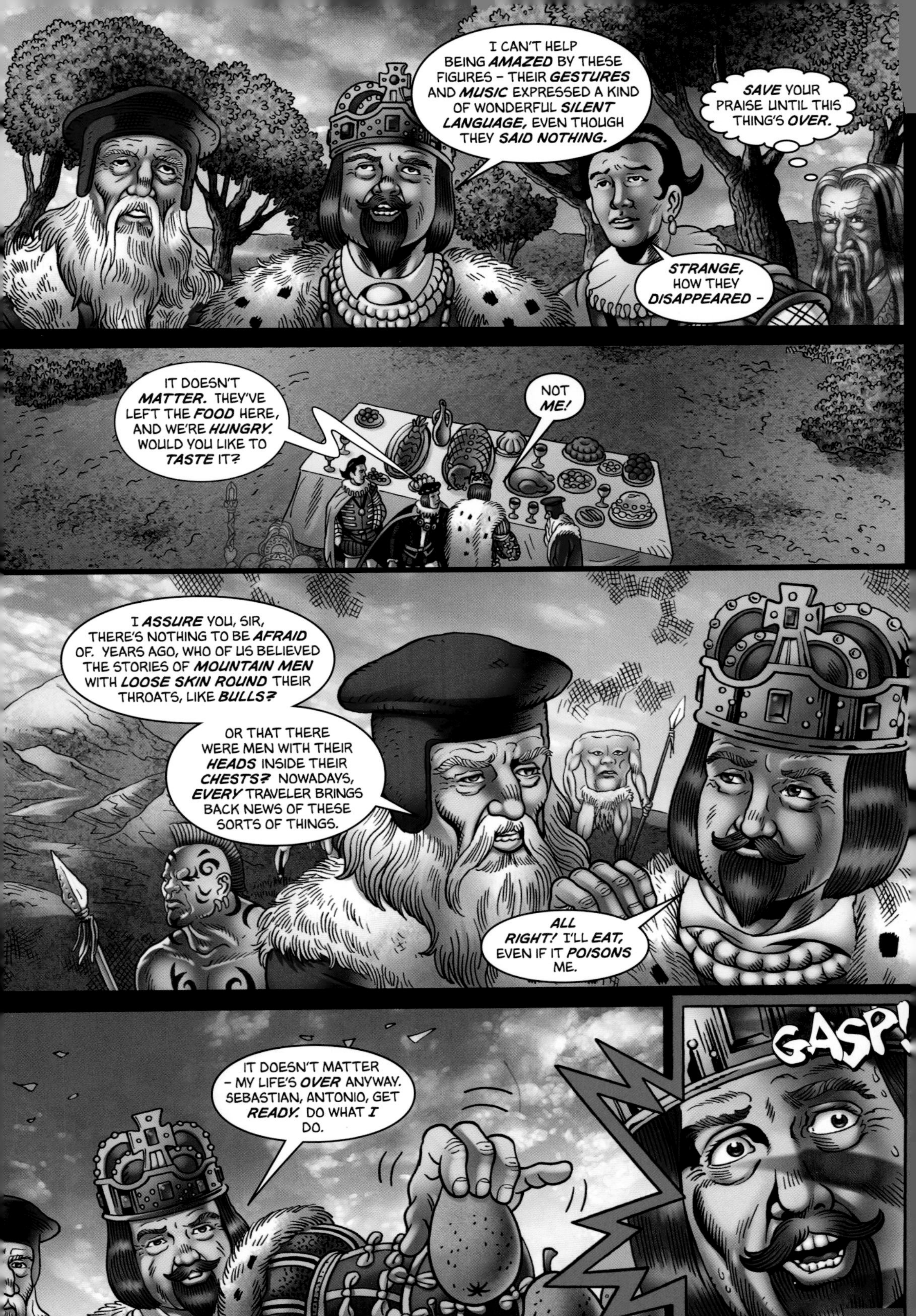
I CAN'T HELP BEING AMAZED BY THESE FIGURES – THEIR GESTURES AND MUSIC EXPRESSED A KIND OF WONDERFUL SILENT LANGUAGE, EVEN THOUGH THEY SAID NOTHING.
SAVE YOUR PRAISE UNTIL THIS THING'S OVER.
STRANGE, HOW THEY DISAPPEARED –
IT DOESN'T MATTER. THEY'VE LEFT THE FOOD HERE, AND WE'RE HUNGRY. WOULD YOU LIKE TO TASTE IT?
NOT ME!
I ASSURE YOU, SIR, THERE'S NOTHING TO BE AFRAID OF. YEARS AGO, WHO OF US BELIEVED THE STORIES OF MOUNTAIN MEN WITH LOOSE SKIN ROUND THEIR THROATS, LIKE BULLS?
OR THAT THERE WERE MEN WITH THEIR HEADS INSIDE THEIR CHESTS? NOWADAYS, EVERY TRAVELER BRINGS BACK NEWS OF THESE SORTS OF THINGS.
ALL RIGHT! I'LL EAT, EVEN IF IT POISONS ME.
IT DOESN'T MATTER – MY LIFE'S OVER ANYWAY. SEBASTIAN, ANTONIO, GET READY. DO WHAT I DO.
GASP!

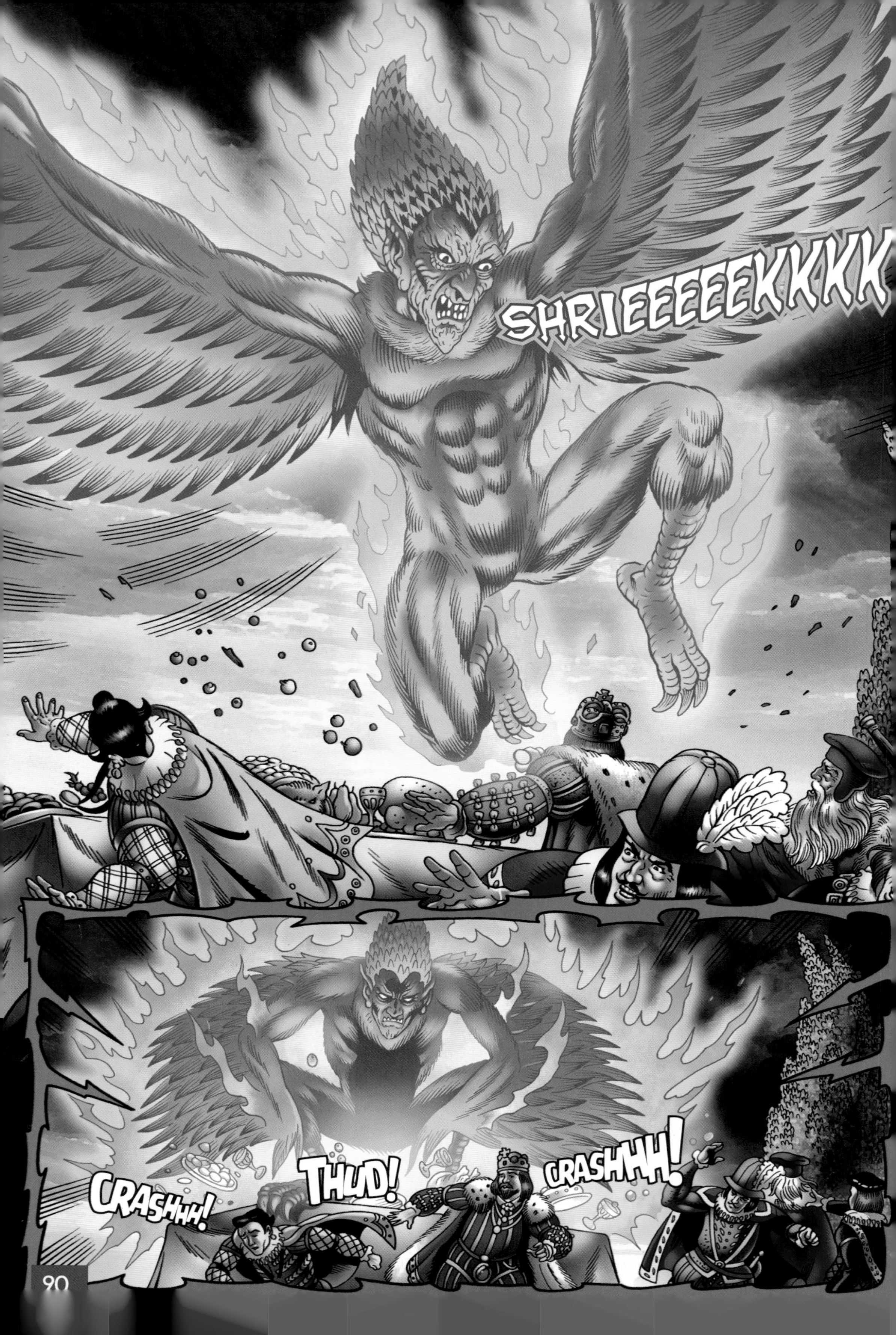
SHRIEEEEEEKKKK
CRASHHH!
THUD!
CRASHHH!

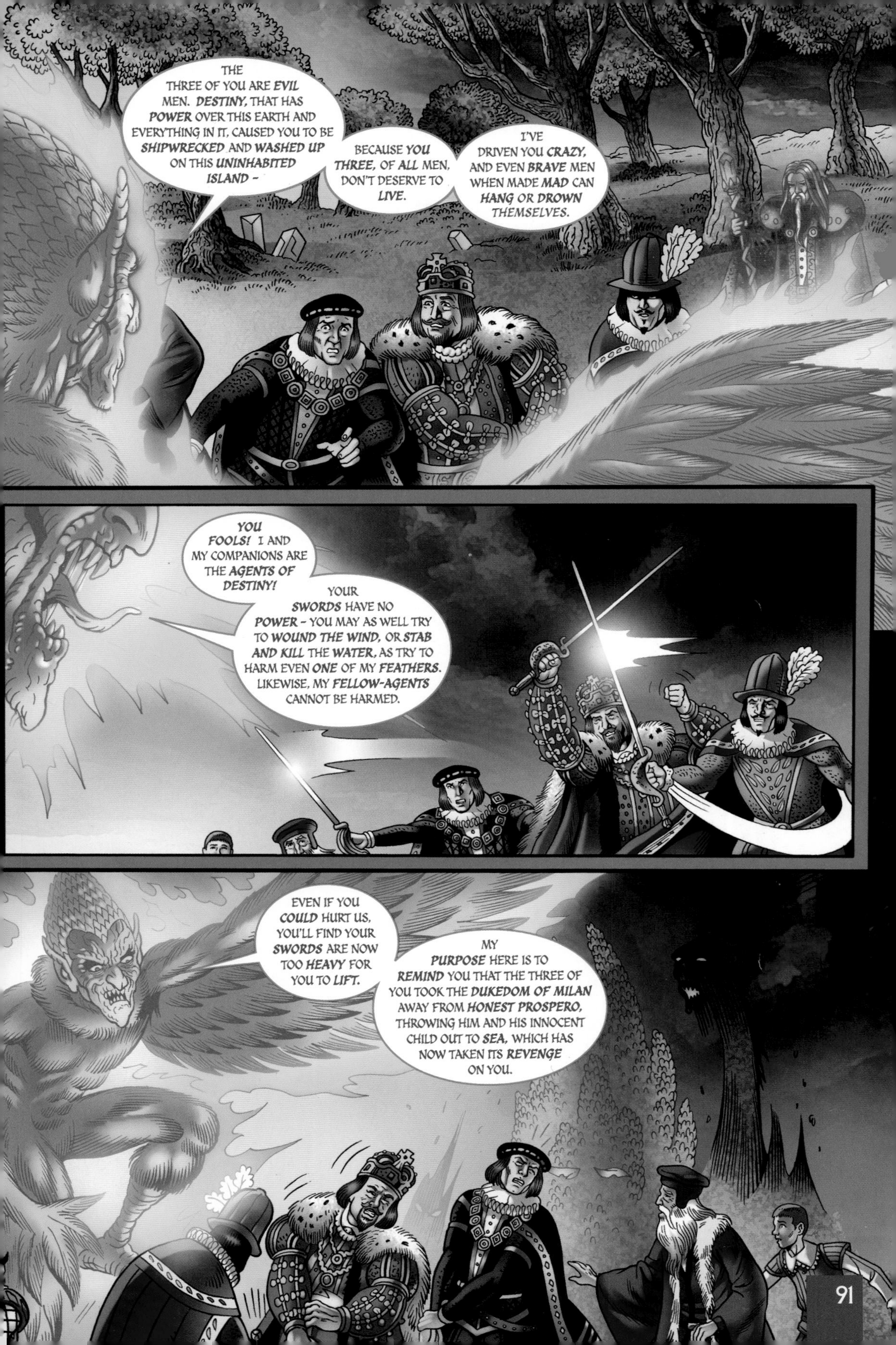
THE THREE OF YOU ARE EVIL MEN. DESTINY, THAT HAS POWER OVER THIS EARTH AND EVERYTHING IN IT, CAUSED YOU TO BE SHIPWRECKED AND WASHED UP ON THIS UNINHABITED ISLAND -
BECAUSE YOU THREE, OF ALL MEN, DON'T DESERVE TO LIVE.
I'VE DRIVEN YOU CRAZY, AND EVEN BRAVE MEN WHEN MADE MAD CAN HANG OR DROWN THEMSELVES.
YOU FOOLS! I AND MY COMPANIONS ARE THE AGENTS OF DESTINY!
YOUR SWORDS HAVE NO POWER - YOU MAY AS WELL TRY TO WOUND THE WIND, OR STAB AND KILL THE WATER, AS TRY TO HARM EVEN ONE OF MY FEATHERS. LIKEWISE, MY FELLOW-AGENTS CANNOT BE HARMED.
EVEN IF YOU COULD HURT US, YOU'LL FIND YOUR SWORDS ARE NOW TOO HEAVY FOR YOU TO LIFT.
MY PURPOSE HERE IS TO REMIND YOU THAT THE THREE OF YOU TOOK THE DUKEDOM OF MILAN AWAY FROM HONEST PROSPERO, THROWING HIM AND HIS INNOCENT CHILD OUT TO SEA, WHICH HAS NOW TAKEN ITS REVENGE ON YOU.

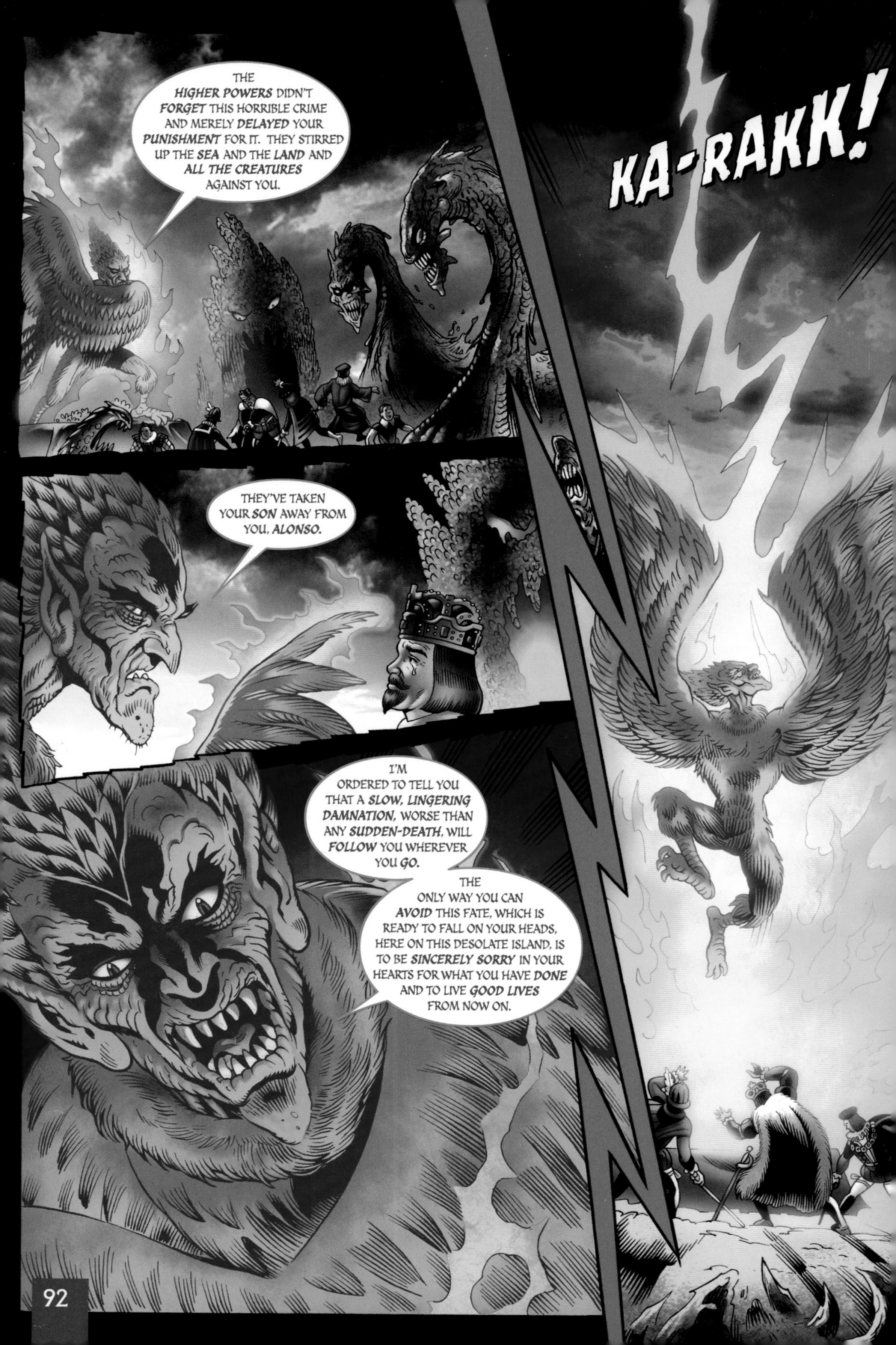
THE HIGHER POWERS DIDN'T FORGET THIS HORRIBLE CRIME AND MERELY DELAYED YOUR PUNISHMENT FOR IT. THEY STIRRED UP THE SEA AND THE LAND AND ALL THE CREATURES AGAINST YOU.
KA-RAKK!
THEY'VE TAKEN YOUR SON AWAY FROM YOU, ALONSO.
I'M ORDERED TO TELL YOU THAT A SLOW, LINGERING DAMNATION, WORSE THAN ANY SUDDEN-DEATH, WILL FOLLOW YOU WHEREVER YOU GO.
THE ONLY WAY YOU CAN AVOID THIS FATE, WHICH IS READY TO FALL ON YOUR HEADS, HERE ON THIS DESOLATE ISLAND, IS TO BE SINCERELY SORRY IN YOUR HEARTS FOR WHAT YOU HAVE DONE AND TO LIVE GOOD LIVES FROM NOW ON.

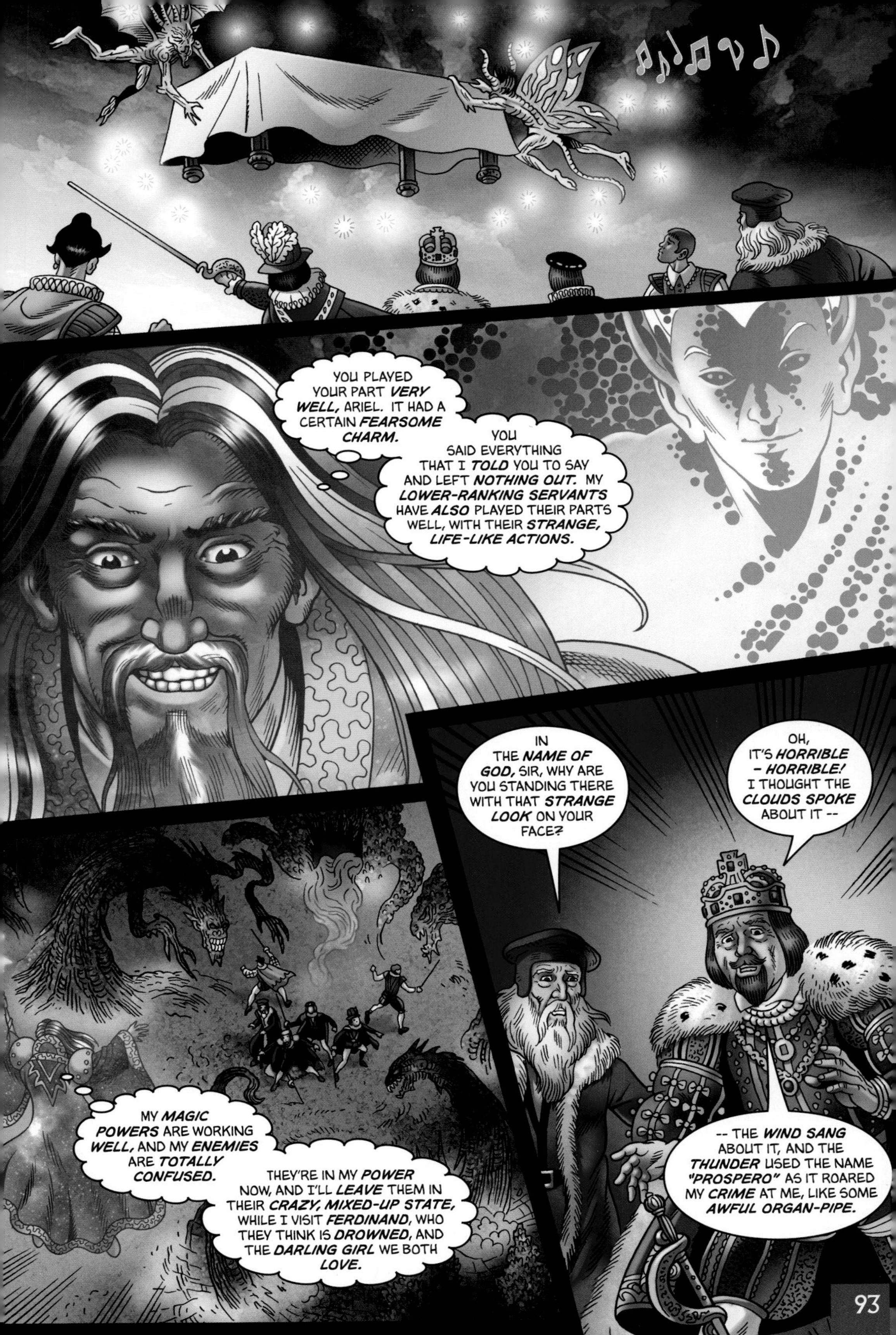

YOU PLAYED YOUR PART VERY WELL, ARIEL. IT HAD A CERTAIN FEARSOME CHARM.
YOU SAID EVERYTHING THAT I TOLD YOU TO SAY AND LEFT NOTHING OUT. MY LOWER-RANKING SERVANTS HAVE ALSO PLAYED THEIR PARTS WELL, WITH THEIR STRANGE, LIFE-LIKE ACTIONS.
MY MAGIC POWERS ARE WORKING WELL, AND MY ENEMIES ARE TOTALLY CONFUSED.
THEY'RE IN MY POWER NOW, AND I'LL LEAVE THEM IN THEIR CRAZY, MIXED-UP STATE, WHILE I VISIT FERDINAND, WHO THEY THINK IS DROWNED, AND THE DARLING GIRL WE BOTH LOVE.
IN THE NAME OF GOD, SIR, WHY ARE YOU STANDING THERE WITH THAT STRANGE LOOK ON YOUR FACE?
OH, IT'S HORRIBLE – HORRIBLE! I THOUGHT THE CLOUDS SPOKE ABOUT IT --
-- THE WIND SANG ABOUT IT, AND THE THUNDER USED THE NAME "PROSPERO" AS IT ROARED MY CRIME AT ME, LIKE SOME AWFUL ORGAN-PIPE.

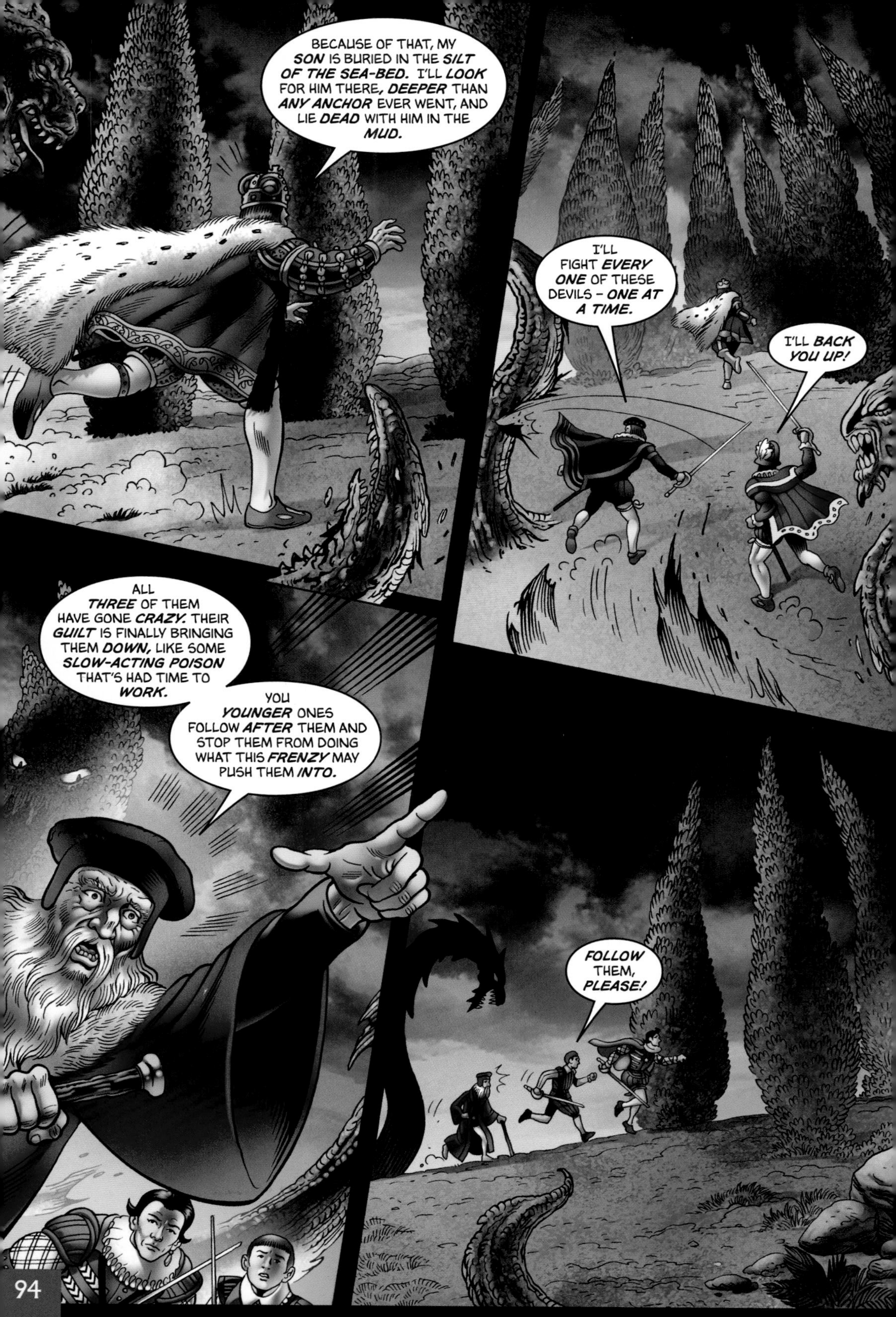
BECAUSE OF THAT, MY SON IS BURIED IN THE SILT OF THE SEA-BED. I'LL LOOK FOR HIM THERE, DEEPER THAN ANY ANCHOR EVER WENT, AND LIE DEAD WITH HIM IN THE MUD.
I'LL FIGHT EVERY ONE OF THESE DEVILS – ONE AT A TIME.
I'LL BACK YOU UP!
ALL THREE OF THEM HAVE GONE CRAZY. THEIR GUILT IS FINALLY BRINGING THEM DOWN, LIKE SOME SLOW-ACTING POISON THAT'S HAD TIME TO WORK.
YOU YOUNGER ONES FOLLOW AFTER THEM AND STOP THEM FROM DOING WHAT THIS FRENZY MAY PUSH THEM INTO.
FOLLOW THEM, PLEASE!

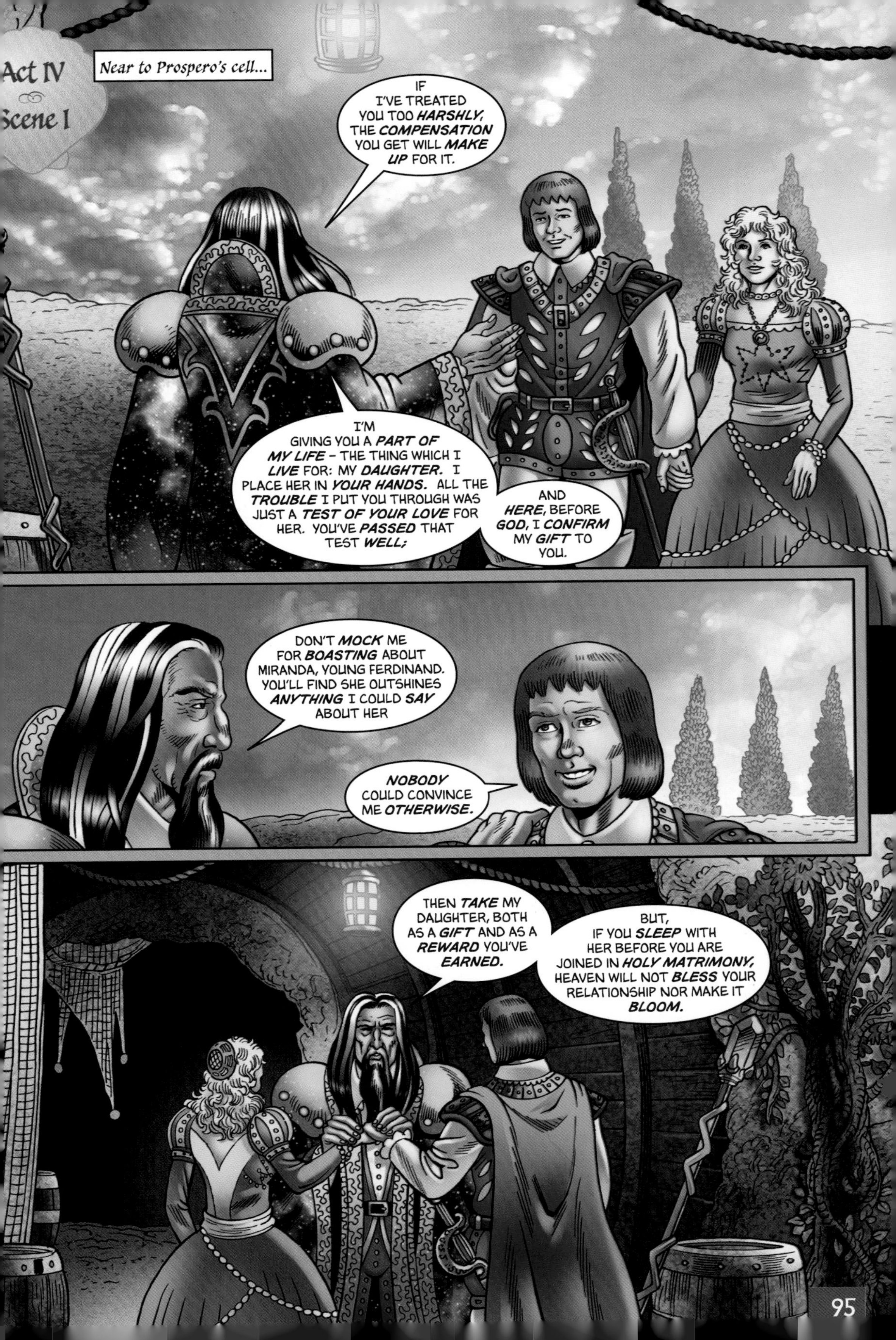
Act IV
Scene I
Near to Prospero's cell...
IF I'VE TREATED YOU TOO HARSHLY, THE COMPENSATION YOU GET WILL MAKE UP FOR IT.
I'M GIVING YOU A PART OF MY LIFE – THE THING WHICH I LIVE FOR: MY DAUGHTER. I PLACE HER IN YOUR HANDS. ALL THE TROUBLE I PUT YOU THROUGH WAS JUST A TEST OF YOUR LOVE FOR HER. YOU'VE PASSED THAT TEST WELL;
AND HERE, BEFORE GOD, I CONFIRM MY GIFT TO YOU.
DON'T MOCK ME FOR BOASTING ABOUT MIRANDA, YOUNG FERDINAND. YOU'LL FIND SHE OUTSHINES ANYTHING I COULD SAY ABOUT HER
NOBODY COULD CONVINCE ME OTHERWISE.
THEN TAKE MY DAUGHTER, BOTH AS A GIFT AND AS A REWARD YOU'VE EARNED.
BUT, IF YOU SLEEP WITH HER BEFORE YOU ARE JOINED IN HOLY MATRIMONY, HEAVEN WILL NOT BLESS YOUR RELATIONSHIP NOR MAKE IT BLOOM.

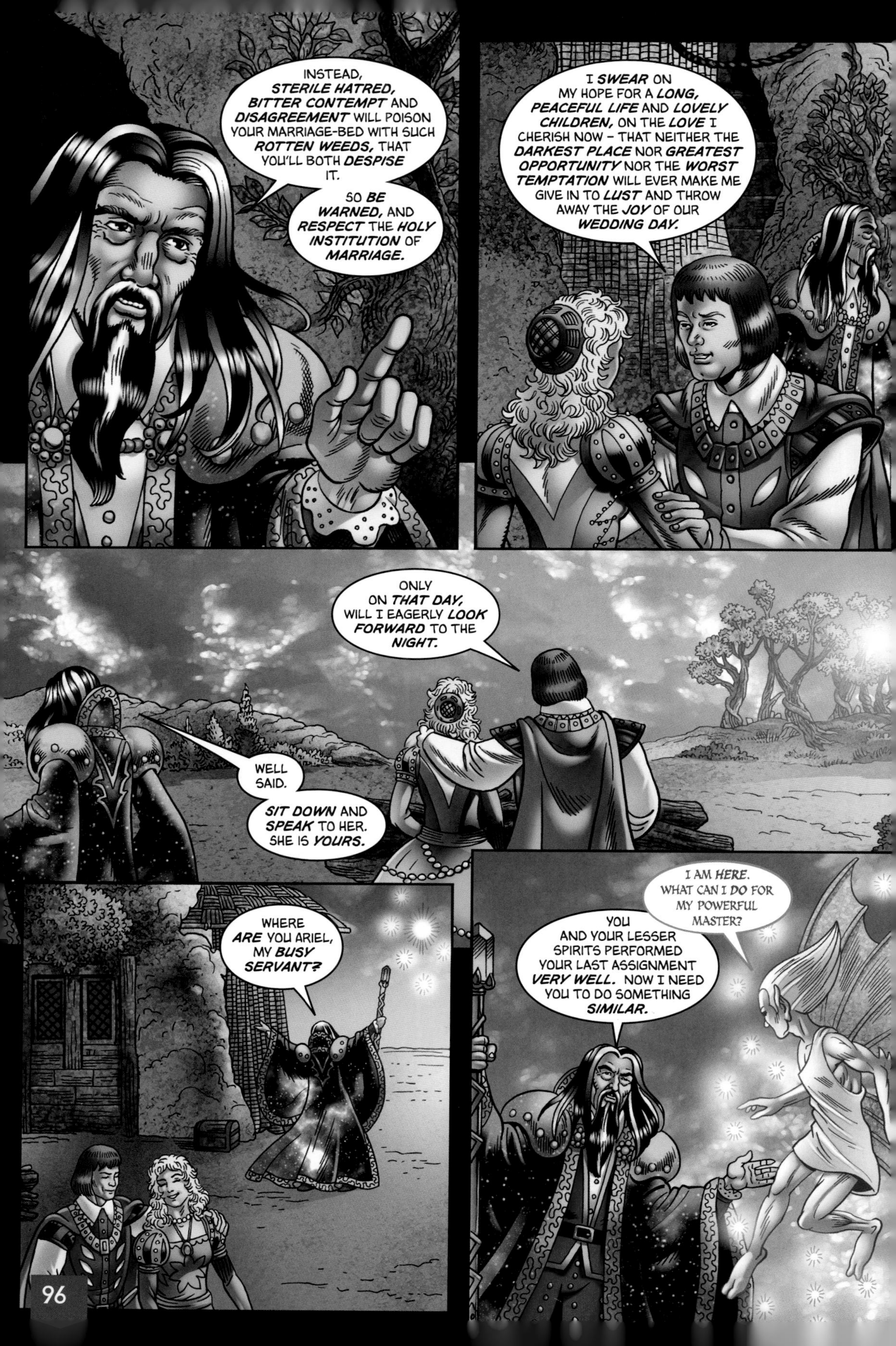
INSTEAD, STERILE HATRED, BITTER CONTEMPT AND DISAGREEMENT WILL POISON YOUR MARRIAGE-BED WITH SUCH ROTTEN WEEDS, THAT YOU'LL BOTH DESPISE IT.
SO BE WARNED, AND RESPECT THE HOLY INSTITUTION OF MARRIAGE.
I SWEAR ON MY HOPE FOR A LONG, PEACEFUL LIFE AND LOVELY CHILDREN, ON THE LOVE I CHERISH NOW – THAT NEITHER THE DARKEST PLACE NOR GREATEST OPPORTUNITY NOR THE WORST TEMPTATION WILL EVER MAKE ME GIVE IN TO LUST AND THROW AWAY THE JOY OF OUR WEDDING DAY.
ONLY ON THAT DAY, WILL I EAGERLY LOOK FORWARD TO THE NIGHT.
WELL SAID.
SIT DOWN AND SPEAK TO HER. SHE IS YOURS.
WHERE ARE YOU ARIEL, MY BUSY SERVANT?
I AM HERE. WHAT CAN I DO FOR MY POWERFUL MASTER?
YOU AND YOUR LESSER SPIRITS PERFORMED YOUR LAST ASSIGNMENT VERY WELL. NOW I NEED YOU TO DO SOMETHING SIMILAR.

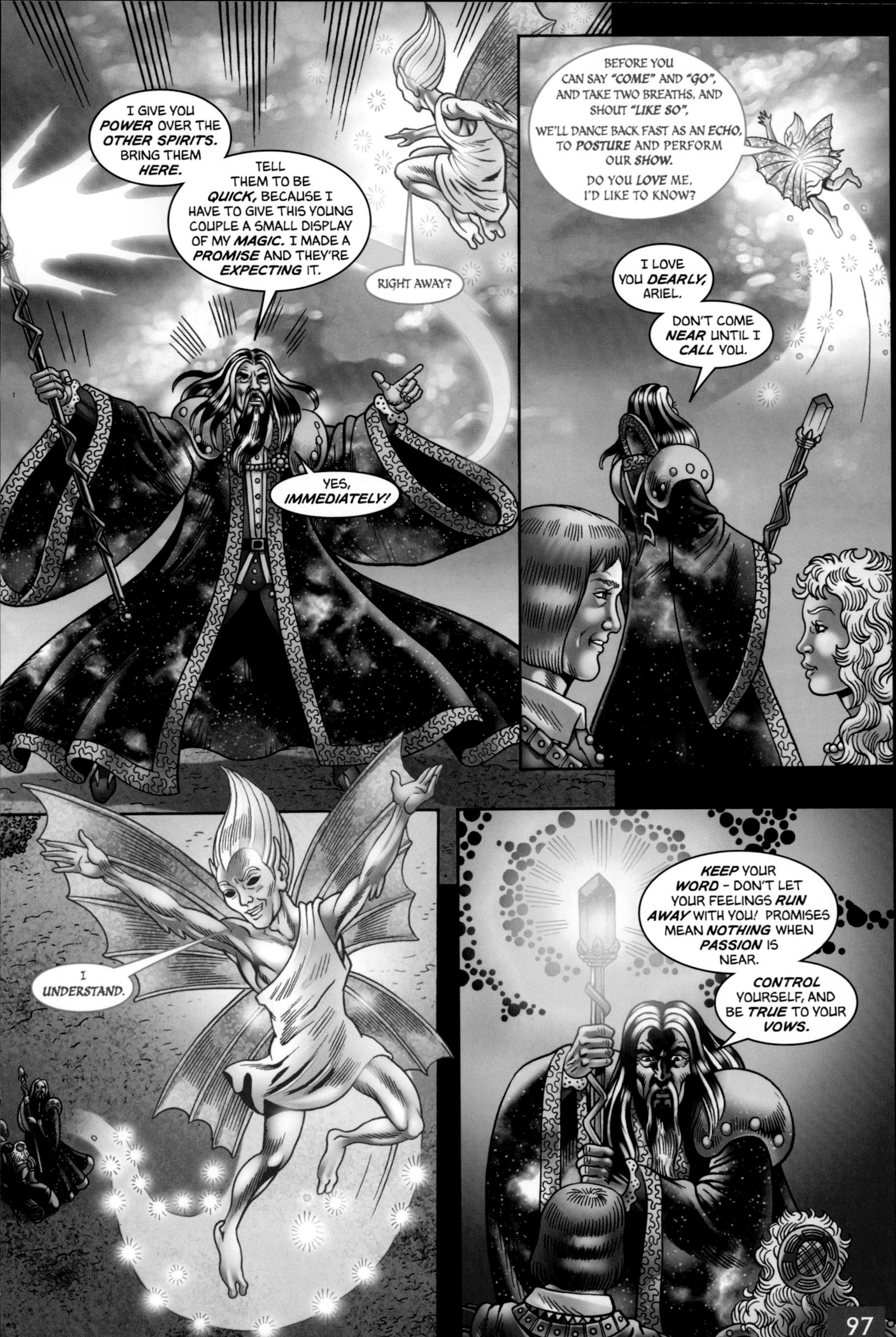
I GIVE YOU POWER OVER THE OTHER SPIRITS. BRING THEM HERE.
TELL THEM TO BE QUICK, BECAUSE I HAVE TO GIVE THIS YOUNG COUPLE A SMALL DISPLAY OF MY MAGIC. I MADE A PROMISE AND THEY'RE EXPECTING IT.
RIGHT AWAY?
YES, IMMEDIATELY!
BEFORE YOU CAN SAY "COME" AND "GO", AND TAKE TWO BREATHS, AND SHOUT "LIKE SO",
WE'LL DANCE BACK FAST AS AN ECHO, TO POSTURE AND PERFORM OUR SHOW.
DO YOU LOVE ME, I'D LIKE TO KNOW?
I LOVE YOU DEARLY, ARIEL.
DON'T COME NEAR UNTIL I CALL YOU.
I UNDERSTAND.
KEEP YOUR WORD – DON'T LET YOUR FEELINGS RUN AWAY WITH YOU! PROMISES MEAN NOTHING WHEN PASSION IS NEAR.
CONTROL YOURSELF, AND BE TRUE TO YOUR VOWS.

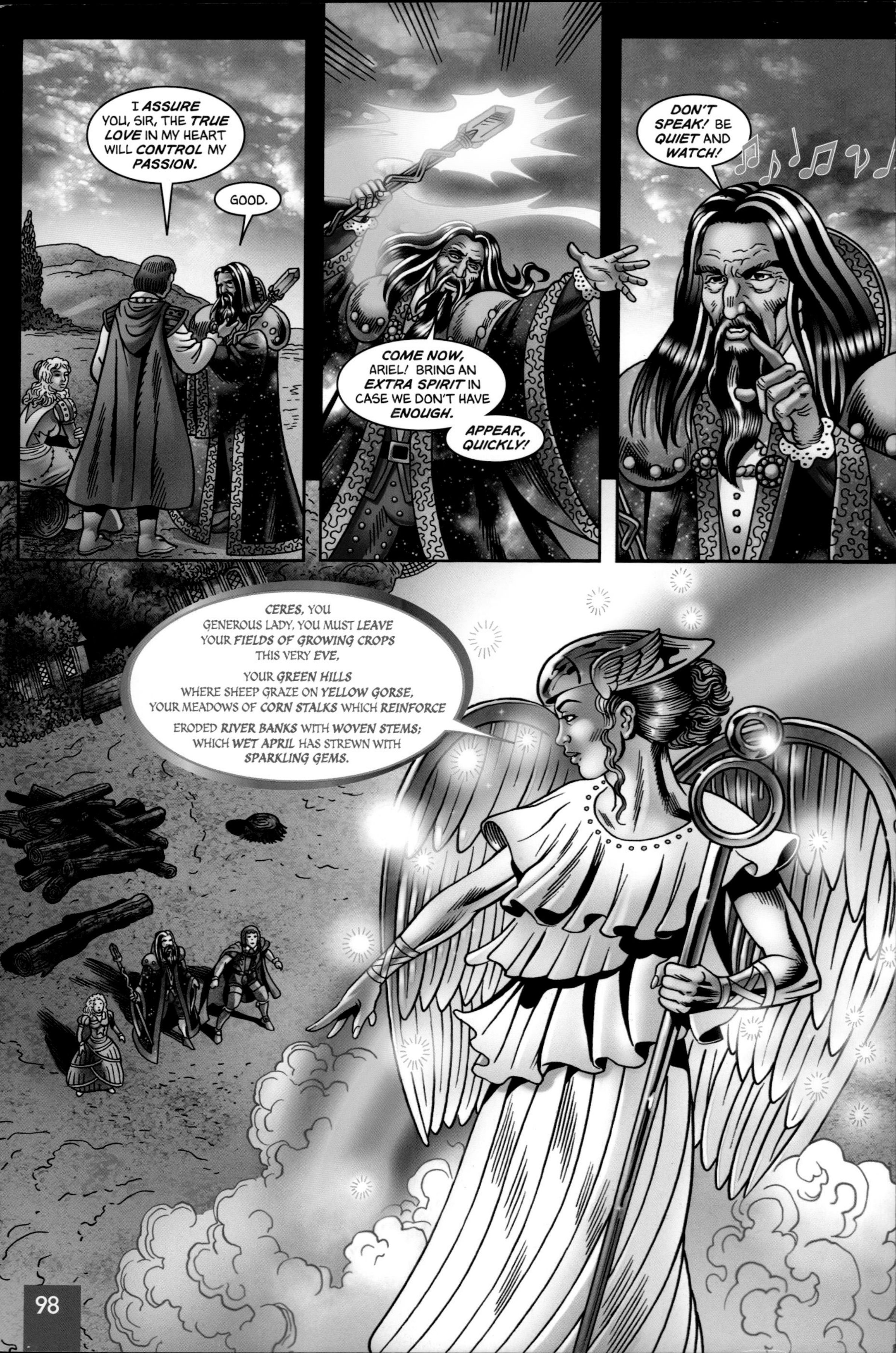

I ASSURE YOU, SIR, THE TRUE LOVE IN MY HEART WILL CONTROL MY PASSION.
GOOD.
COME NOW, ARIEL! BRING AN EXTRA SPIRIT IN CASE WE DON'T HAVE ENOUGH.
APPEAR, QUICKLY!
DON'T SPEAK! BE QUIET AND WATCH!
CERES, YOU GENEROUS LADY, YOU MUST LEAVE YOUR FIELDS OF GROWING CROPS THIS VERY EVE,
YOUR GREEN HILLS WHERE SHEEP GRAZE ON YELLOW GORSE, YOUR MEADOWS OF CORN STALKS WHICH REINFORCE
ERODED RIVER BANKS WITH WOVEN STEMS; WHICH WET APRIL HAS STREWN WITH SPARKLING GEMS.

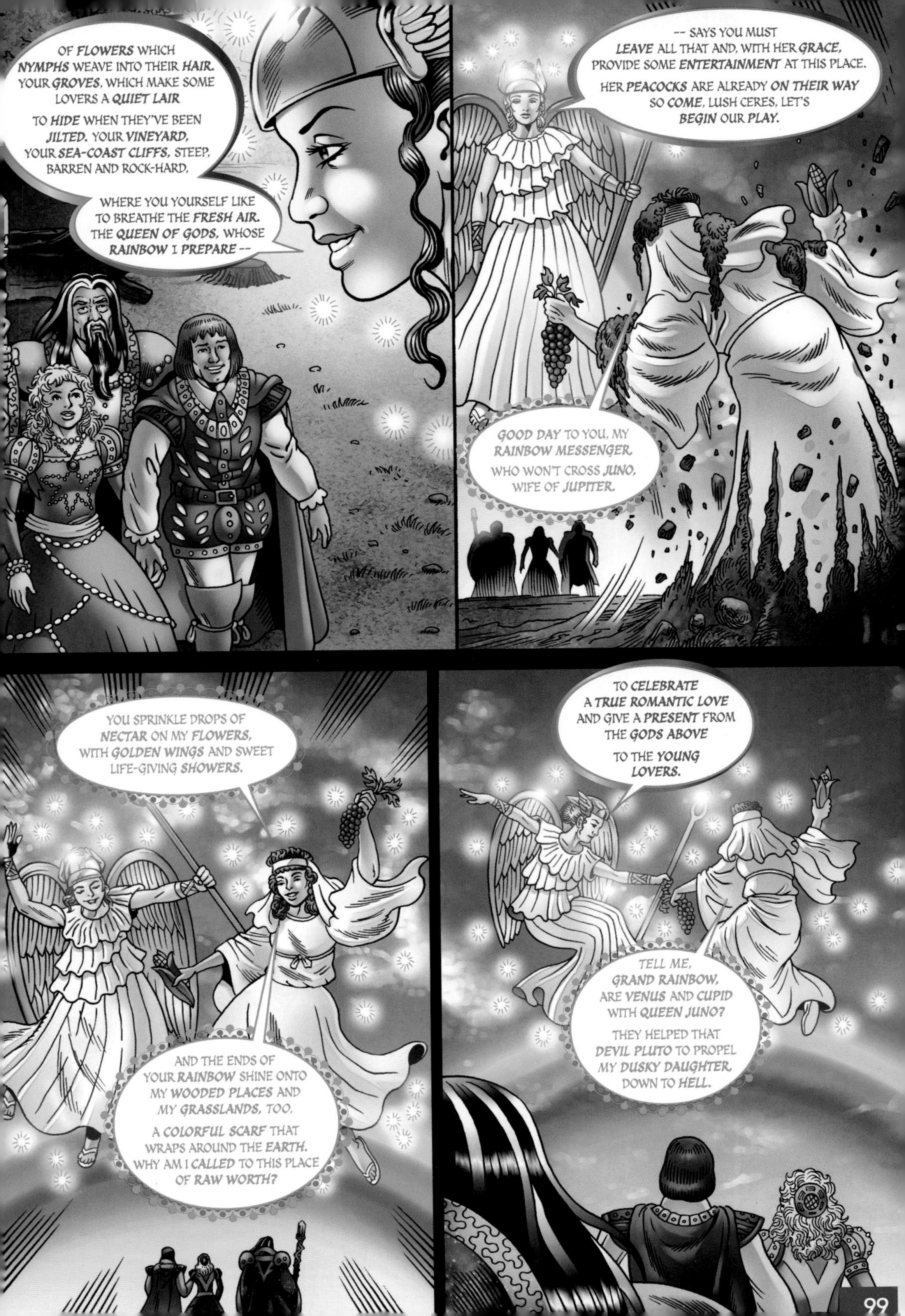

OF FLOWERS WHICH NYMPHS WEAVE INTO THEIR HAIR. YOUR GROVES, WHICH MAKE SOME LOVERS A QUIET LAIR
TO HIDE WHEN THEY'VE BEEN JILTED. YOUR VINEYARD, YOUR SEA-COAST CLIFFS, STEEP, BARREN AND ROCK-HARD,
WHERE YOU YOURSELF LIKE TO BREATHE THE FRESH AIR. THE QUEEN OF GODS, WHOSE RAINBOW I PREPARE --
-- SAYS YOU MUST LEAVE ALL THAT AND, WITH HER GRACE, PROVIDE SOME ENTERTAINMENT AT THIS PLACE.
HER PEACOCKS ARE ALREADY ON THEIR WAY SO COME, LUSH CERES, LET'S BEGIN OUR PLAY.
GOOD DAY TO YOU, MY RAINBOW MESSENGER.
WHO WON'T CROSS JUNO, WIFE OF JUPITER.
YOU SPRINKLE DROPS OF NECTAR ON MY FLOWERS, WITH GOLDEN WINGS AND SWEET LIFE-GIVING SHOWERS.
AND THE ENDS OF YOUR RAINBOW SHINE ONTO MY WOODED PLACES AND MY GRASSLANDS, TOO,
A COLORFUL SCARF THAT WRAPS AROUND THE EARTH. WHY AM I CALLED TO THIS PLACE OF RAW WORTH?
TO CELEBRATE A TRUE ROMANTIC LOVE AND GIVE A PRESENT FROM THE GODS ABOVE
TO THE YOUNG LOVERS.
TELL ME, GRAND RAINBOW, ARE VENUS AND CUPID WITH QUEEN JUNO?
THEY HELPED THAT DEVIL PLUTO TO PROPEL MY DUSKY DAUGHTER DOWN TO HELL.

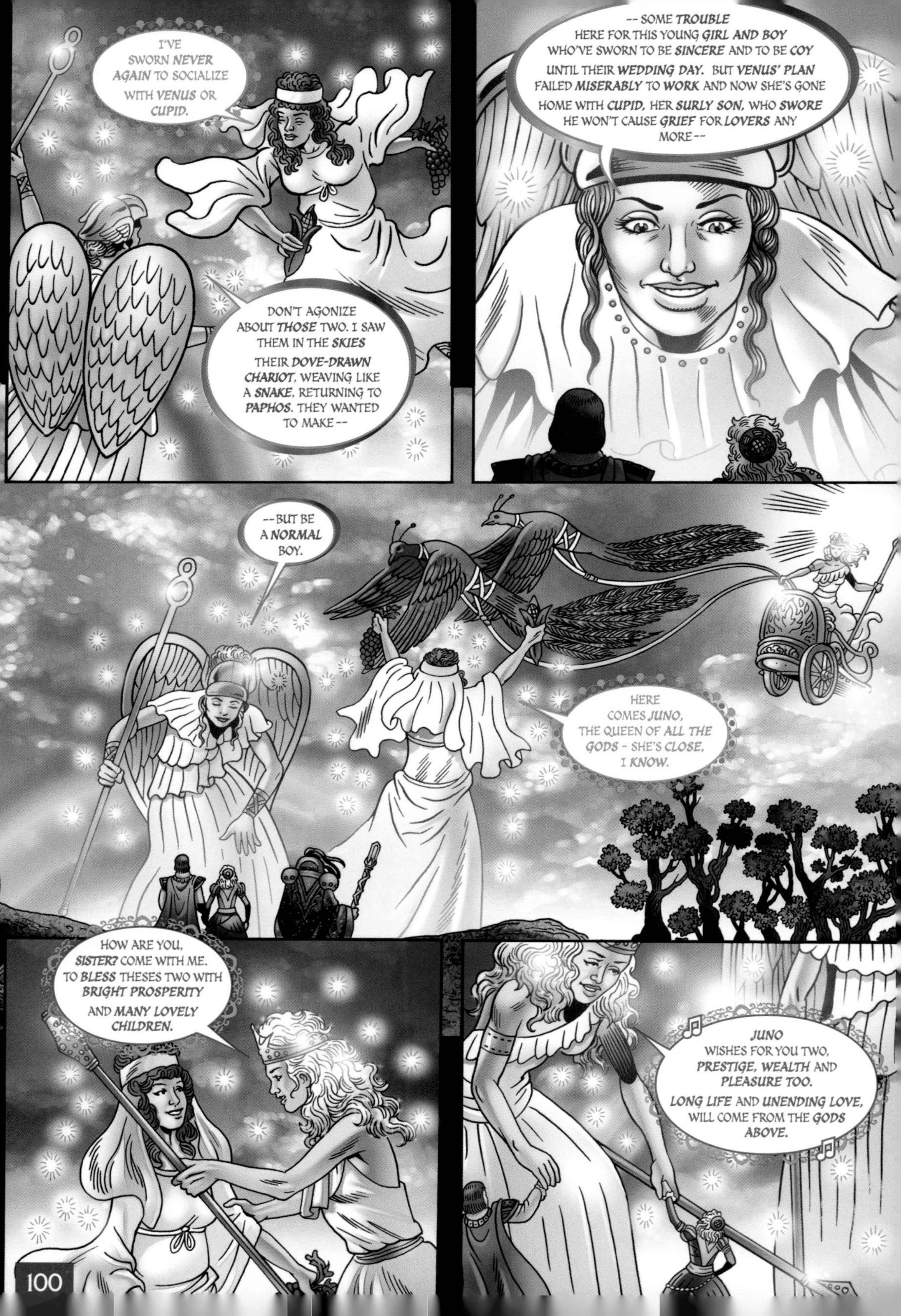

I'VE SWORN NEVER AGAIN TO SOCIALIZE WITH VENUS OR CUPID.
DON'T AGONIZE ABOUT THOSE TWO. I SAW THEM IN THE SKIES THEIR DOVE-DRAWN CHARIOT, WEAVING LIKE A SNAKE, RETURNING TO PAPHOS. THEY WANTED TO MAKE--
-- SOME TROUBLE HERE FOR THIS YOUNG GIRL AND BOY WHO'VE SWORN TO BE SINCERE AND TO BE COY UNTIL THEIR WEDDING DAY. BUT VENUS' PLAN FAILED MISERABLY TO WORK AND NOW SHE'S GONE HOME WITH CUPID, HER SURLY SON, WHO SWORE HE WON'T CAUSE GRIEF FOR LOVERS ANY MORE--
--BUT BE A NORMAL BOY.
HERE COMES JUNO, THE QUEEN OF ALL THE GODS - SHE'S CLOSE, I KNOW.
HOW ARE YOU, SISTER? COME WITH ME. TO BLESS THESES TWO WITH BRIGHT PROSPERITY AND MANY LOVELY CHILDREN.
JUNO WISHES FOR YOU TWO, PRESTIGE, WEALTH AND PLEASURE TOO. LONG LIFE AND UNENDING LOVE, WILL COME FROM THE GODS ABOVE.

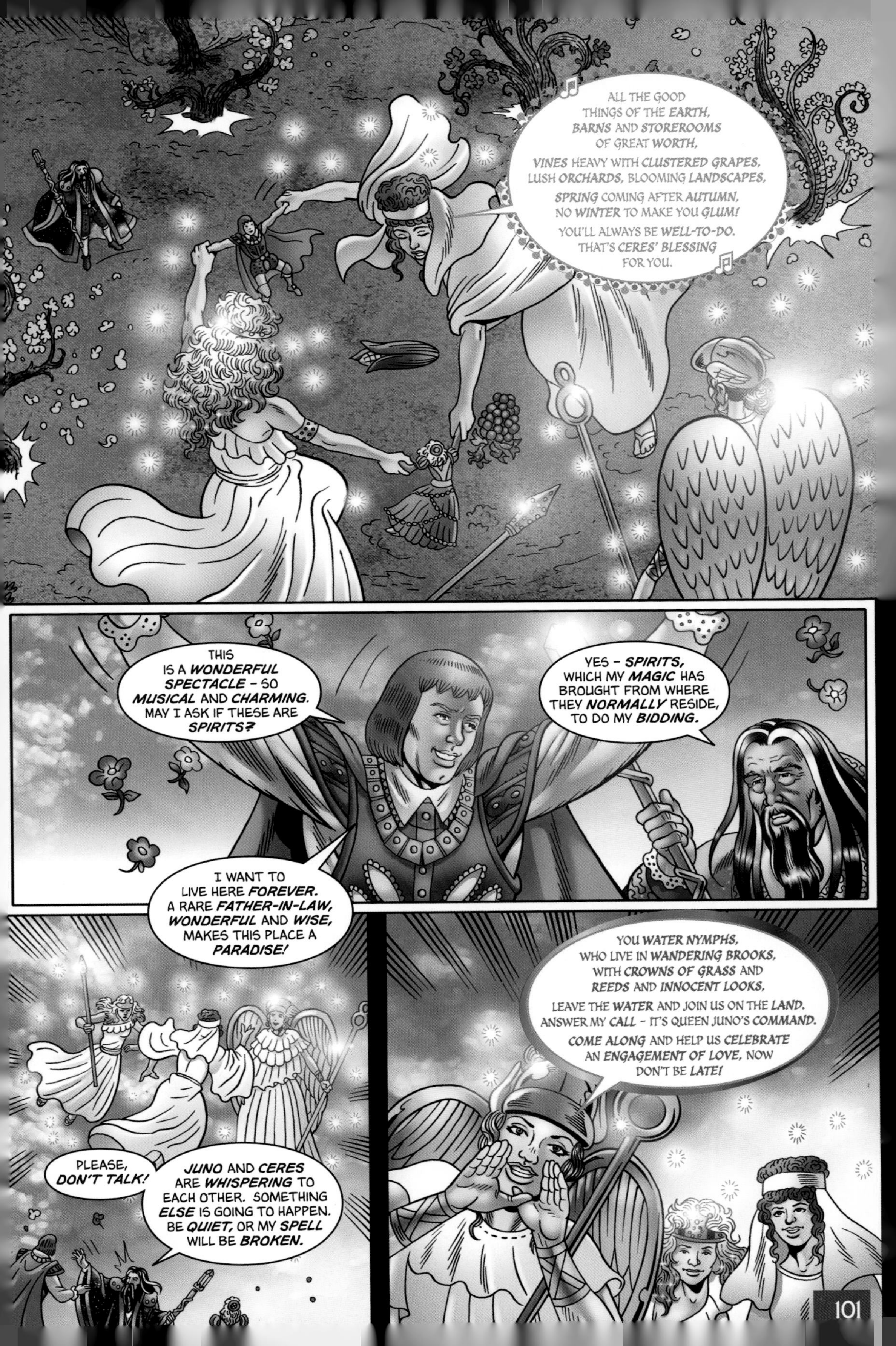
ALL THE GOOD THINGS OF THE EARTH, BARNS AND STOREROOMS OF GREAT WORTH, VINES HEAVY WITH CLUSTERED GRAPES, LUSH ORCHARDS, BLOOMING LANDSCAPES, SPRING COMING AFTER AUTUMN, NO WINTER TO MAKE YOU GLUM! YOU'LL ALWAYS BE WELL-TO-DO. THAT'S CERES' BLESSING FOR YOU.
THIS IS A WONDERFUL SPECTACLE – SO MUSICAL AND CHARMING. MAY I ASK IF THESE ARE SPIRITS?
YES – SPIRITS, WHICH MY MAGIC HAS BROUGHT FROM WHERE THEY NORMALLY RESIDE, TO DO MY BIDDING.
I WANT TO LIVE HERE FOREVER. A RARE FATHER-IN-LAW, WONDERFUL AND WISE, MAKES THIS PLACE A PARADISE!
PLEASE, DON'T TALK!
JUNO AND CERES ARE WHISPERING TO EACH OTHER. SOMETHING ELSE IS GOING TO HAPPEN. BE QUIET, OR MY SPELL WILL BE BROKEN.
YOU WATER NYMPHS, WHO LIVE IN WANDERING BROOKS, WITH CROWNS OF GRASS AND REEDS AND INNOCENT LOOKS, LEAVE THE WATER AND JOIN US ON THE LAND. ANSWER MY CALL – IT'S QUEEN JUNO'S COMMAND. COME ALONG AND HELP US CELEBRATE AN ENGAGEMENT OF LOVE, NOW DON'T BE LATE!

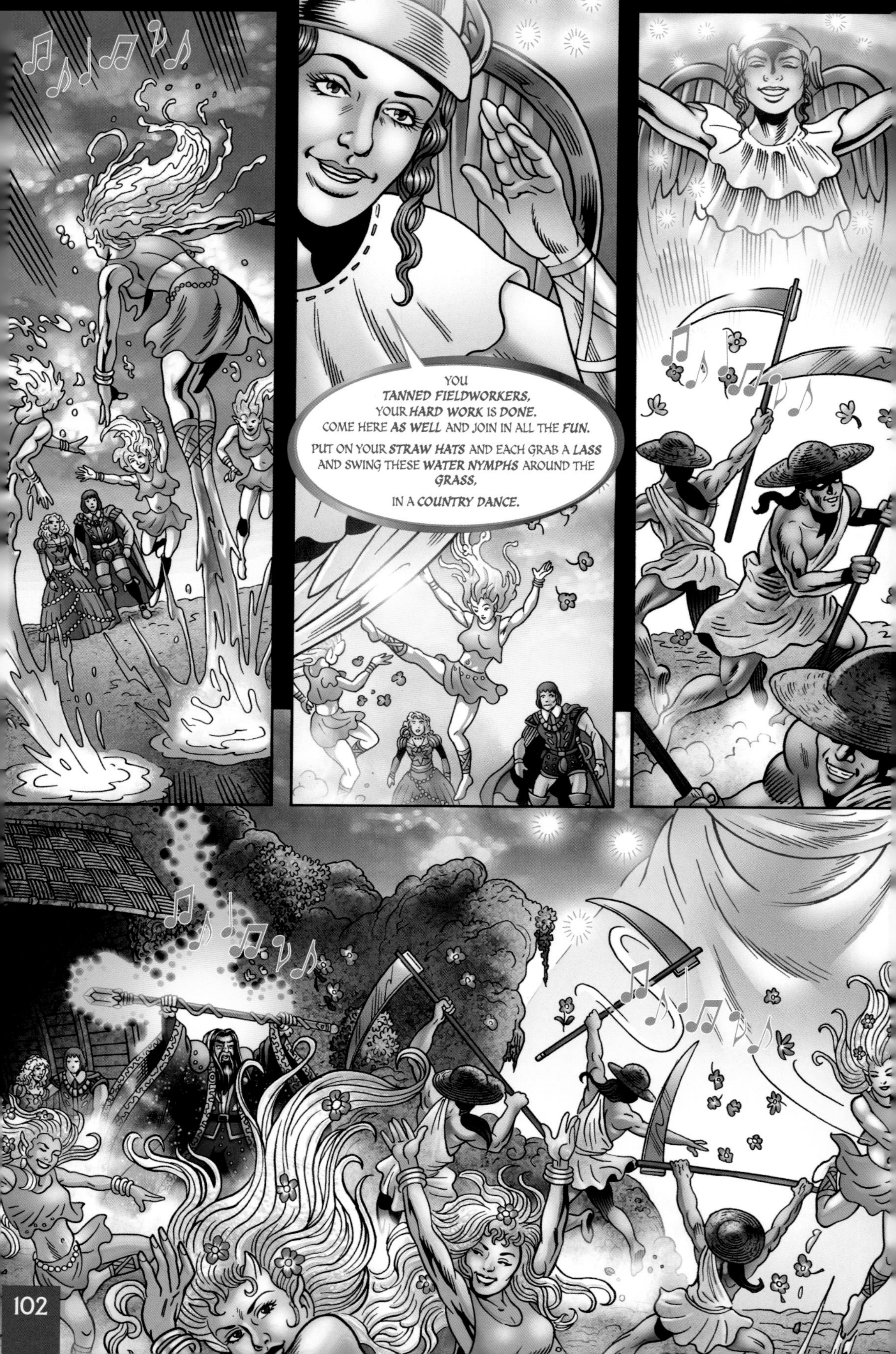
YOU TANNED FIELDWORKERS, YOUR HARD WORK IS DONE. COME HERE AS WELL AND JOIN IN ALL THE FUN.
PUT ON YOUR STRAW HATS AND EACH GRAB A LASS AND SWING THESE WATER NYMPHS AROUND THE GRASS,
IN A COUNTRY DANCE.

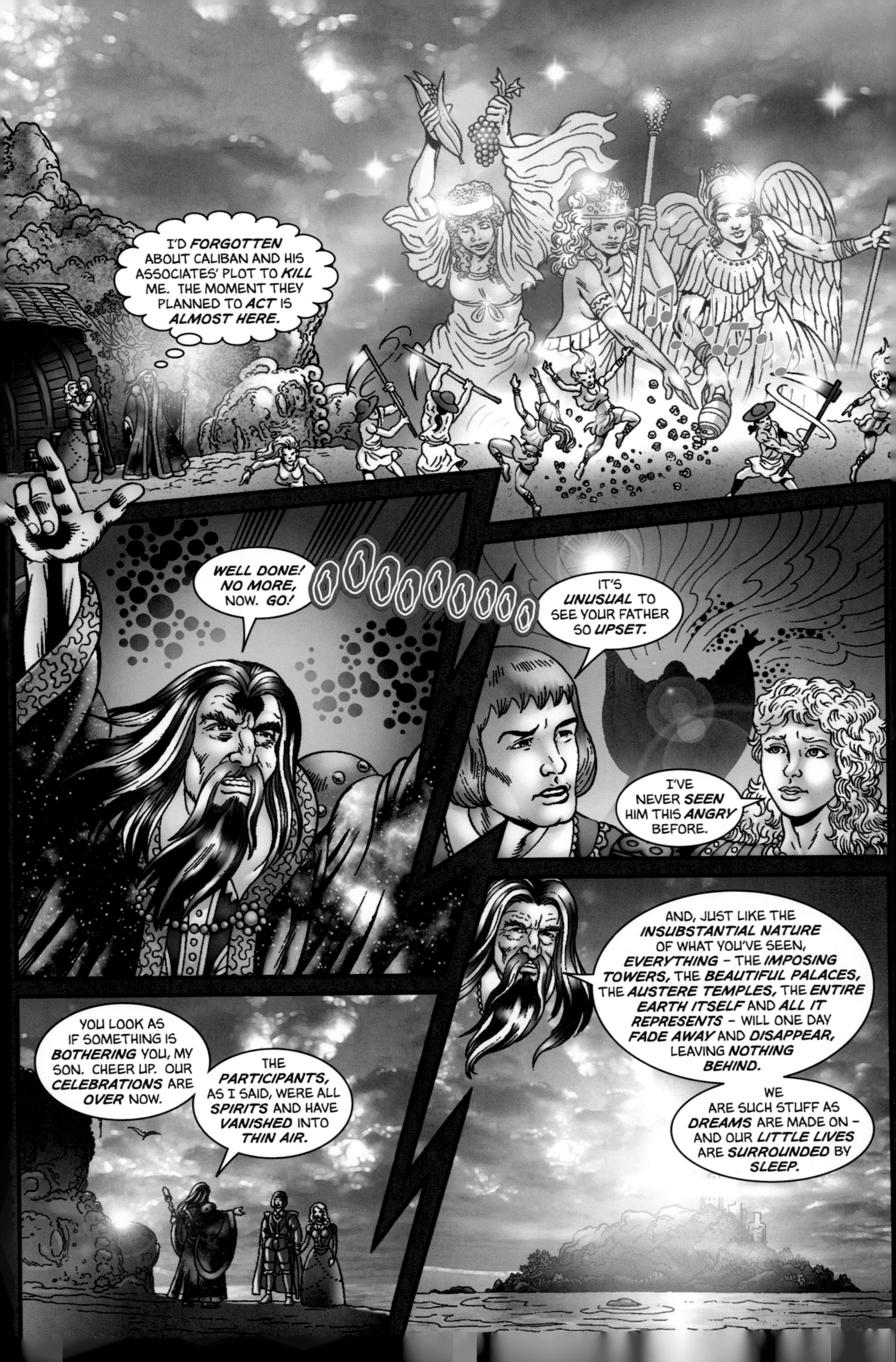
I'D FORGOTTEN ABOUT CALIBAN AND HIS ASSOCIATES' PLOT TO KILL ME. THE MOMENT THEY PLANNED TO ACT IS ALMOST HERE.
WELL DONE! NO MORE, NOW. GO!
IT'S UNUSUAL TO SEE YOUR FATHER SO UPSET.
I'VE NEVER SEEN HIM THIS ANGRY BEFORE.
YOU LOOK AS IF SOMETHING IS BOTHERING YOU, MY SON. CHEER UP. OUR CELEBRATIONS ARE OVER NOW.
THE PARTICIPANTS, AS I SAID, WERE ALL SPIRITS AND HAVE VANISHED INTO THIN AIR.
AND, JUST LIKE THE INSUBSTANTIAL NATURE OF WHAT YOU'VE SEEN, EVERYTHING – THE IMPOSING TOWERS, THE BEAUTIFUL PALACES, THE AUSTERE TEMPLES, THE ENTIRE EARTH ITSELF AND ALL IT REPRESENTS – WILL ONE DAY FADE AWAY AND DISAPPEAR, LEAVING NOTHING BEHIND.
WE ARE SUCH STUFF AS DREAMS ARE MADE ON – AND OUR LITTLE LIVES ARE SURROUNDED BY SLEEP.

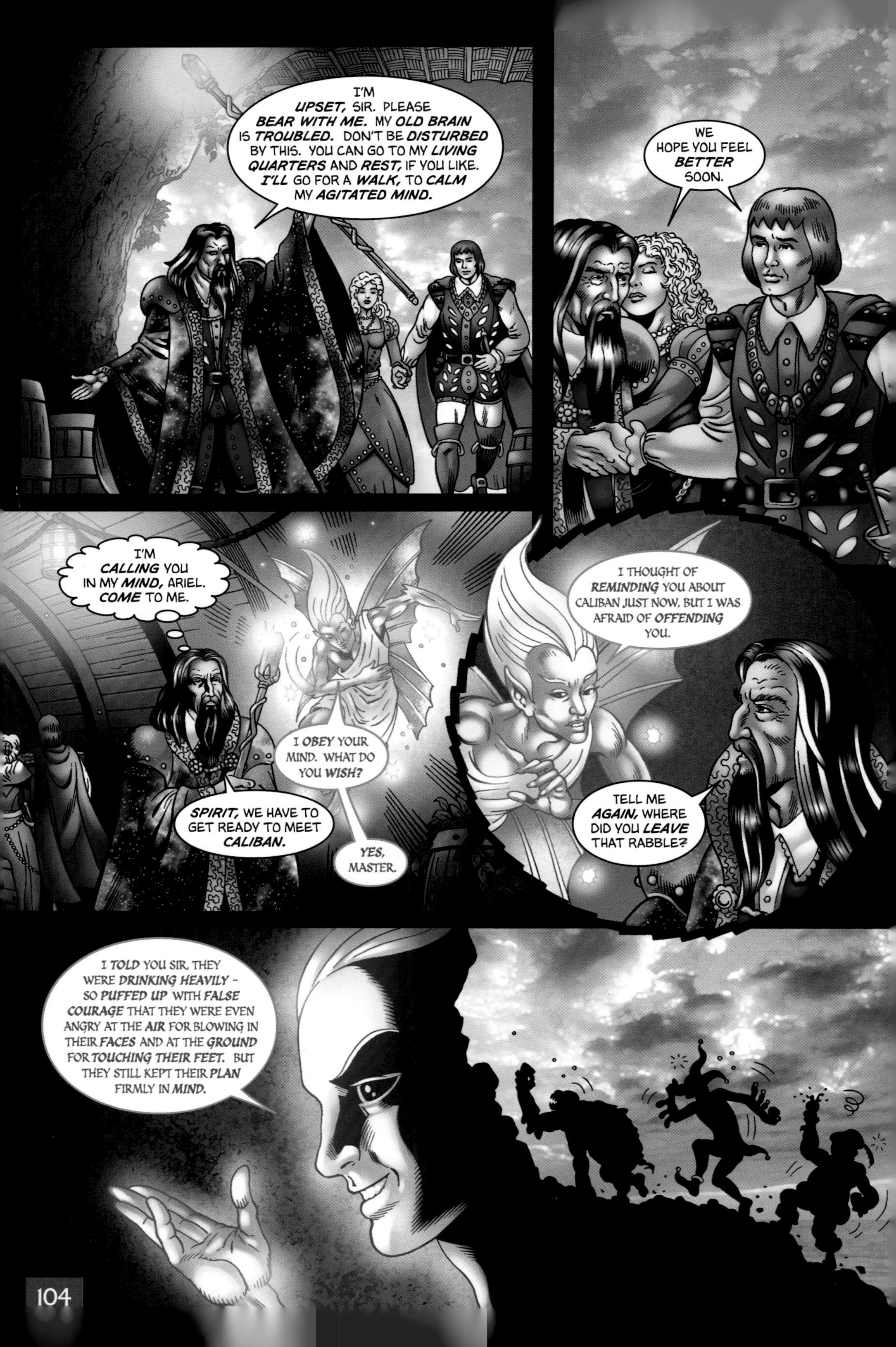
I'M UPSET, SIR. PLEASE BEAR WITH ME. MY OLD BRAIN IS TROUBLED. DON'T BE DISTURBED BY THIS. YOU CAN GO TO MY LIVING QUARTERS AND REST, IF YOU LIKE. I'LL GO FOR A WALK, TO CALM MY AGITATED MIND.
WE HOPE YOU FEEL BETTER SOON.
I'M CALLING YOU IN MY MIND, ARIEL. COME TO ME.
I OBEY YOUR MIND. WHAT DO YOU WISH?
SPIRIT, WE HAVE TO GET READY TO MEET CALIBAN.
YES, MASTER.
I THOUGHT OF REMINDING YOU ABOUT CALIBAN JUST NOW, BUT I WAS AFRAID OF OFFENDING YOU.
TELL ME AGAIN, WHERE DID YOU LEAVE THAT RABBLE?
I TOLD YOU SIR, THEY WERE DRINKING HEAVILY – SO PUFFED UP WITH FALSE COURAGE THAT THEY WERE EVEN ANGRY AT THE AIR FOR BLOWING IN THEIR FACES AND AT THE GROUND FOR TOUCHING THEIR FEET. BUT THEY STILL KEPT THEIR PLAN FIRMLY IN MIND.

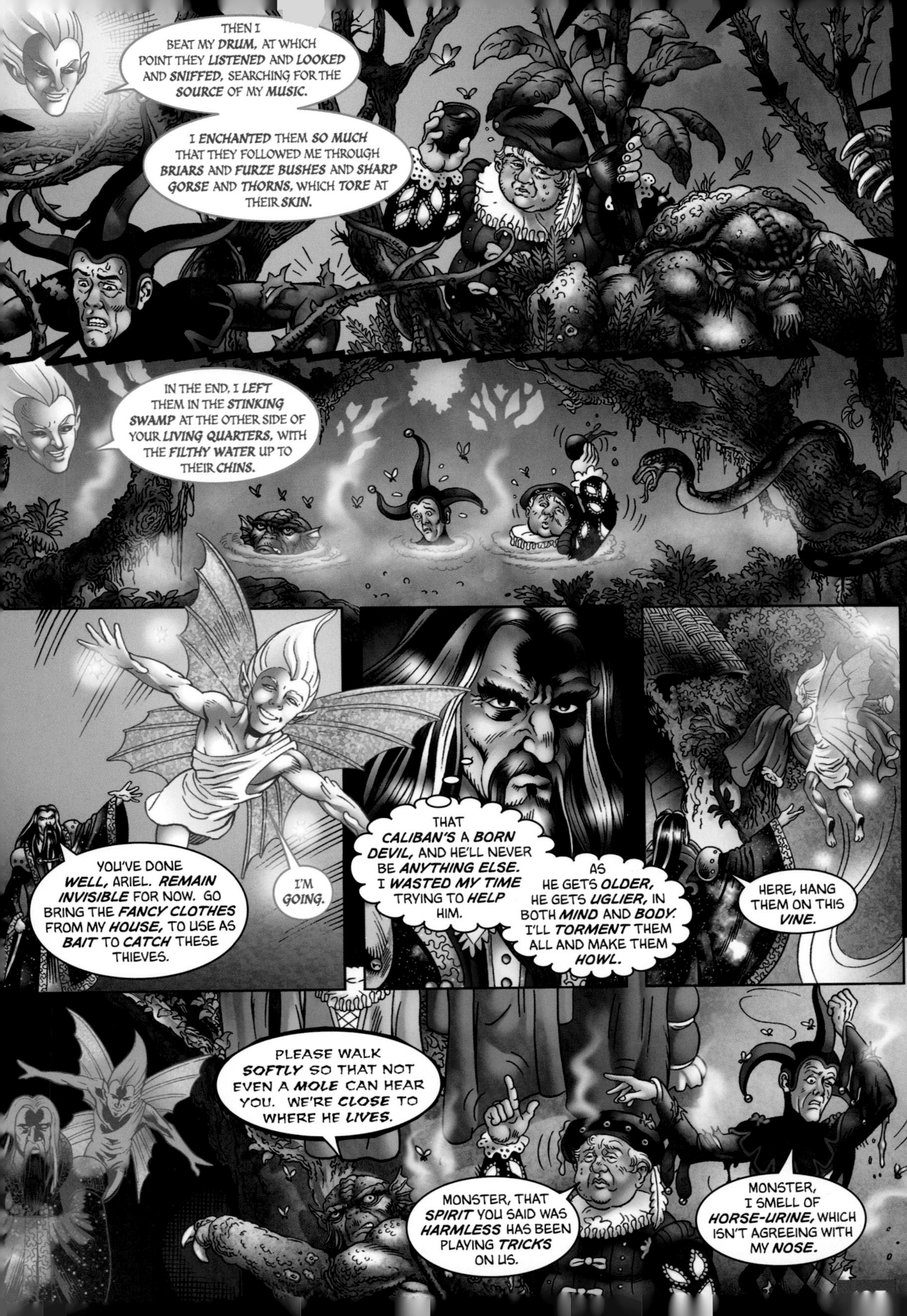
THEN I BEAT MY DRUM, AT WHICH POINT THEY LISTENED AND LOOKED AND SNIFFED, SEARCHING FOR THE SOURCE OF MY MUSIC.
I ENCHANTED THEM SO MUCH THAT THEY FOLLOWED ME THROUGH BRIARS AND FURZE BUSHES AND SHARP GORSE AND THORNS, WHICH TORE AT THEIR SKIN.
IN THE END, I LEFT THEM IN THE STINKING SWAMP AT THE OTHER SIDE OF YOUR LIVING QUARTERS, WITH THE FILTHY WATER UP TO THEIR CHINS.
YOU'VE DONE WELL, ARIEL. REMAIN INVISIBLE FOR NOW. GO BRING THE FANCY CLOTHES FROM MY HOUSE, TO USE AS BAIT TO CATCH THESE THIEVES.
I'M GOING.
THAT CALIBAN'S A BORN DEVIL, AND HE'LL NEVER BE ANYTHING ELSE. I WASTED MY TIME TRYING TO HELP HIM.
AS HE GETS OLDER, HE GETS UGLIER, IN BOTH MIND AND BODY. I'LL TORMENT THEM ALL AND MAKE THEM HOWL.
HERE, HANG THEM ON THIS VINE.
PLEASE WALK SOFTLY SO THAT NOT EVEN A MOLE CAN HEAR YOU. WE'RE CLOSE TO WHERE HE LIVES.
MONSTER, THAT SPIRIT YOU SAID WAS HARMLESS HAS BEEN PLAYING TRICKS ON US.
MONSTER, I SMELL OF HORSE-URINE, WHICH ISN'T AGREEING WITH MY NOSE.

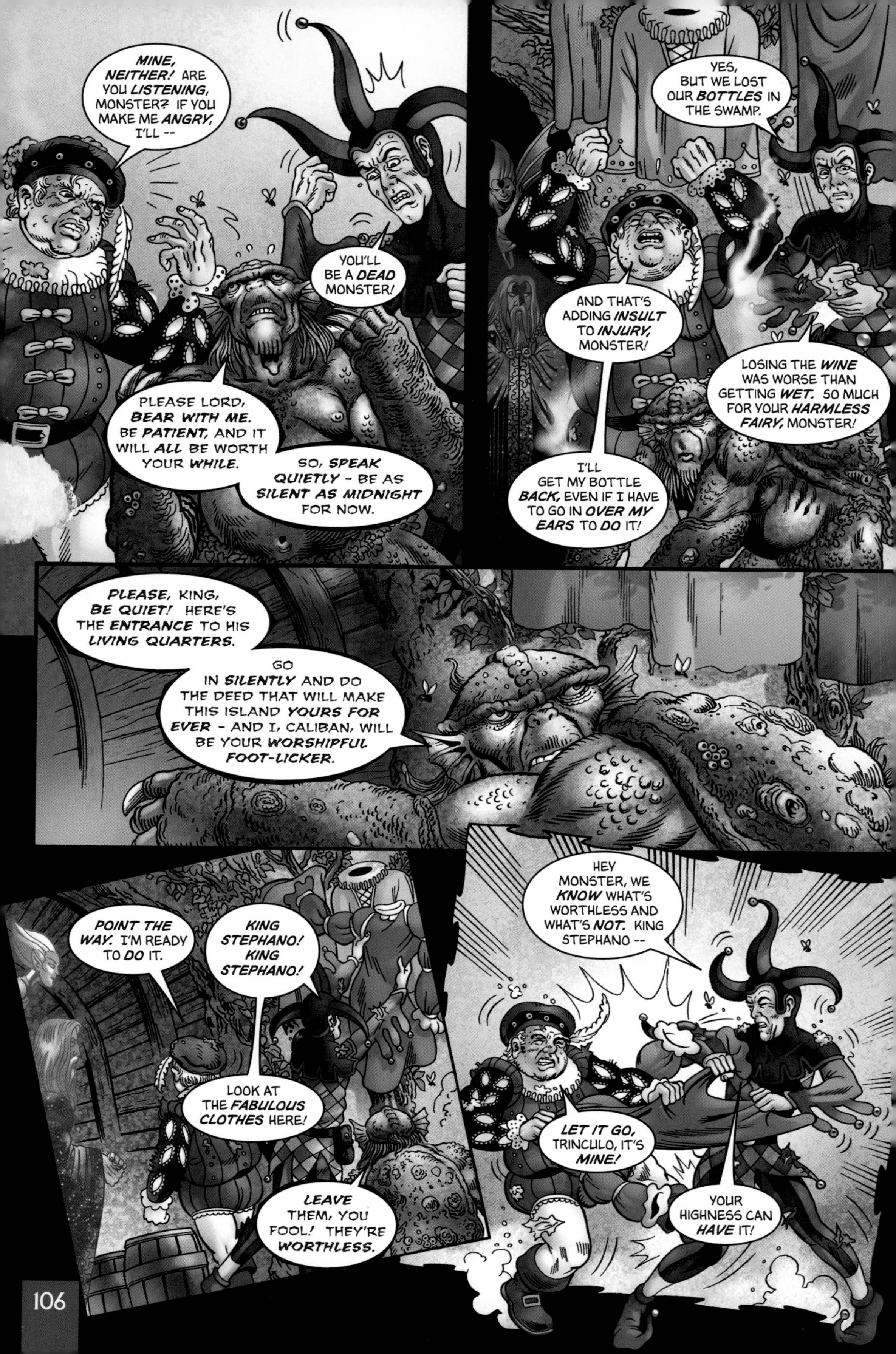
MINE, NEITHER! ARE YOU LISTENING, MONSTER? IF YOU MAKE ME ANGRY, I'LL --
YOU'LL BE A DEAD MONSTER!
PLEASE LORD, BEAR WITH ME. BE PATIENT, AND IT WILL ALL BE WORTH YOUR WHILE.
SO, SPEAK QUIETLY - BE AS SILENT AS MIDNIGHT FOR NOW.
YES, BUT WE LOST OUR BOTTLES IN THE SWAMP.
AND THAT'S ADDING INSULT TO INJURY, MONSTER!
LOSING THE WINE WAS WORSE THAN GETTING WET. SO MUCH FOR YOUR HARMLESS FAIRY, MONSTER!
I'LL GET MY BOTTLE BACK, EVEN IF I HAVE TO GO IN OVER MY EARS TO DO IT!
PLEASE, KING, BE QUIET! HERE'S THE ENTRANCE TO HIS LIVING QUARTERS.
GO IN SILENTLY AND DO THE DEED THAT WILL MAKE THIS ISLAND YOURS FOR EVER - AND I, CALIBAN, WILL BE YOUR WORSHIPFUL FOOT-LICKER.
POINT THE WAY. I'M READY TO DO IT.
KING STEPHANO! KING STEPHANO!
LOOK AT THE FABULOUS CLOTHES HERE!
LEAVE THEM, YOU FOOL! THEY'RE WORTHLESS.
HEY MONSTER, WE KNOW WHAT'S WORTHLESS AND WHAT'S NOT. KING STEPHANO --
LET IT GO, TRINCULO, IT'S MINE!
YOUR HIGHNESS CAN HAVE IT!

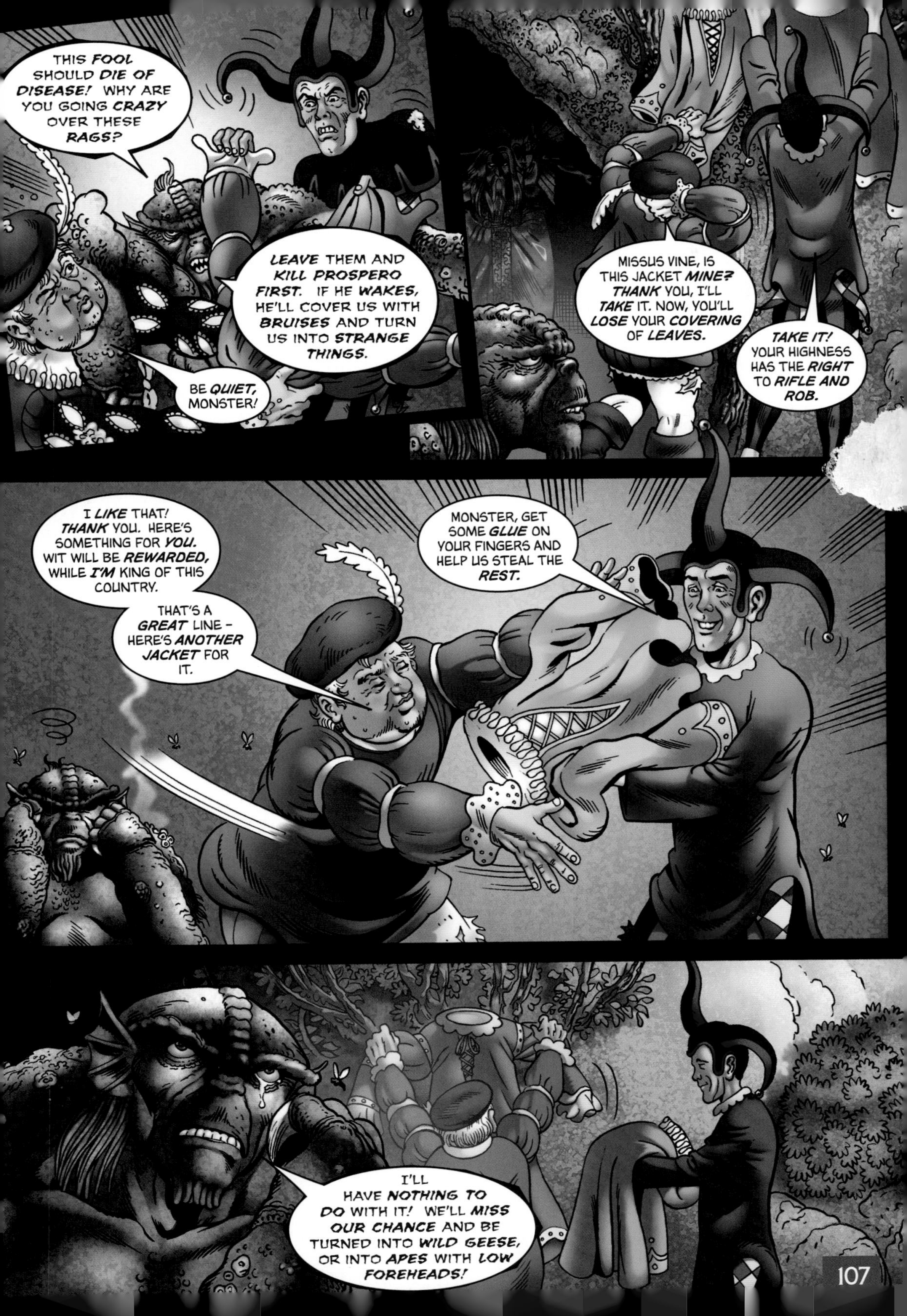
THIS FOOL SHOULD DIE OF DISEASE! WHY ARE YOU GOING CRAZY OVER THESE RAGS?
LEAVE THEM AND KILL PROSPERO FIRST. IF HE WAKES, HE'LL COVER US WITH BRUISES AND TURN US INTO STRANGE THINGS.
BE QUIET, MONSTER!
MISSUS VINE, IS THIS JACKET MINE? THANK YOU, I'LL TAKE IT. NOW, YOU'LL LOSE YOUR COVERING OF LEAVES.
TAKE IT! YOUR HIGHNESS HAS THE RIGHT TO RIFLE AND ROB.
I LIKE THAT! THANK YOU. HERE'S SOMETHING FOR YOU. WIT WILL BE REWARDED, WHILE I'M KING OF THIS COUNTRY.
THAT'S A GREAT LINE – HERE'S ANOTHER JACKET FOR IT.
MONSTER, GET SOME GLUE ON YOUR FINGERS AND HELP US STEAL THE REST.
I'LL HAVE NOTHING TO DO WITH IT! WE'LL MISS OUR CHANCE AND BE TURNED INTO WILD GEESE, OR INTO APES WITH LOW FOREHEADS!

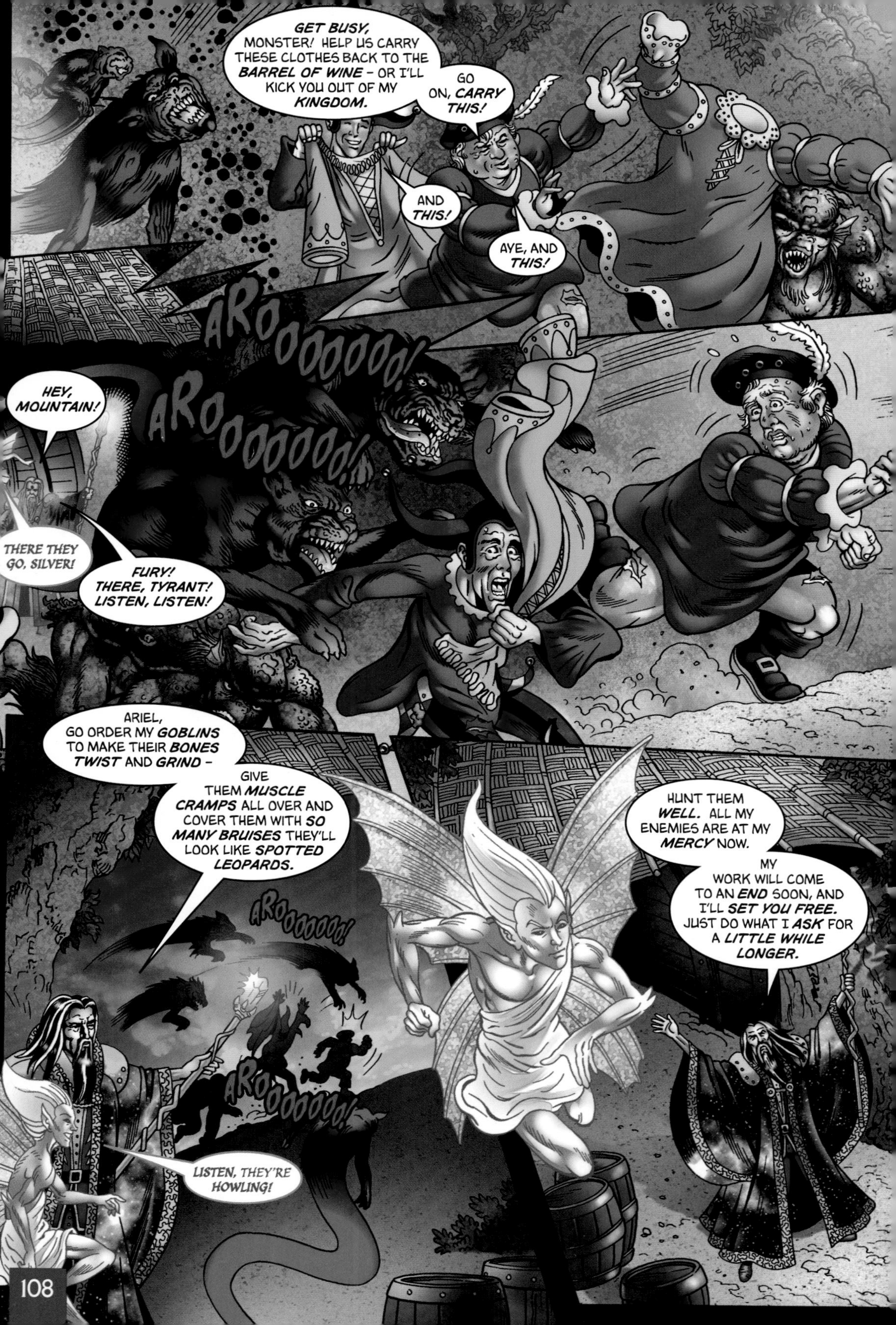

GET BUSY, MONSTER! HELP US CARRY THESE CLOTHES BACK TO THE BARREL OF WINE – OR I'LL KICK YOU OUT OF MY KINGDOM.
GO ON, CARRY THIS!
AND THIS!
AYE, AND THIS!
AROOOOOOO!
AROOOOOOOO!
HEY, MOUNTAIN!
THERE THEY GO, SILVER!
FURY! THERE, TYRANT! LISTEN, LISTEN!
ARIEL, GO ORDER MY GOBLINS TO MAKE THEIR BONES TWIST AND GRIND –
GIVE THEM MUSCLE CRAMPS ALL OVER AND COVER THEM WITH SO MANY BRUISES THEY'LL LOOK LIKE SPOTTED LEOPARDS.
HUNT THEM WELL. ALL MY ENEMIES ARE AT MY MERCY NOW.
MY WORK WILL COME TO AN END SOON, AND I'LL SET YOU FREE. JUST DO WHAT I ASK FOR A LITTLE WHILE LONGER.
AROOOOOOO!
AROOOOOOO!
LISTEN, THEY'RE HOWLING!

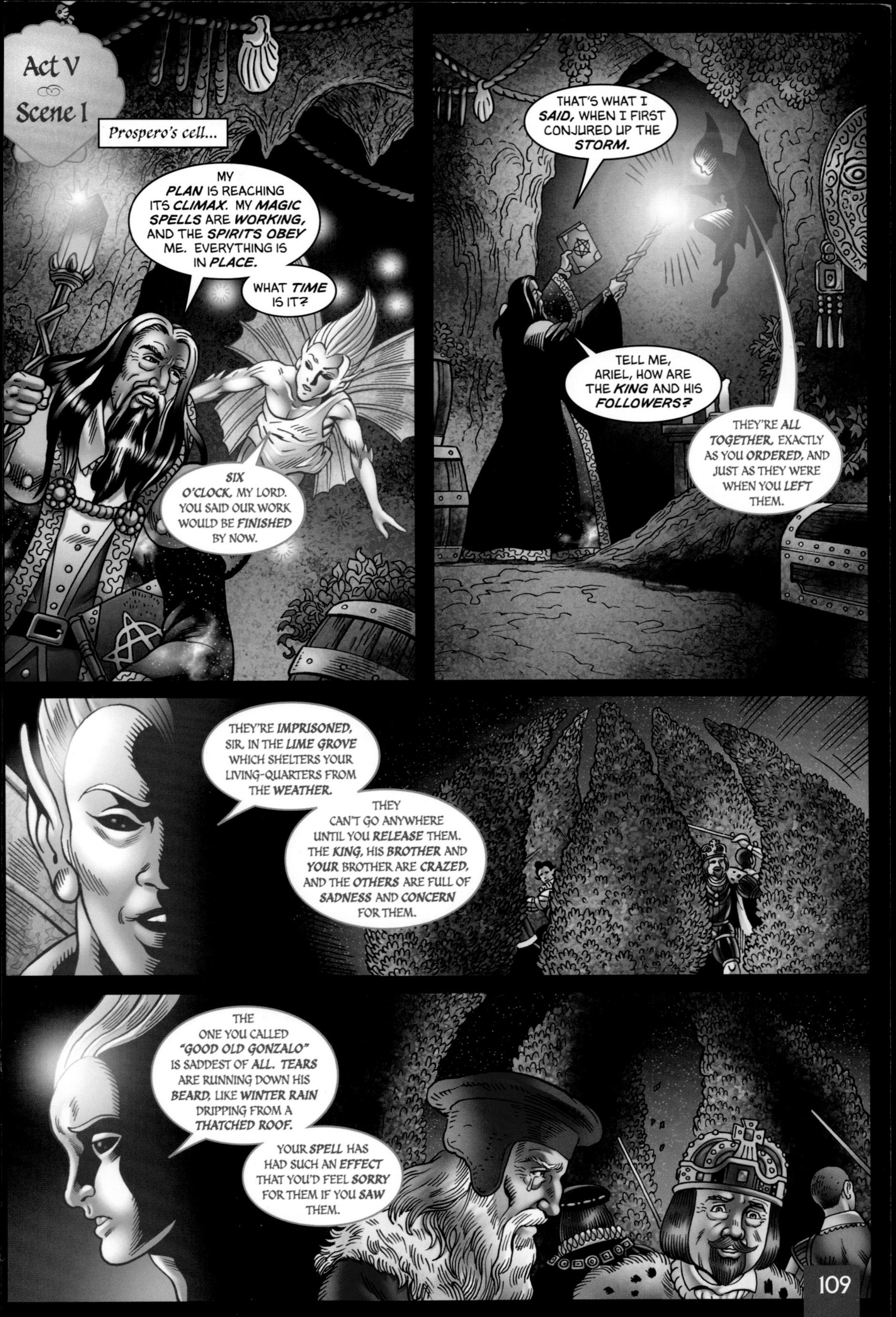
Act V
Scene I
Prospero's cell...
MY PLAN IS REACHING ITS CLIMAX. MY MAGIC SPELLS ARE WORKING, AND THE SPIRITS OBEY ME. EVERYTHING IS IN PLACE.
WHAT TIME IS IT?
SIX O'CLOCK, MY LORD. YOU SAID OUR WORK WOULD BE FINISHED BY NOW.
THAT'S WHAT I SAID, WHEN I FIRST CONJURED UP THE STORM.
TELL ME, ARIEL, HOW ARE THE KING AND HIS FOLLOWERS?
THEY'RE ALL TOGETHER, EXACTLY AS YOU ORDERED, AND JUST AS THEY WERE WHEN YOU LEFT THEM.
THEY'RE IMPRISONED, SIR, IN THE LIME GROVE WHICH SHELTERS YOUR LIVING-QUARTERS FROM THE WEATHER.
THEY CAN'T GO ANYWHERE UNTIL YOU RELEASE THEM. THE KING, HIS BROTHER AND YOUR BROTHER ARE CRAZED, AND THE OTHERS ARE FULL OF SADNESS AND CONCERN FOR THEM.
THE ONE YOU CALLED "GOOD OLD GONZALO" IS SADDEST OF ALL. TEARS ARE RUNNING DOWN HIS BEARD, LIKE WINTER RAIN DRIPPING FROM A THATCHED ROOF.
YOUR SPELL HAS HAD SUCH AN EFFECT THAT YOU'D FEEL SORRY FOR THEM IF YOU SAW THEM.

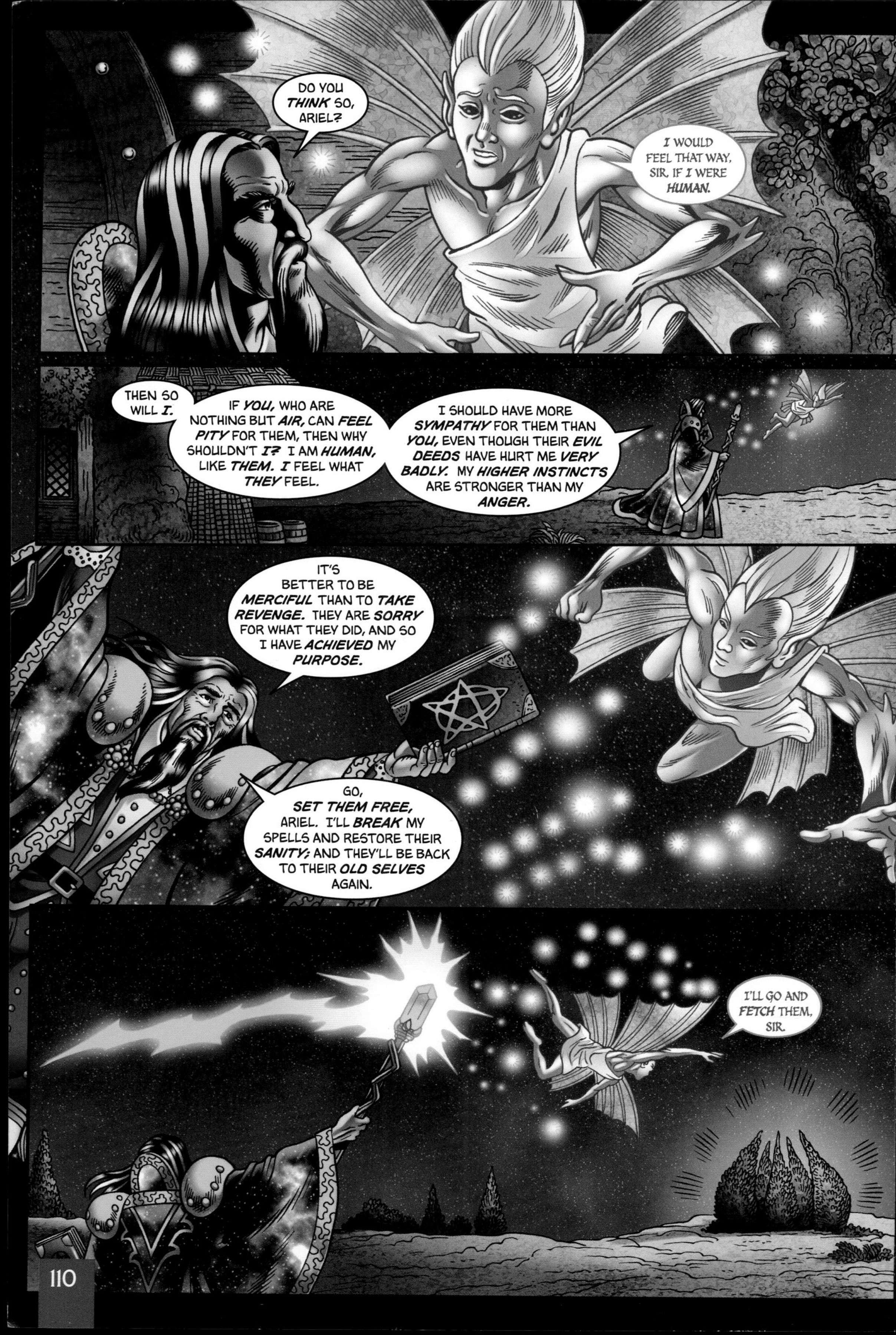
DO YOU THINK SO, ARIEL?
I WOULD FEEL THAT WAY, SIR, IF I WERE HUMAN.
THEN SO WILL I.
IF YOU, WHO ARE NOTHING BUT AIR, CAN FEEL PITY FOR THEM, THEN WHY SHOULDN'T I? I AM HUMAN, LIKE THEM. I FEEL WHAT THEY FEEL.
I SHOULD HAVE MORE SYMPATHY FOR THEM THAN YOU, EVEN THOUGH THEIR EVIL DEEDS HAVE HURT ME VERY BADLY. MY HIGHER INSTINCTS ARE STRONGER THAN MY ANGER.
IT'S BETTER TO BE MERCIFUL THAN TO TAKE REVENGE. THEY ARE SORRY FOR WHAT THEY DID, AND SO I HAVE ACHIEVED MY PURPOSE.
GO, SET THEM FREE, ARIEL. I'LL BREAK MY SPELLS AND RESTORE THEIR SANITY; AND THEY'LL BE BACK TO THEIR OLD SELVES AGAIN.
I'LL GO AND FETCH THEM, SIR.

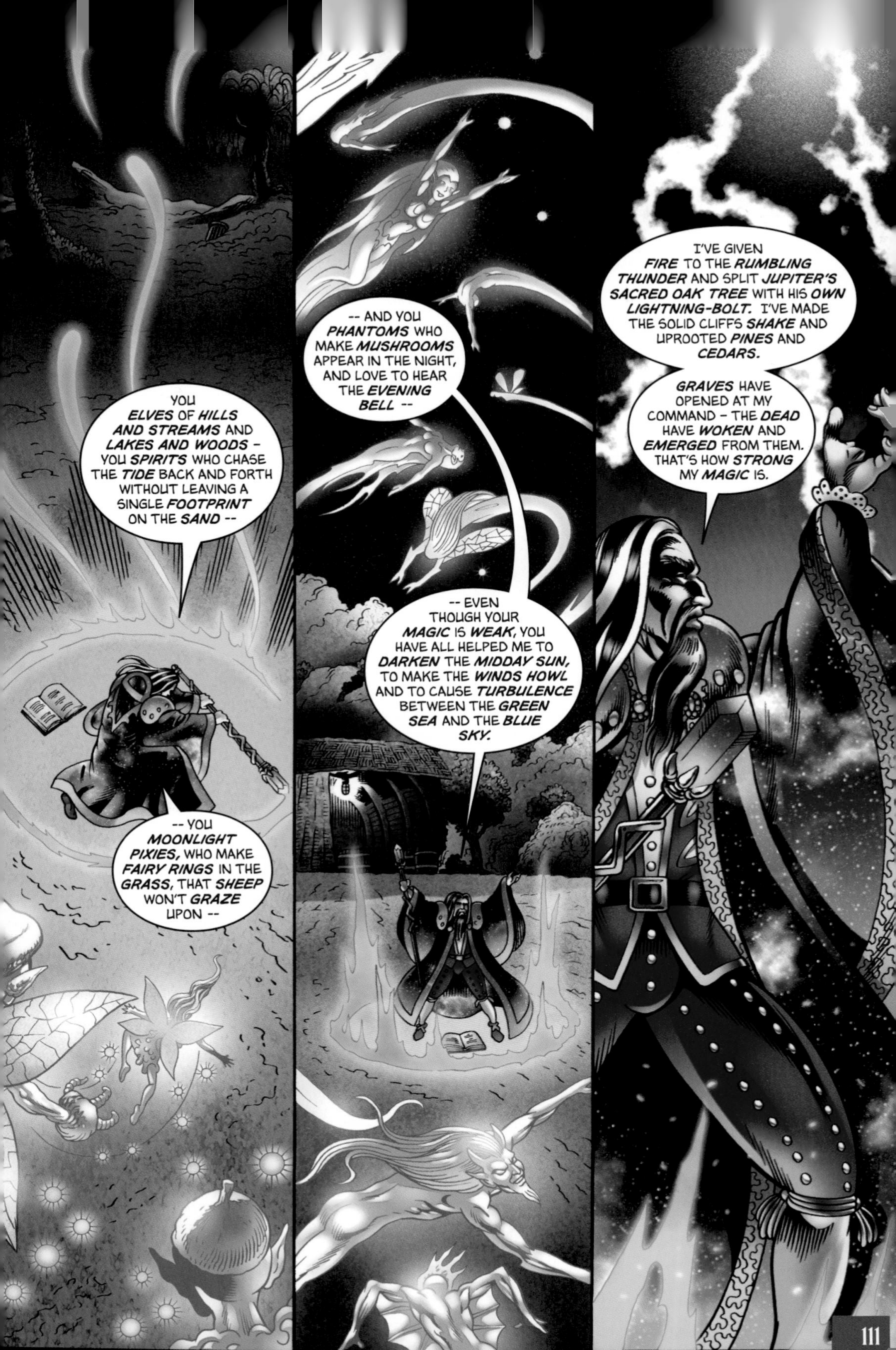

YOU ELVES OF HILLS AND STREAMS AND LAKES AND WOODS – YOU SPIRITS WHO CHASE THE TIDE BACK AND FORTH WITHOUT LEAVING A SINGLE FOOTPRINT ON THE SAND --
-- YOU MOONLIGHT PIXIES, WHO MAKE FAIRY RINGS IN THE GRASS, THAT SHEEP WON'T GRAZE UPON --
-- AND YOU PHANTOMS WHO MAKE MUSHROOMS APPEAR IN THE NIGHT, AND LOVE TO HEAR THE EVENING BELL --
-- EVEN THOUGH YOUR MAGIC IS WEAK, YOU HAVE ALL HELPED ME TO DARKEN THE MIDDAY SUN, TO MAKE THE WINDS HOWL AND TO CAUSE TURBULENCE BETWEEN THE GREEN SEA AND THE BLUE SKY.
I'VE GIVEN FIRE TO THE RUMBLING THUNDER AND SPLIT JUPITER'S SACRED OAK TREE WITH HIS OWN LIGHTNING-BOLT. I'VE MADE THE SOLID CLIFFS SHAKE AND UPROOTED PINES AND CEDARS.
GRAVES HAVE OPENED AT MY COMMAND – THE DEAD HAVE WOKEN AND EMERGED FROM THEM. THAT'S HOW STRONG MY MAGIC IS.

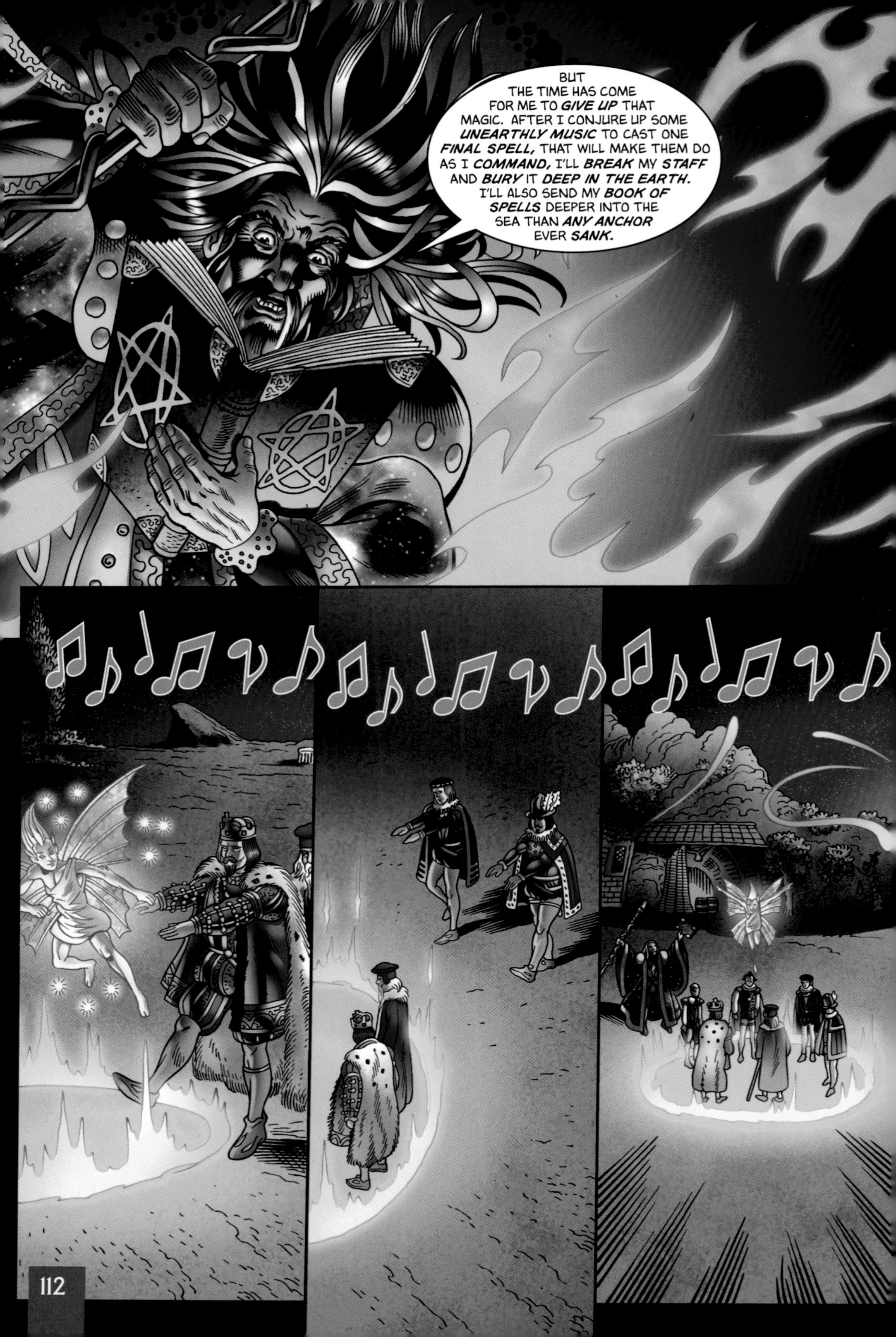
BUT THE TIME HAS COME FOR ME TO GIVE UP THAT MAGIC. AFTER I CONJURE UP SOME UNEARTHLY MUSIC TO CAST ONE FINAL SPELL, THAT WILL MAKE THEM DO AS I COMMAND, I'LL BREAK MY STAFF AND BURY IT DEEP IN THE EARTH. I'LL ALSO SEND MY BOOK OF SPELLS DEEPER INTO THE SEA THAN ANY ANCHOR EVER SANK.

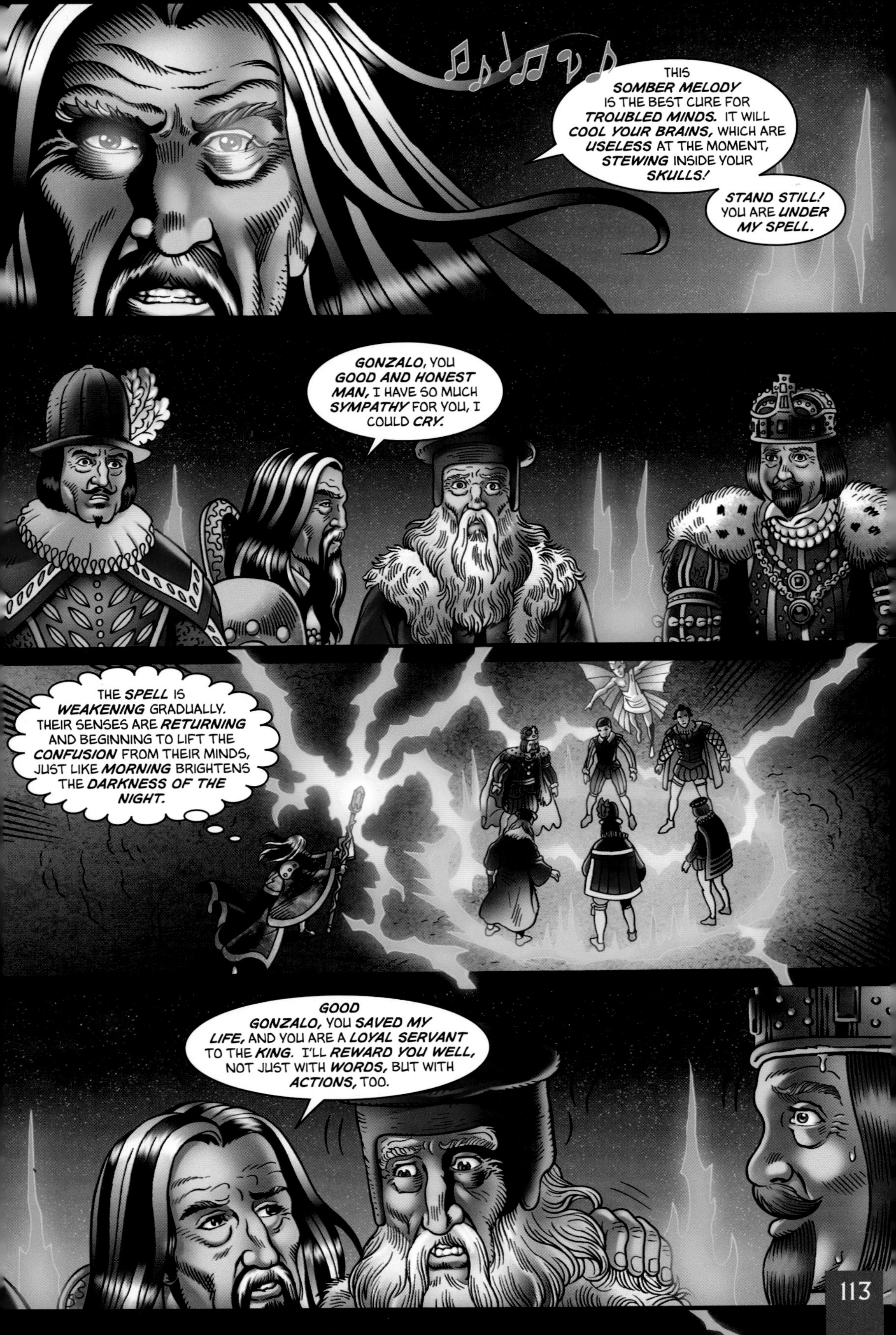
THIS SOMBER MELODY IS THE BEST CURE FOR TROUBLED MINDS. IT WILL COOL YOUR BRAINS, WHICH ARE USELESS AT THE MOMENT, STEWING INSIDE YOUR SKULLS!
STAND STILL! YOU ARE UNDER MY SPELL.
GONZALO, YOU GOOD AND HONEST MAN, I HAVE SO MUCH SYMPATHY FOR YOU, I COULD CRY.
THE SPELL IS WEAKENING GRADUALLY. THEIR SENSES ARE RETURNING AND BEGINNING TO LIFT THE CONFUSION FROM THEIR MINDS, JUST LIKE MORNING BRIGHTENS THE DARKNESS OF THE NIGHT.
GOOD GONZALO, YOU SAVED MY LIFE, AND YOU ARE A LOYAL SERVANT TO THE KING. I'LL REWARD YOU WELL, NOT JUST WITH WORDS, BUT WITH ACTIONS, TOO.

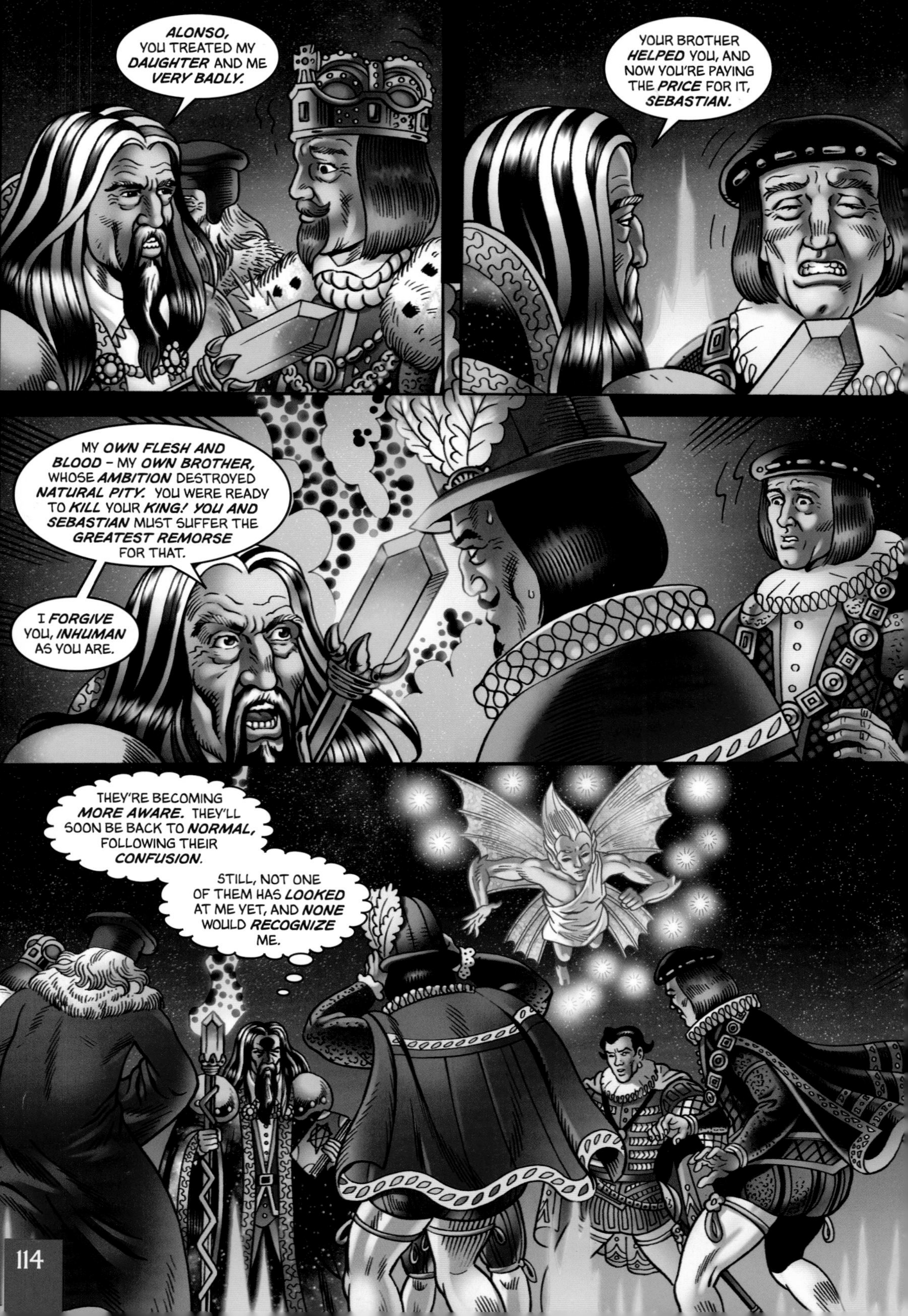
ALONSO, YOU TREATED MY DAUGHTER AND ME VERY BADLY.
YOUR BROTHER HELPED YOU, AND NOW YOU'RE PAYING THE PRICE FOR IT, SEBASTIAN.
MY OWN FLESH AND BLOOD - MY OWN BROTHER, WHOSE AMBITION DESTROYED NATURAL PITY. YOU WERE READY TO KILL YOUR KING! YOU AND SEBASTIAN MUST SUFFER THE GREATEST REMORSE FOR THAT.
I FORGIVE YOU, INHUMAN AS YOU ARE.
THEY'RE BECOMING MORE AWARE. THEY'LL SOON BE BACK TO NORMAL, FOLLOWING THEIR CONFUSION.
STILL, NOT ONE OF THEM HAS LOOKED AT ME YET, AND NONE WOULD RECOGNIZE ME.

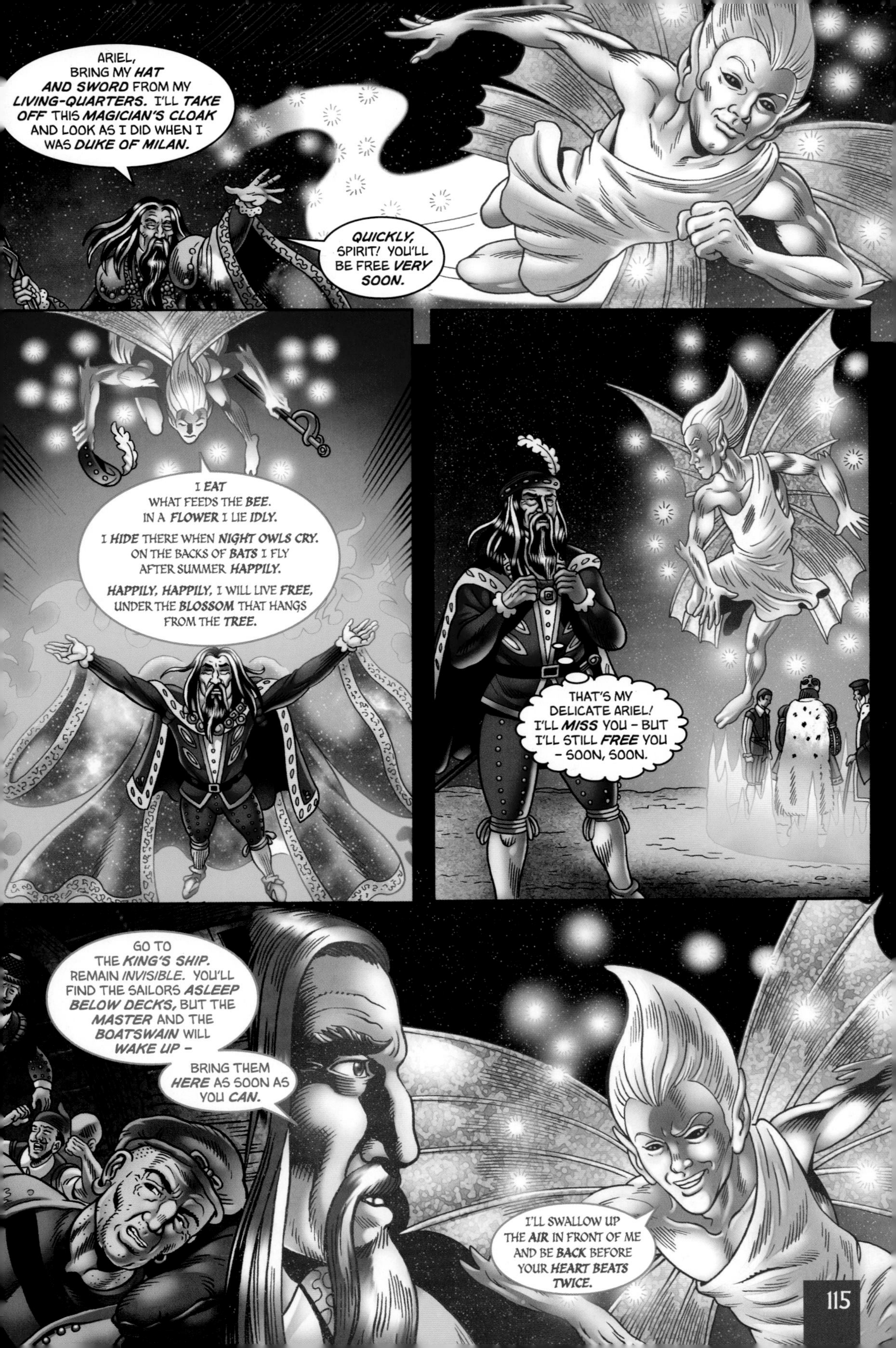
ARIEL, BRING MY HAT AND SWORD FROM MY LIVING-QUARTERS. I'LL TAKE OFF THIS MAGICIAN'S CLOAK AND LOOK AS I DID WHEN I WAS DUKE OF MILAN.
QUICKLY, SPIRIT! YOU'LL BE FREE VERY SOON.
I EAT WHAT FEEDS THE BEE. IN A FLOWER I LIE IDLY.
I HIDE THERE WHEN NIGHT OWLS CRY. ON THE BACKS OF BATS I FLY AFTER SUMMER HAPPILY.
HAPPILY, HAPPILY, I WILL LIVE FREE, UNDER THE BLOSSOM THAT HANGS FROM THE TREE.
THAT'S MY DELICATE ARIEL! I'LL MISS YOU – BUT I'LL STILL FREE YOU – SOON, SOON.
GO TO THE KING'S SHIP. REMAIN INVISIBLE. YOU'LL FIND THE SAILORS ASLEEP BELOW DECKS, BUT THE MASTER AND THE BOATSWAIN WILL WAKE UP –
BRING THEM HERE AS SOON AS YOU CAN.
I'LL SWALLOW UP THE AIR IN FRONT OF ME AND BE BACK BEFORE YOUR HEART BEATS TWICE.

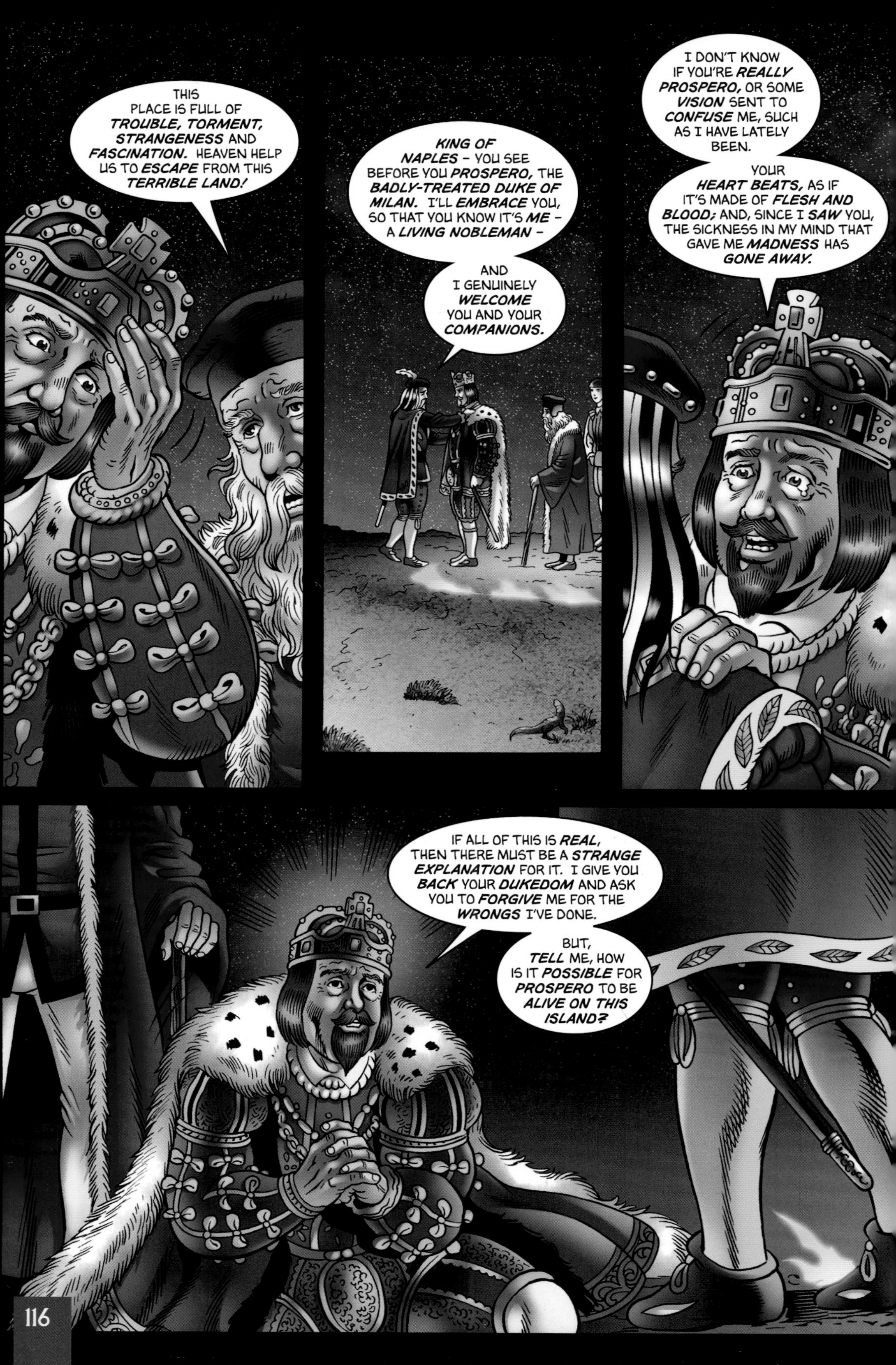

THIS PLACE IS FULL OF *TROUBLE, TORMENT, STRANGENESS* AND *FASCINATION.* HEAVEN HELP US TO *ESCAPE* FROM THIS *TERRIBLE LAND!*
KING OF NAPLES – YOU SEE BEFORE YOU *PROSPERO,* THE *BADLY-TREATED DUKE OF MILAN.* I'LL *EMBRACE* YOU, SO THAT YOU KNOW IT'S *ME* – A *LIVING NOBLEMAN* –
AND I GENUINELY *WELCOME* YOU AND YOUR *COMPANIONS.*
I DON'T KNOW IF YOU'RE *REALLY PROSPERO,* OR SOME *VISION* SENT TO *CONFUSE* ME, SUCH AS I HAVE LATELY BEEN.
YOUR *HEART BEATS,* AS IF IT'S MADE OF *FLESH AND BLOOD;* AND, SINCE I *SAW* YOU, THE SICKNESS IN MY MIND THAT GAVE ME *MADNESS* HAS *GONE AWAY.*
IF ALL OF THIS IS *REAL,* THEN THERE MUST BE A *STRANGE EXPLANATION* FOR IT. I GIVE YOU *BACK* YOUR *DUKEDOM* AND ASK YOU TO *FORGIVE* ME FOR THE *WRONGS* I'VE DONE.
BUT, *TELL* ME, HOW IS IT *POSSIBLE* FOR *PROSPERO* TO BE *ALIVE ON THIS ISLAND?*

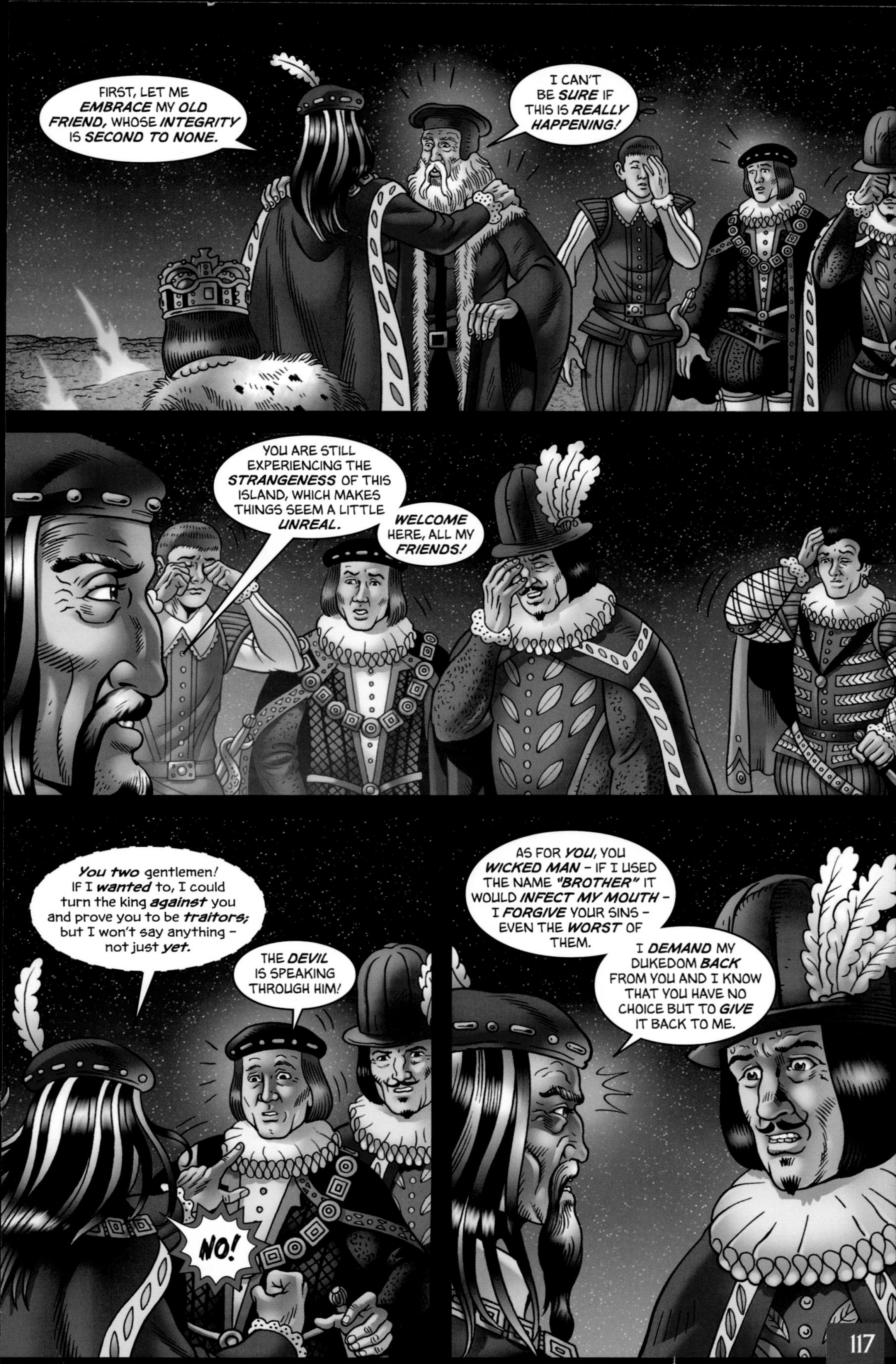
FIRST, LET ME EMBRACE MY OLD FRIEND, WHOSE INTEGRITY IS SECOND TO NONE.
I CAN'T BE SURE IF THIS IS REALLY HAPPENING!
YOU ARE STILL EXPERIENCING THE STRANGENESS OF THIS ISLAND, WHICH MAKES THINGS SEEM A LITTLE UNREAL.
WELCOME HERE, ALL MY FRIENDS!
You two gentlemen! If I wanted to, I could turn the king against you and prove you to be traitors; but I won't say anything – not just yet.
THE DEVIL IS SPEAKING THROUGH HIM!
NO!
AS FOR YOU, YOU WICKED MAN – IF I USED THE NAME "BROTHER" IT WOULD INFECT MY MOUTH – I FORGIVE YOUR SINS – EVEN THE WORST OF THEM.
I DEMAND MY DUKEDOM BACK FROM YOU AND I KNOW THAT YOU HAVE NO CHOICE BUT TO GIVE IT BACK TO ME.

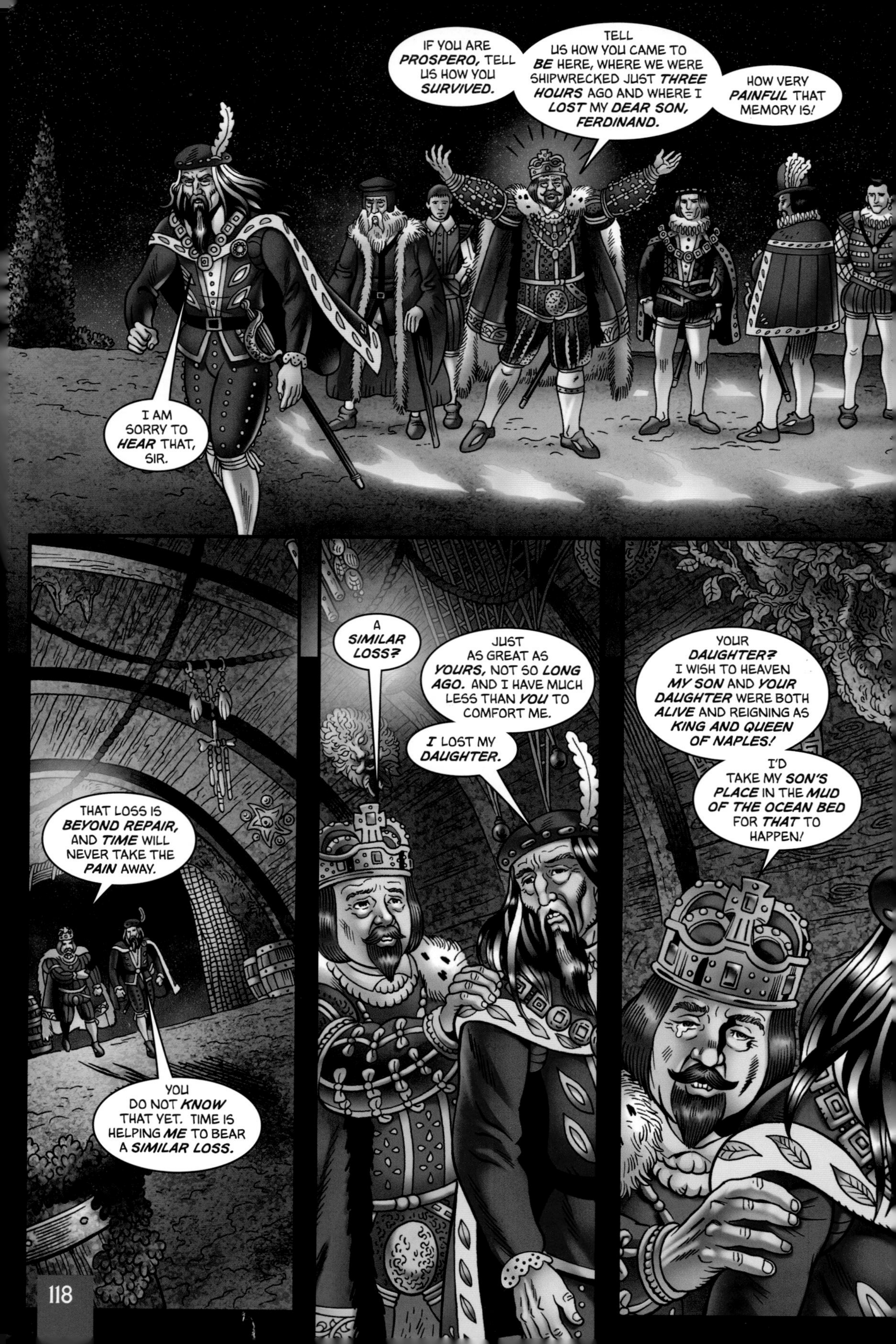
IF YOU ARE PROSPERO, TELL US HOW YOU SURVIVED.
TELL US HOW YOU CAME TO BE HERE, WHERE WE WERE SHIPWRECKED JUST THREE HOURS AGO AND WHERE I LOST MY DEAR SON, FERDINAND.
HOW VERY PAINFUL THAT MEMORY IS!
I AM SORRY TO HEAR THAT, SIR.
THAT LOSS IS BEYOND REPAIR, AND TIME WILL NEVER TAKE THE PAIN AWAY.
YOU DO NOT KNOW THAT YET. TIME IS HELPING ME TO BEAR A SIMILAR LOSS.
A SIMILAR LOSS?
JUST AS GREAT AS YOURS, NOT SO LONG AGO. AND I HAVE MUCH LESS THAN YOU TO COMFORT ME.
I LOST MY DAUGHTER.
YOUR DAUGHTER? I WISH TO HEAVEN MY SON AND YOUR DAUGHTER WERE BOTH ALIVE AND REIGNING AS KING AND QUEEN OF NAPLES!
I'D TAKE MY SON'S PLACE IN THE MUD OF THE OCEAN BED FOR THAT TO HAPPEN!

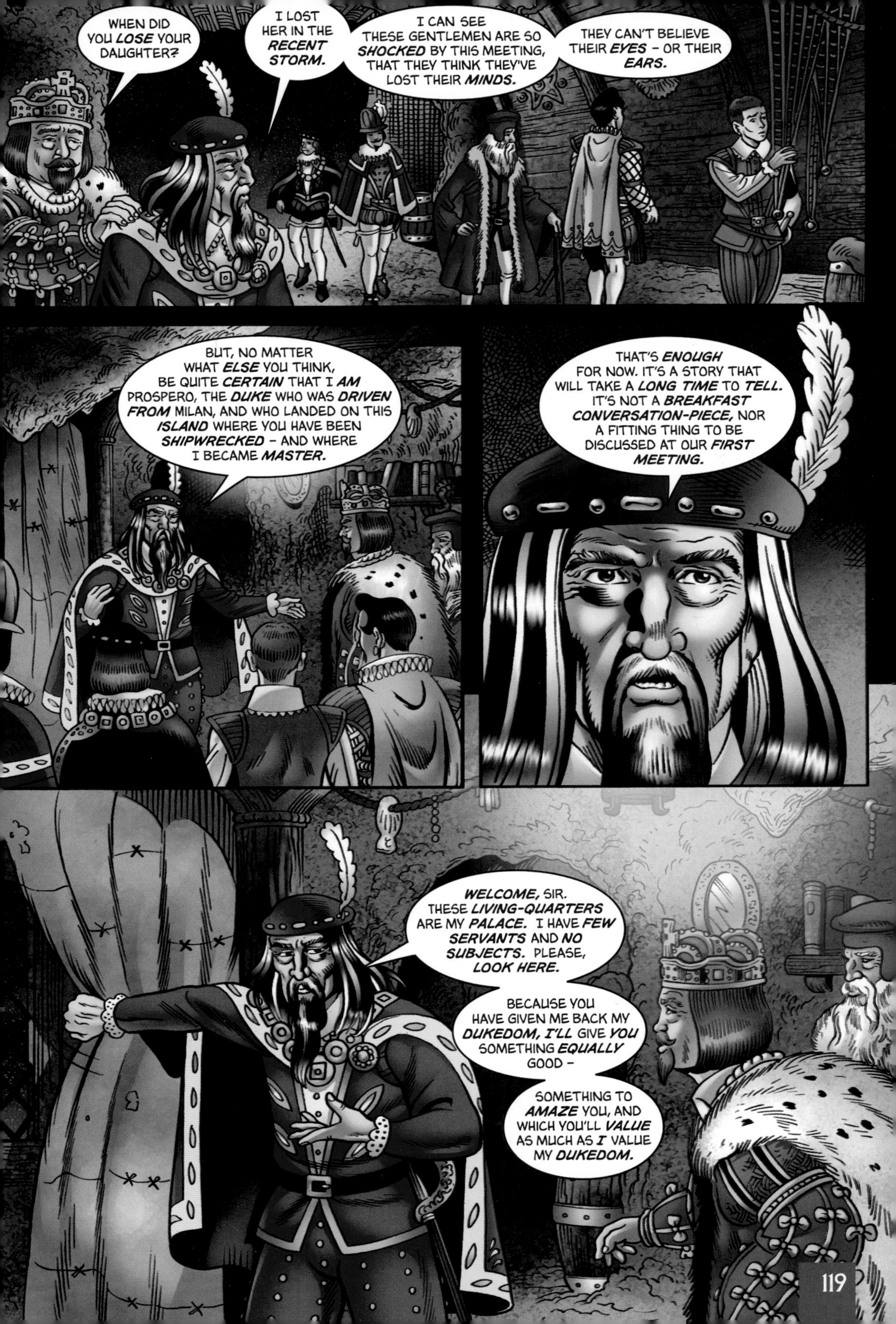
WHEN DID YOU LOSE YOUR DAUGHTER?
I LOST HER IN THE RECENT STORM.
I CAN SEE THESE GENTLEMEN ARE SO SHOCKED BY THIS MEETING, THAT THEY THINK THEY'VE LOST THEIR MINDS.
THEY CAN'T BELIEVE THEIR EYES – OR THEIR EARS.
BUT, NO MATTER WHAT ELSE YOU THINK, BE QUITE CERTAIN THAT I AM PROSPERO, THE DUKE WHO WAS DRIVEN FROM MILAN, AND WHO LANDED ON THIS ISLAND WHERE YOU HAVE BEEN SHIPWRECKED – AND WHERE I BECAME MASTER.
THAT'S ENOUGH FOR NOW. IT'S A STORY THAT WILL TAKE A LONG TIME TO TELL. IT'S NOT A BREAKFAST CONVERSATION-PIECE, NOR A FITTING THING TO BE DISCUSSED AT OUR FIRST MEETING.
WELCOME, SIR. THESE LIVING-QUARTERS ARE MY PALACE. I HAVE FEW SERVANTS AND NO SUBJECTS. PLEASE, LOOK HERE.
BECAUSE YOU HAVE GIVEN ME BACK MY DUKEDOM, I'LL GIVE YOU SOMETHING EQUALLY GOOD –
SOMETHING TO AMAZE YOU, AND WHICH YOU'LL VALUE AS MUCH AS I VALUE MY DUKEDOM.

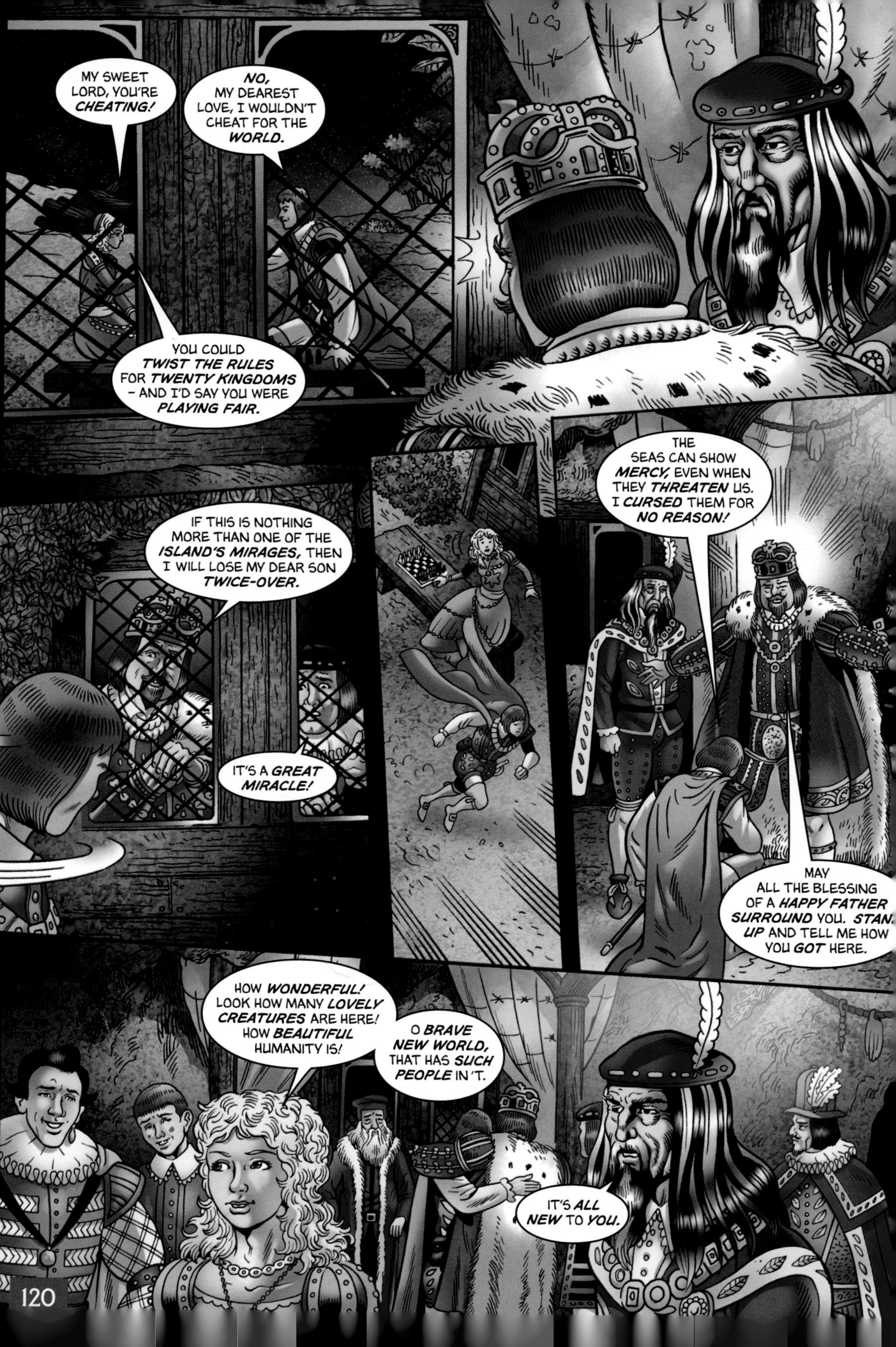
MY SWEET LORD, YOU'RE CHEATING!
NO, MY DEAREST LOVE, I WOULDN'T CHEAT FOR THE WORLD.
YOU COULD TWIST THE RULES FOR TWENTY KINGDOMS - AND I'D SAY YOU WERE PLAYING FAIR.
IF THIS IS NOTHING MORE THAN ONE OF THE ISLAND'S MIRAGES, THEN I WILL LOSE MY DEAR SON TWICE-OVER.
IT'S A GREAT MIRACLE!
THE SEAS CAN SHOW MERCY, EVEN WHEN THEY THREATEN US. I CURSED THEM FOR NO REASON!
MAY ALL THE BLESSING OF A HAPPY FATHER SURROUND YOU. STAN[D] UP AND TELL ME HOW YOU GOT HERE.
HOW WONDERFUL! LOOK HOW MANY LOVELY CREATURES ARE HERE! HOW BEAUTIFUL HUMANITY IS!
O BRAVE NEW WORLD, THAT HAS SUCH PEOPLE IN 'T.
IT'S ALL NEW TO YOU.

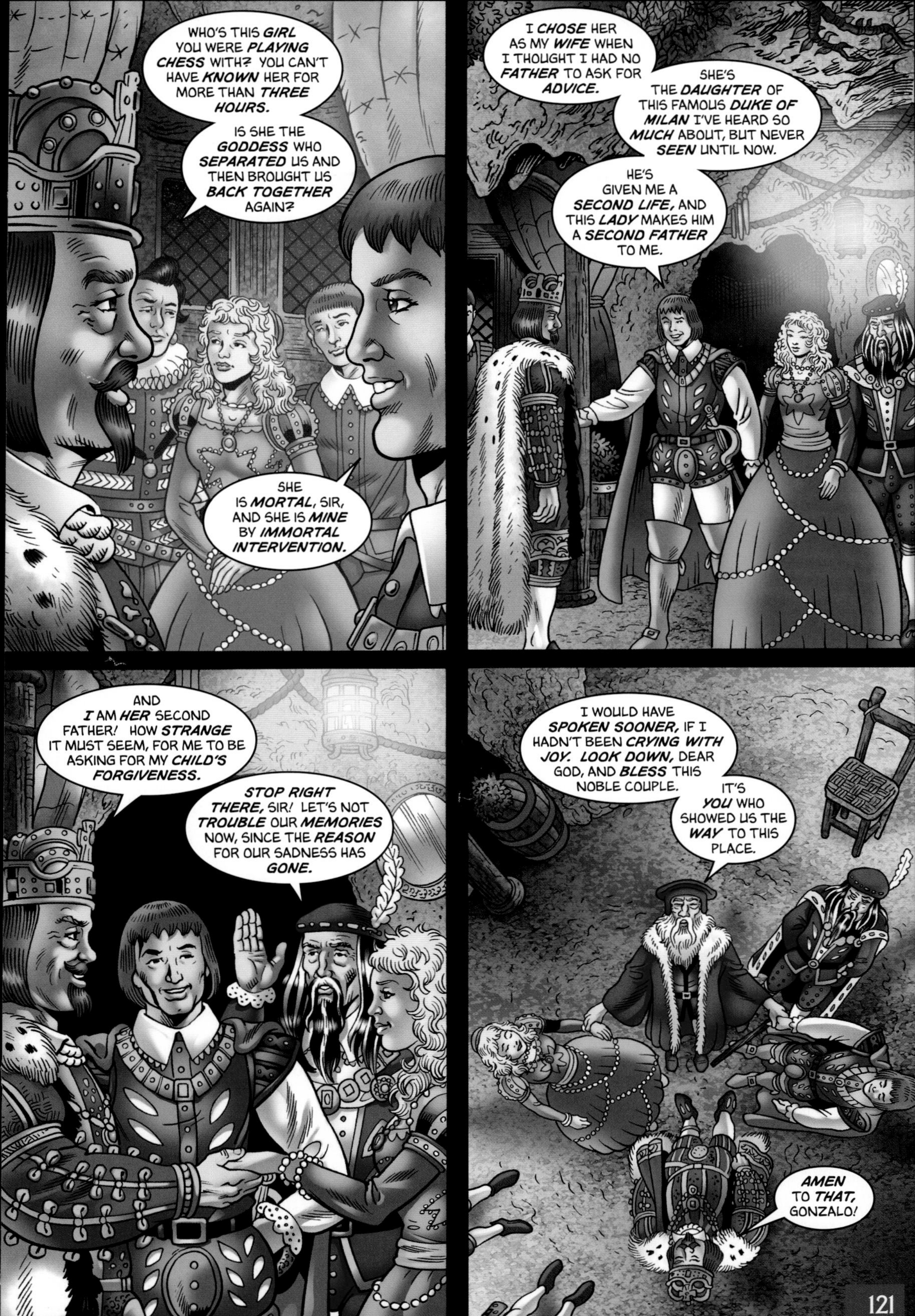
WHO'S THIS GIRL YOU WERE PLAYING CHESS WITH? YOU CAN'T HAVE KNOWN HER FOR MORE THAN THREE HOURS.
IS SHE THE GODDESS WHO SEPARATED US AND THEN BROUGHT US BACK TOGETHER AGAIN?
SHE IS MORTAL, SIR, AND SHE IS MINE BY IMMORTAL INTERVENTION.
I CHOSE HER AS MY WIFE WHEN I THOUGHT I HAD NO FATHER TO ASK FOR ADVICE.
SHE'S THE DAUGHTER OF THIS FAMOUS DUKE OF MILAN I'VE HEARD SO MUCH ABOUT, BUT NEVER SEEN UNTIL NOW.
HE'S GIVEN ME A SECOND LIFE, AND THIS LADY MAKES HIM A SECOND FATHER TO ME.
AND I AM HER SECOND FATHER! HOW STRANGE IT MUST SEEM, FOR ME TO BE ASKING FOR MY CHILD'S FORGIVENESS.
STOP RIGHT THERE, SIR! LET'S NOT TROUBLE OUR MEMORIES NOW, SINCE THE REASON FOR OUR SADNESS HAS GONE.
I WOULD HAVE SPOKEN SOONER, IF I HADN'T BEEN CRYING WITH JOY. LOOK DOWN, DEAR GOD, AND BLESS THIS NOBLE COUPLE.
IT'S YOU WHO SHOWED US THE WAY TO THIS PLACE.
AMEN TO THAT, GONZALO!

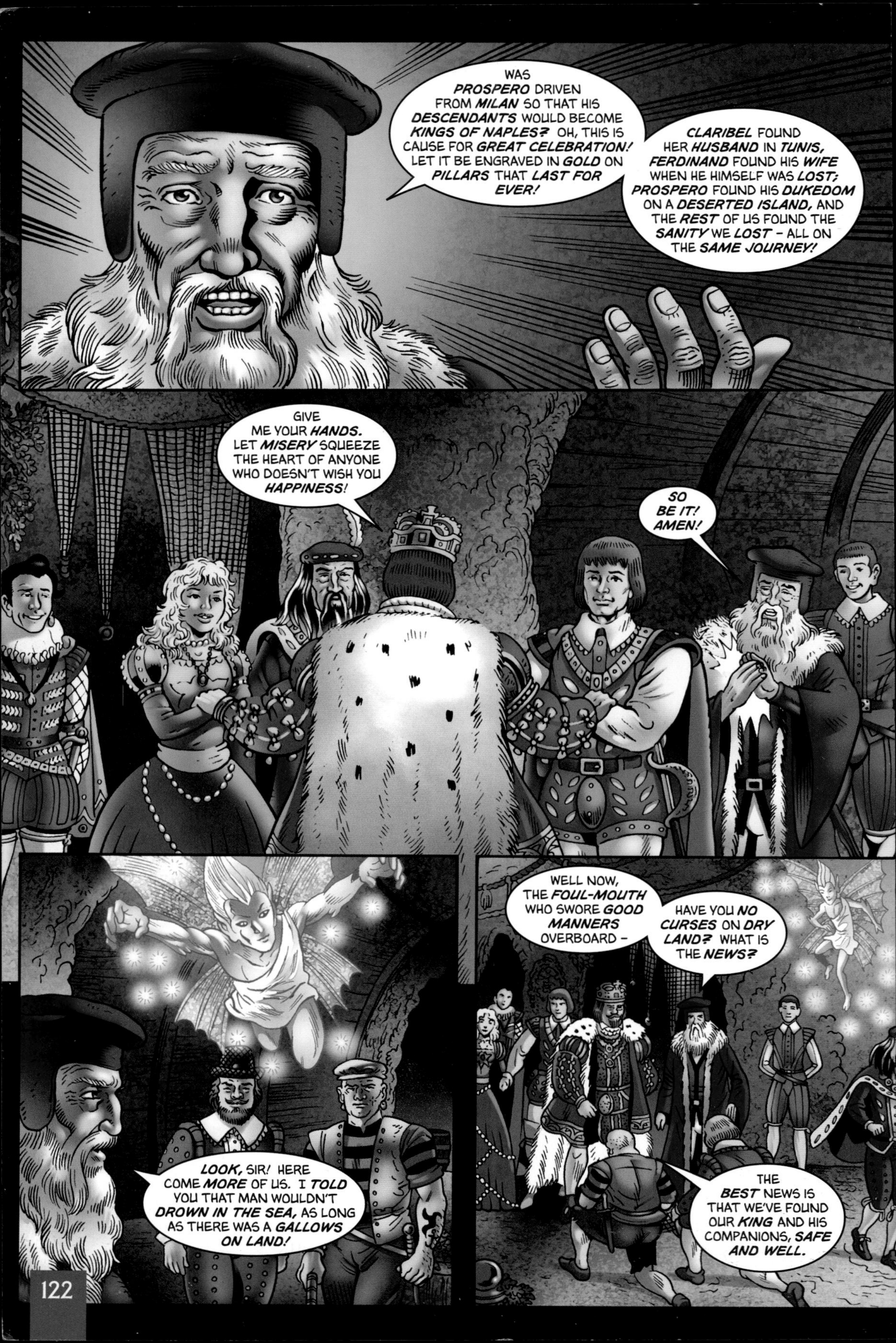
WAS PROSPERO DRIVEN FROM MILAN SO THAT HIS DESCENDANTS WOULD BECOME KINGS OF NAPLES? OH, THIS IS CAUSE FOR GREAT CELEBRATION! LET IT BE ENGRAVED IN GOLD ON PILLARS THAT LAST FOR EVER!
CLARIBEL FOUND HER HUSBAND IN TUNIS, FERDINAND FOUND HIS WIFE WHEN HE HIMSELF WAS LOST; PROSPERO FOUND HIS DUKEDOM ON A DESERTED ISLAND, AND THE REST OF US FOUND THE SANITY WE LOST – ALL ON THE SAME JOURNEY!
GIVE ME YOUR HANDS. LET MISERY SQUEEZE THE HEART OF ANYONE WHO DOESN'T WISH YOU HAPPINESS!
SO BE IT! AMEN!
LOOK, SIR! HERE COME MORE OF US. I TOLD YOU THAT MAN WOULDN'T DROWN IN THE SEA, AS LONG AS THERE WAS A GALLOWS ON LAND!
WELL NOW, THE FOUL-MOUTH WHO SWORE GOOD MANNERS OVERBOARD –
HAVE YOU NO CURSES ON DRY LAND? WHAT IS THE NEWS?
THE BEST NEWS IS THAT WE'VE FOUND OUR KING AND HIS COMPANIONS, SAFE AND WELL.

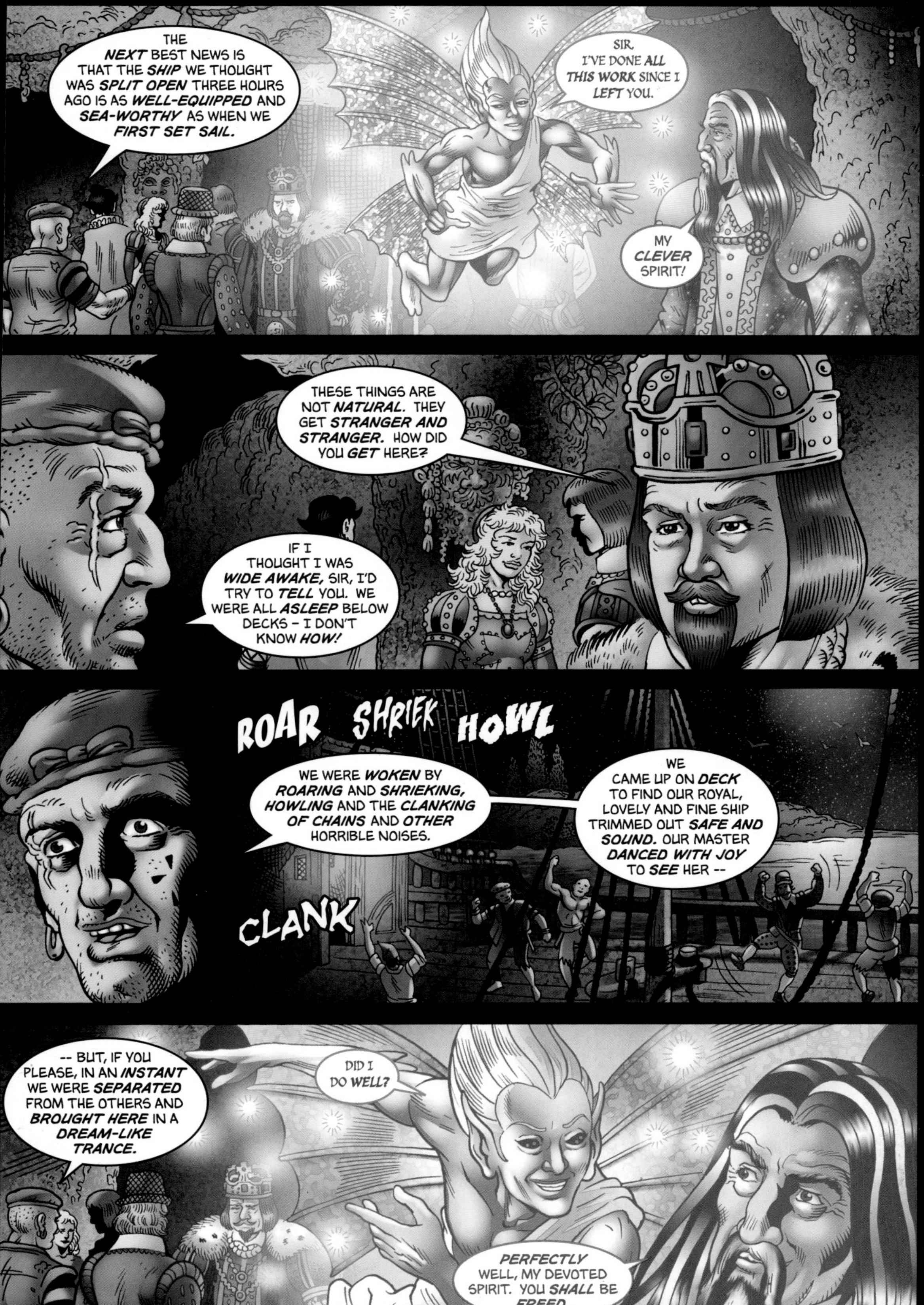
THE NEXT BEST NEWS IS THAT THE SHIP WE THOUGHT WAS SPLIT OPEN THREE HOURS AGO IS AS WELL-EQUIPPED AND SEA-WORTHY AS WHEN WE FIRST SET SAIL.
SIR, I'VE DONE ALL THIS WORK SINCE I LEFT YOU.
MY CLEVER SPIRIT!
THESE THINGS ARE NOT NATURAL. THEY GET STRANGER AND STRANGER. HOW DID YOU GET HERE?
IF I THOUGHT I WAS WIDE AWAKE, SIR, I'D TRY TO TELL YOU. WE WERE ALL ASLEEP BELOW DECKS - I DON'T KNOW HOW!
ROAR SHRIEK HOWL
WE WERE WOKEN BY ROARING AND SHRIEKING, HOWLING AND THE CLANKING OF CHAINS AND OTHER HORRIBLE NOISES.
WE CAME UP ON DECK TO FIND OUR ROYAL, LOVELY AND FINE SHIP TRIMMED OUT SAFE AND SOUND. OUR MASTER DANCED WITH JOY TO SEE HER --
CLANK
-- BUT, IF YOU PLEASE, IN AN INSTANT WE WERE SEPARATED FROM THE OTHERS AND BROUGHT HERE IN A DREAM-LIKE TRANCE.
DID I DO WELL?
PERFECTLY WELL, MY DEVOTED SPIRIT. YOU SHALL BE FREED.

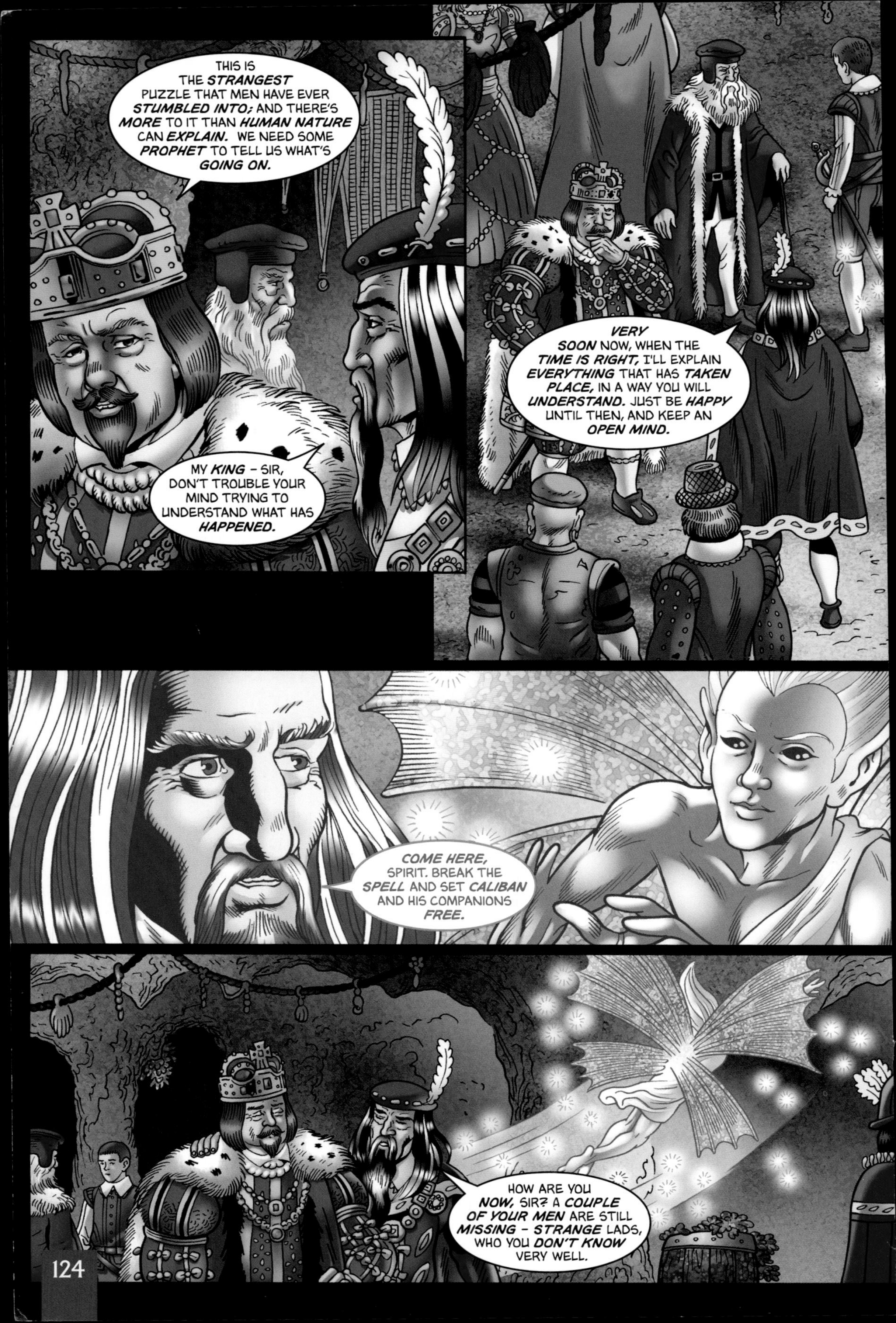
THIS IS THE STRANGEST PUZZLE THAT MEN HAVE EVER STUMBLED INTO; AND THERE'S MORE TO IT THAN HUMAN NATURE CAN EXPLAIN. WE NEED SOME PROPHET TO TELL US WHAT'S GOING ON.
MY KING - SIR, DON'T TROUBLE YOUR MIND TRYING TO UNDERSTAND WHAT HAS HAPPENED.
VERY SOON NOW, WHEN THE TIME IS RIGHT, I'LL EXPLAIN EVERYTHING THAT HAS TAKEN PLACE, IN A WAY YOU WILL UNDERSTAND. JUST BE HAPPY UNTIL THEN, AND KEEP AN OPEN MIND.
COME HERE, SPIRIT. BREAK THE SPELL AND SET CALIBAN AND HIS COMPANIONS FREE.
HOW ARE YOU NOW, SIR? A COUPLE OF YOUR MEN ARE STILL MISSING - STRANGE LADS, WHO YOU DON'T KNOW VERY WELL.

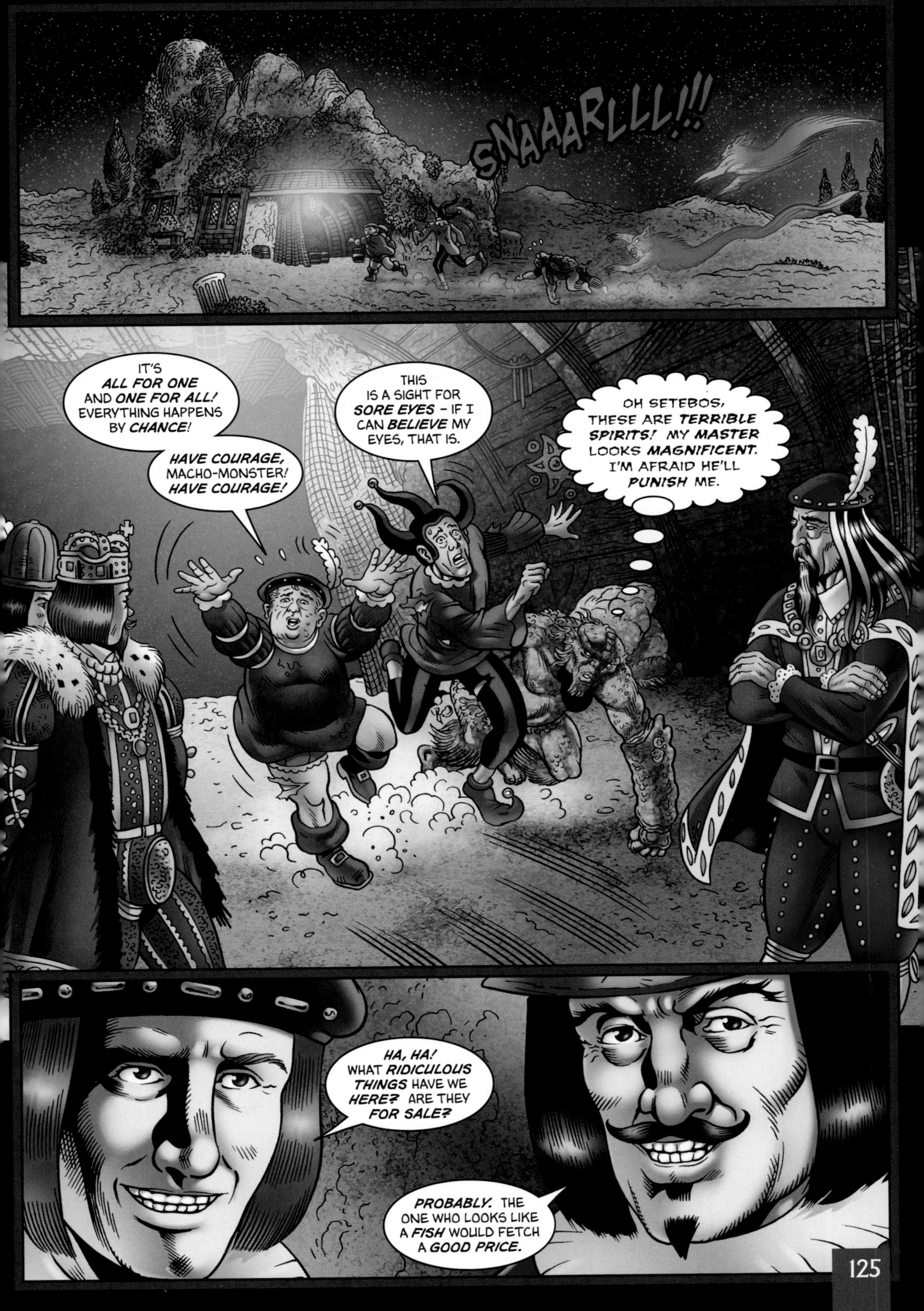
SNAAARLLL!!!
IT'S ALL FOR ONE AND ONE FOR ALL! EVERYTHING HAPPENS BY CHANCE!
HAVE COURAGE, MACHO-MONSTER! HAVE COURAGE!
THIS IS A SIGHT FOR SORE EYES – IF I CAN BELIEVE MY EYES, THAT IS.
OH SETEBOS, THESE ARE TERRIBLE SPIRITS! MY MASTER LOOKS MAGNIFICENT. I'M AFRAID HE'LL PUNISH ME.
HA, HA! WHAT RIDICULOUS THINGS HAVE WE HERE? ARE THEY FOR SALE?
PROBABLY. THE ONE WHO LOOKS LIKE A FISH WOULD FETCH A GOOD PRICE.

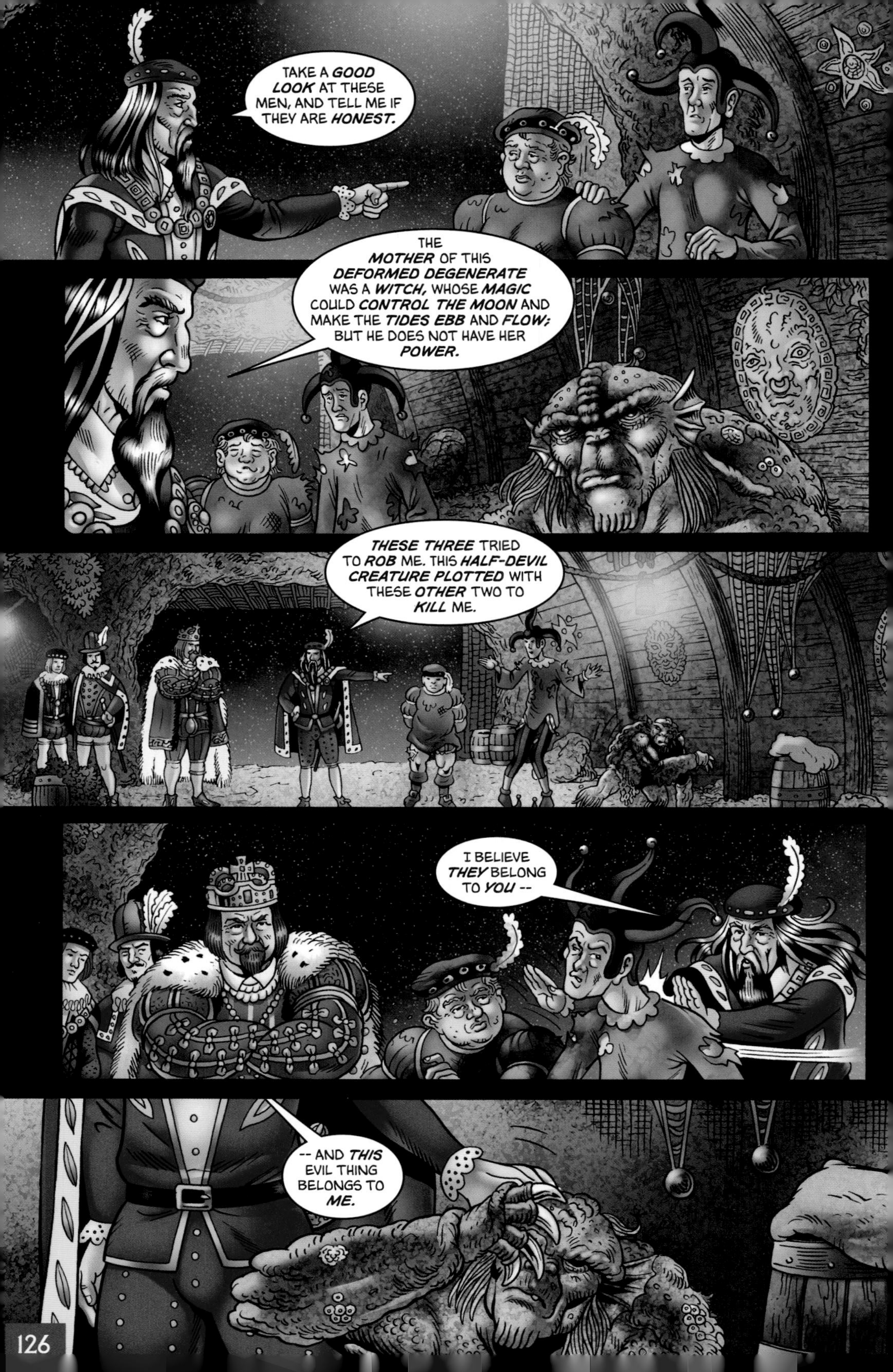
TAKE A GOOD LOOK AT THESE MEN, AND TELL ME IF THEY ARE HONEST.
THE MOTHER OF THIS DEFORMED DEGENERATE WAS A WITCH, WHOSE MAGIC COULD CONTROL THE MOON AND MAKE THE TIDES EBB AND FLOW; BUT HE DOES NOT HAVE HER POWER.
THESE THREE TRIED TO ROB ME. THIS HALF-DEVIL CREATURE PLOTTED WITH THESE OTHER TWO TO KILL ME.
I BELIEVE THEY BELONG TO YOU --
-- AND THIS EVIL THING BELONGS TO ME.

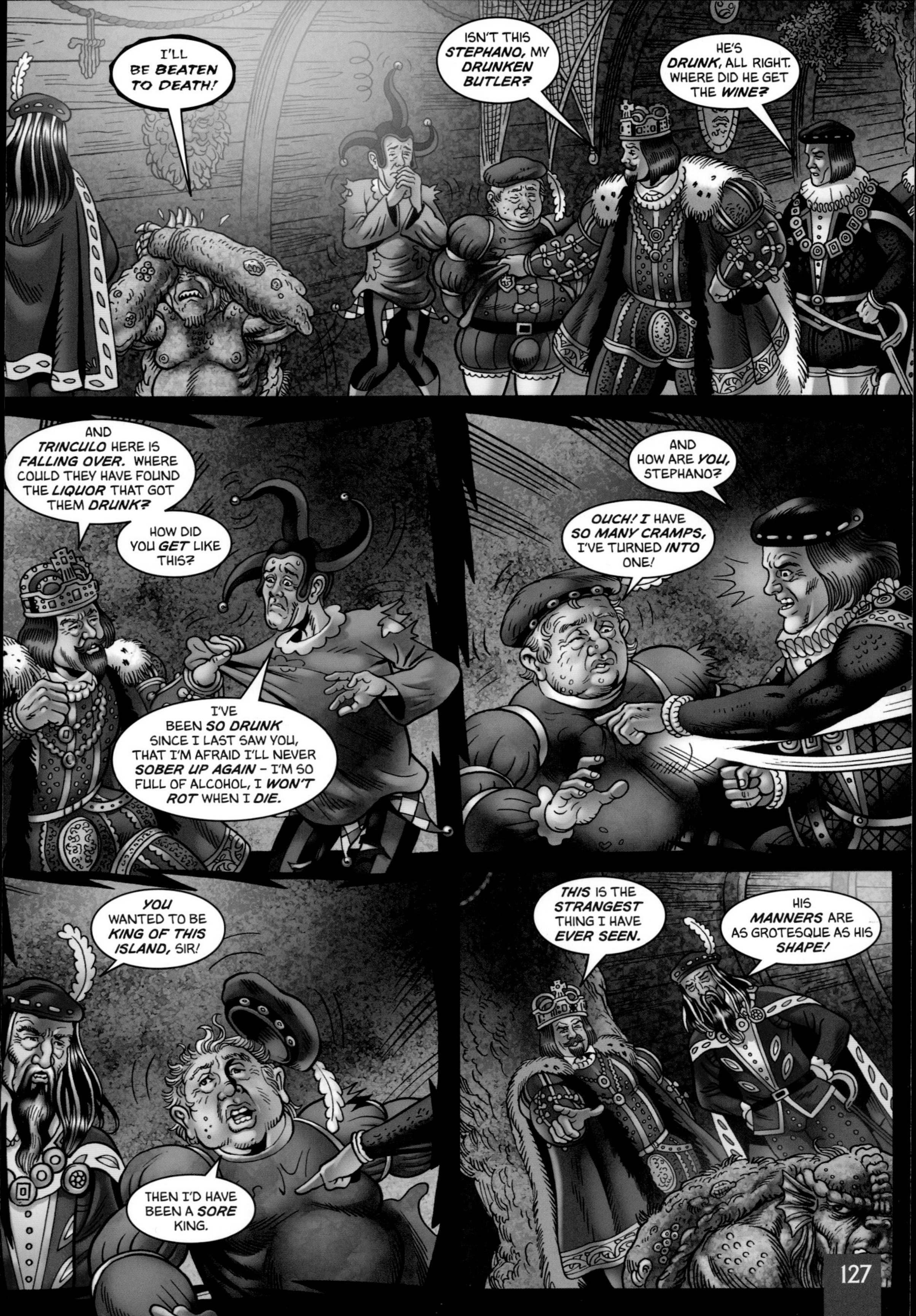
I'LL BE BEATEN TO DEATH!
ISN'T THIS STEPHANO, MY DRUNKEN BUTLER?
HE'S DRUNK, ALL RIGHT. WHERE DID HE GET THE WINE?
AND TRINCULO HERE IS FALLING OVER. WHERE COULD THEY HAVE FOUND THE LIQUOR THAT GOT THEM DRUNK?
HOW DID YOU GET LIKE THIS?
I'VE BEEN SO DRUNK SINCE I LAST SAW YOU, THAT I'M AFRAID I'LL NEVER SOBER UP AGAIN – I'M SO FULL OF ALCOHOL, I WON'T ROT WHEN I DIE.
AND HOW ARE YOU, STEPHANO?
OUCH! I HAVE SO MANY CRAMPS, I'VE TURNED INTO ONE!
YOU WANTED TO BE KING OF THIS ISLAND, SIR!
THEN I'D HAVE BEEN A SORE KING.
THIS IS THE STRANGEST THING I HAVE EVER SEEN.
HIS MANNERS ARE AS GROTESQUE AS HIS SHAPE!

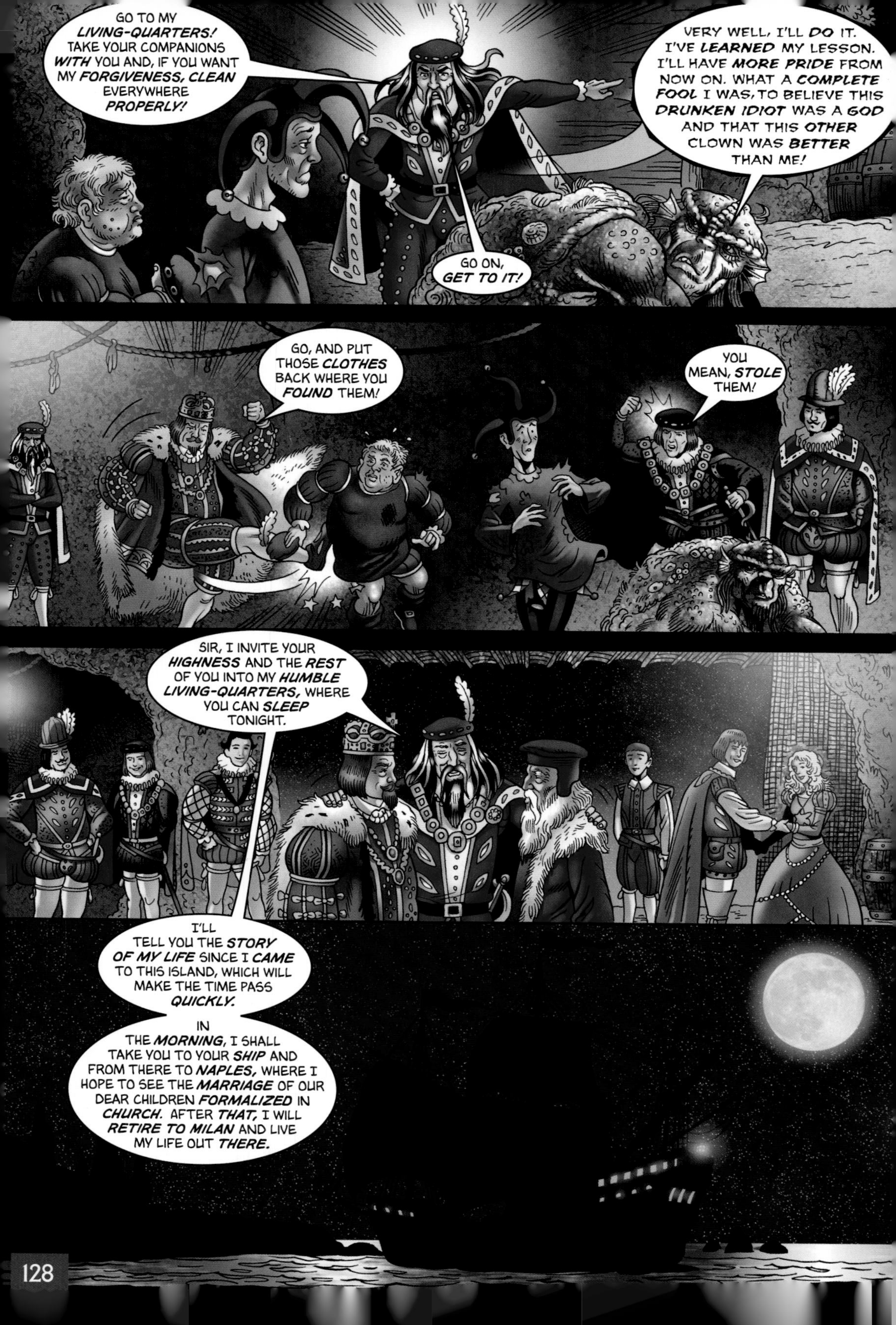
GO TO MY LIVING-QUARTERS! TAKE YOUR COMPANIONS WITH YOU AND, IF YOU WANT MY FORGIVENESS, CLEAN EVERYWHERE PROPERLY!
GO ON, GET TO IT!
VERY WELL, I'LL DO IT. I'VE LEARNED MY LESSON. I'LL HAVE MORE PRIDE FROM NOW ON. WHAT A COMPLETE FOOL I WAS, TO BELIEVE THIS DRUNKEN IDIOT WAS A GOD AND THAT THIS OTHER CLOWN WAS BETTER THAN ME!
GO, AND PUT THOSE CLOTHES BACK WHERE YOU FOUND THEM!
YOU MEAN, STOLE THEM!
SIR, I INVITE YOUR HIGHNESS AND THE REST OF YOU INTO MY HUMBLE LIVING-QUARTERS, WHERE YOU CAN SLEEP TONIGHT.
I'LL TELL YOU THE STORY OF MY LIFE SINCE I CAME TO THIS ISLAND, WHICH WILL MAKE THE TIME PASS QUICKLY.
IN THE MORNING, I SHALL TAKE YOU TO YOUR SHIP AND FROM THERE TO NAPLES, WHERE I HOPE TO SEE THE MARRIAGE OF OUR DEAR CHILDREN FORMALIZED IN CHURCH. AFTER THAT, I WILL RETIRE TO MILAN AND LIVE MY LIFE OUT THERE.

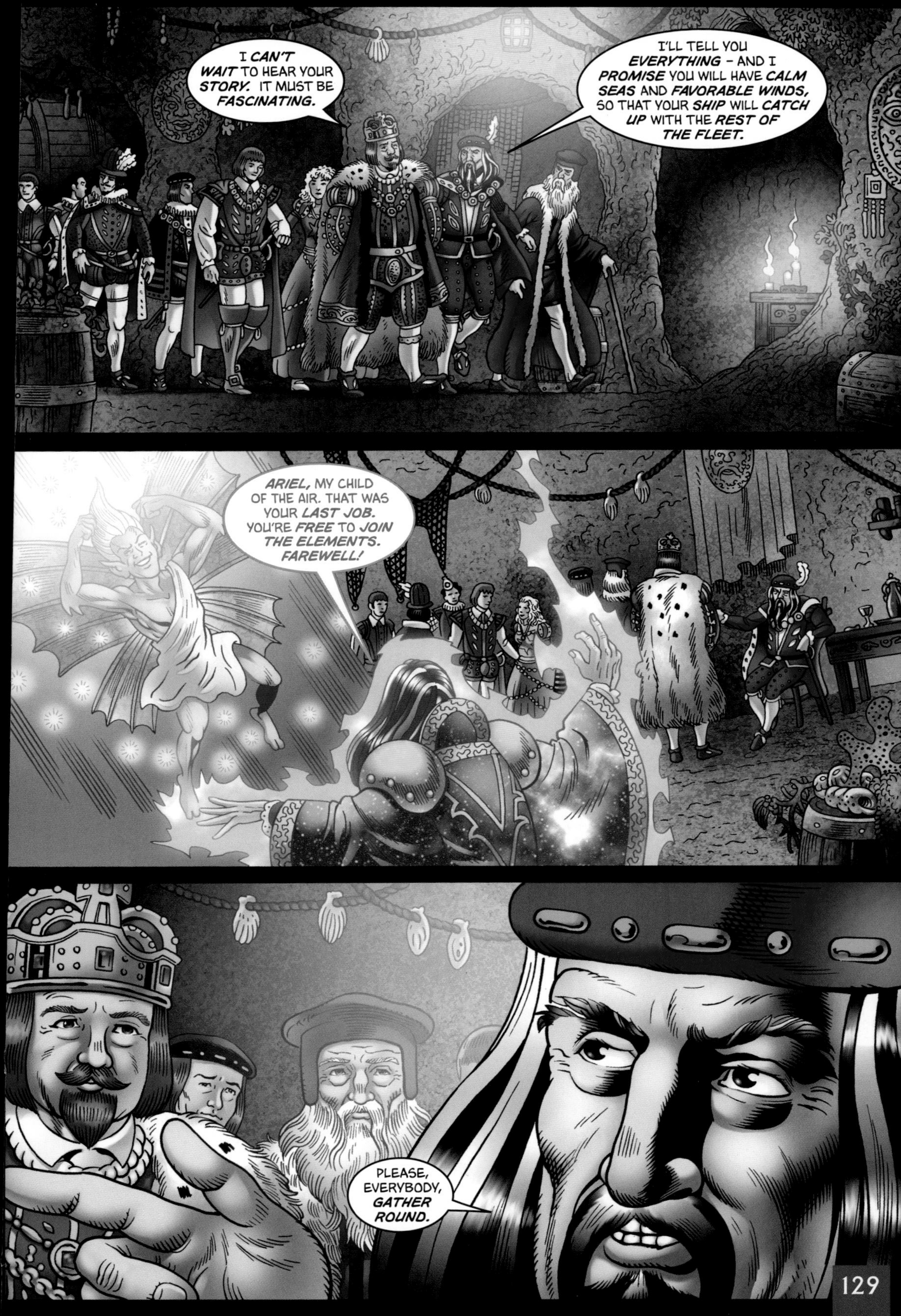
I CAN'T WAIT TO HEAR YOUR STORY. IT MUST BE FASCINATING.
I'LL TELL YOU EVERYTHING – AND I PROMISE YOU WILL HAVE CALM SEAS AND FAVORABLE WINDS, SO THAT YOUR SHIP WILL CATCH UP WITH THE REST OF THE FLEET.
ARIEL, MY CHILD OF THE AIR. THAT WAS YOUR LAST JOB. YOU'RE FREE TO JOIN THE ELEMENTS. FAREWELL!
PLEASE, EVERYBODY, GATHER ROUND.

Epilogue

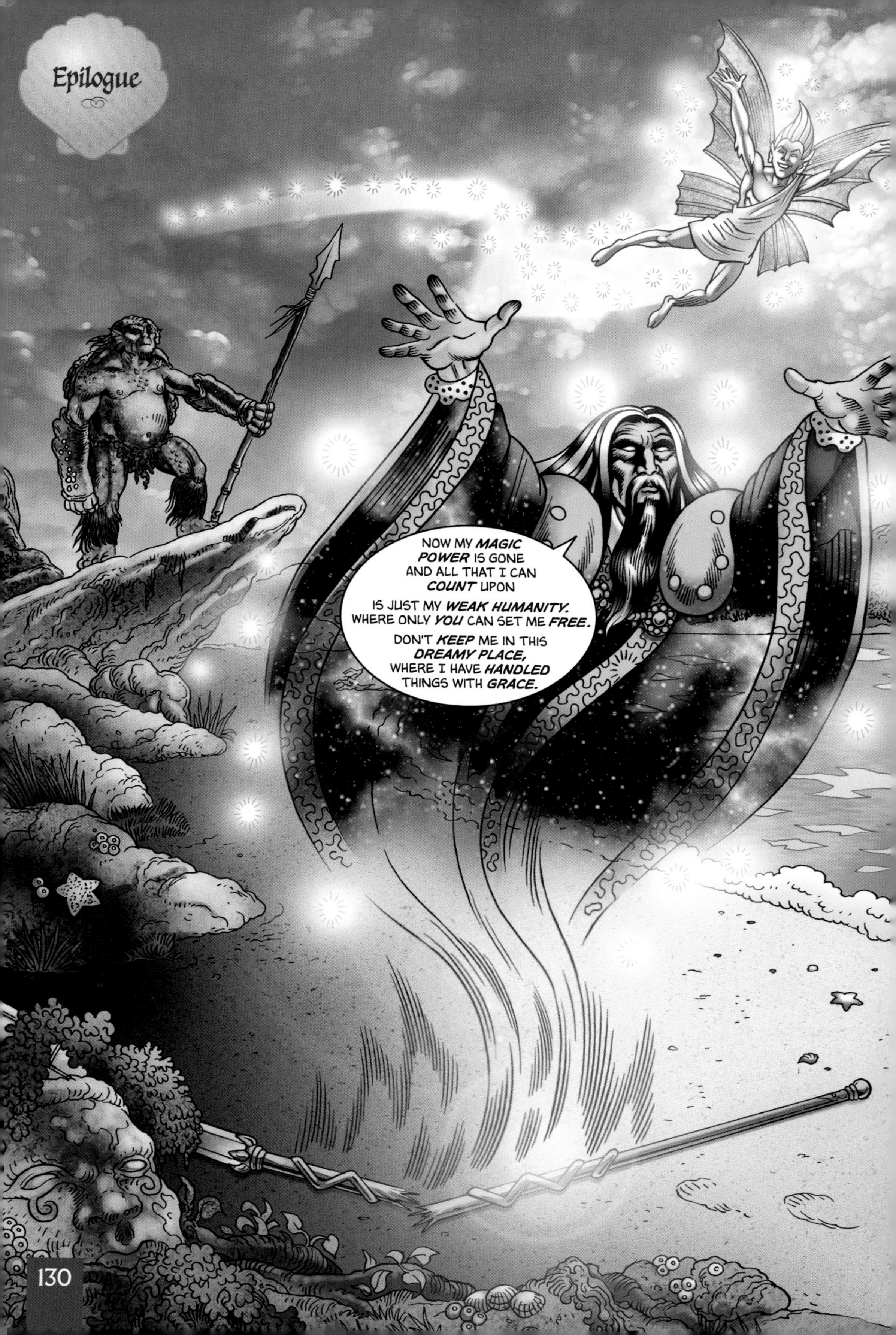
NOW MY MAGIC POWER IS GONE
AND ALL THAT I CAN COUNT UPON
IS JUST MY WEAK HUMANITY.
WHERE ONLY YOU CAN SET ME FREE.
DON'T KEEP ME IN THIS DREAMY PLACE,
WHERE I HAVE HANDLED THINGS WITH GRACE.

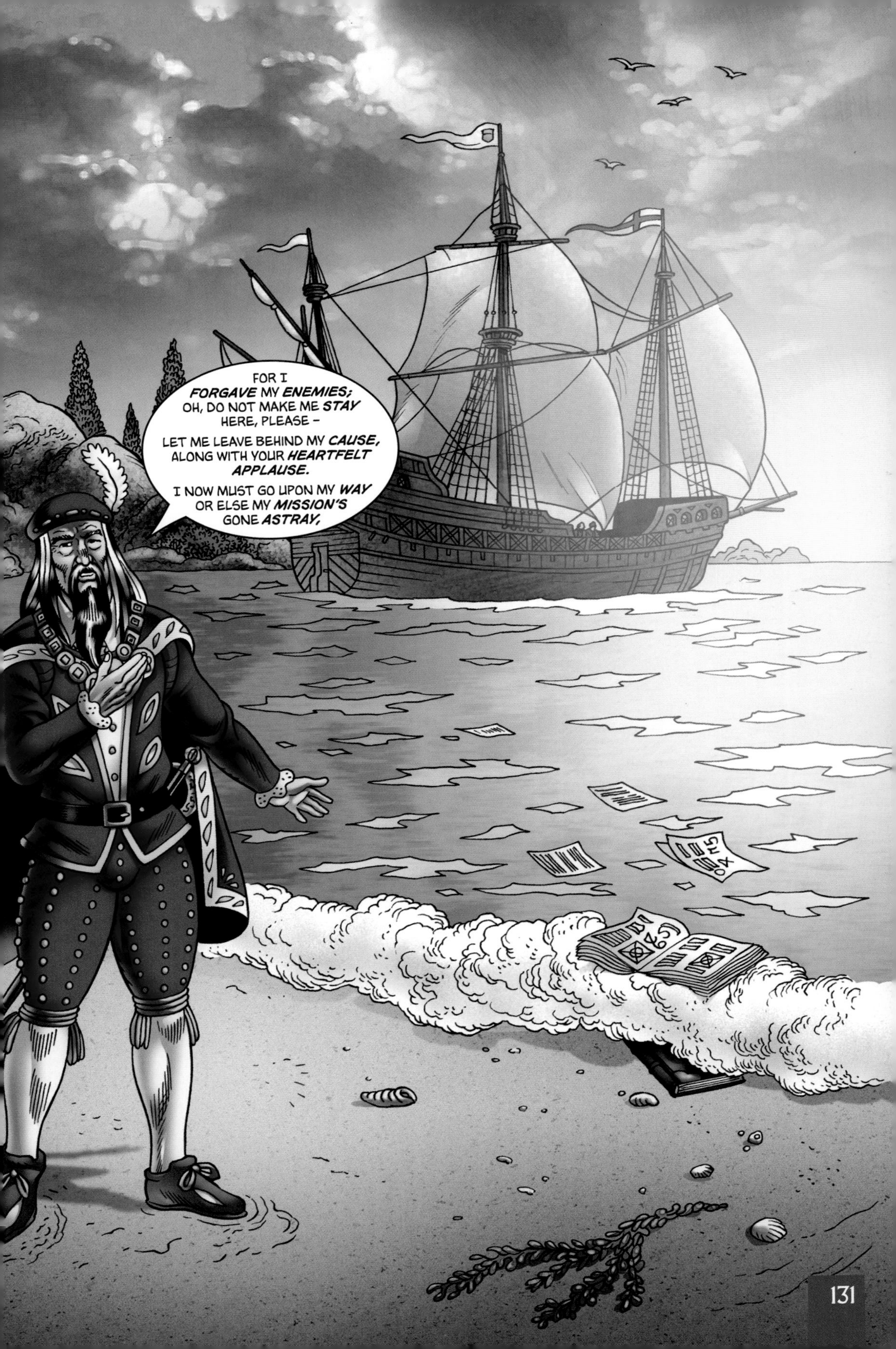
FOR I FORGAVE MY ENEMIES; OH, DO NOT MAKE ME STAY HERE, PLEASE – LET ME LEAVE BEHIND MY CAUSE, ALONG WITH YOUR HEARTFELT APPLAUSE. I NOW MUST GO UPON MY WAY OR ELSE MY MISSION'S GONE ASTRAY,

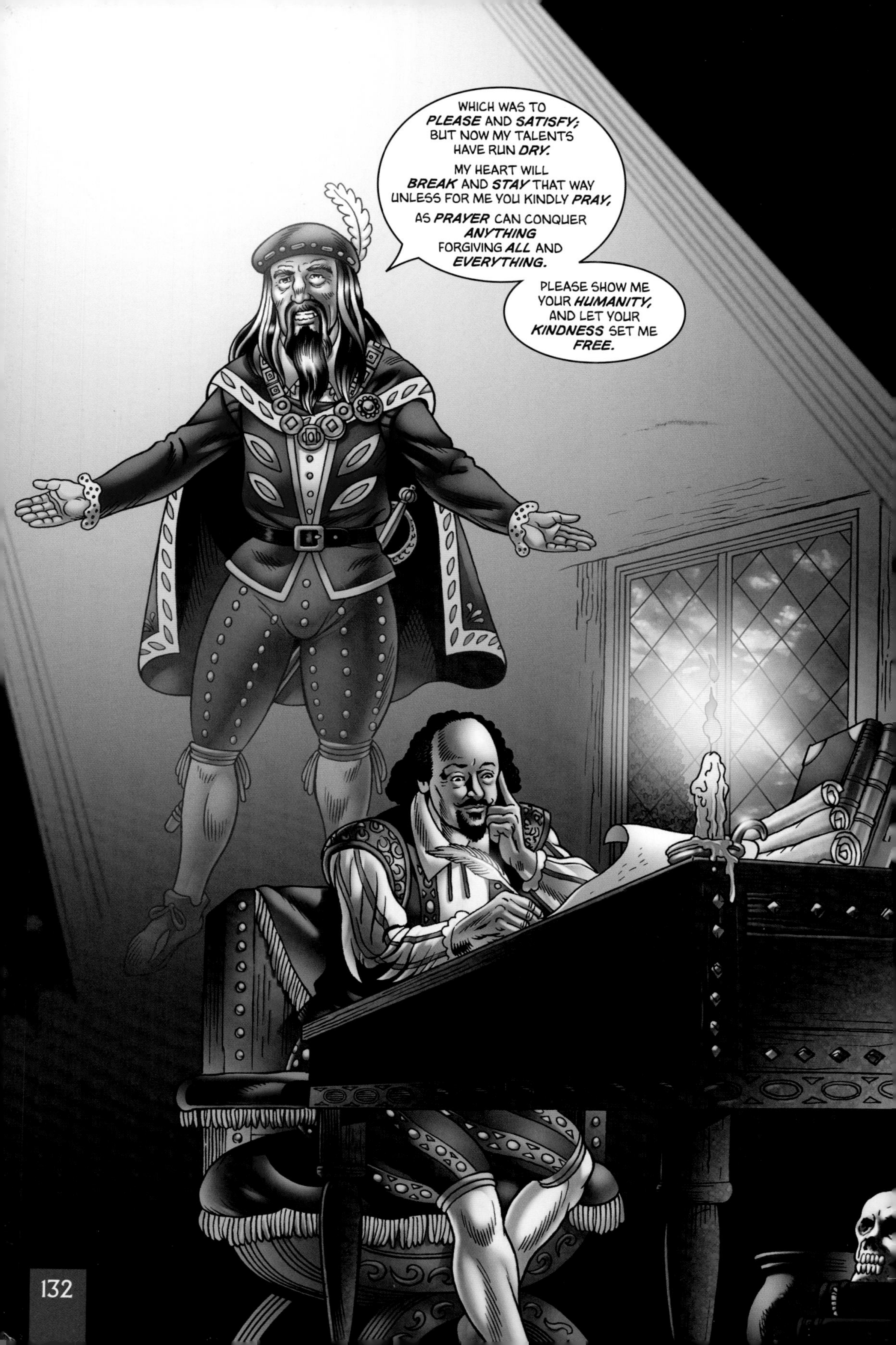
WHICH WAS TO PLEASE AND SATISFY; BUT NOW MY TALENTS HAVE RUN DRY.
MY HEART WILL BREAK AND STAY THAT WAY UNLESS FOR ME YOU KINDLY PRAY,
AS PRAYER CAN CONQUER ANYTHING FORGIVING ALL AND EVERYTHING.
PLEASE SHOW ME YOUR HUMANITY, AND LET YOUR KINDNESS SET ME FREE.

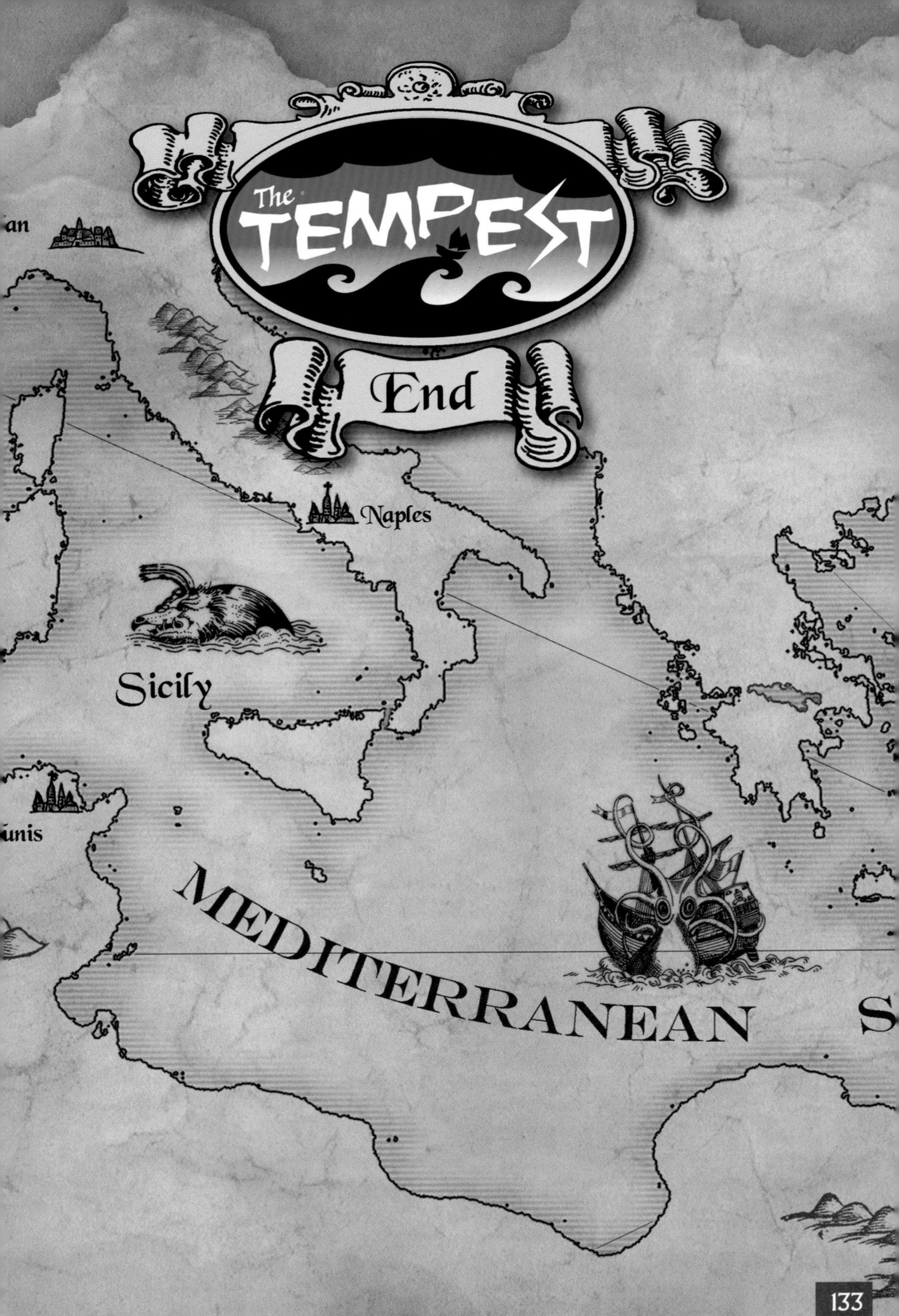
The TEMPEST
End
Naples
Sicily
MEDITERRANEAN

William Shakespeare

(c.1564 - 1616 AD)

National Portrait Gallery, London

Shakespeare is, without question, the world's most famous playwright. Yet, despite his fame, very few records and artifacts exist for him — we don't even know the exact date of his birth! April 23, 1564 (St George's Day) is taken to be his birthday, as this was three days before his baptism (for which we do have a record). Records also tell us that he died on the same date in 1616, aged fifty-two.

The life of William Shakespeare can be divided into three acts.

Act One – Stratford-upon-Avon

William was the eldest son of tradesman John Shakespeare and Mary Arden, and the third of eight children (he had two older sisters). The Shakespeares were a respectable family. The year after William was born, John (who made gloves and traded leather) became an alderman of Stratford-upon-Avon, and four years later he became High Bailiff (or mayor) of the town.

Little is known of William's childhood. He learned to read and write at the local primary school, and later is believed to have attended the local grammar school, where he studied Latin and English Literature. In 1582, aged eighteen, William married a local farmer's daughter, Anne Hathaway. Anne was eight years his senior and three months pregnant. During their marriage they had three children: Susanna, born on

May 26, 1583, and twins, Hamnet and Judith, born on February 2, 1585. Hamnet (William's only son) died in 1596, aged eleven, from Bubonic Plague.

Act Two – London

Five years into his marriage, in 1587, William's wife and children stayed in Stratford, while he moved to London. He appeared as an actor at *The Theatre* (England's first permanent theater) and gave public recitals of his own poems; but it was his playwriting that created the most interest. His fame soon spread far and wide. When Queen Elizabeth I died in 1603, the new King James I (who was already King James VI of Scotland) gave royal consent for Shakespeare's acting company, *The Lord Chamberlain's Men* to be called *The King's Men* in return for entertaining the court. This association was to shape a

number of plays, such as *Macbeth*, which was written to please the Scottish King.

William Shakespeare is attributed with writing and collaborating on 38 plays, 154 sonnets and 5 poems, in just twenty-three years between 1590 and 1613. No original manuscript exists for any of his plays, making it hard to accurately date any of them. Printing was still in its infancy, and plays tended to change as they were performed. Shakespeare would write manuscript for the actors and continue to refine them over a number of performances. The plays we know today have survived from written copies taken at various stages of each play and usually written by the actors from memory. This has given rise to variations in texts of what is now known as "quarto" versions of the plays, until we reach the first official printing of each play in the 1623 *"folio" Mr William Shakespeare's Comedies, Histories, & Tragedies.* His last solo-authored work was *The Tempest* in 1611, which was only followed by collaborative work on two plays (*Henry VIII* and *Two Noble Kinsmen*) with John Fletcher. Shakespeare is strongly associated with the famous *Globe Theatre.* Built by his troupe in 1599, it became his "spiritual home", with thousands of people crammed into the small space for each performance. There were 3,000 people in the building in 1613 when a cannon-shot during a performance of *Henry VIII* set fire to the thatched roof and the entire theater was burned to the ground. Although it was rebuilt a year later, it marked an end to Shakespeare's writing and to his time in London.

Act Three - Retirement

Shortly after the 1613 accident at *The Globe,* Shakespeare left the capital and returned to live once more with his family in Stratford-upon-Avon. He died on April 23, 1616 and was buried two days later at the Church of the Holy Trinity (the same church where he had been baptized fifty-two years earlier). The cause of his death remains unknown.

Epilogue

At the time of his death, Shakespeare had substantial properties, which he bestowed on his family and associates from the theater. He had no son to inherit his wealth, and he left the majority of his possessions to his eldest daughter Susanna. Curiously, the only thing that he left to his wife Anne was his second-best bed! (although she continued to live in the family home after his death). William Shakespeare's last direct descendant died in 1670. She was his granddaughter, Elizabeth.

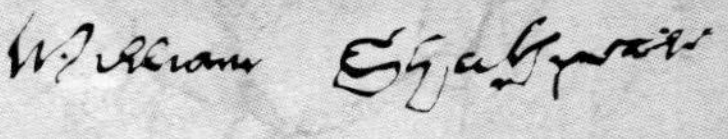

Shakespeare Birthplace Trust

As so few relics survive from Shakespeare's life, it is amazing that the house where he was born and raised remains intact. It is owned and cared for by the Shakespeare Birthplace Trust, which looks after a number of houses in the area:

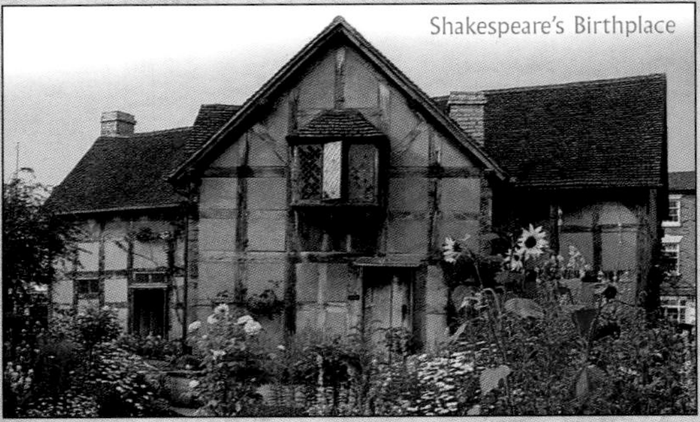
Shakespeare's Birthplace

- Shakespeare's Birthplace.
- Mary Arden's Farm: The childhood home of Shakespeare's mother.
- Anne Hathaway's Cottage: The childhood home of Shakespeare's wife.
- Hall's Croft: The home of Shakespeare's eldest daughter, Susanna.
- New Place: Only the grounds exist of the house where Shakespeare died in 1616.
- Nash's House: The home of Shakespeare's granddaughter.

www.shakespeare.org.uk

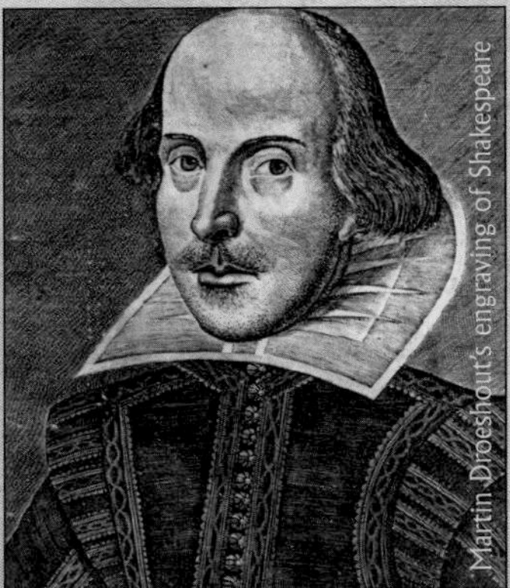
Martin Droeshout's engraving of Shakespeare

Formed in 1847, the Trust also works to promote Shakespeare around the world. In early 2009, it announced that it had found a new Shakespeare portrait, believed to have been painted within his lifetime, with a trail of provenance that links it to Shakespeare himself.

It is accepted that Martin Droeshout's engraving (left) that appears on the First Folio of 1623 is an authentic likeness of Shakespeare because the people involved in its publication would have personally known him. This new portrait (once owned by Henry Wriothesley, 3rd Earl of Southampton, one of Shakespeare's most loyal supporters) is so similar in all facial aspects that it is now suspected to have been the source that Droeshout used for his famous engraving. **www.shakespearefound.org.uk**

History of The Tempest

The Tempest was almost certainly Shakespeare's last solo-authored work. Only *Henry VIII* and *Two Noble Kinsmen* were to follow, and they were both collaborations with John Fletcher. It is also the only Shakespeare play that features an original story — all of his other plays have very clear sources. Perhaps it is these two factors that prompt many to believe it to be his finest work — a view shared by the publishers of his first collected works (the "First Folio" of 1623), who gave pride of place to the play.

As with all of his plays, an accurate dating of *The Tempest* is near-impossible; however, we know that it was performed for King James I in November 1611, and this leads us to believe it was written earlier that same year (it was such a success that it was played again the following year to celebrate the betrothal of King James' daughter Elizabeth).

Shakespeare effectively retired after writing *The Tempest*, returning to Stratford-upon-Avon to live his final few years close to his family. Prospero's closing speech of the play appears to be a metaphor for Shakespeare "saying goodbye" to the profession and bowing out from the theater altogether. The fact that he was soon to write his will and tidy up his business affairs means that this is unlikely to have been a coincidence.

Although it was performed in court, it wasn't written for any particular royal performance; however, it was almost certainly written with the King and his daughter in mind. Not only does it feature magic and witchcraft to pander to the King's interests, but it portrays an all-seeing and all-knowing father who protects and looks after the interests of his own daughter. The play also features a "masque" (the dance performed by the goddesses Iris, Ceres and Juno on pages 98–103). Masques were extremely popular in the royal courts and here also served as an interlude or resting point in the progress of the story.

The opening storm of thunder, coupled with shouting and peril, was a wonderfully effective way to grab the attention of the audience. Shakespeare uses the device brilliantly, as the storm also cuts the characters off from one another and separates reality from fantasy — not only for the players, but also for the on-lookers, as the actors land on the mysterious, magical island.

Sources

Exploration and colonization of the "New World" were topical subjects in the early 1600s. Only 24 years before *The Tempest* was written, Sir Walter Raleigh had returned from his attempts to start colonies in North America. One such colony was established on Roanoke Island, off the coast of North Carolina, Virginia; but when supply ships revisited the colony four years later, all of the inhabitants had disappeared, and they became known as the "Lost Colony". Despite such stories, the expansion of British interests via colonization continued, building up a romantic notion of valiant expeditions and the "taming" of the savage inhabitants of far-off lands.

Travelers brought back many strange tales, and some were documented, giving Shakespeare the inspiration for his masterpiece. The reports talked of cannibals and primitive people who conducted bizarre rituals. They were only vaguely human — much like Shakespeare's portrayal of Caliban (it is thought that the name of Caliban purposefully sounds similar to the word "cannibal"). Caliban's primitiveness, forced into civilization by Prospero, reflects a positive view of colonization that would have found favor with King James, justifying the many expeditions that the King funded. Shakespeare also cleverly portrays Caliban's resentment of Prospero's intrusion

ıd enforced civilization, which ›bbed Caliban of his ruling status n the island. This is quickly smissed within the play. Not only ›es Shakespeare reveal Caliban's ›or character in the recounting of 's attack on Miranda (pages 36-7), but he clearly shows how ›ospero was able to release the idden power of the island, making a better place for his arrival.

he inspiration for the storm itself ame from a pamphlet printed in 10 called *A Discovery of the ermudas, other wise called the Ile of ivels.* It documented the story of ow a convoy of ships, traveling om London to Virginia, ncountered a storm that separated ne flagship from the rest. The agship was blown towards ermuda and, although the ship was ›st, no one drowned. The travelers ved on the island until they could uild boats and sail on to Virginia. he story captured the minds of ne exploration-hungry citizens of ngland and gave Shakespeare a ramatic starting point for his play.

rospero

'rospero is shown to be a caring, rilliant and learned father with nagical powers (which would have ppealed to King James I). Like the King, his power is signified by his ›ooks, his staff and his robe. Books ıot only provided knowledge, but hey were seen as a source of nystical power; particularly by the argely illiterate public. The figure of 'rospero is thought to have been nspired by Queen Elizabeth's strologer, Dr John Dee (1527-1608). Dee had a reputation for ›erforming acts of magic and was enowned for possessing a vast ibrary of books – at one time the

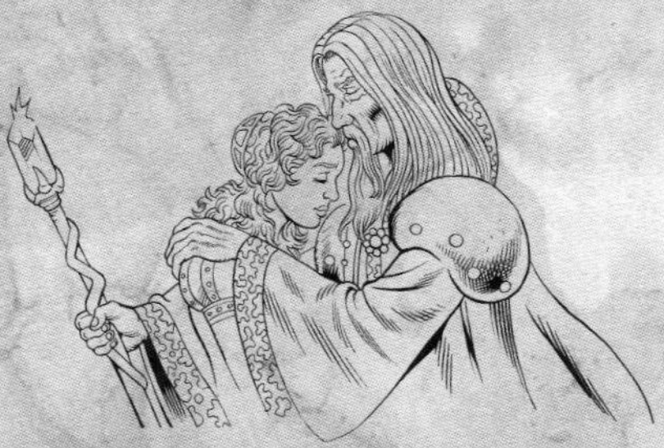

largest library in England. The mystical power that people believed he derived from his books was so feared that a group of people attacked his house and set fire to his library. King James I put an end to his financial support, and Dee was forced to sell his possessions. He died in poverty three years before *The Tempest* was written.

Theater Development

From 1608, Shakespeare's acting troupe started to perform his plays at *Blackfriars Theatre* on the north bank of the River Thames in London. His "spiritual home", *The Globe Theatre,* was an open-air performance space and subject to the effects of weather (the "groundling" audience had no shelter from rain). *Blackfriars Theatre,* on the other hand, was a fully enclosed space that included lighting and a pipe organ. *The Tempest* was shaped by the availability of this facility. The play features the most music of any of his works, using the organ to full effect, as well as the backstage areas for sound effects and other "off-stage" music. Also, the "imaginary banquet" scene (pages 87-93) is stage-directed for the sudden appearance and disappearance of the table and the food. This was made possible by a trap door on the stage, with the area beneath open for the moving of props – something that *The Globe Theatre* didn't possess. This was theater at the forefront of technology in 1611. It was important for Shakespeare always to be coming up with new spectacles, and one can only imagine how ending his fulltime writing career "on a high" with *The Tempest* would have left him satisfied in his final few remaining years.

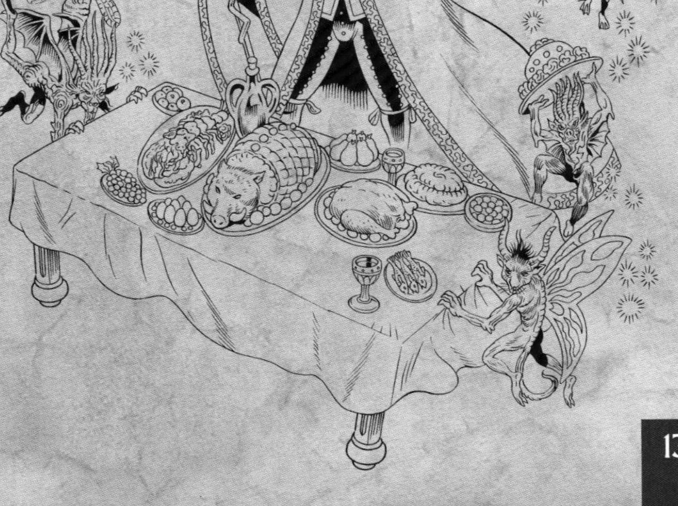

Page Creation

78. Ariel re-appears 'invisible', in the guise of a water-nymph [similar, but not exactly like, those in Frame 349]. Prospero whispers to him.

PROSPERO	Fine apparition! My quaint Ariel, Hark in thine ear.	You look fine, my delicate Ariel. I'll whisper to you –	You look just right, Arial. Listen –
ARIEL	My lord, it shall be done.	It will be done, my lord.	It will be done, master.

79. Prospero turns his attention back to the cave. Caliban is beginning to emerge. Miranda hides behind Prospero.

PROSPERO	Thou poisonous slave, got by the devil himself Upon thy wicked dam, come forth!	You poisonous slave – the devil himself fathered you with your witch-mother! **Come here!**	**Come here, you poisonous slave!**
CALIBAN	As wicked dew as e'er my mother brush'd With raven's feather from unwholesome fen, Drop on you both! a south-west blow on ye, And blister you all o'er!	I hope the evil dew collected by my mother from infected swamps with a crow-feather falls on both of you! I wish a hot south-west wind would blow on you and cover you with blisters.	A curse on both of you!

80. Prospero angrily strikes Caliban with his staff.

FX	**THWAAAAK!!**	**THWAAAAK!!**	**THWAAAAK!!**
PROSPERO	For this, be sure, to-night thou shalt have cramps, Side-stitches that shall pen thy breath up ; urchins Shall forth at vast of night, that they may work All exercise on thee : thou shalt be pinch'd As thick as honey-comb, each pinch more stinging Than bees that made them.	Make no mistake, tonight you'll have cramps for saying that – strong pains in your sides that will hurt when you breathe. My goblins will work on you for most of the night, and you'll be covered with painful bruises – each hurting like a bee-sting.	You'll be sorry for saying that! I'll give you cramps and pains, and cover you with bruises.

81. Caliban grabs a small passing lemur-like creature and bites its head off.

CALIBAN	I must eat my dinner.	I have to eat my dinner.	I need my dinner.

82. Caliban throws away the remains of the animal and stands erect, railing at Prospero and Miranda.

CALIBAN	This island's mine, by Sycorax my mother, Which thou tak'st from me. When thou camest first Thou strok'dst me, and mad'st much of me ; wouldst give me Water with berries in 't ; and teach me how To name the bigger light, and how the less, That burn by day and night :	My mother, Sycorax, left this island to **me!** You took it from me. You were kind to me at first – you petted me and gave me water with berries and taught me about the sun and the moon.	My mother, Sycorax, left this island to **me!** You stole it from me. You were kind to me at first –

Page 35 from the script of *The Tempest* showing the three text versions.

1. Script

The first stage in creating a graphic novel adaptation of a Shakespeare play is to split the original script into comic book panels, describing the images to be drawn as well as the dialogue, captions and sound effects. To do this, not only does the script writer need to know the play well, but he also needs to visualize each page in his head as he writes the art descriptions for each panel (there are over 460 panels in *The Tempest*).

Once this is created, the dialogue is adapted into Plain Text and Quick Text to create the three versions of the book, which all use the same artwork.

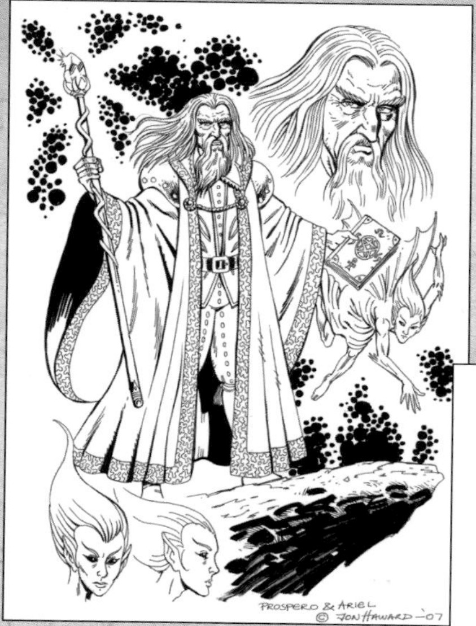
PROSPERO & ARIEL
© JON HAWARD -07
A character sheet of Prospero and Ariel.

2. Character Sheets

As well as creating the script, the scriptwriter (John McDonald) also supplies descriptions of each character. The artist (Jon Haward) couples these with his own ideas to create a number of character sheets. These sheets provide a point of reference when drawing the pages, but more importantly they allow the artist to familiarize himself with the characters – to the point where they almost take on a life of their own.

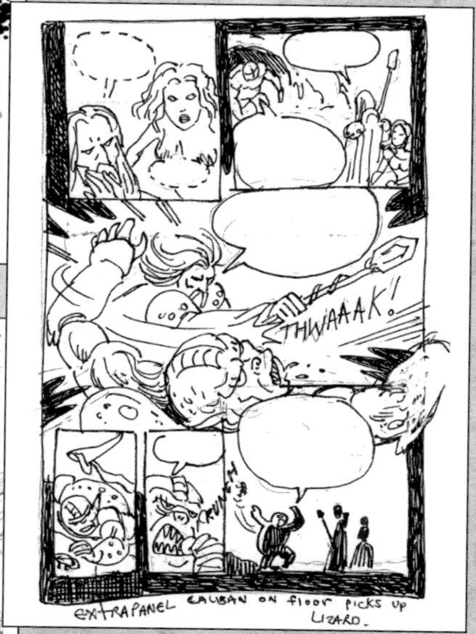
THWAAAK!
EXTRA PANEL CALIBAN ON floor PICKS UP LIZARD.
The rough sketch created from the script.

3. Rough Sketch

There is a wealth of detail in each panel of this book, and therefore it is important to solve any problems in the layouts through the use of rough sketches of each page. Here is Jon's sketch of page 35. Comparing it to the finished page, you can see how slight alterations were made during the artistic process.

Note how the characters were reversed in panel 2, to help with the lettering and also to have Prospero continuing in speaking from left to right, leading the reader on through the page.

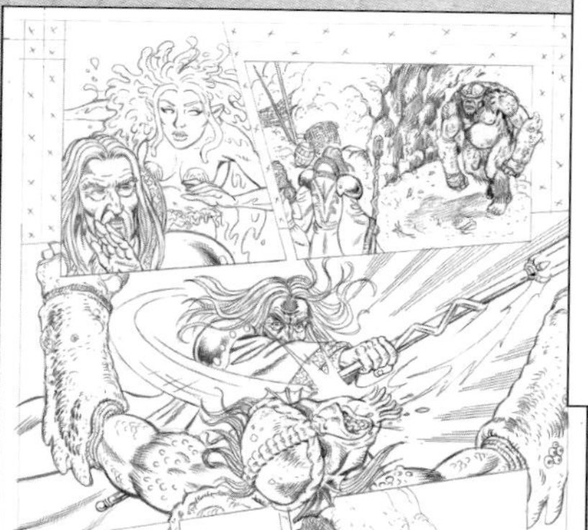
The pencil drawing of page 35.

4. Pencils

As soon as the rough sketch is approved by the editor, work starts on penciling the page. The artwork is drawn on A3 art board at approximately 150% of the finished printed size. Here you can clearly see the change to panel 2, and the amount of detail that goes in to each and every panel, even at this early stage.

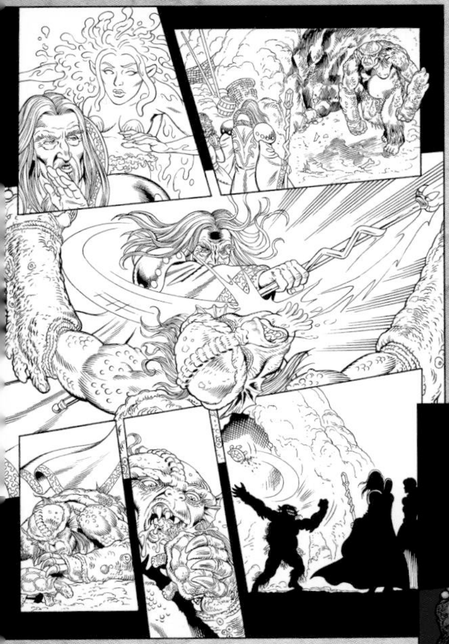

The inked image, ready to be colored.

5. Inks

The inking stage is important because it clarifies the pencil lines and finalizes the linework. There is far more to this than simply tracing over the pencil lines! The best way to view inking is as a pre-coloring stage, where deep blacks are created, and certain textures added. Different line weights are used to create a sense of depth in the image, and also to imply the types of edges being portrayed in the various materials.

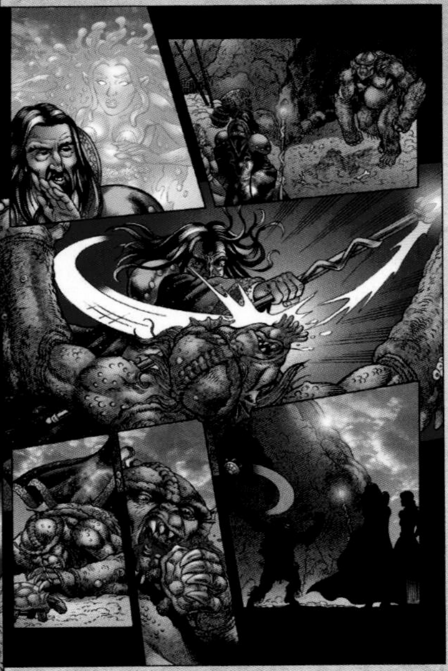

The final colored artwork.

6. Coloring

Adding color really brings the page and its characters to life. Coloring isn't merely a process of replacing the white areas with flat color. Some of the linework itself is shaded, while great emphasis is placed upon texture and light sources to get realistic shadows and highlights. Effects are also considered, such as the glow from Prospero's staff.. Finally, the whole page is color-balanced to the other pages of that scene, and to the overall book.

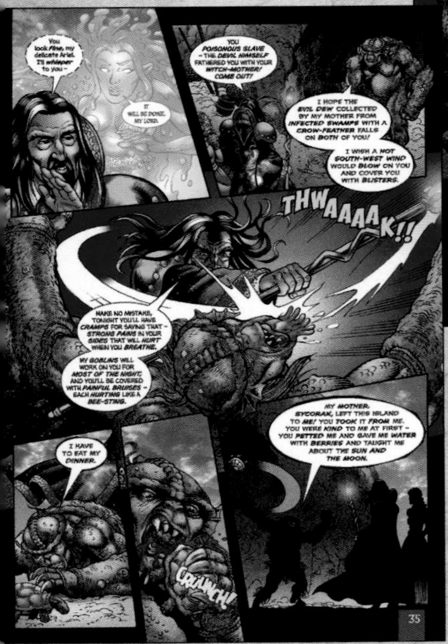

You look fine, my delicate Ariel. I'll whisper to you –
IT WILL BE DONE, MY LORD.
YOU POISONOUS SLAVE – THE DEVIL HIMSELF FATHERED YOU WITH YOUR WITCH-MOTHER! COME OUT!
I HOPE THE EVIL DEW COLLECTED BY MY MOTHER FROM INFECTED SWAMPS WITH A CROW-FEATHER FALLS ON BOTH OF YOU!
I WISH A HOT SOUTH-WEST WIND WOULD BLOW ON YOU AND COVER YOU WITH BLISTERS.
THWAAAAK!!
MAKE NO MISTAKE, TONIGHT YOU'LL HAVE CRAMPS FOR SAYING THAT – STRONG PAINS IN YOUR SIDES THAT WILL HURT WHEN YOU BREATHE.
MY GOBLINS WILL WORK ON YOU FOR MOST OF THE NIGHT, AND YOU'LL BE COVERED WITH PAINFUL BRUISES – EACH HURTING LIKE A BEE-STING.
I HAVE TO EAT MY DINNER.
CRUNCH!
MY MOTHER, SYCORAX, LEFT THIS ISLAND TO ME! YOU TOOK IT FROM ME. YOU WERE KIND TO ME AT FIRST – YOU PETTED ME AND GAVE ME WATER WITH BERRIES AND TAUGHT ME ABOUT THE SUN AND THE MOON.
35

The finished page 35 with Plain Text lettering.

7. Lettering

The final stage is to add the captions, sound effects, and speech bubbles from the script. These are placed on top of the finished colored pages. Three versions of each page are lettered, one for each of the three versions of the book (Original Text, Plain Text and Quick Text).

Original Text

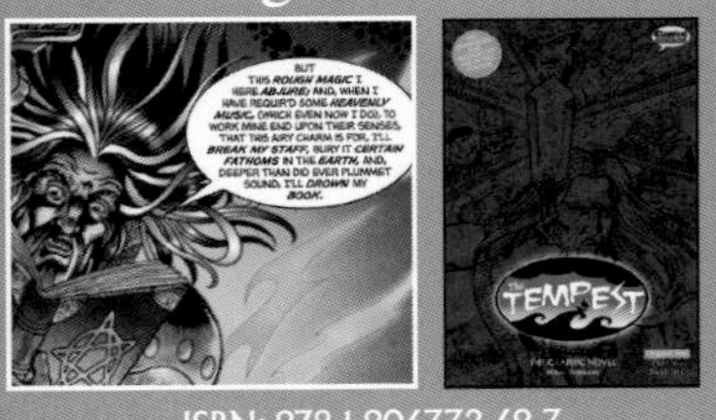

BUT THIS ROUGH MAGIC I HERE ABJURE) AND, WHEN I HAVE REQUIR'D SOME HEAVENLY MUSIC, (WHICH EVEN NOW I DO), TO WORK MINE END UPON THEIR SENSES, THAT THIS AIRY CHARM IS FOR, I'LL BREAK MY STAFF, BURY IT CERTAIN FATHOMS IN THE EARTH, AND, DEEPER THAN DID EVER PLUMMET SOUND, I'LL DROWN MY BOOK.
TEMPEST

ISBN: 978-1-906332-69-3

Plain Text

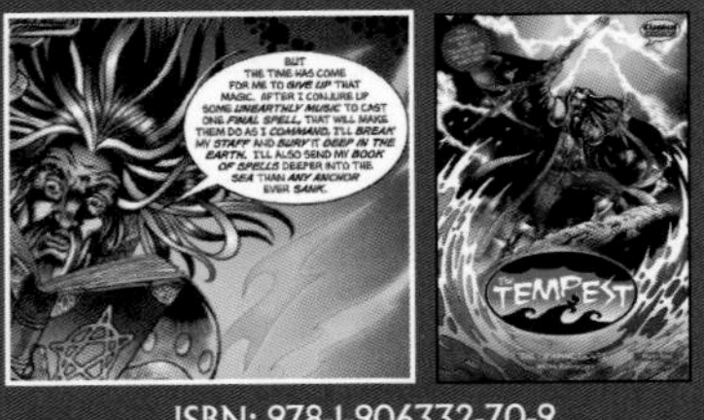

BUT THE TIME HAS COME FOR ME TO GIVE UP THAT MAGIC. AFTER I CONJURE UP SOME UNEARTHLY MUSIC TO CAST ONE FINAL SPELL, THAT WILL MAKE THEM DO AS I COMMAND, I'LL BREAK MY STAFF AND BURY IT DEEP IN THE EARTH. I'LL ALSO SEND MY BOOK OF SPELLS DEEPER INTO THE SEA THAN ANY ANCHOR EVER SANK.
TEMPEST

ISBN: 978-1-906332-70-9

Quick Text

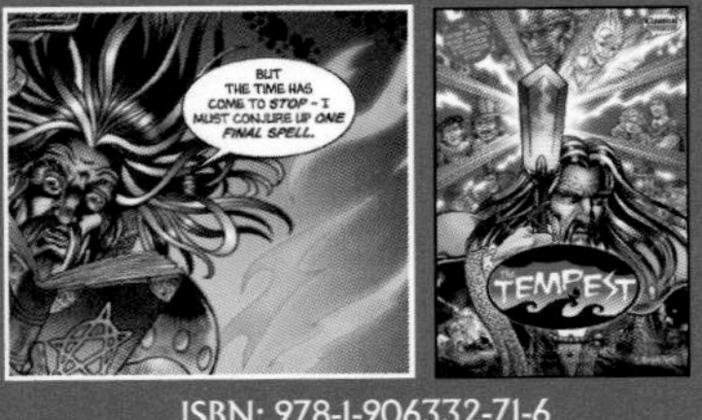

BUT THE TIME HAS COME TO STOP – I MUST CONJURE UP ONE FINAL SPELL.
TEMPEST

ISBN: 978-1-906332-71-6

Shakespeare's Globe

The Globe Theatre and Shakespeare

It is hard to appreciate today how theaters were actually a new idea in William Shakespeare's time. The very first theater in Elizabethan London to only show plays, aptly called *The Theatre*, was introduced by an entrepreneur by the name of James Burbage. In fact, *The Globe Theatre*, possibly the most famous theater of that era, was built from the timbers of *The Theatre*. The landlord of *The Theatre* was Giles Allen, a Puritan who disapproved of theatrical entertainment. When he decided to enforce a huge rent increase in the winter of 1598, the theater members dismantled the building piece by piece and shipped it across the Thames to Southwark for reassembly. Allen was powerless to do anything, as the company owned the wood - although he spent three years in court trying to sue the perpetrators!

The report of the dismantling party (written by Schoenbaum)

says: *"ryotous... armed... with divers and manye unlawfull and offensive weapons... in verye ryotous outragious and forcyble manner and contrarye to the lawes of your highnes Realme... and there pulling breaking and throwing downe the sayd Theater in verye outragious violent and riotous sort to the great disturbance and terrefyeing not onlye of your subjectes... but of divers others of your majesties loving subjectes there neere inhabitinge."*

William Shakespeare became a part owner of this new *Globe Theatre* in 1599. It was one of four major theaters in the area, along with the *Swan*, the *Rose*, and the *Hope*. The exact physical structure of the *Globe* is unknown, although scholars are fairly sure of some details through drawings from the period. The theater itself was a closed structure with an open courtyard where the stage stood. Tiered galleries around the open area accommodated the wealthier patrons who could afford seats, and those of the lower classes - the "groundlings" - stood around the platform or "thrust" stage during the performance of a play. The space under and behind the stage was used for special effects, storage and costume changes. Surprisingly, although the entire structure was not very big by modern standards, it is known to have accommodated fairly large crowds - as many as 3,000 people - during a single performance.

The Globe II

In 1613, the original *Globe Theatre* burned to the ground when a cannon shot during a performance of *Henry VIII* set fire to the thatched roof of the gallery. Undeterred, the company completed a new *Globe* (this time with a tiled roof) on the foundations of its predecessor. Shakespeare didn't write any new plays for this theater, which opened in 1614. He retired to Stratford-Upon-Avon that year, and died two years later. Despite that, performances continued until 1642, when the Puritans closed down all theaters and places of entertainment. Two years later, the Puritans razed the building to the ground in order to build tenements upon the site. No more was to be seen of the *Globe* for 352 years.

Shakespeare's Globe

Led by the vision of the late Sam Wanamaker, work began on the construction of a new *Globe* in 1993, close to the site of the original theater. It was completed three years later, and Queen Elizabeth II officially opened the *New Globe Theatre* on June 12th, 1997 with a production of *Henry V*.

The *New Globe Theatre* is as faithful a reproduction as possible to the Elizabethan theater, given that the details of the original are only known from sketches of the time. The building can accommodate 1,500 people in all, across the galleries and the "groundlings".

www.shakespeares-globe.org

Teaching Resource Packs

HELPING YOU PREPARE MOTIVATING AND STIMULATING LESSONS

CLASSICAL COMICS
TEACHING RESOURCE PACK
The TEMPEST
THE GRAPHIC NOVEL
SCENE BY SCENE SYNOPSIS
CHARACTER SHEET
WORD SEARCH
Includes CD-ROM

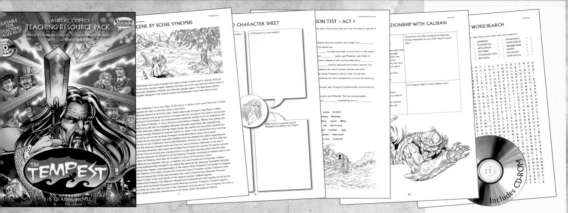

o accompany each title in our series of raphic novels and to help with their pplication in the classroom, we also publish eaching resource packs. These widely cclaimed 100+ page books are spiral-ound, making the pages easy to photocopy. hey also include a CD-ROM with the ages in PDF format, ideal for whole-class eaching on whiteboards, laptops, etc or for irect digital printing. These books are ritten by teachers, for teachers, helping tudents to engage in the play or novel. uitable for teaching ages 10-17, each book rovides exercises that cover structure, listening, understanding, motivation and character as well as key words, themes and literary techniques. Although the majority of the tasks focus on the use of language and comprehension, there are also many cross-curriculum topics, covering areas within history, IT, drama, reading, speaking, writing and art. An extensive Educational Links section provides further study opportunities. Devised to encompass a broad range of skill levels, they provide many opportunities for differentiated teaching and the tailoring of lessons to meet individual needs.

"Thank you! These will be fantastic for all our students. It is a brilliant resource and to have the lesson ideas too are great. Thanks again to all your team who have created these."
B.P. KS3

"As to the resource, I can't wait to start using it! Well done on a fantastic service."
Will

"...you've certainly got a corner of East Anglia convinced that this is a fantastic way to teach and progress English literature and language!"
Chris

OUR RANGE OF TEACHING RESOURCE PACKS AVAILABLE

CLASSICAL COMICS
TEACHING RESOURCE PACK
The TEMPEST

he Tempest
78-1-906332-77-8

CLASSICAL COMICS
TEACHING RESOURCE PACK
Romeo & Juliet
THE GRAPHIC NOVEL

Romeo & Juliet
978-1-906332-74-7

CLASSICAL COMICS
TEACHING RESOURCE PACK
Macbeth
THE GRAPHIC NOVEL

Macbeth
978-1-906332-54-9

CLASSICAL COMICS
TEACHING RESOURCE PACK
Henry V
THE GRAPHIC NOVEL

Henry V
978-1-906332-53-2

CLASSICAL COMICS
TEACHING RESOURCE PACK
Frankenstein
THE GRAPHIC NOVEL

rankenstein
78-1-906332-56-3

CLASSICAL COMICS
TEACHING RESOURCE PACK
Jane Eyre
THE GRAPHIC NOVEL

Jane Eyre
978-1-906332-55-6

CLASSICAL COMICS
TEACHING RESOURCE PACK
A Christmas Carol

A Christmas Carol
978-1-906332-57-0

CLASSICAL COMICS
TEACHING RESOURCE PACK
GREAT EXPECTATIONS
THE GRAPHIC NOVEL

Great Expectations
978-1-906332-58-7

- Only $22.95 each
- 100+ spiral-bound, photocopiable pages.
- Electronic version included for whole-class teaching and digital printing.
- Cross-curricular topics and activities.
- Ideal for differentiated teaching.

AVAILABLE IN THREE TEXT VERSIONS

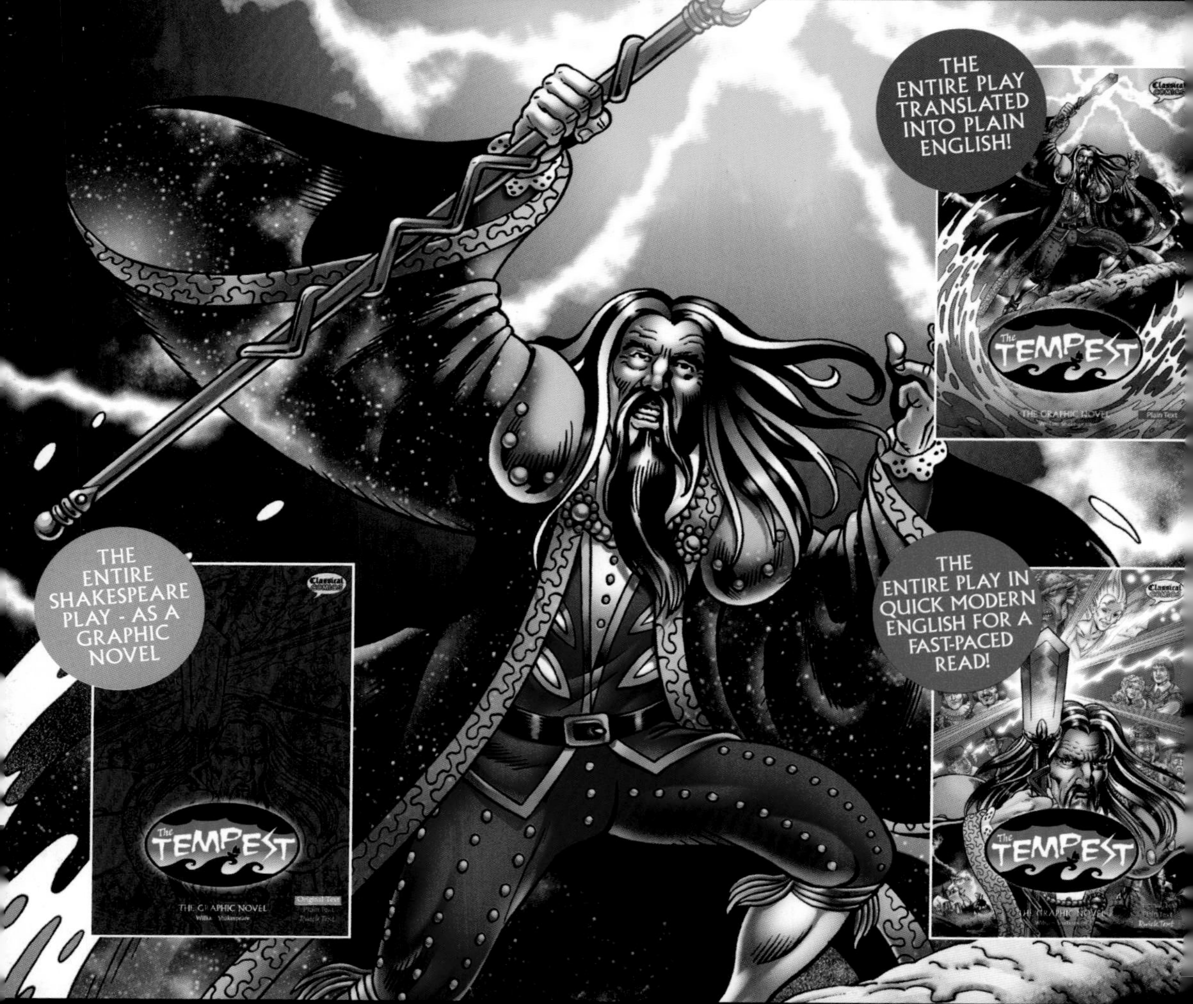

THE ENTIRE PLAY TRANSLATED INTO PLAIN ENGLISH!
The TEMPEST
THE GRAPHIC NOVEL
Plain Text
THE ENTIRE SHAKESPEARE PLAY - AS A GRAPHIC NOVEL
The TEMPEST
THE GRAPHIC NOVEL
Original Text
THE ENTIRE PLAY IN QUICK MODERN ENGLISH FOR A FAST-PACED READ!
The TEMPEST
THE GRAPHIC NOVEL
Quick Text

CHOOSE FROM ONE OF THREE TEXT VERSIONS, ALL USING THE SAME HIGH QUALITY ARTWORK

Original Text

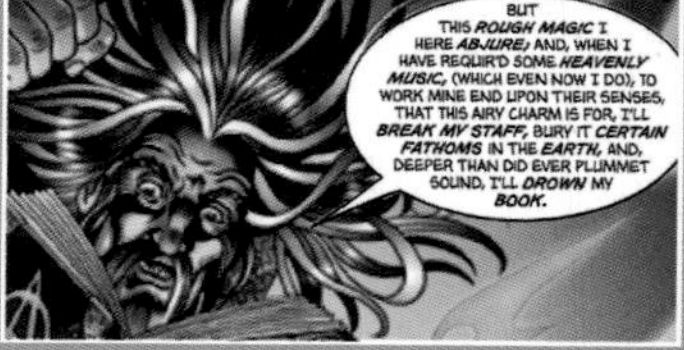

BUT THIS ROUGH MAGIC I HERE ABJURE; AND, WHEN I HAVE REQUIR'D SOME HEAVENLY MUSIC, (WHICH EVEN NOW I DO), TO WORK MINE END UPON THEIR SENSES, THAT THIS AIRY CHARM IS FOR, I'LL BREAK MY STAFF, BURY IT CERTAIN FATHOMS IN THE EARTH, AND, DEEPER THAN DID EVER PLUMMET SOUND, I'LL DROWN MY BOOK.

ISBN: 978-1-906332-69-3

Plain Text

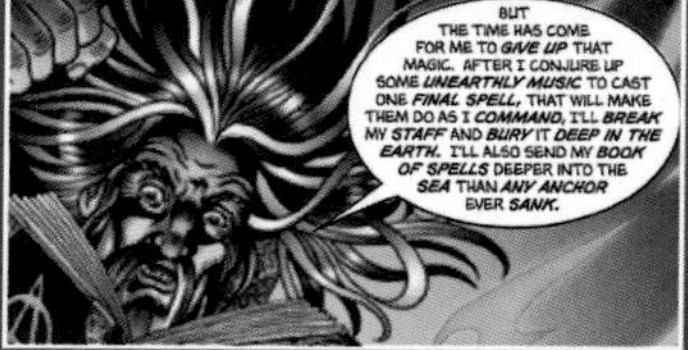

BUT THE TIME HAS COME FOR ME TO GIVE UP THAT MAGIC. AFTER I CONJURE UP SOME UNEARTHLY MUSIC TO CAST ONE FINAL SPELL, THAT WILL MAKE THEM DO AS I COMMAND, I'LL BREAK MY STAFF AND BURY IT DEEP IN THE EARTH. I'LL ALSO SEND MY BOOK OF SPELLS DEEPER INTO THE SEA THAN ANY ANCHOR EVER SANK.

ISBN: 978-1-906332-70-9

Quick Text

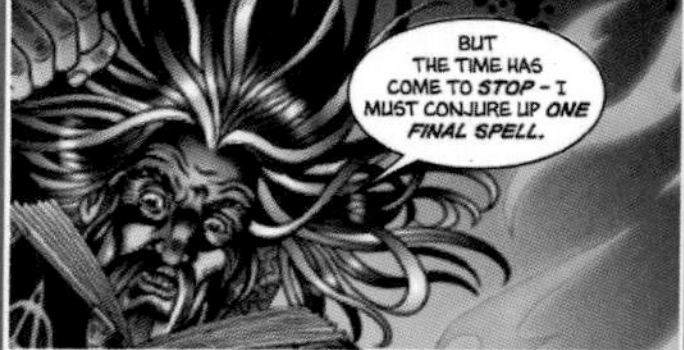

BUT THE TIME HAS COME TO STOP - I MUST CONJURE UP ONE FINAL SPELL.

ISBN: 978-1-906332-71-6

This is the full, original script - just as The Bard intended. This version is ideal for purists, students and for readers who want to experience the unaltered text: all of the text, all of the excitement!

We take the original script and "convert" it into modern English, verse-for-verse. If you've ever wanted to appreciate the works of Shakespeare fully, but find the original language rather cryptic, then this is the version for you!

A revolution in graphic novels! We take the dialogue and reduce it to as few words as possible while retaining the full essence of the story. This version allows readers to enter into and enjoy the stories quickly.

ALL SHAKESPEARE TITLES ARE AVAILABLE IN THREE TEXT VERSIONS